Firefly
Beach

Firefly Beach

Luanne Rice

BOOKSPAN LARGE PRINT EDITION

Bantam Books

NEW YORK TORONTO LONDON SYDNEY AUCKLAND

This Large Print Edition, prepared especially for Bookspan, contains the complete, unabridged text of the original Publisher's Edition.

FIREFLY BEACH

ISBN 0-7394-1831-9

Published simultaneously in the United States and Canada

Bantam Books are published by Bantam Books, a division of Random House, Inc. Its trademark, consisting of the words "Bantam Books" and the portrayal of a rooster, is Registered in U.S. Patent and Trademark Office and in other countries. Marca Registrada. Bantam Books, 1540 Broadway, New York, New York 10036.

PRINTED IN THE UNITED STATES OF AMERICA

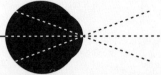

This Large Print Book carries the Seal of Approval of N.A.V.H.

For Bill and Lois,
Bob and Anne

ACKNOWLEDGMENTS

With love and thanks to Carol Cammero, Rosemary McGinn, Jim Silvia, Jan Watson, Emily Andrews, Lisa Billingsley, Gerry Chylko C.Ss.R., William "Rip" Collins C.Ss.R., Ed Dunne C.Ss.R, Maureen Gaffney R.S.M., Inge Hanson, Jayne Libby, April Fishgold, George Rose, and to all my friends from Westbrook, Old Saybrook, Old Lyme, and New York.

Firefly
Beach

DECEMBER 1969

The house smelled like Christmas cookies.

Butter, sugar, ginger, and spice. The aroma filled the warm kitchen; carols played on the radio. All their senses told Caroline and Clea that something wonderful was about to happen. The sisters were five and three, baking cookies on a snowy night with their mother. When the cookies cooled, they decorated them with white icing, silver balls, and red and green sprinkles.

Whenever the girls saw a crèche, they thought of their own family. Their mother was going to have another baby soon. The baby would be their new brother or sister, and the girls already loved him or her. The baby's crib was ready, just like the crib in the manger. The family had decided to name a boy Michael, a girl Skye. Caroline and Clea hoped for a Skye.

The doorbell rang.

Augusta Renwick, the girls' mother, wiped her hands on her dark green apron. The sight of floury handprints on their mother's big, pregnant belly made both girls laugh like crazy, and they ran with her to the door. On a night like this, anything could happen: Maybe Santa was there early, or maybe a small family in need of lodging had come to their house. Their father was away, painting the winter waterfront in Newport, but maybe he had come home early to surprise them.

It was a man with a gun.

He forced his way into the house. His gun was shaking in his hand. He closed the door behind him, as if he were a polite guest instead of a robber. Caroline and Clea huddled tight against their mother's legs. Her voice was calm but high, and she asked the man please to leave her children alone, to let them go, to not hurt them.

The man started to cry.

He pointed the gun at Caroline. Then at Clea. Then at Augusta. The black gun waved in the air as if it had ideas of its own. It kept coming back to point at Caroline.

She stared at it, its small, mean-looking hole, and she knew that was where the bullet was. Even more awful than the gun was the man crying. Until that moment, Caroline had not known adults ever cried. She had never seen her mother or her father cry. The terrible sight choked her throat. She clutched her mother's thigh. The man's eyes kept darting to the photograph of their house, Firefly Hill, a study for a famous painting by her father.

"He's taken her," the man said. "Taken her away from me. Stolen her love, stolen everything I ever wanted, and now I've come to take what's his."

"What do you mean? Who are you talking about? You're wrong, it's a mistake—" Augusta began, her voice stronger than his.

"Your husband, Mrs. Renwick," he said. "I have the right man. He's with my wife at this moment. Do you doubt me? He's taken what I love from me, and I'm going to take what he loves from him."

"What he loves?" Augusta asked, and Caroline noticed her mother's hands shaking on her shoulder.

"His daughters."

Augusta gasped. Caroline heard that horrible high sound and couldn't believe it was coming from her mother. She pressed closer to her mother's legs, face-to-face with Clea. Clea looked scared and worried, her lower lip pushed out like when she was a baby, her thumb inching toward her mouth. Caroline gave Clea's thumb a small push, and in it went.

"Let them go," Augusta said softly. "They've done nothing to hurt you. They're innocent children. Let them be safe. You don't want to hurt them. I can see you're a good man. You're crying, you're a sensitive person. They're just little girls. . . ."

"We have a son," the man said. He pulled out his wallet, flipped it open to a picture. His hand fumbled, and the picture fluttered. At the sight of it, the man choked and sobbed. "My boy," he cried. "Oh, God."

Caroline saw the smiling face of a little boy about her age. He had blond hair and big blue eyes, and he looked like his father. "He's her pride and joy. We were so happy, all of us together. So happy. Oh, the day he was born . . ." The man hung his head and wept.

"What's his name, Mr. . . . ? What's your little boy's name?" Caroline asked suddenly.

"Joe. Joe Connor. That's his name. Come here," the man said, roughly grabbing

Caroline's arm and pulling her away from her mother. He held her tight, and she heard a click come from the gun.

"No," Augusta wailed. "Please, Mr. Connor. Don't hurt her!"

"Shut up," the man said.

Caroline had never heard anyone tell her mother to shut up before, and she recoiled as if she'd been slapped. She looked up at the man and wondered if he was crazy. His eyes were terribly sad, sadder than any picture or real-life person Caroline had ever seen. Because of the excruciating sorrow in his blue eyes, she didn't feel afraid. She felt sorry for him instead.

"Don't say shut up to my mommy," Caroline said firmly.

"I want my sister," Clea cried, reaching her arms toward Caroline as their mother restrained her.

"Joe wouldn't want you to do this, Mr. Connor," Augusta said. "He wouldn't want you to scare my little girls, he wouldn't like to think of his father with a gun. . . . I'll do whatever you want. I'll make my husband stop seeing her. You have my word."

"What good is a person's word," the man asked, "when her husband doesn't love her anymore? When he loves someone else? You might as well promise me you'll stop the year from ending. It's over. It's all over now."

Caroline stood with the man's arm around her. She watched her mother's face. It melted like a warm candle. Her eyes drooped and her mouth frowned and tears poured down her cheeks. Caroline was watching her mother cry, now the second adult she had ever seen, and the sight of her mother's tears, more than the man's threat, suddenly filled Caroline with real panic.

"Take me," Augusta begged. "Let Caroline go. Take me and the baby instead. If you have to kill someone, kill us. But let her go!"

Her mother's voice rose on the word "go." It soared like a scream, like the wind howling through the trees on the hill.

"Let her go," the man repeated, blinking suddenly and swallowing his own tears. He looked at Caroline, then away, as if he didn't really want to see her.

"Please," Augusta said. "Take me. Take our baby."

"Don't say that," the man said, staring at Augusta's big belly.

The man gazed back at Caroline; he let himself linger on her eyes. They stared at each other, and Caroline felt herself getting less scared. A smile flickered on the man's lips. His hands trembling, he reached down to brush the hair out of her eyes.

"What's your name?"

"Caroline."

"You're Joe's age."

"I'm five now."

"Caroline," the man said, talking directly to her with tears running freely down his cheeks. "I came to take what your father loves, but I can't do it. I can't shoot a little girl like you."

"No," she agreed, and she had a sudden good feeling. As if everything would work out well.

"But he did this. Your father did this."

"Did what? My daddy did what?" Caroline asked, wanting to understand. Her mouth was dry. Reaching for the man's hand, her fingers ruffled the picture of Joe. "My daddy did what?" she asked again.

"Killed my family," the man said with a sob just as he raised the gun to his head and pulled the trigger.

The shot exploded in Caroline's ears. The burning smell of gunpowder made her gag, and the weight of the man crushed her to the floor. Blood poured out of his mouth and from the hole where he had shot out the side of his head. Her black hair was wet with it. She couldn't breathe because his body was on top of her. She screamed for her mother, crying with terror.

But her eyes were on the boy. Smiling up at Caroline was Joe Connor, six years old, his picture lying on the floor right under her face. The little boy whose father had just killed himself instead of Caroline or Clea or their mother and the new baby, whose mother didn't love him enough, who would never see his father again.

When Augusta Renwick, weeping, managed to pull the man's dead body off her daughter, she clutched Caroline to her breast and wiped some of the blood off her face and tried to hear what Caroline was saying to the picture of the little boy.

"I want my daddy," Caroline was crying. "I want my daddy now."

December 30, 1969

Dear Joe Connor,

I am your friend. Because your father came to our house and showed me your picture. I am sorry that he died, very very sorry.

Sincerely yours,
Caroline Renwick

January 14, 1970

Dear Caroline Renwick,

My father showed you my picture? He was nice and laughed a lot. We played baseball at Cardine Field. My father had a heart attack with you. I am glad you were with him.

Your friend,
Joe Connor

CHAPTER ONE

JUNE 2000

It was the longest day of the year. The full moon was rising out of the sea. The old dog lay on the grass beside Caroline, his chin resting on folded paws. Caroline, her mother, and her sisters sat in white wicker chairs. The gathering had an edge; family ghosts were circling around.

Caroline Renwick felt like a matriarch, but she was just the oldest sister. She loved her family. They were strong yet vulnerable, ordinary women who happened to be exceptional. Sometimes she felt she spent too much time with them, shepherding them along like a flock of eccentric sheep. Whenever that happened, she would jump on a plane, go on a business trip. It didn't matter where, as long as it was far enough away to give her mind a rest. But for right now, she was home.

As the moon rose, it grew smaller and colder, lost its pinkness and became silver. Stirred and panting, Homer raised his head from his paws . . . to watch. "Oh, girls," Augusta Renwick said, looking at her three daughters once it was entirely up.

"Isn't it incredible?" Augusta asked, staring out at Long Island Sound.

"A full moon on the longest day of the year," said Caroline. "That has to be a good omen."

"You're always looking for signs," Clea teased. "A full moon, shooting stars . . ."

"The North Star," Skye said. "Caroline taught me how to find it the last night I was ever really happy."

"The last *what?*" Augusta asked, smiling.

"Mom . . ." Caroline warned.

"My last happy night," Skye said sadly. She stumbled slightly on the words, making Caroline wonder how much she had already had to drink.

"You're happy *now,* darling," Augusta said. "Don't be ridiculous. How can you say something like that?"

"Easily," Skye said softly, staring at the old dog Homer.

"Mom . . ." Caroline started again, racking her brain for something light and conversational.

"Oh, Skye. Stop now," Augusta said, looking wounded. "We're celebrating the summer solstice! Let's get back to talking about stars. . . ."

"The North Star . . ." Clea said, laughing. "I don't need it anymore. If I want to go somewhere, I'll call my travel agent. No more hiking, no more hunting for this girl."

"Don't need *any* stars," Skye said.

"We all need stars," Augusta said. Then she said it again, as if it were very important: "We all need stars."

"We need cocktails," Skye said. "Isn't it time? The sun's down, the moon's up. There: I've got signs too. It's the cocktail hour. Right, Homer?" The ancient golden retriever thumped his tail.

"Well, it is," Augusta agreed, checking her small gold watch for added confirmation. She glanced at Caroline and Clea as if she expected them to interfere. Watching her mother, Caroline was reminded of a teenage girl on the brink of doing something her parents would disapprove of, daring them to stop her. Hearing no objections, Augusta walked into the house.

"Cocktails," Skye said to Homer.

"Drinking's not the answer," Caroline said. Instead of acting offended, Skye blew her a kiss. After all this time, their roles in life were clear: Skye misbehaved, and Caroline cleaned up.

Caroline shifted in her chair. She felt an unease deep down, worry mixed with fear. Lately she had been restless, cranky, dissatisfied with her bountiful life. She looked at Skye and saw a person she loved throwing herself away. She had to fight to keep from saying something sharp. For all these years, Caroline had been the glue holding her youngest sister together, and she felt as if Skye might finally be coming undone.

"Simon's not back, is he?" Clea asked, referring to Skye's scoundrel artist husband. "He's not coming tonight?"

"No, is Peter?" Skye asked, referring to Clea's husband, a hospital chaplain.

"No, he took the kids out for pizza," Clea replied.

"Peter's such a good guy," Caroline said, "wanting a night out with his kids."

"Caroline, how was your date the other night?" Clea asked.

"Fine," Caroline said, smiling as she shrugged.

"Who, that poor investment banker who drove all the way up from New York just to learn he doesn't have a snowball's chance in hell—" Skye began.

"Okay." Caroline laughed, getting up. "Enough." Thirty-six and never been married. The only Renwick girl never to tie the knot or even come close, she knew her sisters wished they could do something about her die-hard singleness.

"Seriously," Skye teased, tripping over the "s's." "Two hundred miles in his 500SL to find out you don't kiss on the first—"

"I'll see what Mom's up to," Caroline said, walking away so she wouldn't have to hear how drunk Skye sounded.

* * *

She walked across the wide green lawn into her mother's house. Firefly Hill had been her childhood home. Hugh and Augusta Renwick had named their house on the Connecticut shoreline after Noël Coward's house in Jamaica, because on still June nights like these, when the moon rose out of the Sound, the dark fields around the old Victorian house and the thicket behind the beach below sparked with the green-gold glow of thousands of fireflies. The three sisters would run barefoot through the grass, catching the bugs in cupped hands.

And they had named it Firefly Hill because Noël Coward, to the Renwick family, meant martinis and conversation, wicked gossip and wit, wild parties and lots to drink—but never too much until way after dark. Caroline's father had been a famous artist; her mother had celebrated him with legendary parties here in Black Hall, the birthplace of American Impressionism.

The house smelled like home. Whenever she entered the place, the smell of her childhood was the first thing Caroline noticed. Salt air, wood smoke, oil paint, gin, her mother's perfume, and her father's gun oil all mingled together. She wandered through the cool rooms and couldn't find her mother.

There, sitting on the wide steps of the side porch, tucked back from her daughters' view, the sea breeze ruffling her mane of white hair, was Augusta Renwick.

Caroline hesitated in the darkened living room. Even alone, thinking herself unobserved, her mother had such poise, such theatricality. She gazed across the ocean with such intensity, she might have been awaiting her husband's return from a dangerous voyage. Her cheekbones were high and sculpted, her mouth wide and tragic.

She wore a faded blue shirt and khakis, tattered old sneakers. Around her neck were the black pearls Hugh Renwick had given her ten Christmases before he died. Augusta wore them always; to a party, to a ball, in the garden, to the A&P, it didn't matter. Her black hair had gone white when she was only thirty years old, but she had never dyed it. It was long and luxuriant, halfway down her back. Her eyebrows remained dark. She was still a dramatic beauty.

"Hi, Mom," Caroline said.

"Darling," Augusta said, emotional. "I just made the drinks and I was sneaking a quick one. Have one with me before we go back to your sisters."

"No, thanks."

Augusta patted the spot beside her. Caroline grabbed a seat cushion off the wicker rocker and placed it on the top step.

The martini shaker, condensation clinging to the deep monogram in the sterling silver, rested between them.

"I was just sitting here, thinking of your father," Augusta said. Shielding her eyes, she looked across the waves, violet and silver in the moonlight. "He loved the June full moon. Didn't he? Couldn't he do a beautiful picture of that sky?"

"He could, Mom," Caroline said.

"Here's to Hugh," Augusta said, raising her glass at the moon, "and to the picture he could make of this moment. His wife and his oldest daughter and the longest day of the year. First one of the summer."

"First one of the summer," Caroline said, raising an imaginary glass.

"Oh, I miss him."

"I know you do."

There was a moment of silence, and Caroline could almost feel her mother waiting for Caroline to say "I do too." Augusta carried an air of sadness and longing around with her, and Caroline knew it had to do with the past, deep love, and missed chances. Hugh had died seven years before, of stomach cancer. As life unfolded, there seemed to be more things they all had to say to him, but he wasn't there to hear them. Her mother had loved him madly till the end.

Across the Sound, the lighthouses of Long Island had flashed on. To the west, the bright lights of some enormous fishing boat or work platform, moored over the Wickland Shoals, blazed like a small city.

"Come on," Caroline said, tugging her mother's hand. "Let's go back to the others and watch the moon."

Her mother left the drink things on the porch steps. Caroline felt relieved. As they crossed the yard, they felt the breeze in their hair. This was the time of day that reminded Caroline of her father more than any other. Her mother was right: She did hold things against him, but that couldn't stop the lump in her throat. Not all the memories were of bad things.

* * *

The fireflies had begun to come out. They twinkled in the rosebushes. They spread across the field, lighting the tall grass like a million candles. The fireflies made their beach magical. They danced down the gently sloping grassy hill, darting through the reeds and spartina above the sandy white strand. No other beaches along the shoreline glowed so intensely. Her father said his girls were special, that the fireflies lit their way and illuminated their beach so they could always find their way home.

Sometimes he would catch the fireflies and kill them, rubbing their lightning juice across Caroline's cheeks, anointing her with glowing war paint. Or he would pinch them between his big fingers and drop them into his glass, making his martini sparkle with stars, laughing with pleasure as he enchanted his daughters. For so long, Caroline had loved her father more than anything.

Clea and Skye were silent in their wicker chairs, watching the fireflies. Were they thinking of their father too? It seemed impossible that they weren't. Homer watched Caroline's progress across the yard, head on his paws. As she took her seat, he lifted his white face to kiss her hand. The night felt magical, as if the moon and the past and the ghost of Hugh had cast a spell upon them all. The Renwick women gazed at the moon and listened to the waves.

"What are you thinking?" Clea asked suddenly, leaning forward to tap Caroline's shoulder.

"About Dad," Caroline said.

Skye brooded in the moonlight, seeming to shiver. Their father was buried in the cemetery through the woods on the western edge of Firefly Hill, and Caroline watched Skye's gaze go there now.

"What are those boats?" Clea asked, pointing at the cluster of lights out by Wickland Shoals. "That's what I'm wondering."

"They anchored there today," Augusta said. "Two big white boats and a lot of little launches running in and out."

Leave it to Clea to be thinking something simple, uncomplicated, Caroline thought. She was the happiest Renwick sister, the least encumbered, the only one who had put the past behind her. Caroline gave her a smile. She turned to Skye.

"How about you?" she asked. "Why are you so quiet, Skye?"

"Just thinking," Skye said. But of course she would not say what about.

"We're all together, Caroline," Augusta said. "Let that be enough."

"I thought someone said something about

cocktails," Skye said, rising unsteadily. "Can I get anyone anything?"

"I don't think so," Augusta said with a sidelong glance at Caroline.

But when Skye turned to walk precariously across the moonlit lawn, Augusta followed, linking arms with her youngest daughter. Homer rose, as if to follow. He seemed torn. Caroline scratched his ears, and he turned his eloquent eyes to hers. He had always sensed that Skye was the one who needed protection. But his great love was for Caroline, and both of them knew it.

Duty won. When Skye and Augusta headed up the gentle incline, Homer followed behind with his old head bent and his tail wagging. They disappeared inside the house. Caroline and Clea sat still, waiting. The music started: the tinkle of ice against silver, the complicit laughter, the clink of heavy crystal.

* * *

Unable to sleep that night Caroline turned her head and looked at the framed photo on her bedside table. It showed her, Clea, and Skye, all in summer dresses, at yet another party for their father, when Caroline was about sixteen.

Sisterhood is amazing. Caroline had known it almost forever, from when she was two, the moment she first realized her mother was growing large. It never ceased to amaze her: She and her sisters came out of the same womb.

Caroline knew it was the same for sisters everywhere. Whenever she met women who had sisters, she knew they *knew*. They understood the incredible connection. Staring at the picture, she tried to remember those girls from long ago. Her eyes focused on the image of herself: smiling but guarded, standing slightly behind Clea and Skye, as if to protect them.

"What were you thinking?" she whispered to her old self, to her younger sisters.

They grew up in the same house, with the same smells, the same sights, the same sounds. They had the same parents. They shared a room, fell asleep every night to the sound of one another's soft breathing. They shared the same images in dreams. They knew each other's nightmares. Some of their sweetest dreams were of one another.

"We walked each other to school," she said to herself, to her sisters.

When she looked at her sisters' bare legs,

she knew every single scar. She knew the
crescent-moon scar just under Clea's left
knee, where she tripped in the night and fell
on a piece of broken glass. She knew the
inch-long scar on Skye's right ankle, from
the time she snagged her foot on barbed
wire, cutting through a pasture where none
of them were supposed to be.

She knew the boys they liked. She had
teased them about every single one. She
helped them write love notes, she dialed boys'
phone numbers for them so Clea or Skye
could hear that boy answer and then hang up.
Sometimes, and she would feel ashamed
about this until she died, she flirted with them
when her sisters weren't there. She wanted to
see whether they liked her better.

Gazing at the picture, she knew they all
had secrets. What about the different expe-
riences, the things they'd never know about
each other? They don't tell you everything,
Caroline thought. The fights they heard
their parents have when she was asleep.
The only time in her life she ever cheated,
on a math test in seventh grade, even
though Caroline had helped her with her
homework, she had pretended to "get it"
just to please her.

The bad things that happened to her, the very bad things. The men she let touch her when she knew she shouldn't. The times she was scared. The times she didn't have a choice. The times she was in a place she didn't know, with no one to call, not even her sisters. The way it feels to kill another human being.

And even the miraculous times, the times when she was overtaken by the thrill of love, when the light of the moon on the water seemed to promise something Caroline could never understand, no matter that she was her sister, that they came out of the same womb.

Three sisters, three separate realities. Lots of combinations, lots of possibilities. Take one, get three. Two against one. Odd girl out. Secrets told to one but not the other. Then that one tells the first one, and everyone's mad at each other. Or secrets told to tell no one. Secrets she knows but would never tell. Secrets you imagine but don't know. Mistakes of life and death. The geometry of sisterhood.

CHAPTER TWO

A week later, the sisters went out for a movie. Dropping Skye off at Firefly Hill, where she had been living since the departure of Simon, Caroline hitched a ride home with Clea. They all lived in Black Hall, within six miles of one another. Tonight they drove slowly, taking Clea's Volvo the long way around. Clea's husband and kids were out for the night, and she didn't have to rush home. Caroline loved driving around the shoreline with her sister. The car felt enclosed and warm, a sister-capsule orbiting the towns. They didn't speak for a few miles.

"What's with Skye?" Clea asked finally.

"I wish I knew," Caroline answered.

Caroline pictured Skye's handsome and ego-laden husband. Skye and Simon, both extraordinary artists, had lived a wild, bohemian lifestyle for as long as it had suited Simon. Running off with his model, he left Skye just before their fifth anniversary. Skye's dark moods had worried Caroline when they were kids, but they had gone dormant recently, until Simon met someone else.

"It's not because of Simon," Caroline said.

"What, then?"

"I think it's history catching up with her," Caroline said.

"What history?"

"She killed a man, Clea."

"But she didn't mean to," Clea said plaintively.

"That can't bring him back."

"She's drinking away her guilt," Clea said, "like Dad."

"Like Dad."

They drove on. Caroline lived in a small cottage of the Renwick Inn. Capitalizing on the family name, Caroline ran it as a hostelry that catered to artists. The inn itself was two hundred years old, a rambling white saltbox with seven chimneys and four secret closets. It had gardens and pine woods and outbuildings and a big red barn.

It occupied one hundred acres on the Ibis River, a tributary of the Connecticut River, and it had once belonged to their grand-parents.

Every year artists came to the Renwick Inn for the summer and parts of the other seasons to paint and escape the city and fall in love with each other. Every August at the end of the season Caroline held a renowned ball to celebrate love and creativity and new work and money in the bank. As Clea drove into the winding drive, Caroline saw that the parking lot was full.

"Good," she said. "Paying guests."

"Artists these days have to be pretty prosperous to afford the rates you charge." Clea laughed, counting the cars.

"Well, they're not all artists," Caroline said. "I just advertise as an artists' retreat because that seems to pull them in."

"It always did," Clea said, probably remembering their own childhood, all the would-be protégés and hangers-on who would congregate around their father, hoping for some of his talent or glamour or mystery to rub off.

Outside, the air was muggy, hot, and still. Heat rose from the lazy river, shimmering in the moonlight. The inn guests loved their ceiling fans, screened porches, mosquito nets, kerosene lamps. They paid extra for a certain rusticity. They wanted flickering candles, tangled gardens, dinners al fresco on weathered picnic tables, mismatched plates and glasses, a cozy bar with a fireplace, and plenty to drink. They disdained modern conveniences, so Caroline obliged by not providing air-conditioning, television, telephones, or electric alarm clocks.

"Will you come in?" she asked Clea, not wanting their night to end. "We have a great new chocolate cake I want you to try."

"Sure," Clea said.

Inside, they walked straight through the lobby. Guests were milling around, drinking and waiting for dinner. Michele, the manager, had everything under control. They walked straight past a row of their father's paintings to the back porch. Caroline settled her sister on a glider and ran to the kitchen. She set up a tray with chipped china coffee cups, a pot of coffee, and two big slices of cake.

"Hold me back," Clea said when she saw the cake.

"Wait till you taste it," Caroline said.

While conversation buzzed in the other room, the sisters hid out on the porch, eating the dense chocolate cake and watching a flock of geese land on the moonlit river twenty yards away.

"The river's pretty, but it's not the ocean," Clea said.

"We're saltwater girls," Caroline said. "Dad always said that."

They were facing the river, when suddenly an arc of headlights illuminated the trees. A line of cars pulled into the inn's circular drive. A truck rumbled up, and another. The sound of boisterous male voices carried across the property.

"Maybe they have us mixed up with the Catspaw Tavern," Caroline said, referring to the roadhouse five miles north.

"Let's go set them straight," Clea said, curious.

The two sisters walked into the lobby, where a pack of sunburned, unshaven men wearing frayed and grimy clothes were pouring through the front door. Michele, alarmed, stood at the reservations desk, ready with directions to the Catspaw. The Renwick Inn was refined, genteel. These men clearly had the wrong place.

"Got any vacancies?" asked one man. He had a mop of salt-damp black hair, a faded tee-shirt advertising a bar in Key West, and a chipped front tooth. His massive gut stretched the shirt to its limits; his tattooed biceps were as thick as Michele's waist.

"For rooms?" Michele asked, frowning.

"Yeah." The man laughed. "What'd you think I meant?"

"Well . . ." Michele said, gracefully ignoring the innuendo. She perused the reservations book. "How many rooms do you need?"

"Six," the man said. "We can double up. And some of us'll be staying on the boats."

"On the boats?" Michele asked, grabbing her chance. "You might be happier with a place nearer the marinas. I have a list of motels . . ."

"The boss wants this place," the man said, shaking his head. "He was definite about it."

"How long do you need the rooms?" Michele asked.

"Indefinitely. All summer, maybe. We're working offshore, got a big salvage operation going—"

"Loose lips sink ships," another man interrupted. He chuckled, but his eyes were serious. "Quit trying to impress the ladies."

"Offshore?" Caroline asked. "Just a little east of here?" She was thinking of the boats she had seen from Firefly Hill, their lights glowing like downtown.

"That's right," the first man said. He grinned proudly, revealing a broken tooth.

"We definitely don't have individual rooms available all summer," Caroline said. "But Michele might be able to find one or two for tonight, then move you around as things come available."

"Shit," the man said. "Boss'll be disappointed. Danny, you'd better run outside and tell him. Maybe he'll want to head back to the marina after all."

Some of the men had drifted into the dark, cozy bar. Candles flickered on every table, some of the old oak surfaces carved with artists' drawings and initials. Landscapes and nudes covered the walls. One by one, the houseguests looked up. They were either artists or people attracted by artists, and they regarded the seafarers with a mixture of alarm and curiosity.

Behind the bar was a particularly lush and decadent nude, depicting a large-breasted blond woman with tragedy in her eyes. The trick of the painting was that the background was money. At first glance it appeared to be foliage, but if you looked closely, it was coins and currency. To the artists, the picture was a sophisticated conversation piece, an excellent execution of trompe l'oeil done by one of Caroline's guests, who had gone on to become well known. But to the new visitors it was lewd and lascivious, and they stood around making loud toasts to the model's erect nipples.

Caroline stood quietly, listening to Clea and Michele ask each other what should be done. The language was growing raunchy. Some of the guests were squirming, staring with distaste at the men. Clea and Michele began to circulate among the tables, attempting damage control by offering drinks on the house.

"Are my guys behaving themselves?" came a deep voice from behind her.

"Not exactly," Caroline said, turning to see who had spoken.

The man was tall and fair. He had tousled blond hair, streaked from the sun and salt. His blue eyes were wide and clear, and their serious expression was deep, in contrast with his smile. He wore a faded blue polo shirt, the tails untucked and the collar frayed. His arms were tan and strong.

"Hey, captain," called the man with the broken tooth and tattoos. "We want to buy you a drink."

"How about remembering you're not at sea anymore," the blond man said good-naturedly to his crew at large. "Be scientists and gentlemen." They listened with no apparent rancor, nodding and raising their glasses. One of them bought the man a drink, and it appeared to be a glass of cranberry juice. He held it, and Caroline could see how big his hands were.

"Danny says you're all booked up?" the man asked.

"I'm sorry," she said. "I can offer you two rooms for tonight, but that's just because we had unexpected cancellations. I think you'll have a hard time finding enough rooms for as long as you want them. Black Hall gets pretty busy in the summer."

"I'm disappointed," the captain said. "I've always wanted to stay at the Renwick Inn."

"Really?" she asked, skeptical but flattered.

"Really," he said.

"We get a lot of artists here," she said. "Not many sailors and . . . what did you say? Scientists?"

"Hard to believe, isn't it?" he asked, surveying his ragtag crew, desperately in need of razors and shampoo, drooling over the sad-eyed nude. "Half those guys are oceanographers and the other half are pirates."

"Which half are you?" she asked.

"I'm definitely a pirate," he replied.

"No kidding," she said. They stood there, smiling at each other. He had a sultry sexiness about him, but in spite of his easy way, there was something secretive behind his eyes.

"I run a salvage company in Florida," he said. "We dive on sunken ships, bring up what we can. Sometimes we contract out for government work, and sometimes we do our own thing."

"What do you salvage?" Caroline asked.

"Treasure." He grinned.

"Treasure?" she asked, still skeptical.

"Yeah," he said. "Sometimes it's just fishing gear and a water-logged outboard motor. A drunken captain who didn't know the water and went aground. Or a family sailboat the father didn't know how to navigate and hit a rock."

"I'm sure you didn't come all the way up from Florida to raise a family sailboat," Caroline said.

"That's right," he replied. "Earlier this year I went off Louisiana and brought up a chest of yellow topaz. A mound of silver pesos four inches high and eighty feet long. All from a Spanish brig that went down in 1784."

The romance of wrecks had always intrigued Caroline. Growing up at Firefly Hill, she and her sisters would look out to sea and imagine the ships that had gone down on the rocky shoals. There were legends about pirates and wreckers on this coast, and one memorable tale about an English ship lost in a terrible storm. "Do you expect to find something like that up here?" she asked, growing excited at the prospect. "Real treasure?"

"Maybe," he said, smiling enigmatically.

"The English ship. Is that what you've come for?" Caroline asked, suddenly understanding. She pictured the boats offshore, the secrecy in the men's expressions. The man had come north to excavate the old shipwreck.

Caroline had learned about it in third grade; all the Black Hall kids had. An English sea captain came to the colonies, his hold full of arms and the king's gold. He fell in love with the lighthouse keeper's wife, and she was going to run away to England with him. But their ship sank on the Wickland Shoals in a great gale. "Tell me her name, the ship that sank," Caroline said finally.

"The *Cambria*," the man said, watching her face.

"That's right!" she said, looking into his eyes. As she did, she had the feeling she knew him, had known him for a long time and knew him well. A strange sensation came over her: Her skin tingled, and the hair on the back of her neck stood on end.

"How did you find out about it?" she asked. "It's only a legend. People have looked before, and they've never found any trace. It happened nearly three hundred years ago, if it happened at all."

"It happened," he said softly.

"But how did you hear? It's a local story. I've never read anything about it."

"You told me about it," the man said.

"I told you?"

"In one of your letters you wrote about a ship that had sunk within sight of your house. The *Cambria*. You'd learned about it in school, and you could see the spot from your bedroom window. You're Caroline Renwick, aren't you?"

She felt the blush spread up her neck. Reaching out, she took his hand. It felt rough and callused, and his grip was tight and didn't let go. She recognized him now. He looked so much like his picture, that smile and the light in his eyes. She had carried his picture around for ten years, and she was surprised she hadn't recognized him the minute he walked in the door.

"Joe," she said. "Joe Connor."

"I should have called first," he said. "But we came north kind of suddenly."

"Joe," she said again.

"The Renwick Inn," he said. "I've always wondered whether it was you. Or your family, at least."

"It's hard to believe," she said. "That we've never met before. Of all the times for you to show up . . ."

"Life's strange," he said, still smiling. But something about the cast of his eyes made her see he was backing off. Whatever friendliness he had initially shown was tempered by their past, the secrecy of his business, or something else. He glanced around, nodded at his men in the bar.

"It is," Caroline said. "Strange that you wanted to stay at my inn, considering . . ."

"Considering what?"

"Everything. Considering everything."

"That's ancient history," Joe said. "You run an inn, and I need a place to put my crew."

"Your crew? Not you?" Caroline asked.

Joe shook his head. "I stay at the site, on board one of the ships. So do most of my guys, but we need a base on land. Showers, a bar, a restaurant."

"Looks like they're enjoying the bar," Caroline said, watching the bartender frown as he poured shots of Southern Comfort. "Can't say I remember the last time I saw someone drinking shots in there."

"My guys a little too rough for you?" Joe asked with an edge. He grinned. "Good thing you're booked. We wouldn't want to coarsen your place up. We'll finish our drinks and clear out."

Caroline brushed back her hair. She felt stiff, off balance. He'd be leaving soon, and she wanted to be glad. Meeting him brought back bad memories, a lot of hurt. She'd done plenty to block the pain out of her life, and she didn't need to open the door and invite it back in. So when she opened her mouth, her words surprised herself. "Like I said, we have two rooms free."

"Yeah?" he asked. "We'll take them."

Clea came forward, a worried look in her green eyes.

"Someone just made a pass at Leo Dumonde's wife," she said, "and Leo wants to fight him outside. I think he's trying to be Dad."

Caroline exhaled; she didn't have the patience just then. Leo Dumonde was an abstract expressionist from New York, a man with a bigger reputation for investing than painting, and he was one of the artists who tried to live what he thought was the Hugh Renwick way: paint fast, fight hard. Exhibit timber, cheat on your wife, drink too much, hunt and fish enough to get noticed by the sports writers.

"Your father was the real thing," Joe said. "Leo Dumonde's a fake. He won't be stepping outside with anyone from my boat."

"You knew our father?" Clea asked, twinkling.

"Knew of him," Joe said. "The bastard."

Clea's smile evaporated.

"Clea, meet Joe Connor," Caroline said evenly, every one of her senses on guard.

"*The* Joe Connor?" Clea asked.

"I think so," he said, flashing her a wicked grin and shaking her hand.

"We've been wanting to meet you for a long time," Clea said.

"He's a treasure hunter," Caroline said. "He's here to raise the *Cambria,* and then he's going home to Florida."

"That's right," Joe said. "Renwick territory is a little too dangerous for me. Or at least it was when Hugh was around."

"We're our father's daughters," Caroline said sharply, the pain of Joe's rejection as sharp as it had been at fifteen. Amazed that it could still hurt, she felt her eyes fill with tears. He had been her friend, and he had cut her off without a second chance. Not even for her own sins, but for their fathers'. "You'd better not forget that."

"I never have," Joe Connor said softly.

* * *

Closing her office door behind her, Caroline went to her desk. Her hands were shaking, her heart pounding as if she'd just climbed a steep trail. Clea had driven away, and

Caroline was glad to be alone. Pulling the curtains, she sat down.

The bar was noisy. She heard the loud voices, the excited laughter. It was a busy night at the Renwick Inn, and she knew she should feel pleased. Friends and acquaintances from the past often walked through her door. Sometimes they knew she owned the place, often they were surprised to find out. It never mattered: Caroline viewed those visits as serendipitous, lucky business.

Joe Connor was different.

Very slowly, she opened the top drawer of her desk. It was cluttered, filled with pens and receipts and mementos. Reaching back, rifling through the papers, she found what she was looking for. She pulled out the old picture and laid it on her desktop.

It was Joe's first-grade school picture, taken long ago. The little boy was smiling, his front tooth missing. He had blond hair, the back sticking up in a cowlick. The picture was stained brown, and dark flecks covered the boy's face. The flecks were his father's blood.

Caroline had held James Connor's hand while he shot himself. Crushed beneath his body, she had pulled his son's picture from the spreading pool of blood. Silent now, she sat at her desk and stared at Joe's face.

Her mother had given her permission to write to him. Against her better judgment, Augusta had let her find his address in Newport, even given her the stamp. Caroline, five years old, had written to Joe Connor, six years old, to tell him she was sorry his father was dead. She didn't mention the gun, she left out the blood. Her emotions were enough, her sorrow for another child who had lost his father. Her mother had helped her print the words, and the letter was short.

Joe wrote back. He thanked her for her letter. She could still remember his first-grade printing, his confusing words: "My father had a heart attack with you. I am glad you were with him."

Caroline responded. They became pen pals. On and off during the years, they wrote to each other. They sent Christmas cards, birthday cards, valentines. As the years went by, Joe began to ask about his father. From the questions, Caroline could tell that he had been lied to, that he had a totally wrong idea about his father's death.

Joe seemed to have the idea that their fathers had been friends. James Connor had met Hugh Renwick during one of his painting forays to Newport, guys from different walks of life who liked to drink together. Somehow James had ended up visiting the Renwicks and had a heart attack in their kitchen.

To Augusta's consternation, Joe's letters began to arrive more regularly. He and Caroline liked each other; when they became teenagers, they liked each other more. It drove Augusta crazy, seeing the name Connor in the return address. She'd grill Caroline about the letters, tell her to stop writing back. Reminded of her husband's infidelity, she couldn't stand Joe Connor.

The letters stopped. Caroline hadn't thought about that part in years, but the memory still carried power. She felt the color rising in her neck. Joe finally learned the truth, and not from Caroline.

Joe's mother had been too ashamed to tell him how his father had died, and one day someone in his family let it slip. An uncle or a cousin, Caroline couldn't remember. Joe finally learned that his father had committed suicide. The heart attack had been a lie, and so had the story about their fathers being friends.

James Connor had died among enemies.

That was terrible, enough to break the heart of any teenage boy. But what was worse, the thing that brought tears to Caroline's eyes now, was the betrayal. She had been his friend. All along, reading his letters, she had known she should tell him the truth.

At the end, he couldn't forgive her. She had known and he didn't. He was seventeen and needed to know all he could about his father, and Caroline had held back a crucial fact: Her father had been having an affair with his mother, and James Connor had killed himself because of it. She had withheld the most important thing one friend could ever give another: the truth.

Truth was never big in the Renwick family, but that was no excuse. Sitting at her desk, staring at the bloody picture, she thought of Joe Connor out in her bar. If he were still a friend, she could buy him a drink, catch up on old times, get to know the man in person. But as it stood right now, he was just another customer.

September 20, 1972

Dear Joe Connor,

We have a shipwreck near our house! It happened long ago. The Cambria came from England loaded with treasure. My sisters and I look for coins on Firefly Beach. If we find some, I will send you one. Our beach is magical. Instead of lighthouses we have fireflies. Are you in fourth grade? I'm in third. The Cambria was a barquentine. It is buried in the mud.

Sincerely yours,
Caroline Renwick

October 16, 1972

Dear Caroline,

Why do you always write Dear Joe Connor? No other Joe lives here. Shipwrecks are cool, as long as you're not on them. Newport has plenty. Lots of barques. (The nickname for barquentine.) Yes I'm in fourth. How many sisters do you have? Keep looking for the treasure.

Your friend,
Joe

P.S. Of course it is buried in the mud. Otherwise, it would decompose. (That means "rot" to you third-graders.)

CHAPTER THREE

Joe Connor drove his truck down to the dock, feeling the air grow thick with sea mist. Behind him was a convoy of vehicles returning to the ship. Bill Shepard sat across the seat, but Joe wished he were alone. He hadn't been prepared for his reaction to meeting Caroline Renwick. He felt wired, as if he had either just landed or lost a black marlin. His hands were actually shaking on the steering wheel. He needed a drink, and he had quit drinking ten years ago.

For one thing, she was beautiful. Five-six and slender with incredible curves, the kind of body that sailors spend their lives dreaming about. Her face belonged on magazine covers, porcelain-pale with wide gray-blue eyes and high cheekbones, a tender mouth that wanted to smile but didn't right away. Her dark hair was long and wavy, and with her pallor it gave her a mysterious black-Irish look that made Joe think of whispers and passion and how her fingernails might feel digging into his back.

For another thing, the main thing, she was Caroline Renwick.

They had a past. All the letters and then, when he'd found out the truth, the rage. He had seen her father's famous portrait of her, *Girl in a White Dress,* hanging at the Metropolitan Museum of Art. But by then he was deep into his hatred of the Renwicks. The lies had already come to light.

"Nice place, the Renwick Inn," Bill said, yawning as he gazed out the open window.

"It is," Joe said.

"So, we'll be keeping a couple of rooms there, sort of like a land base?" Bill asked. He was new to Joe's crew, a diver they'd picked up at the tail end of the last excavation. He was young and eager, but he liked to talk too much. Joe wasn't big on getting to know his team. They did their work, he paid their salary.

"Yes," Joe said.

"Pretty girls," Bill said. "That owner chick and her sister. They friends of yours?"

"Not exactly," Joe said. "But close enough."

"I wouldn't mind getting to know her better, that Caroline. Very hot, very hot. But she has that New England–reserved look, real hard to get. You know?"

"That's because she is," Joe said harshly.

"Hey, you never know." Bill laughed in that drawn-out southern way of his. He had a spooky cast to his eyes, and his manner managed to make most things he said sound snide. Joe felt a big knot of anger balling up in his stomach, feeling like the right thing to do was defend Caroline and not really knowing why.

"Listen," Joe said. "You want to drink, do it somewhere besides the Renwick Inn. When it's your turn to bunk there, stay away from Caroline and her sisters."

"Sister," Bill corrected Joe. "There was only one."

There are two, Joe thought, remembering Caroline's letters. He didn't bother to enlighten Bill.

"I'll tell everyone, not just you, but the

Renwicks are off limits. Let's just say they're friends of the family. Okay?"

"Gotta respect that," Bill conceded. "But they're sexy as all hell. Too bad."

"Too bad," Joe agreed.

They were nearing the water. The saltier the air got, the easier Joe breathed. Going to sea, he always felt like a freed man. All the bonds of dry land, the problems and worries, slipped away. He loved the movement of waves under his feet, the sense of wind and tides having more power than he did. It had always been that way, since around the time he stopped writing to Caroline. He had escaped life by shipping out.

The road curved around, the coast grew rocky. In the back of his mind, Joe wondered where it was: Firefly Hill, the place where his father had shot himself. He could locate it on a chart—had done so a million times—but being so physically close sent chills down his neck.

On the USGS charts, the town was called Black Hall and the point of land, jutting like a crooked elbow into Long Island Sound, was called Hubbard's Point. Firefly Hill was a dot on the chart, the apostrophe in the name "Hubbard's Point," the highest point of land on the shoreline from Branford to Stonington.

Firefly Beach was the family's name for their private beach; Joe recalled Caroline's story about having fireflies instead of a lighthouse.

Joe had dived for treasure in five of the seven seas, gotten rich doing it, found artifacts he still couldn't believe. But the *Cambria* was his Holy Grail. His Atlantis. Diving off Bosporus, his hold filled with Turkish gold and casks of Russian rubies, he had rocked the nights away in his cramped bunk, plotting his excavation of the *Cambria.* Finally, he laid legal claim to the wreck and brought his equipment and team and fleet north from Florida.

Was it just because the *Cambria* had sunk off the Black Hall shore? Within sight of Firefly Hill? Staring at the foggy road ahead of him, Joe thought to himself: Black Hall should be marked by a skull and crossbones on nautical charts. His reaction might have been less intense if the same name hadn't made him feel so happy for all those years, seeing it postmarked on Caroline's letters. He was bitter about the way she had held back the truth. But she had piqued his interest early with her letter about the *Cambria,* and here he was. In Renwick territory.

In too many ways, the Renwicks had shaped

his life. Hugh had come to paint in Newport. Joe's mother worked for a lobster company, just a pretty fish lady with rough hands and sore feet, and when the artist with his easel on the dock had asked her to have a drink with him, it had been too exciting to turn down.

Although the affair didn't last long, from the very beginning Hugh owned Joe's mother's heart. When his father found out, it broke his. She spent her life loving a man she could never have, and the years and events made her bitter. She remarried, had another son, tried to live her life better the second time. But she could never stop loving Hugh Renwick and she had never been accessible to Joe.

After all these years, no one had ever told him the whole story of his father's death. Only the Renwicks knew what had happened in that house. Roman Catholic, his mother had kept even the fact of his suicide buried for as long as she could. That, plus the guilt she must have felt over the affair and what it drove his father to do, had turned the truth into a black secret that she had never talked about before her death. Joe felt the bitterness rising. He wanted to turn around and ask Caroline questions. But too many years had passed between them in silence.

He pulled into the sandy parking lot at Moonstone Point, parked his pickup truck next to the dockmaster's office. Half the trucks in the shabby old lot belonged to Joe's crew, and more were pulling in. Most of them were already headed out to the *Meteor,* the research vessel his guys referred to as "the mother ship." He used the truck's CB radio to call the launch.

"Meteor, this is Patriot One, we're at the dock. Over," he said into the microphone.

"Roger, Patriot," came the crackling voice. "Coming to get you straightaway. Over."

"Make it fast," Joe said, his chest hurting with an old pressure. "I'm getting land legs, I've been here so long."

"Don't worry, skipper. We're on the way."

Joe clicked off, settling back to wait. He listened to Bill talk about the site, what they'd seen earlier that day. The project was exciting; in spite of himself, Joe breathed the salt air and began to relax.

Lives lost, hopes gone down. With the sunken ship came a hold of old dreams, the very specific lives of a ship captain and his mates. That's how Joe saw it: Raising a vessel's treasure was like meeting the dead. Their families, their habits, their fragile old bones.

He heard the high pitch of the launch's engine, the slap of its hull. Grabbing his chart case and duffel bag, he climbed out of the pickup truck. The sea was dark gray and choppy; clouds were thick on the horizon. The big mako bounded across the waves, sidled up to the dock.

Dan Forsythe, the launch driver, wore an orange foul-weather jacket over khaki shorts. "Hey, captain," he said.

"Hi, Dan," Joe said, climbing down the ladder. It was dead-low tide, a long drop from the dock to the water. In his mind, he was already back at work, calculating tomorrow's tides and currents, thinking of the operation.

"Water's rough. Hope that doesn't work against us," Dan said. "We going to try stabilizing the aft timbers tomorrow?"

"If the bottom hasn't shifted," Joe said.

They wheeled away from the dock, through the harbor crowded with pleasure boats, and out to sea. Lights were beginning to come on in the houses along the shore. Joe's eyes were drawn to them; he couldn't help it.

He tried to concentrate on work, but it was a lost cause. Black Hall stole his attention.

Which one was Firefly Hill? He brushed the salt spray out of his eyes, gazing at the salt marshes and granite ledges. The houses slid by, and Joe thought of Caroline, of the darkness and trouble in her beautiful gray-blue eyes, her toughness and secrets. Now that he had met her, he couldn't get her out of his mind.

But then, he never could.

* * *

"What's he like?" Skye asked Clea.

"Can Mom hear you?" Clea asked, wanting to be sure they had privacy.

They were on the telephone. It was late, but Clea had called Firefly Hill the minute she got home from the Renwick Inn, after meeting Joe and leaving Caroline. The news of Joe Connor dropping into their midst was too crucial to keep from Skye.

"No," Skye said, "Mom's in the other room. Tell me."

"He's all grown up," Clea said. "Isn't it weird? All these years have passed, but I imagine Joe Connor still looking like that old picture Caroline always used to carry around."

"Six years old," Skye said, "with that cowlick and his front tooth missing."

"He's handsome," Clea said, "in a seaside kind of way. Very bright blue eyes, and he's tall. Strong, the way I guess men get when they go around lugging sea chests up from the bottom of the ocean." She spoke softly, not wanting to hurt Peter's feelings. As the hospital chaplain, he didn't do much heavy lifting. He visited the sick and soothed the bereaved, and Clea loved him more than she believed humanly possible. He was upstairs, reading one last story to Mark and Maripat.

"What is he, a fisherman?" Skye asked. "Like his father?"

"No, he has a marine salvage business. You know those boats we can see from Mom's? Those are his. He's a treasure hunter."

"How did Caroline seem, meeting him?"

"Well, she . . ." Clea began, but she was distracted by the sound of clinking ice cubes. "What's that? Skye, you're not still drinking, are you?"

"I'm having a nightcap," Skye said. "Here I am, in my old room at Mom's. Thirty-one years old, and I've moved back home. What a loser."

"That's not true," Clea said. Was Skye as bereft as she suddenly sounded? Or was it just booze talking? Clea had watched alcohol work its black magic before on their father.

"Tell me, Clea," Skye said calmly. "How did Caroline take meeting him?"

"She was shocked," Clea said.

"Because she loved him," Skye said in a low and dangerous voice.

"She didn't love him," Clea said. "She was only fifteen when they stopped writing to each other. It was just a crush."

"She loved him," Skye said. "She loved him more than anything."

Clea heard the tense edge in Skye's voice again, and she sat still, listening.

"Caroline used to talk about him," Skye said. "I remember. And she didn't stop carrying his picture. She kept it with her for ages afterward. She took it on every horrible trip, every time Dad left us alone."

"I know."

"Kept it in her backpack, one of those waterproof pockets."

"Don't, Skye," Clea said, feeling her heart start to pump.

"Joe would understand."

"Understand what?" Clea asked.

"Me," Skye said. "Caroline. Redhawk. The universe."

"He's a scruffy pirate with holes in his shoes," Clea said, her anxiety growing. "He's not an oracle."

"Where's he keep his pirate ship when it's not off Mom's?" Skye asked.

"Meteor, it's called. I saw the name painted on the side of his truck. At Moonstone Point, I guess. What do you want to say to him?" Clea pressed.

"That maybe it was an accident," Skye said. "Maybe his father didn't mean to shoot himself."

"Skye."

"It could have been," Skye said, her voice suddenly thick with tears, drunkenness making her sound maudlin. "You can see why I'd think that, can't you?"

"Skye, listen to me," Clea said. "You've had too much to drink. Go to bed, and you'll feel better in the morning."

"I think I could help him," Skye said. "I really think I could help him."

The sound of Skye's muffled sobs filled the phone.

Clea put her head down. She tried to gather her thoughts, to say something soothing that would defuse Skye's contorted grief, make her want to go to sleep.

But before she could speak, Skye hung up the phone.

Clea sat still, wondering what to do. Was Skye going to do something crazy? Go to bed, she prayed. Go to sleep, Skye. Climbing the stairs, she decided to check on her children. For so long, she and her sisters had faced their past by not facing it. They busied themselves to avoid it. Clea had a family. If her family was happy, she could be too. Happiness was so cleansing.

She tiptoed into her children's rooms, kissed them each as they slept. Whispering "sweet dreams" into Maripat's ear, she wished for her daughter's dreams to be free of all fear. She kissed Mark, wishing the same. Kissing her kids, Clea suddenly knew she had to call Skye back. She felt so frantic, she fumbled the buttons as she dialed the telephone.

Augusta answered. Clea heard the pleased warmth in her mother's voice that one of her daughters would call, even this late, even to talk to Skye instead of her. She called upstairs for Skye, and told Clea she must have gone out. Clea felt her heart banging. Her hands felt clammy. "Thanks, Mom," she said, blowing kisses into the phone as if nothing were wrong. Then she called Caroline.

"I think I just did something stupid," she said. "I just spoke to Skye. She's very upset, and I think she's gone down to the dock. She's drunk."

"You let her hang up?"

"What was I supposed to do?" Clea asked.

"I know," Caroline said. "I'm sorry, Clea. It's not your fault."

"It feels like it is," Clea said.

* * *

The town was small. Everyone knew Skye, and Caroline got the phone call. She immediately telephoned Clea to tell her, and sped to the Shoreline General Hospital. All three Renwick girls had been born there. Her heart racing, not knowing what she was going to find, Caroline tried to gain courage from that fact: Skye had come to life in this place.

"She's alive," the policeman said.

Caroline nodded, her knees going weak with relief.

"She's drunk out of her mind. No one's going to look the other way on this," he said. "She's going to get a DWI."

Caroline read his badge: Officer John Daugherty. She knew him from around town;

sometimes he brought his wife to the inn for dinner. "Did you find her?" she asked.

"Yes, I did."

"Thank you," Caroline said.

"She's a lucky person," he said. "She really cracked up good, and she could have gotten herself killed."

They stood outside the emergency entrance, the summer breeze soft and warm. Police cars had pulled in helter-skelter, their blue lights silently flashing, as if the hospital itself were the scene of a crime. Officer Daugherty had kind eyes and a calm voice, and he spoke with the soft regret Caroline remembered from the officers who had sometimes come to the inn to tell them they had picked up Hugh for drunk driving.

"Nature saved her," he said. "She left the pavement going eighty miles an hour, but her wheels hit a bog. There's a marsh along Moonstone Road, and her tires sank in deep. Even so, she had enough speed going to take down a fence and total her car."

"Moonstone Road?" Caroline asked.

"Yes. Heading for the docks. I can't help knowing she's married to Simon Whitford, but that's not the name she was saying when I got to her."

"What name was she saying?"

The officer lowered his voice, trying to be discreet. "Joe," he said. "She was calling for someone named Joe."

* * *

Caroline found Skye in a private cubicle in the emergency room.

Skye Renwick Whitford looked like an angel in white. White bandages, white sheets, pearlescent white skin. Except for the bruises' purple, black, wine-red. Her light lashes rested on high cheekbones. She was so thin, so small, she looked more like a child than a woman. The sight of her filled Caroline with such powerful love, she shook her head and had to take a step back.

Love expanded Caroline's chest and made her heart hurt. She stood at Skye's side, gazing down at her. She lay so still. Was she even breathing? Caroline watched for her chest to rise and fall. Skye's small mouth was open slightly under the cool green oxygen mask, her upper lip gashed and swollen. Her bruised eyelids twitched with dreams.

Caroline gently took Skye's hand. It was a sculptor's hand, rough as a workman's. Her fingernails were dirty with paint and clay. Bringing the tiny hand to her lips, Caroline smelled turpentine.

"Skye," she said. "Can you hear me?"

Skye didn't reply.

"You didn't mean this one, did you?" Caroline asked. "You didn't drive off the road on purpose. You were on your way somewhere."

"Skye?" Caroline tried again. "Why did you want to see Joe?"

The sight of Skye's face made Caroline stop. Her eyes were closed, but tears were sliding out of them, down her cheeks. Were her lips moving under the mask? The rushing oxygen sounded loud, a little unreal. Skye reached up and pulled the mask away.

"I didn't get to the dock," she said.

"No," Caroline said.

"It sounds stupid now," she said. "But it made sense at the time."

"Tell me anyway."

"I hate sobering up," Skye whispered. "My head hurts, and I feel like an idiot. Will you get me out of here?"

"I can't," Caroline said. "Not right now."

"Maybe his father made a mistake," Skye said, touching her bruised face. "Shot the wrong person."

"The wrong person?" Caroline asked, feeling sick. "Who would he have shot instead?"

"Me," Skye said.

"You weren't born yet," Caroline said. "You were still in Mom's womb."

"I wish he had," Skye said. "Then I wouldn't have been born."

"If you hadn't," Caroline said, putting her face right beside Skye's "I wouldn't have had you for a sister. Clea and I wouldn't have known you at all. Don't say those things."

"I wouldn't be a killer," Skye said.

"Oh, Skye," Caroline said, her eyes filling with tears. It always came back to this. How could she think it wouldn't?

Skye twitched, from pain or vodka or Demerol. Her voice was choked, her words hard to understand. Caroline wished her father were there. She wanted him to see Skye's agony, soothe her head with his rough, kind hands, tell her to forgive herself. His mistake had brought her here. Caroline squeezed Skye's hand. She searched her mind for something to say, something wise and comforting, but she felt too churned up herself.

"Joe," Skye said.

"Why are you calling for him?" Caroline asked. "What do you want him for?"

"We're connected. Don't you feel it?" Skye asked, her eyes wide open.

"I used to," Caroline said.

"More than ever now," Skye continued, almost unhearing.

Caroline held her hand and didn't answer.

Later, in the waiting room, she bowed her head so no one could see her face. How had they gotten here?

* * *

Six-feet-three, Hugh Renwick was a large man, and very strong; his ideas were huge to match.

He had been a great outdoorsman, as excessive in his sport as he was in his art and life, and he had wanted to teach his daughters the things other men taught sons. He gave them compasses and Swiss Army knives. He taught them to read the sky and mountain trails, to hunt for food.

His home had been violated by a stranger. The reason didn't count. Hugh, thinking that dangers lurked in every corner now, wanted his daughters to be able to defend themselves. Even if his affair with James Connor's wife was the cause of the attack.

They would drive away from the sea, north through pine woods and meadows of yellow flowers. The road followed a lazy brown river, and when Skye was young they would keep her occupied by telling her to count the red barns and black cows. Her father was so famous, the whole world wanted him, but on those trips he was theirs alone.

When they got to New Hampshire, to Redhawk Mountain, they would unload all the camping things. The trees were tall, and skinny green caterpillars dangled from branches by silken threads. Her father would help them pitch their tents; he would take the guns out of their cases. The .22-caliber rifles were heavy, especially when the girls were young, but their father taught them how to lift them slowly, to aim carefully.

Hugh's face by the campfire was shadowed with worry, for the fact that he had three daughters and the world was a cruel place.

Caroline had sat between Clea and Skye, listening to him, hearing the sounds made by wild things in the woods. He had told them that learning to shoot was necessary, to protect themselves against predators. His girls were sensitive and kind. Others were not, and bad men existed in a kill-or-be-killed world.

They knew he was right, he had said, because of the man who had come to their house. Their father had spoken so gently, as if he were telling a bedtime story.

The fire crackled. Her sisters were warm beside her, and her father drew them close. He knew they loved wildlife, kept lists of the birds they'd seen. Each had her own garden at Firefly Hill. In some ways, hunting was like a nature walk. The softer you walked, the more creatures you saw. When it was time to kill, you became one with the animal. Mysteriously thrilling, the hunt stirred instincts most humans had long forgotten, a fantastic surging of life deep inside. He talked about hunting the way he talked about art: the ecstasy of life and death.

Caroline didn't believe it for a minute. She was thirteen, Clea was eleven, Skye was eight. Listening to their father, faces aglow in the firelight, the three girls were terrified. But they trusted him. He saw to their welfare with passion and kindliness, and if he said they should learn to shoot animals, they would.

Caroline's first kill was a squirrel. It sat on the branch of an oak tree, its tail curled over its back. She aimed the way her father had taught her, and squeezed the trigger. The squirrel toppled over. Just like a toy on a shelf, it fell off the branch. It lay on the ground, a black hole in its white fur. Caroline felt sick.

Her father wanted them to go their own ways, to explore the mountain and hunt on their own. If such independence was terrifying for Caroline, she could only imagine how it was for her younger sisters. She used to follow Skye. She would track her, fifty yards back, as if Skye were her quarry, just watching out for her.

Once Skye was crossing a narrow bridge across a fast stream. Halfway across she lost her footing, falling into the water. Caroline laid her gun down, kicked off her shoes, and went in after her. It was early spring, and the water came from melting river ice, farther north. The frigid water slashed around her, freezing her limbs, plastering them with the dead leaves of last winter. Her wool clothes weighed her down. Up ahead, Skye kept disappearing under the water.

By the time Caroline got her arms around Skye, they were in the rapids. The white water hissed in their ears. She spit out mouthfuls of cold water. Blinded by icy spray, she caught nightmare glimpses of snakes sunning themselves on the flat rocks they passed. Bumping into logs, tearing their clothes on sticks, Caroline clutched Skye with one arm and tried to grab branches and vines with the other.

Crashing down the river, Caroline felt the stones underwater. The force would drive the sisters into deep, swirling pockets, and they would be sucked under and spit out. Craggy boulders blocked their way, too slippery to grasp. The river pulled them forward. Caroline wondered how high the falls would be; she knew they were going over. She wondered if they would die.

But then the river evened out. The rapids gave way to a wide, peaceful stream. The roar faded away to silence and birds singing. Overwhelmed with her own life, the sense of safety, Caroline began to laugh with joy. She hugged Skye. But Skye didn't hug back. Her lips were blue. Weighed down by her jacket and boots, she felt like a sack of grain. Caroline pulled her to the riverbank. Skye was alive, and her eyes were open. But they wouldn't blink, wouldn't meet Caroline's.

"Skye, we're safe," Caroline said, rubbing her small hands.

"Did you see?" Skye asked, her voice small and frozen. "All those snakes on the rocks back there?"

"Yes, but—"

"I want to go home, Caroline," Skye said, the feelings breaking out. She began to cry hard. "Take me home. Please take me home."

But Caroline couldn't. She couldn't talk her father out of what he thought was best. Falling in the icy river was part of learning how to be tough. Seeing snakes on the rocks was how you learned to keep from getting bitten. The lesson Caroline learned that day was slightly more disturbing: Just because she felt thrilled to be alive, overcome with rapture and gratitude, didn't necessarily mean her sister felt the same way. It didn't mean that at all.

Hugh had been so wrong. Caroline knew that now. Her father was dead, officially of cancer, but he had died years before, of a broken heart. Unable to bear what had finally happened to Skye, his baby, their beautiful girl, he had drunk himself to death, turning away from his family in the process. That more than the hunts themselves had filled Caroline with the bitterness she now felt. Because Skye was doing the same thing.

March 14, 1973

Dear the only Joe,

I have two sisters. Clea and Skye. Clea is better than a best friend, and Skye is our beautiful baby sister. I wish we were all in the same grade together. Sometimes we want to talk so no one else can understand, and we do. It's hard to explain, but I know what they're thinking and they know what I'm thinking. It's like magic, only it's not. It's having sisters.

Your friend,
Caroline

June 19, 1973

Dear Caroline,

   Well, he's definitely not magic, but he's pretty cute. Sam. Good old Sam, my baby brother. Only he's a real baby—as in just born. Squawks like a seagull all night long. I took him out in my boat the other day, and my mother called the Coast Guard. She was really worried. Something about him not knowing how to swim (he's about the size of a flounder), but she missed the point. The kid loves water. Loves boats too. I swear, he wanted to row.

                    See you later,
                    Joe

CHAPTER FOUR

"Mom admits Skye must have had a little too much to drink," Clea said, raising her eyebrow. The night before, while Caroline had maintained watch at the hospital, Clea had stayed home with her family, in touch only by telephone. She felt guilty, and it came through in the too-bright tone of her voice.

"Like a fifth of vodka?" Caroline asked.

The day was new, and they were on their way to Firefly Hill, to pick up Augusta and drive her to the hospital. Clea was at the wheel of her Volvo, and as they rounded the headland, Caroline caught sight of the big white ships on the horizon. They reminded her of Skye's last words the previous night.

"Did you tell Skye that Joe Connor was here?" Caroline asked.

"Oh, God," Clea said. "Why?"

Caroline was almost too angry to say. She felt tired and rumpled from spending the night at the hospital, and she hated these triangles of sisterhood, when two would know something the other wasn't supposed to. When she confided a worry to Clea and heard it come back from Skye. Or when she told some gossip to Skye and two hours later got a phone call from Clea, reporting the big news. Secrets among sisters were dangerous and nearly impossible to keep.

"Because she was on the way to see him," Caroline said flatly.

"She was?"

"She thinks if she hadn't been born, none of the rest would have happened."

"She was drunk. I thought she'd just go to bed," Clea said. "When she asked me about Joe's boat . . . I didn't think she'd drive. I can't stand thinking she crashed because of me," Clea said.

"Don't blame yourself, Clea," Caroline said.

"I can't help it. I should never have let her off the phone. Or I should have had her put Mom on the line."

"Blame has never gotten any of us very far," Caroline said. "So don't do it to yourself now."

They had arrived at Firefly Hill. The two sisters sat very still, staring at the door and wondering what kind of mood their mother was in. Would she be enthusiastic, ready to Visit the Sick with a big basket of freshly cut snapdragons? Or would she be frail, focused on her own arthritis or migraine headache to avoid noticing that her youngest child was going downhill fast?

The sun shone through a layer of high gossamer clouds. Not quite bright enough to throw dark shadows, it bathed the house and yard in an overall muted whiteness. A cold front was moving in, and the wind blew hard. Augusta appeared in the kitchen window. She was dressed, ready to go. At the sight of Caroline and Clea, she gave a hearty wave.

"Here we go," Caroline said, opening the car door.

"Have you seen Homer?" Augusta called, looking around.

The old dog sometimes disappeared. No one knew where he went. He could be gone for hours, or even overnight, but he always came back. Caroline didn't reply, knowing that Augusta's defense and denial were already locked in place. She just walked across the yard, to kiss her mother and drive her to the hospital.

* * *

At the hospital, all was quiet and blue. The lights at the psychiatric nurses' station had a shaded violet tone. Various monitors beeped and whirred melodically. The white-clad nurse pushing the medicine cart along the hall seemed to be swimming in contemplative slow motion.

From the far end of the hall, a patient let forth an eerie, ungodly howl, like someone in extreme agony. Standing with her mother and sister, Caroline had the impression of lurking in a strange undersea environment. For no reason at all, she wondered how it might feel to dive for treasure.

When signaled by the charge nurse, Caroline and Clea took their mother's hands and walked with her into Skye's room. The sight of Skye so still and pale, even more so than last night, made Caroline draw a deep breath. But her mother actually gasped. Caroline recognized this as a moment of truth: Her mother hadn't had time to polish, encode, or reinvent the situation. Unguarded, Augusta simply stared at Skye lying in her hospital bed. With frail fingers she touched her black pearls while tears ran down her cheeks.

The heart monitor glowed green in the otherwise dark room. Caroline and Clea stood back, letting their mother bend close to Skye, kiss her bandaged forehead. Augusta was silently crying, her shoulders shaking under her mink coat. A storm of emotion shivered through her thin body, but Caroline watched her force it down. She wiped her tears. She squared her shoulders.

"Skye. I'm here," Augusta said out loud.

"She can't hear you," Clea whispered.

"Skye. Wake up. Wake up, dear. It's your mother." Augusta spoke to Skye the way she talked to her daughters' answering machines, as if she knew someone was sitting there listening, unwilling to pick up the phone.

"Mom, she's sedated," Clea said.

"Caroline told me she spoke to her," Augusta said, sounding injured.

"Just a few words," Caroline said, wanting to cushion the fact that she had been there and her mother had not. That had always been the case, and Augusta was very sensitive about it. Caroline felt the all-too-familiar pressure in her chest. Skye was so injured and troubled, her mother was so infuriating and needy, and Clea was kowtowing to beat the band. Caroline wanted to rush out, slam the door behind her, head for the airport, and get on a plane to anywhere.

"If she needs her sleep, let's let her be," Augusta said, sounding frustrated. "She'll talk to me tomorrow. In the meantime, let's go find Peter. He's here, isn't he?" And she left Skye's bedside without another word.

Caroline and Clea drew together. With their mother gone, the old feelings came back: just the three of us, Caroline thought, holding Clea's hand and looking at Skye. The way it's always been. Three sisters on a lonely mountaintop, told to hunt by their father, holding hands when he turned his back. They had always taken care of each other.

Catching up with Augusta at the nurses' station, the women heard the charge nurse say that Peter was with Skye's doctor, who was just finishing up with another patient.

Augusta raised her dark eyebrows. No one could mistake her displeasure. She watched with silent disdain as the nurses moved methodically about their tasks. What did she want them to do? Caroline wondered. Make Skye's doctor finish with his other patients faster? Serve cocktails?

"I'm going to go mad if that doctor doesn't hurry," Augusta said. She spoke in her normal voice instead of a whisper, and nurses up and down the corridor turned to look. "They'll have to admit me to this very floor if I have to stand here another minute."

"Mother, shhhh," Clea said.

"I have no respect for a doctor who makes the mothers of his patients wait like this," Augusta continued. "I think it's very rude."

Caroline and Clea exchanged a glance. Whenever their mother became this imperious, it meant she was very scared. She refused to accept the things she couldn't stand, the details of life she found too awful. Twisting reality was Augusta's way of marshaling her own sanity. Clea slid her arm around Augusta's slender shoulders, snuggling against the fur coat their mother had thrown on over her jeans and sneakers. Caroline felt her own rage start to abate.

"Doctors do it on purpose," Clea said. "They like to make the mothers really squirm, waiting to talk to them. Ministers do it too. Peter learned it in divinity school."

Augusta shook her head, her lips tightening. She was not about to laugh at anything. She was putting forth her best lofty grande-dame air, gazing appraisingly down the corridors as if she owned them. Like Caroline,

Augusta Renwick had contributed to this hospital. Since Hugh's death, her sojourns here had been for opening ceremonies, board meetings, or events involving her chaplain son-in-law. Coming to the psychiatric floor to visit her youngest daughter was most assuredly not in her realm.

Finally Peter came along, wearing his clerical collar and dark trousers. He was talking to another man. He kissed Augusta and Caroline, then pulled Clea into a massive hug. Caroline watched the way they held each other, whispered a few words, looking deeply into each other's eyes until a slow smile came to Clea's troubled face. Then he introduced Dr. Jack Henderson, the head of their substance abuse unit.

"How do you do?" Dr. Henderson said.

"Pleased to meet you," Augusta said warily.

"Hi, Jack," Clea said, stepping forward.

Augusta shuddered, possibly at the idea of this doctor getting too close, at the prospect of him knowing anything too personal about the family. Caroline had met him before, seen him at a retrospective of her father's work.

"Hi," Caroline said, shaking his hand.

"Do you know each other?" Augusta asked.

"I collect your late husband's work," Dr. Henderson said.

"Really?" Augusta asked, lightening up slightly. "That's good to hear. Then you probably know that Skye takes after him. She's an artist herself."

The doctor nodded.

"She's a genius, doctor. Truly brilliant, and I am not saying that just because I am her mother." Augusta looked around the group for confirmation. Her eyes were glittering, as if tears were close by. "She's a sculptor. She was recognized by the art world years ago, when she was very young. Right, girls?"

"She was," Clea said. Caroline said nothing. She felt her mother lean against her slightly, and she held her hand for support.

"She's so talented . . ." Augusta choked up. Touching her throat, she pulled herself back together. "But she seems to be blocked."

"Blocked?" he repeated.

"I'm not an artist, so I don't know," Augusta said, "but her father used to say he'd kill himself if he couldn't paint. An artist who can't make art . . . She's suffering so. Right, Caroline? We can see it, can't we?"

"Mom . . ."

"That's all it is," Augusta said, trying to convince herself and everyone else.

"Hmmm," Dr. Henderson said noncommittally.

"Mom, let's wait for Skye to wake up," Caroline said. "Let her talk to the doctor herself."

Augusta shook Caroline off.

"Artist's block," Augusta said, her voice trembling. "It explains everything, I think. She's so afraid she can't work anymore. And her husband left her. It's awful, it's just so terrible. . . ."

"Yes," Dr. Henderson said inscrutably.

"Who wouldn't drink a little under such trying circumstances? And I'm sure you know, alcohol fires the creative spirit. My God, could Hugh put it away! Skye takes after him even there, perhaps a little too much. If she could just moderate—"

"Excuse me?" Dr. Henderson asked.

"Perhaps you could suggest moderation!" Augusta said gingerly, offering the doctor his solution. "Half-measures don't come easily to any Renwick, that's for sure—"

"Mom," Caroline interrupted, stopping her.

"I believe moderation would help Skye. If she could just cut back a bit. You know, just stick to cocktails and wine with dinner.

Don't you agree?" Augusta continued, unfazed, her hand cupping her chin as if she were a consulting physician.

"No, I'm afraid not," the real doctor said.

"Excuse me?" Augusta asked.

"Moderation rarely works with alcoholics. Total abstinence is the only way."

"Skye is not . . . an *alcoholic*," Augusta said, shocked and wounded.

Linking arms with Caroline and Clea, she glared at the doctor. Insulated by her family, she felt safe. She wanted him to see that the Renwicks were good people who loved one another. She wanted him to understand that although eccentric, they were not crazy, not the sort of people who became alcoholics. Bad things had happened to them, but adversity had built their characters. Caroline ached for her mother, recognizing that in her vulnerability she was terrified for Skye.

"Last night," the doctor said, "she told me about the hunting incident."

"Well," Clea said, holding Peter's hand. "Then you know."

Just then the doctor's beeper went off. He gave everyone an apologetic look, shook Augusta's hand, and hurried down the hallway. Everyone watched him go. Caroline had expected her mother to look relieved at his departure, but instead her pallor had increased. She had a thin film of sweat on her brow.

"Augusta, sit down," Peter said, leading her to a cluster of chairs at the end of the hall.

"It was an accident," Augusta said out loud. Her tone was quiet, almost humble. Tears spilled down her cheeks. Her hands trembling, she pulled at her pearls.

"It was," Caroline said quietly.

"Skye was just a child," Augusta said to Peter, her eyes wide. "She had no business shooting a gun in the first place. Haven't I always said that?"

"Yes, Augusta," he said. "You have."

"Skye wouldn't hurt a soul. She never meant to harm that man. A hunting accident, that's all it was. No one ever suggested otherwise, there were never charges brought."

"Skye isn't bad," Caroline said. "No one is saying that."

"He called her an alcoholic!" Augusta said.

"She drinks," Caroline said.

"Dad's drinking changed," Clea said, "after it happened."

"It was a tragedy," Augusta said, "a horrible thing that happened a long time ago.

But there's no reason Skye should pay for it the rest of her life." Bewildered, she looked at Caroline. "Is there?"

Caroline shook her head. She was picturing the young man. She had heard the gunshot and Skye's scream, and she had been the first to find him. It had been fall, a bright blue day with yellow leaves covering the trail. He lay on the ground, the blood pouring from his chest. His eyes were bright and clear. His name was Andrew Lockwood, and he was twenty-five years old.

"Tell me why," Augusta said, staring straight into Caroline's eyes.

Caroline remembered taking her jacket off, pressing it into the hole in his chest. She could still feel the heat of his blood, see the question in his eyes. All the time, Skye, her voice as high as a baby bird's, asking what had she done, what had she done.

"Because she killed him, Mom," Caroline said quietly. "She didn't mean to, but she did."

January 7, 1977

Dear Joe,

I remember one of my letters to you, all about Clea and Skye and the magic of having sisters. Well, this one's not quite so nice. Did I mention my father? He's an artist. Okay, he's a famous artist. He tells us that he wants us to know How the World Works. (Boys have it easy, in case you're wondering) (according to him, anyway.) (I'm going parentheses-crazy.)

Girls have to be tough. Learn how to take care of ourselves. So he takes us hunting on Redhawk Mountain.

He loves us, you see.

He wants us to learn everything we can, really taste life. We camp out, go fishing and hunting. We go pretty far out in the country, and we have to fend for ourselves. I hate the hunting part. Killing is very hard—I know he'd be upset to know how much I hate hunting even squirrels.

At night, the woods are so dark, and we get scared. Sometimes very scared, especially Skye. I love her so much, Joe. Just writing this letter makes me cry, because if anything happened to Clea or

Skye, I don't know what I'd do. They are the best, sweetest sisters in the world.

Write back soon. I'm starting to think you might be my best friend.

Love,
Caroline

Feb 2, 1977

Dear Caroline,

Hunting, cool! Your dad sounds great. Okay, I'll be your best friend. On one condition. Tell me the scariest thing that ever happened on the mountain.

Love,
Joe

March 4, 1977

Dear Joe,

The scariest thing. Okay, I'll tell you. It's how I feel. My father made Skye shoot a gun. She didn't want to, Joe. I'm so mad at him. He took something innocent and destroyed it. So I'm scared by how much I hate him right now. Hunting's not cool, not the way you said. It's horrible. Do you still want to be my best friend? Probably not. Even I don't.

Caroline

March 21, 1977

Dear Caroline,

I can tell you're upset by the way you didn't sign your letter "love." It's a little thing, but we best friends can be pretty sensitive. The gun thing sounds lousy. Poor Skye. I don't even know her, but since she's your sister, I figure she's okay. Your dad should forget about hunting and go back to painting. Or better yet, treasure hunting. He can teach you to dig for gold doubloons.

Love,
Joe

P.S. I'm only joking to make you smile. So smile!

P.S. again: Thought I forgot about the *Cambria,* didn't you?

P.S. double again: Smile, C.

CHAPTER FIVE

Caroline was preoccupied.

Michele Brady saw it right away, the way Caroline strode into the inn so purposefully, past the guests eating breakfast in the parlor, grabbing the phone messages off Michele's desk with barely more than a "good morning." Caroline looked gorgeous, as always: sleeveless black linen dress, black sandals, silver hoop earrings, silver necklace. She smiled, but it seemed forced.

Or pained, Michele thought, concerned. From certain phone messages, she had gathered that Skye was in the hospital again. That girl certainly gave Caroline plenty to worry about. Her whole family did. Even Clea, whom everyone in town considered to be the picture of respectability, was always calling

Caroline for something. And Augusta didn't butter her toast without phoning Caroline for a consult.

Michele had been Caroline's assistant for ten years. At forty-two, she was just enough older than Caroline to feel rather protective of her. She was always telling her husband Tim about Caroline's crazy family, the things that went on. He was a professor of English at Connecticut College. Tim would listen with wry detachment, amusedly saying that Skye was New England's answer to Zelda Fitzgerald, or that the Renwick girls were like three divas in three different operas on the same stage.

Michele couldn't help laughing at Tim's take on the family, but she loved Caroline nonetheless. Caroline had hired her the year she opened the inn. They had spent the last ten years in separate offices, side by side, and although Caroline didn't specifically confide in her, Michele had been privy to the major moments in her life. She had watched Caroline transform from a . . . well, crazy Renwick girl into an astute and respected businesswoman. Caroline had always been loyal and kind, and those qualities had served her well.

Michele answered the phone, so she knew the general workings of Caroline's love life, business life, and family life. Over time she had watched Caroline build the Renwick Inn from a quirky little artists' retreat into an inn that attracted guests from all over the world. Some came for the location, others for the charm, still others because of the Renwick name.

Caroline's father was famous in a way usually reserved for actors or politicians, a man whose work hung in museums in New York, Paris, and London and whose wild nature had made him a favorite of magazine writers. One story in *Esquire* had called Hugh Renwick "the Hemingway of twentieth-century landscape painters." The author cited his bravery in World War II, his drinking and adultery, violence and self-destruction, the way his talent seemed to engulf everything—and everyone—in his life.

Doing the story, the author got drunk with Hugh. So did the photographer, who was famous in his own right. Their drunken escapades became part of the piece. They photographed him in a hunting jacket, with a rifle, somewhere in the woods at the edge of a bay in Maine. Hugh had told the story of an intruder that made it into the piece, a man who had entered his home and held his family hostage, finally blowing his own brains out.

Michele remembered Hugh's fury. It had saturated the magazine story: *his* home had been violated, *his* daughters threatened. He couldn't protect them twenty-four hours a day, but he could damn well teach them how to shoot a gun. He was sorry about the event on Redhawk Mountain, the hunting accident involving his daughter Skye. As Michele remembered it, the story didn't actually mention the name of the man she killed. All Hugh's sorrow and self-doubt had been edited out of the piece, leaving only rage and bluster.

Michele knew differently. Hugh Renwick was heartsick. As much as he had loved hunting, he celebrated life more. He loved nature. His adored his daughters. The world couldn't hold his passions; he had wanted excess and abundance for everyone, especially his family. But after the accident he turned inward. Michele had watched him mourn that young man every day, drinking alone in a dark corner of the Renwick Inn bar, his head bowed in silence.

Artists would approach him. He would be polite, sometimes let them buy him drinks. He could stare at the spot on the bar between his elbows for hours, watching the level of scotch in his glass rise and fall. Although he chose to drink at her inn, he couldn't stand to be with Caroline. It had killed Michele to watch her approach him, try to talk to him. He would turn surly, even belligerent. It was as if she reminded him of what was most precious in life, what he had failed to protect again and again. More than once, Michele heard him say that he had ruined Skye's life.

Three of his paintings hung in the bar. Hugh had done them when his daughters were young. Vivid and pure, they left no doubt about the love he had for the girls. Hunting scenes, set on Redhawk Mountain, each portrait depicted a different season, with each subject holding a different dead creature and weapon. Clea, in spring, held a rainbow trout in one hand and a fly rod in the other. Skye, in autumn, held a large knife and a writhing snake.

But it was Caroline in winter who took your breath away. Cradled in her arms was a small red fox. Blood dripped from its mouth. Snow covered the mountain and Caroline's cheeks were red. Her black hair blew across her eyes, but they showed through, clear blue and haunted. In her left hand she held the rifle that she had used to kill the fox. Her father had caught her compassion and regret; he had flooded the portrait with love for his oldest daughter. Michele shivered every time she looked at it.

Caroline walked out of her office. She had on her half-glasses, which gave her the look of a sexy librarian.

"What's this message?" she asked, ruffling a sheet of paper.

"Oh," Michele said, reading it. "He called first thing this morning. He left some rather complicated instructions about dialing ship-to-shore. I think he's one of those sailors who was here last night, drinking in the bar. They have Rooms Six and Nine, but I guess he's out on his boat."

"Did he say what he wanted?" Caroline asked.

"No. Just for you to call."

"Thanks," Caroline said. She walked into her office and closed the door.

* * *

Caroline dialed the marine operator and asked to be put through to the R/V Meteor. She held the line while the connection was made, staring out her window at the Ibis River, at egrets striding the shallows. She watched a kingfisher dive straight down, craning her neck to see what he came up with.

"This is Research Vessel *Meteor,*" a man's voice said, the transmission crackling with static. "Over."

"This is the high seas operator. I have a call for a Mr. Joe Connor."

"Hold for Captain Connor," the man said.

A minute passed. Finally Joe's voice came over the line. The operator signed off, and Caroline said hello.

"It's Caroline," she said. "I got your message."

"Is your sister okay?" he asked.

"Why do you ask?" Caroline asked, surprised that he would know.

"She left a message at the dock office," Joe said. "Last night. Something about needing to see me, it was important."

"Did you talk to her?"

"Not in person. She said she was coming right over, but she never showed up. I wasn't sure where to reach her. So I called you."

"She's in the hospital," Caroline said tensely.

"Oh, no," Joe said, shocked. "What happened?"

"She had an accident," Caroline said.

"I'm sorry," Joe said. "Is she okay?"

"Not yet," Caroline said, her eyes welling up. His voice was kind. Speaking to him about Skye reminded her that they had once been close friends. She didn't feel friendship now, but the memory of their letters was powerful.

"Why did she want to see me? Do you know?"

"She was confused," Caroline said, not wanting to tell him more.

"I'm sorry," Joe said again.

"Thanks," Caroline said.

* * *

The dream had been so real, she had been back on the mountain.

She could smell the gunsmoke. The mountain air was fresh and cold, the yellow leaves twinkling down like falling stars. Skye was holding her breath, standing just behind her. Caroline crept through the brush until she saw the deer Skye had shot. Big and brown, crumpled in a heap. She didn't want to look at it, but she made herself, for Skye's sake.

It was a man. He wore a brown corduroy

jacket, the color of a buck. His hair was red, glinting in the sun. His eyes were wide, so amazed at it all. They held Caroline's as she crouched beside him. She knew she had to look into the man's eyes and never away, so she barely glanced at the wound in his chest, the blood pumping out of it like a natural spring.

She heard Skye start to whimper and then cry. She felt the man's dog, a young golden retriever, bumping against her with his wet nose, trying to kiss his owner and the stranger bending over him. She felt the cold air as she unzipped her red jacket, pulled it off. She felt his blood on her fingers, so incredibly hot as she pressed the jacket into the wound.

"Did I shoot him?" Skye asked. "Did I? Did I? What have I done?"

Caroline, who had never ignored her sister in her life, ignored her now.

"What's your name?" she asked, looking into the man's eyes.

"Andrew," he answered. He was not much older than Caroline, the age of some of the younger teachers at her college.

His eyes were so bright. They were calm and kind, reassuring Caroline that she was doing her best, that he understood she was trying to help. At first there was no fear in his eyes at all. Every second seemed longer than a heartbeat. Caroline felt the blood pumping out of his body, soaking her jacket, flowing through her fingers into the ground. Their campsite was only five miles down the dirt road, but that was too far. They would never make it for help. Time had paused for them, Caroline and Skye Renwick, Andrew and his dog.

"I thought he was a deer," Skye sobbed.

The sky was too blue. The day was too beautiful. The dog wanted to sniff the man's blood, kiss the man's face.

"Homer," Andrew said.

"He's just a puppy, isn't he?" Caroline asked, noticing the dog's puff-ball body, his eager yellow face. He was barely full grown.

"Yes," Andrew said.

"Call him, Skye. Call Homer," Caroline said, because the dog had blood on his muzzle from kissing Andrew, and she thought Andrew would look at him and see his blood and be afraid.

"Homer," Skye said, her voice thin and high, trying so hard. "Here, boy."

The dog ran to her. Only then did

Andrew's eyes look away from Caroline. He watched his dog go, and then his gaze came back to Caroline.

"I'm going to die, aren't I?" he asked.

Caroline knew he was. She saw his lips turning white, felt his blood moving slower. She heard her sister crying behind her, felt the dog return to Andrew, wriggling between them as he snuggled closer to his master. Caroline thought of Joe Connor, of the lesson she had learned about how important it was to tell the truth about death, about how it was the least one person could do for another.

"I think you are," she said.

"Oh, God," Andrew said. His eyes turned afraid. It was so terrible to see. Caroline pressed harder on his chest, but she knew she wasn't doing any more good. His hands clenched and unclenched. Homer made a sound like a human crying, a mournful sob that came from deep inside. Skye stood right behind Caroline, her legs shaking against her sister's back.

"I didn't know," Skye wept. "I thought he was a deer."

"Homer," Andrew said.

The dog licked Andrew's face. There was

comfort in that, Caroline knew. Even at that moment, with his life flowing through her fingers, she could see that he found peace in the presence of his dog. She could see it in the way he closed his eyes and let everything slip away. He didn't open his eyes again.

* * *

"A big bouquet," Joe Connor said to the woman at the roadside stand.

"Do you want just zinnias and sunflowers, or wildflowers too?" the woman asked.

"Everything," Joe said.

He watched her work. She stood under the yellow-and-white-striped tent, pulling flowers from big buckets of water. She was heavy and very tan, dressed in a faded red housecoat, a scarf tied around her brown hair. She frowned. Watching an unhappy woman work hard reminded Joe of his mother.

"Did you pick the flowers?" Joe asked.

"Yes. And planted them too," she said, smiling proudly.

"They're pretty," Joe said, reaching into his pocket. The flowers cost five dollars, but he gave her a twenty. She started to make change, but Joe shook his head. The woman cast a quick glance at her husband, but he was sitting on a stack of milk cartons engrossed in the sports page. She nodded her thanks. But she put the money in the cash box instead of her pocket.

"Hey," Joe said, startling the man. "You should take your wife out for dinner."

The man grunted. His eyes were small and red. He looked mean, like a pig. Joe wanted to knock him off the milk crates.

"You should buy her a lobster," Joe said, "at her favorite restaurant."

"Yeah," the man said.

Joe drove away. He had problems in the area of unhappy women. He hated seeing women frown. He had watched his mother transform from a pretty, enthusiastic woman into a bitter, hurt, disappointed shadow. Working double shifts at the shellfish company, she had spent her free time waiting for Hugh Renwick to call. Drowning in guilt after her husband died. She had married again, but by then she had spent some miserable years.

Joe had wanted to bash heads. Everyone who had ever hurt his mother. The shellfish company owners, for making her work too hard. Hugh Renwick, for breaking both his parents' hearts. Joe's father had died in the Renwicks' kitchen, friendless and alone. And his gold watch: his father had died wearing his watch, the watch he had always let Joe play with, and Joe's mother had never bothered getting it back. The missing watch had been a symbol of everything Joe thought he had lost.

Staying friends with Caroline after learning the truth would have taken a miracle. For Joe's seventeenth birthday, his uncle had taken him out to the Spindrift to get him drunk. Joe was underage, but that was beside the point. They had sat on barstools, drinking boilermakers, while Uncle Marty told him the truth about his father's death. He was a jealous man, Uncle Marty said, out of his mind. Killed himself right in the Renwicks' kitchen. The kids had been there, Uncle Marty had said: Caroline and Clea. Caroline had watched his father die, heard his last words.

How could a friend know something like that, such a brutal part of his life, and not tell him? His friendship with Caroline was over. Whiskey numbed the initial shock, so Joe kept it flowing. He turned to the sea, studies, and drinking to forget. To block out how bad he felt, how angry it made him.

After a while he cut out drinking, but the first two still worked.

Trying to forget the flower stand lady, Joe did his errands. He had supplies to pick up for the *Meteor,* letters to mail, packages to send. His divers had collected some timber fragments and rust scrapings, and he was sending them to Woods Hole for analysis, in order to date the vessel. Today he planned to enter the wreck, when the tide was right, so he was in a hurry to get back. Nothing like a dive to take his mind off his emotions.

Before returning to sea, he had one final stop to make. He drove down Main Street, away from the small business district, through the outskirts of town. He pulled into the shady parking lot of Shoreline General Hospital.

"I'd like to leave these flowers for a patient," he told the blue-smocked lady at the information desk.

"What's the name, please?" she asked politely.

"Skye Renwick."

"Whitford's her married name," the lady said, smiling. She didn't even bother typing Skye's name into the computer, and Joe recognized the doings of a small town. "I'm afraid she can't have visitors quite yet."

"All right," Joe said, relieved because he didn't want to meet her anyway. He scribbled a note and handed the lady his flowers. "Would you please see that she gets these?"

"Aren't they beautiful?" the woman exclaimed. "I certainly will."

"Thanks," Joe said. He turned to walk out of the hospital. The air-conditioning stifled him. He couldn't wait to breathe the sea air. In an hour or so he'd be in the water, diving down to the wreck. He'd be away, he'd be free.

* * *

Caroline knew Skye wasn't supposed to see anyone, even family, but she stepped off the elevator with authority, a folder of papers under her arm, and she said a brisk hello to the nurses she passed instead of stopping to ask if it was okay for her to visit. No one questioned her. She had known they wouldn't, from all the times she had sneaked in when her father was sick.

Skye was awake. She was propped up in bed, staring at a card someone had sent her. It was a large, expensive greeting card with bluebirds, roses, a waterfall, and a rainbow on the front. It was supposed to be painterly and beautiful, but the artist had, perhaps unintentionally, given the bluebirds leering expressions in their large eyes. They looked like winged lechers.

"The word is out," Caroline said. "Fan mail is arriving."

Skye looked up and forced a smile. Her bruises had darkened and yellowed. The bandages around her head were disheveled from sleep; they hadn't been changed yet that morning. It was painful to look at her hands shaking from withdrawal, but Caroline couldn't take her eyes away.

"Who sent the card?" Caroline asked. Although, of course, she knew.

"Mom," Skye said, and with that she really did smile. She passed the card to Caroline, and her smile grew wider. It was a fact in the Renwick family that their mother bought and sent cards for all occasions, the more sentimental and glittery, the better. In turn, when Augusta herself received a card in the mail, she always checked the back to see how much the sender had spent on her.

Caroline turned the card over, to see the price.

"Wow," she said. "You really rate."

"A four-dollar card," Skye said, smiling harder. "You're not jealous, are you?"

"Don't rub it in," Caroline said, pretending to scowl. She read the handwritten message:

Darling,
   When will you learn to ask when you need something? My car is yours whenever you need it. You had no business driving that old junker anywhere—never mind all the way to Moonstone Point. What ever possessed you to go there anyway? Come home soon! I am rattling around this big house without you!
                    Love,
                    Mom

"Vintage Mom," Caroline said, laying the card beside Skye's breakfast tray.

"She misses me," Skye said.

"She misses the point," Caroline said.

"Hmmm," Skye said.

"Not one word about vodka in that whole four-dollar card."

"Caroline, I feel bad enough," Skye said.

"Don't rub it in, okay? I was an idiot, driving in the first place. I'm sure Joe Connor thinks I'm out of my mind. I know you don't understand, and I don't really feel like explaining it right now, but I had something I wanted to tell him."

"Tell *me*," Caroline said. She sat on the bed, waiting to hear Skye try to talk her way out of the situation. Skye's expression turned sullen.

"Don't torture me. I was hammered. I admit it."

"You don't remember, do you?"

"Blackout city," Skye confessed.

"It's not funny, Skye," Caroline said. "Last night your doctor told us you're an alcoholic."

"They say that about everyone," Skye said. "Look where I am: the rehab unit. It's how they make their money. They think everyone who has more than two beers is an alcoholic."

"Do you think you are?"

"No! Of course not! But I'm going on the wagon."

"You are?" Caroline asked, surprised. It wasn't something she had expected Skye to say.

"For now. I've been drinking too much. I admit it, okay? But things with Simon . . .

and I can't get my work to go right . . . Does Homer miss me?"

"I'm sure he does. I stopped by to walk him this morning."

"Good, he was there?" Skye smiled, wanting to divert Caroline with speculation about Homer's secret life. He would take off, and they never knew when to expect him back. But Caroline wanted to stay focused on Skye. She sat still, not saying anything.

"I was worried," Skye went on. "What if he didn't come back? I mean, he's so old now. Doesn't it seem like he was just a puppy?"

"Something about Joe coming to town," Caroline said as if Skye hadn't spoken.

"What about it?"

"Stirring everyone up. Upsetting you."

"Not *me,*" Skye said, smiling expectantly. Trying her best to cajole Caroline, Skye hadn't noticed her bandage slipping over one eye. Reaching over, Caroline gently straightened it.

"When you were drunk," Caroline said carefully, "you said maybe Joe's father didn't mean to kill himself, and I know you had to be thinking about what happened with you. About shooting Andrew Lockwood."

"The beauty about it . . ." Skye said. She

was sitting upright in bed, her knees drawn up. A white cotton blanket was spread over the sheets, and she had worked one of the threads loose, tugging the loop with her index finger. "Is that I don't really remember what I had in mind."

Both sisters seemed engrossed in the loop of thread. Skye wove it back into the blanket so seamlessly, Caroline couldn't detect where it had been. After a few minutes, Skye closed her eyes and faked being asleep. Caroline sat quietly at her side, wondering what to say. A candy striper walked in, wheeling a cart of flowers. She placed a large vase of beautiful flowers on Skye's table.

"Look," Caroline said, causing Skye to open her eyes. She handed her the small card.

"Oh," Skye said, frowning at the flowers. She read the card, then smiled up at Caroline. "They're from your boyfriend."

Caroline read the small card: " 'Get well soon. Call me when you want to talk again. Joe Connor.' My boyfriend? Not quite."

"He has nice handwriting," Skye said, grabbing the card. "Very masculine. Here, let me analyze it for you." She squinted, examining the words.

In spite of herself, Caroline was curious. Skye was no handwriting expert, she was just playing around. Even so, Caroline's interest was piqued. "What?" she asked.

"He is very lonely," Skye said, trying to sound mysterious. "He has no one to talk to. He searches for treasure to replace that vital thing missing in his life."

"Which is?"

"Hope? Love?" Skye asked. "His long-lost sweetheart. I don't know. You'll have to ask him. That will be three dollars."

"Sorry, I forgot my checkbook," Caroline said.

"It's okay," Skye said. "I owe you anyway."

* * *

When Caroline pulled up to Firefly Hill, her mother's car was gone. She walked up the porch steps and went in through the kitchen door. Homer was lying on his rug. At the sound of Caroline, he glanced over. Without actually moving, his eyes changed expression and he looked deeply happy to see her. Then his tail began to wag. It swished once, twice, across the tile floor. He clambered to his feet, wobbling on his legs. Then, with a little forward momentum, he came across the room to greet her.

"Hi, boy," she said, rubbing his head. "Good dog. You're a good dog, Homer."

He carried a faded blue hand towel in his mouth. The towel, or one like it, had been his toy ever since he came to live at Firefly Hill fourteen years ago. Her father had given him the first one. Caroline tugged the towel. Homer tossed his head, playfully pulling back.

"You win, Homer," Caroline said.

He stood at the door, waiting to be let out. Caroline walked across the yard, and he stayed close by: Today wasn't a day for one of his mystery sojourns. The ships were visible on the horizon, Joe Connor searching for treasure. Caroline stared at them for a minute, but Homer was eager to get to the beach.

He left his towel at the top of the tall stairway leading down the grassy bluff. It was painful to watch how slowly he moved, how every step seemed to tire his legs and hurt his back. His thick golden coat had turned thin and brittle, bald in patches. Watching him descend the steps, Caroline remembered him as a grief-stricken young puppy, his face dark with his owner's blood.

They walked down Firefly Beach, along

the high-tide line. Bits of dry kelp and eel-grass stuck to his tufty fur, but he didn't care. He was happy to be outside with Caroline, the human he had loved most since Andrew Lockwood. When they turned back toward home, Caroline heard someone call her name.

It was Maripat. Her niece was nine, and she came running full tilt down the beach, holding a book in her hand. Homer barked, overcome with joy at the sight of another family member. His back leg faltered, and he went down. But he was up in time, panting happily, when Maripat got there.

She wore blue shorts and a tee-shirt Caroline had brought her from Nantucket. Her silky brown hair was long, pulled back in a French braid. She had the Renwick eyes, wide and clear, and she wore glasses with enameled green wire rims.

"Brought you something," Maripat said, kissing her aunt and patting the dog.

"For me or Homer?" Caroline asked.

"For you," Maripat said, smiling.

"What is it?" Caroline asked, accepting the book Maripat held out to her.

"Mom told me about your friend," Maripat said, "the pirate. Is he really a pirate?"

"He says so," Caroline said. "That's him, out there."

Maripat shielded her eyes, looking at the big white boats shining in the late sun.

"They look like yachts to me," she said doubtfully.

"Modern pirates," Caroline said. "They don't know what they're missing. Too much luxury and not enough creaky old planks. What's the book?"

"The ship that sank?" Maripat said, her eyes bright as she got to tell her aunt something she didn't know. "The *Cambria?* Well, she was an English barquentine, or brigantine, the one with more masts, I forget which."

"Barquentine, I think," Caroline said, thinking back to third grade.

"The captain was a rat," Maripat said. "Considering he went to the lighthouse and fell in love with the lady who lived there. And that she was married to the lightkeeper."

"What a stinker," Caroline agreed.

"The lady had a little girl," Maripat said.

"That's right. I forgot," Caroline said, watching Homer dig a hole in the cool sand and lie down in it. "What were their names again?"

"The captain was Nathaniel Thorn, and the lady was Elisabeth Randall. The little girl was

Clarissa." Maripat paused, her eyes shining, her excitement so palpable, there might have been an imaginary drumroll. "And that's her diary!" She thumped the book.

"Whose diary?"

"Clarissa's! Some old lady, her husband was in the Coast Guard and took over the light, found the diary, and had it printed. I'd kill my mother if she ever did that to me. But we had to read it in school, and when Mom told me about the treasure guy, I said oh-my-God. Read it!"

Together they opened the book, and Caroline read the first entry:

July 19, 1769

Today I found a finback whale which had run ashore. She was bigger than the lifeboat and the same color as the rocks of our island, and she was lying on the south shore with her eye wide open, just staring at the sky. Mama and I tried to free her for hours, until darkness fell. We kept her wet with sea water carried in the fire bucket, because Mama said if her skin dried out, she would die. And she bade me watch the whale's blowhole, because that was where she breathed, and if water got in, she could drown. The tide took so long to rise! Tonight my arms ache from carrying water, from pulling on her tail to free her from the rocks. But it is worth it. Mama and I watched our whale swim away when the tide finally came to its full height, with a fat orange moon full on the water.

"I like her," Maripat said. "Don't you? Doesn't she sound cool?"

"Very," Caroline said, touched that her niece had brought her Clarissa's diary. "This wasn't around when I was in third grade."

"Maybe they just didn't bother printing it back then," Maripat said helpfully. "Did you and Mom and Aunt Skye ever free a finback whale? Did there used to be many around here?"

"No, we never did," Caroline said, smiling. It cracked her up, the way Maripat thought her mother and aunts had lived "back then," in olden times, historical days like Clarissa Randall, when finback whales were as thick in the water as minnows.

"Are you going to show the diary to that guy?"

"Which guy?"

Maripat pointed out to sea. She seemed to be suppressing a smile, and Caroline wondered what Clea had told her about Joe. "Him," she said.

"I might, come to think of it," Caroline said.

"He's down in the shipwreck," Maripat said reasonably. "I think he should know about the people involved."

"That makes excellent sense. After I read it, I might let him borrow it. Is this from the library?"

"The school library. Only students can borrow there, but I signed it out till September. For you," Maripat said with shy pride.

"Thank you," Caroline said.

"He was like a brother to you, right?" Maripat asked, blushing slightly. "You were pen pals?"

"Sort of, when we were young," Caroline said. She sensed Maripat wanting to ask more. Her niece came from a totally stable home, with parents who had been married to each other forever, and she seemed fascinated with her two aunts and their troubled world of men. Ex-boyfriends, stormy love affairs, even broken friendships with boys intrigued her and got her curiosity working.

"Where's your mother?" Caroline asked.

"Up there," Maripat said, glancing up at the house.

"Let's go find her," Caroline said.

Together they waited for Homer to get to his feet. Caroline moved down to the hard sand, where it would be easier for him to walk. A fly buzzed around his nose, and it made her sad to see him ignore it. Not so long ago he would have chased that fly until he snapped it in his mouth.

"Poor Homer," Maripat said. "It's hard for him to walk."

"He's sixteen. That's old for a dog."

"You love him, don't you?" Maripat said. "He's like your baby."

"I've had him since he was a puppy," Caroline said.

"A brand-new puppy?"

"Well, not quite brand new," Caroline said.

"I wish Mom would let us get a dog," Maripat said. "And that she'd let her sleep on my bed. I'd get a girl dog. Not that Homer isn't nice—I know he's a boy and all—but one boy is enough in our house. Mark drives me crazy. . . ."

Caroline nodded, listening to Maripat chatter on, happily complaining about her brother, their lack of pets, her rival in swimming class, her father's thinning hair, her recent discovery of lemon Popsicles shaped like great white sharks. Caroline was grateful Maripat hadn't kept asking about Homer. Questions came as easily to the child as her next breath, and Caroline was pretty sure her mother hadn't told her the story of Homer's first owner. Caroline certainly didn't intend to tell her now.

Maripat led the steep parade up the stone steps. Caroline and Homer brought up the rear. Petting the dog, encouraging him along, Caroline took one last glance at the ships at sea. Joe Connor. Telling the truth about life and death could get you in trouble, no matter which way you went.

When they got to the top, Homer paused for a moment. The western edge of the property was a nature sanctuary, a small forest of oaks and scrub pines. The woods were cool and wild, and they sounded their mysterious call. Homer cast Caroline an articulate look of love. Then he swung around, walking quickly, disappearing into the trees.

Never forgetting that she had first come upon him in woods, Caroline watched him go.

April 2, 1978

Dear Joe,

I can't believe I've never asked you this, but do you have any pets? People always say it's possible to be a cat person or a dog person, but never both. I guess that makes me weird. I'm both. The problem is, I love saltwater so much, I want my animals to, too. I taught my first puppy how to swim. He sank first, and I dove down and found him walking through the seaweed. But then he floated up and swam like a champ. (Actually, I had to rescue him—but he ran right back in!) Cats are another story. They'd rather curl up on the window seat and listen to the waves.

Time for me to listen to my sisters. They want me to stop writing you and go outside with them. Until later!

Love,
Caroline

April 15, 1978

Dear Caroline,

This has to be short because I want to go sailing and the wind's perfect. Right now my only pet is my boat. She's fifteen feet, very fast, doesn't eat much. If I could live on the water for the rest of my life, I'd be happy. Maybe I will. You're a dog person and a cat person, and I'm a boat person.

Love,
Joe

CHAPTER SIX

"What are you staring at?" Augusta Renwick asked, hating the silence. Her oldest daughter was standing at the big picture window facing seaward, looking across Long Island Sound with Hugh's shooting scope. When Augusta arrived home a few hours earlier, a troubled silence had billowed in, settling on the room like a great gray fog bank and encouraging Clea and Maripat to cut their visit short.

"Just a minute," Caroline said. Augusta felt hurt by her tone. She sat on the down love seat, curled up under a cashmere throw, needlepointing a pillow for Skye: swans and a castle, the motif from *Swan Lake.*

"I'm halfway finished," Augusta said just to make conversation. "*Swan Lake.* Wasn't that a happy memory for you and your sisters? The night your father took you to the ballet? Down to New York City in those black velvet dresses . . . You all came home wanting to be ballerinas. Maybe we should have encouraged Skye to study dance."

"Hmmm."

"She's always been so *critical* of herself. She thinks she can't paint, and now that she's having such a time, so blocked with her sculpting, it would be wonderful if she had something else to fall back on."

"You don't fall back on being a prima ballerina, Mom."

Augusta glanced over. Of course she had said the wrong thing. Speaking of Skye, she walked on eggshells with Caroline; she had no confidence in herself whatsoever.

But then, as if Caroline could suddenly read her mind, she smiled, trying to unhurt her mother's feelings, and said, "I just mean dancing's a life's work, like sculpting. I think it would be either-or, not both. Obsessive professions."

"Like loving your father," Augusta said, trying to joke.

But Caroline wouldn't laugh. She shut down on that subject. She had always seemed so sternly competent, looking after her sisters like a mother hen when Augusta had abdicated her position, at times when things with Hugh had been the most precarious. Looking back, Augusta had a million regrets, but she knew one thing: She had never loved her daughters less than ferociously. That knowledge gave her courage to keep going.

"Any one of you could have danced the ballet," Augusta said. "Maybe not as your life's work, but you certainly had the grace and spirit for it. And your legs! Your father would look at your legs and say they were over the legal limit."

No comment. Augusta did her needlepoint, accepting Caroline's silence. All three girls were exquisite, temperamental beauties; right now, in Caroline's case, with an accent on the *temperamental.* Staring at her daughter, Augusta could only imagine the bad-parent accusations swirling around in her head.

Caroline had always been on edge, watching for something to happen, defending her little sisters against everything. Even their parents, Augusta thought, trying not to feel hurt. Watching Caroline now, staring off to sea, Augusta imagined her as a sentinel maintaining watch over the ones she loved.

Her heart ached for her daughter, who didn't have enough love in her life. Always the one protecting other people.

She needed a man, Augusta thought. Beautiful but rather severe, with her dark hair all swept up, her clothing the colors of rocks or architecture: shades of granite and slate and brick and sandstone. Such a successful businesswoman, she intimidated all the men in town—scared them half to death. In her free time she traveled constantly, much too much. Or she hiked in the woods, alone.

"Caroline," Augusta said, rising. "What can be so interesting out there?"

"Come see," Caroline said. She handed the glass to Augusta, helped her steady it against her right eye. "There."

Augusta held the brass tube and tried to focus. The metal felt warm under her hands, from Caroline's grip. She blinked against the lens, twisted the eyepiece, trying to make sense of what she was looking at. A big circle of open ocean with a few boats in the middle.

"Fishermen," she said.

"No," Caroline said. "They're not."

Augusta laughed. Was Caroline joking? She lived here, looked out this window a hundred times a day. She knew fishing boats when she saw them. They'd surf the rip at Moonstone Reef, throw their lines over-board, hoping to catch bluefish and sharks. Hugh had fished there himself, although most of his sportfishing had been for big game in the Canyon beyond Block Island, or south, in the Bahamas or the Keys. Still, she stared at the boats. What was that plume shooting like a jet of water?

"What are they doing?" she asked.

"Diving for treasure," Caroline said.

Augusta lowered the lens. She gazed at Caroline's lovely gray-blue eyes and saw them so alive, so full of fire, she couldn't speak. Something was going on. It was like looking at a person having a religious vision.

"Darling, are you kidding?" Augusta asked.

"They're bringing up a shipwreck," Caroline said.

"Really?" Augusta asked. She adored things like shipwrecks. Why else would she live in a godforsaken mansion on the Sound if she didn't? Even more, it felt like a bond with Caroline. A shipwreck was something they could enjoy together. Curious, she raised the glass to her eye again. "How do you know?"

"A friend told me," Caroline said. "It's the *Cambria*."

"The *Cambria* . . ." Augusta said. The name sounded familiar.

"That fountain thing you're seeing is actually sand. They have a compressor on board their boat that blows sand away from the wreck so they can get to the gold."

"How exciting," Augusta said. She watched the spray of sand, tried to see the people on board the boats. At this distance, they were tiny and faceless, like toys. Even the big boats tossing on the waves looked miniature. Augusta smiled with pride. Leave it to Caroline to know everything going on in the area.

"How do you hear about these things?" Augusta asked, beaming. "It must be terribly top secret. I haven't seen a word about it in the papers. And no one's talking."

"I suppose it is a secret," Caroline said.

"You know I keep a secret better than anyone," Augusta said. But the awful look on Caroline's face made her heart sink.

"I know you do," Caroline said, making it sound like an indictment. She walked across the room, sat down in the Windsor rocker. In the time it took, she composed herself. When she directed her gaze at Augusta, her face was placid and neutral. Augusta swallowed. She was in for something she wasn't going to like.

"We have to talk about Skye," Caroline said.

Involuntarily Augusta touched the pearls around her neck. Why were they called "black" when they were actually the most amazing shade of dove gray? She glanced at Caroline.

"Have I ever told you your eyes are exactly the same color as my pearls?" she asked, smiling, still touching the pearls.

"Yes," Caroline said, patiently rocking.

"Eyes the color of black pearls. So rare . . . Some wonderful man will see that someday. He will. Ordinary men would look at you and say your eyes are blue, or blue-gray, but the right man will know immediately. He will tell you your eyes are the color of black pearls."

"Mom, you heard what Dr. Henderson said," Caroline said, leaning forward. "That she's an alcoholic."

Augusta shook her head. She had had time to process what the doctor had said. While she knew Skye was emotional, she refused to lend credence to the idea of her being an alcoholic. But Caroline was rocking away, determined to discuss it.

"He's crazy," Augusta said. "He doesn't know her. She's an artist, like your father. It's normal for artists to drink."

"Don't compare her to Dad."

"Such a terrible resentment," Augusta said sadly. "You and your sisters feel so angry at your father for those hunts, and all he wanted was to spend a little time alone with his girls."

"Turn us into boys," Caroline said, patting the dog.

"That is not true. He would attack anyone who suggested that he wished even one of you were a son instead of a daughter. He just wanted you to enjoy the outdoors, the way he did."

"It was a little more complicated than that," Caroline said kindly after the briefest of pauses.

"Well," Augusta began, but she trailed off. She didn't have the heart for an argument. Augusta was nonviolent. She didn't believe in guns or knives. She hadn't wanted her daughters exposed to danger, wild animals, or the thin night air. But she had adored her husband beyond all reason. When he had wanted to take the girls hunting overnight on the mountain, she hadn't spoken up, even though her heart had told her he was wrong.

"What do we do, then, Mom? Without blaming Dad or calling Skye an alcoholic, how do we help her?"

"We bring her home. We encourage her and love her."

"We will do all those things. We always have. But they're not enough anymore."

Augusta watched Caroline kneel next to Homer, who had started to scratch himself.

Working a seed pod free from where it had tangled in a clump of fur, Caroline pulled too hard. Yelping, he looked over his shoulder at Augusta, his big brown eyes liquid with injury.

"I didn't do it," Augusta said to the dog.

"Remember when we brought him home?" Caroline asked, stroking the old dog. His eyes were closed, his ribs visible through his rough yellow coat.

"He's a big pain in the neck," Augusta said, sounding less affectionate than she felt and ignoring Caroline's question. He had gotten Caroline and Skye through those first awful weeks after the hunting accident, although she knew that Caroline thought the opposite was true: that she had helped the dog in his grief.

"You love him, Mom," Caroline said. "You can't kid any of us."

"He'd be a stray if it weren't for me," Augusta said, watching him slobber all over Caroline. "I wonder if anyone remembers that."

The young man had lived in New Hampshire, on a fellowship to Dartmouth, but his family was from San Francisco and wanted no part of shipping a dog across the country, to live in the middle of a city. The police had taken him to the pound in Hanover. Augusta had allowed Homer into her house because Caroline had been unable to bear thinking of him abandoned, because she had convinced Augusta that saving the dog would help Skye. And because Hugh had needed to do it as well.

"What about Skye, Mom?" Caroline asked now.

"I don't know what's set her off," Augusta said carefully. "What's making her so upset all of a sudden. I think we should let her come home, get some rest, and not go looking for trouble. The past is a minefield, and I for one am tired of it."

"Mom—"

"End of the story. Hear me, Caroline?" Augusta asked sharply. She pulled off her half-glasses and glared over Homer's head at Caroline.

"You're wrong, Mom," Caroline said, rising. "It won't be the end of the story."

"And what is? You and your sisters crying about your father to any stranger who'll listen? While I sit there and try to defend him? He loved you all. And I defy you to tell *anyone,* especially yourself, otherwise."

"Mom, the end of the story is Skye's funeral," Caroline said, her voice thick with anger and tears. Her black-pearl eyes were brimming, furious.

"Don't you dare say that," Augusta said.

"Maybe she'll fall and hit her head, or maybe she'll take too many pills. Maybe it won't be a car wreck next time. Or maybe it will. She killed a man, Mom, and I think it makes her want to die herself."

"Caroline," Augusta said dangerously, feeling her head starting to shake, the way it did when she got upset.

Caroline came across the room. She knelt before her mother's chair and held her hands. Seeing her elegant daughter kneel before her in such abject supplication was too much for

Augusta to bear. She tried to push Caroline away, but Caroline wouldn't move. She stared straight into Augusta's eyes.

"Please, Mom," Caroline said, the tears just running down her cheeks. "It's you I'm thinking of almost as much as Skye. I know how you'll feel if something happens. You won't be able to stand it. You love Skye so much. Let's pull together now. Do whatever it takes to help her. Let's start by being honest, okay?"

Augusta took a deep breath. She leaned forward, touched the tip of her nose against Caroline's. Their eyes met, and, as always, Augusta was struck by the depth, the beauty, the compassion in Caroline's eyes. The emotion was enough to take your breath away. Hugh had caught it once, just once, in that portrait he had done of her, his famous *Girl in a White Dress*.

Backing away, Augusta brushed a stray wisp of raven hair off Caroline's forehead. She set her needlepoint aside. Arching her back, she stood tall. Looking down at Caroline, still on her knees, she thought of her own childhood, of going to church to pray for help. She wondered whether her children remembered their Catholic up- bringing, whether they ever turned to

prayer. Or whether they had stopped be-
lieving at the same time as Augusta and
Hugh, right after the accident at Redhawk.

"Your father did love you," Augusta said,
watching Caroline's face. It remained im-
passive. "Those hunts were his way. . . . He
was larger than life, and he showed his love
in extraordinary ways."

"I know," Caroline said.

"Would you like a cocktail?" Augusta
asked. "I'm going to have one."

Caroline bowed her head. She didn't say
yes, she didn't say no. She seemed to be
thinking it over. She gave the appearance of
devotion, of praying. Augusta would mix
enough for two. She patted Caroline's head.
Then she walked away, toward the flower
room, where they kept the bar.

* * *

Extraordinary ways. Caroline sat at the top
of the beach stairway with Homer, remembering her father. On the way to Redhawk,
she was the navigator. She was supposed
to say "head northeast" instead of "take a
right," and when they came to an intersec-
tion and looked both ways, she would tell

her father "clear," just like a copilot would say. She knew the things that made him happy, and she liked to do them.

One time she had a fever. Leaving for the mountain she had been healthy, enthusiastic. But that night, alone in her tent, she got sick. Her throat blazed, and her head ached. The hair on her head hurt. She had chills. She was fifteen, and when she got sick at home she knew how to take care of herself, but way out there she felt scared. Crying, she just wanted the sun to come up.

Her father heard her. He came into her tent, felt her head, held her in his arms while she shivered. In all the times they had camped out in their separate tents, she had thought she was all alone. Having her father come when she called was a surprise, and in her feverish state made her cry harder.

"You're sick, sweetheart," he said. "We have to go home right away."

He bundled her up, told her to sit still while he got her sisters. Caroline waited, unable to believe what was happening. She was fifteen, unused to being taken care of. The hunts were her chance to be with her father, but nothing had ever made her feel so loved as having him tell her they were going home. Knowing that she was sick, and giving her what she needed.

While her sisters took down her tent and their own, Caroline's father walked her to the car. He started it up, settled her in the front seat, frequently touching her head to see if the fever had gone down. He was so big and tough, with gray eyes that never showed his feelings, but Caroline remembered how worried he looked that night. It was after midnight; her sisters should have been sleepy, but they were excited. Leaning against her father, shivering in spite of the blasting heat, Caroline had felt so happy.

She had scarlet fever.

But then she thought of another time, years later, driving home from the same mountain after Skye had shot Andrew Lockwood.

They had spent the day at the police station. Skye was in one interrogation room, Caroline in another. So many questions: Did you know the man? Ever see him before? Was there any conversation before the shot was fired? A confrontation? Did your sister seem angry? What was her mood like?

Caroline was in shock. She understood that now, but at the time she had thought she was just tired. All she wanted to do was put her head on the desk and fall asleep. She kept seeing the man, hearing her own calm voice ask him his name. Hearing his voice say "Andrew." His eyes, his mouth, the feeling of his hand in hers. He was hers forever; no one would ever know him as well. Thinking of Andrew, she promised herself she would take care of his dog.

After the inquest, they drove home. They climbed into the station wagon, solemn but relieved. Everyone rallied around Skye. She had just been cleared of homicide. Augusta was at Firefly Hill, waiting to greet them. But Caroline was—as always—the surrogate mother. She wrapped Skye in a plaid blanket. She settled her in the backseat and Clea sat beside her. Caroline rode in front with their father.

The way-back was for Homer. They stopped by the pound to pick him up. Walking into the concrete building, they could hear the heartbroken howling. Handing Hugh papers to sign, the attendant went to get the dog. Caroline was sick with anticipation. She was afraid he would see his master's killers and bare his teeth. But at the sight of her, Homer stopped his noise.

Clea had the rear hatch up to let the dog into the way-back. She had made him a bed with an old beach blanket. But walking over to the car, Hugh shut the hatch door. He looked at Caroline.

"He likes you," he said.

"I don't know why," she said, looking away. "I was there when—"

"You're helping him, Caroline," Hugh said. "Let him ride in front with you. It'll make him feel safe." Her father's expression was unfamiliar, and looking back, Caroline realized she was seeing the first signs of agonized sorrow.

Homer traveled the whole way to Connecticut with his head on Caroline's thigh. He whimpered at first, but then he stopped. Clea had her earphones on, and she recited her French dialogue to herself. Skye, Caroline, and Hugh didn't speak at all. But every so often Hugh would reach across the seat to pat Homer's head. To look at Caroline and try to read her eyes. To pretend to smile.

Extraordinary ways.

* * *

Joe Connor stood in the *Meteor*'s cabin, watching the calm water. The wind had been steady all day, making waves that churned up the sea column. It had died at six, and now that it was too dark to dive, the surface was glass. He gazed forward as the line of the bow tilted up to meet the sky, then settled down. Overhead the sky was a jumble of stars. Joe looked back on his day, wishing he could have done more.

Strong currents had kept his crew away from the wreck. A weather system off Hatteras was making big waves offshore, creating a dangerous undertow. Joe had sent divers down every hour, had gone down himself in the morning, and again just before dark. But the water had been moving too fast to attempt much of anything.

Yet in the short time they had been onsite, they had moved forward. They had charted the wreck, cleared mud and sand. They had taken underwater photos, analyzed the timbers, examined the ship's construction. Their consensus was that the ship had been built in England before 1800, probably before 1750. Based on Caroline's letter written to Joe in 1971, he knew they had located the *Cambria.*

Caroline's letter and the gold.

They were beginning to uncover gold coins.

The sea bottom was treacherous, a forest of broken spars: the vessel's splintered masts and yards. The jagged wood could snag a diver's air hose or slice through his wetsuit to the skin. Getting through the wreckage took care and concentration, like cutting a path through dense woods. But along the way they were finding treasure.

It cost a fortune to find a treasure. Joe was paying out of his own pocket, and he hated to see a day pass without real progress. He wanted to finish this project fast. A bunch of the guys had gone ashore to carouse at the Catspaw Tavern, and he was beginning to think he should have gone with them.

One of the launches was coming back. He heard the drone of the engine getting closer. He watched it circle the *Meteor* once, then tie up to the stern. Dan climbed aboard.

"Hey, skipper," Dan called, coming into the wheelhouse.

"Forget something?"

"No, I just don't feel like going out. Tired of everyone, I guess."

"I know what you mean," Joe said. The crew got cranky on days when they couldn't dive much. Too much togetherness, hearing each other complain. Everyone began to miss their shore lives, their wives and children or girlfriends or whomever they cared about, and it began to show. Joe, who had never really made himself a shore life, missed having one at all.

"These came for you," Dan said, tossing some letters and a big brown envelope on the chart table. "The dockmaster asked me to deliver them."

There was a letter from his brother Sam. He'd been feeling lonely, restless at sea, and the sight of the letter made him glad. At first glance the big envelope looked official. Probably lab work on the sail and timber fragments he'd sent to Woods Hole, or historical documentation from his friend in the map department at Yale. But then he saw the familiar handwriting. He would have known it anywhere. He wondered why Caroline would be writing to him now. Only one way to find out. Laying the other mail aside, he ripped open the package.

It contained a thick sheaf of photocopied papers. Joe glanced at them; they were dated 1769, written in small, neat penmanship. Caroline had sent a note on pale blue stationery. He could see by the telltale smudges that she had used a fountain pen, and he remembered that she had sometimes used one when they were kids.

Dear Joe,

My niece showed me this diary, and I thought it might interest you. It was written by Clarissa Randall, whose mother was the woman who ran away with the captain of the Cambria. I haven't read it all the way through, but it tells a little about what life was like living at a lighthouse in the 1700s, having one of your parents run away for the love of someone else and never come back home. Sounds too familiar . . .

It made me wonder if that's why you're diving on the Cambria. Not that it's any of my business, of course. I can't imagine how you're going to react to getting this from me, but I hope you'll take it in the spirit of scholarship. I do feel partly responsible for you being here, after all. Visiting my mother at Firefly Hill, I looked out the window and saw your boats. I felt kind of proud, actually.

The flowers you sent Skye were beautiful.

Yours,
Caroline

Joe glanced at the diary. Starting out, he had control of his feelings. He read the first few entries; it looked like the real thing, a faithfully reproduced handwritten account by a member of the woman's family. It contained descriptions of the area, a little about her family life. But as the meaning of Caroline's letter sank in, he felt the heat rising in his neck. Dan was right beside him, and Joe kept his face free of expression.

"She's a brave woman," he said.

"What?" Dan asked.

"Nothing," Joe said. Brave or crazy, he thought. What the hell kind of nerve did she have, making parallels between the *Cambria* and his family? Death and infidelity. Not exactly the kind of stuff he wanted to think about. Coming up here, he knew he'd have to face complicated emotions connected to his father. But he was a grown man, sober a long time, and he had put the past behind him, regardless of what Caroline Renwick might think.

Then, to make his night complete, he opened the letter from Sam. Knowing what it said, he read it anyway. He must have groaned, because Dan looked over.

"The kid still coming?" Dan asked.

"Yep," Joe said.

"He likes shipwrecks, huh? How's it feel to be a role model?"

"Fucking wonderful," Joe said, smiling ruefully.

"Kid's got balls, I'll give him that," Dan said, chuckling. "You send him packing every time, but he keeps coming back for more."

"He's tough," Joe said quietly.

The night was still. The *Meteor* rocked on the quiet sea. Joe stood at his chart table, staring at the letters. The green-shaded lamp threw soft light, easy on the eyes. Waves slapped the hull. Maybe he should ask Caroline out here so she could see that the excavation was about gold and scholarship, nothing messy and emotional. He wanted daylight, so he could work and dive. He didn't want to think about the people in his life, the people who could make him feel the way he did inside right now. Sad and angry, and as though he had lost something he couldn't quite name.

* * *

Caroline stood at the top of Serendipity Hill and stared out to sea. She was out of breath from climbing the steep and narrow trail. She gazed over the towns of Hawthorne and Black Hall, followed the Ibis River to where it met the Connecticut, then into Long Island Sound. Lights twinkled throughout the area. Caroline counted two lighthouses along the Connecticut coast and four across the Sound, on Long Island. She saw lights on a ship and wondered whether it was the Meteor.

A nightbird called up the hill. It sounded lonely and beautiful and reminded Caroline of nights on the mountain. She rested for a minute, sitting very still and trying to locate the bird in the trees. Its song was clear, coming from a grove of dark pines. The air smelled spicy. An owl swept through, its wings beating loudly.

As much as Caroline had hated the hunts, there had been parts of them she loved. The feeling of solitude, hiking up narrow paths that gave onto vistas of sweeping beauty, blue valleys heavy with summer haze. Sleeping outside, the feeling of air moving on her bare arms, had made her feel free. Caroline had always loved nature. She had loved the surprise of hiking, of coming across an animal or bird she hadn't expected to see. She just hadn't liked killing them.

Her father had tried to teach his daughters his sport, but you can't impose blood lust on those who don't have it. Caroline remembered killing the fox. She had felt like a murderer. It had been December, and that night she had seen the northern lights for the first time. She had held the fox in her arms. Its body had kept her warm.

Now, alone on her mountain perch, she looked for a star to wish on, in memory of Andrew Lockwood. She always did. Finding one, she shivered, even though the summer night was warm. Then she found one for her father. Thinking of her father wasn't always easy. But she made herself do it anyway.

Breathing the sea air, Caroline wondered whether Joe had received her package. She wondered whether her note would anger him, but it didn't matter. She hadn't written it for his reaction. Standing on the hilltop, watching the ship she imagined to be Joe's, Caroline felt a mystical communion with him. He had to love nature to spend so much time at sea.

Hating to hunt, Caroline was guilty of loving to catch fish. She loved the initial grab, the pull on the line, the tension between her and the fish. When she looked in its eye, she felt a strange kinship with the creature. Usually she let it go. She had spent time trolling Moonstone Reef. Stripers and blues were common in August; tautog and flounder lived on the bottom. She knew the wreck attracted fish, and she wondered whether Joe saw them or whether he had eyes only for the gold.

Maybe he wouldn't care about Clarissa's diary at all. Perhaps he only wanted the treasure, didn't care about the story behind it. He had run from his own story. By the time Caroline had been ready to tell him her part in it, he had been too angry to hear.

Or too afraid.

By the time Caroline walked down the trail, the half-moon had traversed the sky. She heard night creatures rustling in the trees, but she didn't feel afraid. Her feet were sure on the steep path; she held a walking stick in her hand. She followed the Ibis River to the inn's grounds, where the guests were having a party. She heard their music, their drunken cries. A group had taken off their clothes and were standing in the shallow water.

When she got to her cottage, she heard her phone ringing.

She almost didn't answer. At this hour it would be her mother. She would have been drinking, and she want to apologize for their unpleasant visit earlier. Caroline stared at the phone. She counted the rings: five, six . . .

But what if it were Skye? What if something had happened? Caroline picked up.

"Hello?" she said.

No one spoke. The line crackled with static. The call seemed to be coming from a long way away, from halfway around the world, or from another hemisphere, from an airplane over the ocean . . .

Or from a boat.

Caroline imagined she could hear the wind and waves. She listened hard. She could almost hear someone breathing. But no one was there. The call was nothing more than crossed wires. The static buzzed like a ferocious swarm of bees, and then it was gone.

The line was silent.

Caroline hung up.

* * *

Early the next morning, Michele teetered on a wooden ladder, starting to hang Japanese lanterns. The ball was days away, but it took time to get the inn ready. The trees were hung with a hundred candelabra, the dance floor was installed. Caroline called it the Firefly Ball, in honor of her parents, and she wanted candlelight to do the night justice. She had ordered beeswax candles from the Bridal Barn, and May Taylor had just brought them over.

May and her family—three generations of women—ran the Barn, planning weddings for women of the shoreline, making products from their herb garden. May and her five-year-old daughter, Kylie, seemed so excited about the ball, about the fact their wonderful, luminous candles would light every table.

Thirty round tables were stacked behind the barn, the long white damask tablecloths were expected back from the laundry that afternoon. The Japanese lanterns were bright and fragile; they danced on a wire strung around the perimeter of the inn's back lawn. She hoped the heat would return, as it always did, every year, for the night of the ball.

A tropical depression was chugging up from Savannah, bringing muggy air and temperatures in the nineties. Michele knew Caroline wished the night of the ball to be hot and steamy. Caroline loved the look of men without their jackets, their starched white shirts clinging to their sweaty backs; she wanted the women with bare shoulders and bare feet, dancing in the cool grass. The Firefly Ball was a night for artists to be wild and expressive, free of constraints and inhibitions.

Every year, Caroline chose a different theme—taking cues from various art forms. This year the theme was to be "My Favorite Painting." People really showed their different styles. Clea and Peter always attended in costume. Last year, for their favorite song, they had dressed as "Rhapsody in Blue," two lovers wrapped in blue chiffon. Skye and Simon had come straight from their studios in the barn, still in their paint-and-clay–stained work clothes, many of which were strewn, as the night progressed, in various bushes around the property. But Caroline the hostess always simply wore a gown.

Michele wondered what everyone would wear this year. She and Tim planned to dress as characters from Seurat's *Grande Jatte*. Michele had a long white dress and a parasol, and Tim would look adorable in his spats and bowler hat. Caroline always insisted that they attend as her guests—not to work, but to revel.

Standing halfway up the ladder, a crimson lantern in her hand, Michele spotted Simon Whitford. He was on the inn's porch, hands on his hips, squinting into the sun. He had that dark artist look to him, one of the brilliant ones who couldn't be held to the rules of ordinary men. But Simon was trompe l'oeil: a fake trying to be Hugh Renwick.

Poor Skye, Michele thought. Marrying a man with her father's fierce moods and none of his tender heart. Michele wondered why he was there. To see Skye, no doubt. Caroline certainly hadn't invited him to the Firefly Ball. The confrontation was coming: From her perch on the ladder Michele could see Caroline coming out of the inn, straight into Simon's path. She held on tight, leaning out for a better view.

* * *

Caroline had lain awake too long the previous night. The telephone call with no one there had unsettled her. She had tossed and turned, unable to get comfortable. After midnight, fog had closed in, swaddled the property, and given her a headache. The foghorns had wailed. Caroline had waited for the phone to ring again, but it never did.

But that morning at work, first thing, Michele had placed a message on her desk. It was from Joe Connor, an invitation to dinner aboard the *Meteor.* The telephone connection had been terrible, Michele said. So filled with static, it sounded like the ship might be riding out a thunderstorm. Afraid he would lose the transmission, Joe had talked fast, asked Michele to tell Caroline if she wanted to visit the excavation, she should be at the dock at eight on Thursday.

Bleary and frazzled, Caroline felt confused. He cut her out of his life, and now he wanted to have her over for dinner. Unsure of any of it, she walked down the back steps of the inn, straight into her brother-in-law.

"What the hell are you doing here?" Caroline asked, unable to believe her eyes.

"Hello to you too, Caroline," Simon said, grinding out his cigarette on the flagstone step.

"I don't want you here," she said.

"I'm here to see Skye," he said. "Where am

I supposed to stay? We gave up our place. I'm hardly welcome at your mother's house."

"So you thought you'd stay at my inn? I think I'm safe in assuming you don't intend to be a paying guest. You lost your brother-in-law privileges when you walked out on my sister."

"Let me stay, please, Caroline? I'll sleep in the barn, in my old studio. I already checked—no one's using it right now. I need to see Skye. I want to help her."

Caroline chewed the end of her pen. She stared at Simon. He was tall and lean with wild black hair and gaunt cheekbones, sunken black eyes with that sexy fire that drove Skye crazy and made Caroline and Clea mistrust him to their bones. He was ingratiating and manipulative. He wore black jeans that rode low on his skinny hips and a clean white tee-shirt with laundry-faded paint stains. He looked malnourished, dissipated, and artistically tormented.

At her most cynical, Caroline wondered whether he had married Skye to complete the picture.

"Well. Speak of the faithless devil," came a voice from across the garden.

At the sound of Clea's voice, Caroline

looked over her shoulder. Her beautiful sister came sauntering across the lawn, stunning in a salmon-pink sundress and big dark glasses. She circled Simon like a great white shark on a bleeding surfer.

"Hi, Clea," Simon said. Caroline didn't want to give him the benefit of the doubt, but he did sound miserable. Together, she and Clea were his worst nightmare. He had hurt their little sister—hurt her badly—and she wondered how he felt, standing in their midst, bearing the brunt of their scorn and derision.

"What brings you back to town? Is there a bank account you forgot to clean out?" Clea asked.

"Clea, I'll tell you what I just told Caroline. I want to help Skye. I made a mistake, okay? I love her, and I want her to take me back."

"Really?" Caroline asked, frowning. He hadn't told her that part.

"Yeah. Can I stay? In the barn?"

"I don't want you here," she said.

"Skye does."

"Why the hell would she want to see you?" Caroline asked, amazed at his arrogance, wondering how it could possibly help Skye to confront the man who had scorned her love.

"How do you think I found out about her accident?" Simon asked, palming another cigarette, wanting to light it so badly, his hand shook. "She called me. She needs me, just like I need her."

"She called him," Caroline said to Clea. The sisters gazed at each other for a few seconds, weighing this new information.

"That does make a difference," Clea said. "Although she's not in her right mind."

"She may have called you, but she doesn't need you," Caroline said to him, narrowing her eyes. "Let's get that straight."

"Think what you want."

"I'll let you stay," Caroline said. "I'll make sure something's free for you."

"I'll stay in the barn—"

Caroline shook her head. "In the inn, not the barn. You have one more chance to be good to Skye, and I'm not going to make you sleep in the hay."

"Thanks," he said. He moved forward, as if to embrace Caroline, but her look stopped him. Lowering his head, he backed away. Then he went toward the parking lot to get his things.

"Scum of the earth," Clea said, sighing, "but Skye loves him."

"For now," Caroline said.

The sisters walked across the brilliantly green lawn to the old red barn where Caroline had been headed before her encounter with Simon. Surrounded by stone walls and white fences, the soft red paint picturesquely peeling, the barn was a painting waiting to happen. Many artists, especially Hugh Renwick, had made it famous. Paintings of the Renwick barn hung in the Clark Institute, the Phillips Collection, the Guthrie, the Farnsworth, the Corcoran Gallery, and the Metropolitan Museum of Art.

Inside, the barn was cool and dark. It smelled of hay. Caroline's grandfather had kept horses and cows. Her father had taught his daughters to ride here; the box stalls were now individual artists' studios. The more expensive rooms at the inn came with barn rights. The stalls were occupied now, with guests painting, sculpting, and getting to know each other better. The unmistakable sounds of passion came from a stall/studio at the far end, making Caroline and Clea laugh softly.

"I lost my virginity in this barn," Clea whispered.

"At least twice." Caroline laughed.

"The Firefly Ball is upon us," Clea said,

surveying the scene, feeling the excitement. Sunlight slanted down from the hayloft.

"Did I do the right thing, letting Simon stay?" Caroline asked.

"Skye is a grown-up," Clea said. "We forget sometimes. We can't protect her forever."

"Or at all," Caroline said. Then she heard herself say, "I sent Joe a copy of the diary Maripat gave me."

"You did?"

"And he invited me to his boat for dinner on Thursday night."

"Really!" Clea said, her eyes sparking as she smiled.

"Yes. But I don't know if I should go. Or if I want to."

"Why not?" Clea asked.

"Oh," Caroline said, shredding a piece of straw, "mainly because we don't like each other very much, I guess."

"Maybe you'll find out he's not so bad. I already know you're not. You'll both be in for a nice surprise."

"I was thinking about a quick trip to Scotland. Just for a few days, to check out a brand-new place that opened on one of the western islands. It's an old priory with great views of mountains and the sea, and there's a labyrinth. Doesn't a labyrinth sound fascinating? I read about it in the airplane magazine on my way back from Venice last time, and I need some new ideas for the inn. . . ."

"And you have to leave tomorrow? How convenient. I think you should stay, have dinner with Joe."

"I might." The pull to travel was strong. She had always done it to get her out of her own life. She went to beautiful country inns, visiting them with a vengeance, telling everyone it was for inspiration. Traveling like a fugitive—got to get there, got to check in, looking over her shoulder. If she kept moving, she wouldn't think too much. With Joe Connor in town, this might be one of those times.

Caroline yawned, shrugging.

"You look tired," Clea said.

"I am," Caroline admitted. "I hiked up Serendipity Hill last night—"

"Caroline, *Jesus*," Clea said.

"What?" Caroline asked, surprised by Clea's expression.

"I hate thinking of you on those cliffs at night . . . You could fall. Besides, you never know who else might be up there. You could get raped. I just read about two girls hiking the Appalachian Trail, they were raped and murdered—"

"Clea, it's okay. I didn't get into any danger on Serendipity Hill."

"No, but you'd fly to Scotland to avoid having dinner with a man on his boat."

Caroline opened her mouth to speak, paused, stopped.

"What?" Clea asked.

"You caught me," Caroline said, smiling. "I was just working out flight times in my head."

* * *

"I brought some old pictures," Augusta said to Skye.

"Mom, I'm tired," Skye said. She lay in her hospital bed. They had cut her pain medication down to Tylenol. But she felt so tired, so lethargic, all she wanted to do was sleep.

"These will cheer you up," Augusta said.

Skye stared at the picture album. Her parents had taken pictures of everything. Skye wasn't one of those youngest children who complained her parents had taken photos of the older siblings but lost interest when she came along. No. The Renwicks had four albums full of Skye alone. Each album was identical, Moroccan leather monogrammed *H & A*.

Augusta turned the pages. This selection of photos covered the early seventies, when Skye was very young. There were the girls on the beach, on the carousel, in a rowboat. Hugh at his easel, appearing young and intense.

"He looks like Simon," Augusta said, pointing. "You and I have the same taste in men."

"Mmm," Skye said.

A nurse came in. Shifts were changing, and she had to get Skye's vital signs. She slapped on the blood pressure cuff, gave the black bulb a few hard squeezes.

"What do we have here?" she asked, looking at the album.

"Family pictures," Augusta said, beaming.

"Beautiful," the nurse said. She wrote on her pad, stuck a thermometer in Skye's ear, glanced at the reading, and wrote it down.

"That's your patient, age two," Augusta said, tapping a photo of Skye holding a paintbrush.

"Quite the artist!" the nurse said.

"You have no idea," Augusta said proudly. She turned the page. "Those are Skye's sisters. They adored her, as you can see. That's her father . . . there he is again. Oh, don't look, that's me with short hair. God, what a mistake that was! That's my husband on his horse, that's the barn . . . there he is painting on the Quai de Tournelle . . ."

"Who are they?" the nurse asked, bending down for a closer look.

The black-and-white photo depicted a group of men wearing tuxedos. They appeared elegant and proud, some holding a paintbrush, a palette, or a small canvas. Others held rifles, bows, and arrows. They stood outside a massive stone building, reminiscent of a French château.

"Oh, they're members of a men's club," Augusta said with a concerned glance at Skye. Sensing Skye's discomfort, she seemed about to turn the page, but then her eyes lit on Hugh. Augusta sighed. Her fingers trailed across the plastic sleeve, caressing the photo.

"There's my husband, right there," she said softly.

The nurse peered at Hugh Renwick, standing in the center of the second row. His big shoulders filled his dinner jacket; his face was set, his eyes focused on the camera as if he wanted to attack it. He held a sable brush like a scepter. Glancing at the picture, Skye recognized where it had been taken and felt her heart start to race. She closed her eyes.

"They look so elegant," the nurse said. "So old-fashioned."

"Yes, courtly," Augusta said, furnishing what she considered the proper word. "They met twice a year, always wore black tie. They'd talk about their work, I suppose. They all had rather substantial careers. My husband was quite a well-known painter, you know."

"What's the place?" the nurse asked. "It's gorgeous. Is it in Europe?"

"No. New Hampshire, actually. Way up in the mountains, the Redhawk Club. It had marvelous gardens and secret places to paint. Places to hunt. Quite a few of the men enjoyed shooting."

"Only men?"

"Yes," Augusta said, and her voice took on a strange note of pride and self-defense. "Although my husband thought it was ridiculous. Our girls could shoot as well as any man."

Skye felt her heart pounding out of her

chest. Her eyes were shut tight. She wanted a drink, she wanted a shot of morphine, she wanted to get out of where she was at that moment.

"Artists and hunters?" the nurse asked. "Seems like an interesting combination."

"They share an ecstasy for life," Augusta said. "My husband thought the two went hand in hand," Augusta said. As if she had just remembered Skye, the effect this conversation might be having on her, she quickly turned the page.

Skye breathed, and it came out a gulp.

The nurse, who had been taking her pulse, frowned and tightened her grip. As if she couldn't believe that her patient, lying down, could have such a quick heartbeat. Skye's eyes were shut tight. Her head was on the pillow, her face turned away. She tried to think of Caroline, to stop her heart from racing.

"Let me do this again," the nurse said, adjusting her grip on Skye's wrist. Skye felt the nurse's fingers on her vein, moving gently to find the right spot. "I got so sidetracked looking at those handsome men, I must have counted wrong."

Handsome men, Skye thought. The only

face she could see belonged to Andrew Lockwood, with his brown eyes and straight nose and wide mouth, dying five miles down the trail from that beautiful château. She tried to push it from her mind, cover his eyes with darkness. The black peace of a moonless night, when the creatures of the hillside are safe from the hunter.

Safe, Skye thought, lying in her hospital bed, thinking of Andrew in his grave.

June 4, 1978

Dear Joe,

So many secret places in the world . . . Driving through the mountains, through forests and beneath cliffs, do you ever think about where the hidden roads lead? Some rich men with too much money built a palace that belongs in Europe. They say it's about sport and art, but it's just about showing off. It's so out of place, stuck right in the middle of the wilderness where there should be only pine trees and granite, not mahogany and marble. I think true artists would know better.

My sister Skye is a true artist. Not just her spirit, which is so beautiful and tender I can hardly write about it. No, not only that. You should see her work. One line from her pencil can become the beach or a cliff or a face. She is more talented than anyone I know. Even my father. How are you? As an artist, I mean.

Love,
Caroline

June 15, 1978

Dear Caroline,

Art, shmart. Secret places, though. Now, there's a subject. Newport has plenty. I can get into any mansion on Bellevue Avenue. I know a lot of the caretakers. Those places all have wine cellars, tunnels, secret staircases.

Sam drew a picture of my boat for you, but then he spilled orange juice on it. Oh well. Me, I'm no artist. Wind's blowing—got to go.

Love,
Joe

CHAPTER SEVEN

Her mother had left the book behind, and when Skye was alone, she opened it again, to the picture of Redhawk. Seeing it had shocked her earlier; she had forgotten the picture existed. Now she stared at it, the cold stone and the men frozen on film, and her heart barely moved. The picture hardly stirred her at all.

The Redhawk Club. It had incensed her father to belong to a club that excluded his daughters. He had taken them everywhere. Taught them to shoot better than boys, talked with such pride about their accomplishments. People would tease him, saying maybe he should have had sons, and he'd start fights.

One day Hugh had driven his daughters

through the club's wide gates, parked the car, and walked them over to the skeet range. Right in front of everyone, he had had the girls shoot clay pigeons, hitting every one. Turning away, just as the club manager walked over for a discreet reprimand, Hugh handed in his letter of resignation.

He had felt so victorious. If only they had loved his sport. Augusta had used the phrase "ecstasy of life"; Skye could hear her father saying it now. He felt wildly alive when he was painting, inspiration surging through his being, flowing onto his canvas, and the same thrill when he was on the hunt, tracking live things that fled before him under the fire of stars.

He had taught her to draw. They had studied anatomy, dissecting the creatures she had killed. She had drawn the muscle and bone and sinew while he told her that was *her;* she was an animal just like the ones they hunted. He wanted her to understand how primitive it was, that joyful surge she felt when she drew and sculpted, how closely connected to the deep and ancient need to hunt. That the burning passion of creation, when she forgot who she was, *that* she was, was no more or less beautiful or exultant than death.

Loving her father, Skye had tried to love hunting. Desiring the ecstasy and self-forgetting she knew in the studio, she fought so hard to fight her fear of the mountain. She felt shame and revulsion when she killed something, but she was afraid to tell him. Now, staring at the picture of Redhawk, she remembered how desperately she had tried to avoid those trips. Knowing how effective Caroline's fever had been, Skye always pretended to have a sore throat, hoping her mother would keep her home.

"Hey, baby," Simon said.

Surprised by the sound of a human voice, as if one of the men in the picture had spoken from the grave, she jumped.

"Hi," Skye said, her voice coming out in a slight croak.

They stared at each other, husband and wife. She swallowed hard at the sight of him: so dark and sexy and concerned. She could see he hadn't been eating right.

"What are you trying to do to me?" he asked, leaning against the doorjamb, his eyes full of worry. He moved slowly toward her hospital bed, gently moving the covers aside, bending down to give her a tentative kiss.

"*Do* to you?" Skye asked, confused.

"Cracking up the car," he whispered. "You'd kill me if you killed yourself."

"It wouldn't kill you," Skye said. "Don't say that it would."

"Want to bet?" Now that he was with her, he couldn't keep from touching her. Her bruised cheek, her hands, his lips against hers. She felt the heat of his body, the electricity in the air between them, and suddenly they pressed together, the skin between them an almost unbearable barrier.

"I love you, Skye," he whispered, "more than anything. I'm sorry, so sorry."

She didn't want to hear his apologies. She felt his arms around her, his hands stroking her back, and she felt she had been only half alive—an animal left to die on the trail—without him in her life.

"Say something," he said.

"Why?" she asked, because it was the only word she could imagine.

"Because I'm a jerk. Is that what you're asking? Why I left?"

Skye didn't know. She just wanted him to keep holding her. She felt their blood flowing together, just under their skin, and she felt the comfort of love, of affection, of human contact come over her. It soothed away her grief and despair. It pushed away her thoughts of Andrew. But because he wanted her to say something, he might pull back if she didn't, she said, "Yes."

"It was her fault, you know. Biba's." He said her name apologetically, as if the sound itself could hurt Skye. But Skye was numb. She closed her eyes and felt him rub her back. "She came at me full blast. You know artists' models, they take off their clothes for pay. What did I expect? For her to respect our marriage?"

"That's for us to do," Skye said quietly, before she could stop herself.

Simon stopped rubbing her back. He sat up straight, pushed his dark hair out of his eyes. Peering at Skye, he seemed to check her out.

"You okay? They planning to let you out of here soon, or what?"

"I hope so," she said. "I do."

Now that Simon had pulled back, her feelings changed. They went cold. It was as if his physical nearness had an anesthetic effect on her, as if the illusion of their love calmed her down, quelled the storms raging inside. She wanted him to hold her again, but she understood that a drink would work just as well. Or a painkiller.

"What's this?" Simon asked, glancing at the photo album.

"Just family pictures," Skye said, turning the page to a series of shots taken in St. Lucia, when she and her sisters were young. They stared at the images of palm trees, big white clouds in a bright blue sky, the black marlin their father had caught hanging above the dock beside their chartered boat.

"Hugh strikes again," Simon said with an admiring laugh. "Or did you kill that one?"

"He did," Skye said quietly.

"What you said before," she heard herself say to Simon, "that it would kill you, what I did. I'd never kill you. I'd never do anything to hurt you. You know that, don't you?"

"Yeah, baby," he said, rubbing her back again, sitting so close, their bodies were nearly one again. "I know that."

* * *

Augusta Renwick was curious about the treasure hunters. Ever since Caroline had been here—pointed out the ships at Moonstone Reef—Augusta had been glued to the window. Watching through Hugh's shooting scope, she kept hoping for a glimpse of some shining objects being raised from the depths.

Focusing on such glamorous activity, she was able to forget the fact that her youngest child was in the hospital. Not forget precisely, but set aside. She had seen Dr. Henderson in the hall outside Skye's room. They had circled each other warily. She mistrusted him. That eager voice with its phony warmth made her shiver.

Standing at the picture window, Augusta tried to see what the men on the boat were doing. Bending over something, raising it to the light. Must be something exciting, she thought. She adjusted the eyepiece for a clearer look.

That tiny act, the slight movement of her two hands as she twisted the spyglass, took her back twenty years: She had taken this very same shooting scope with her to spy on Hugh and one of his women in a glade north of Hawthorne, and she felt a rush of shame and fury. She had taken the girls with her. They had been young: nine, seven, and four. She hadn't told them what she was doing, but she suspected they knew.

Her girls were cursed with exceptional powers of perception.

She narrowed her eyes, focusing on the ship, but the thrill was gone. That flash of guilt from the past had destroyed it. What kind of woman took her daughters to spy on their father?

Maybe she should have a cup of tea. She walked into the kitchen. A cool breeze ruffled the white curtains at the windows. The air smelled fresh, of the sea and herbs from the garden. Augusta set a kettle on to boil, then walked out the screen door to the small, sunken herb garden. Homer followed her, panting.

Set in a circle, the garden had plants that dated back one hundred years. Augusta had taken snips and cuttings from her mother's garden in Jamestown and her grandmother's garden in Thornton. Whenever she came out to pick rosemary, sage, or thyme, she felt the endless love of those two wonderful women. Augusta had had no sisters of her own. She was an only child, and when she had borne three girls, she thought it was the most amazing blessing possible.

That she had daughters, and that they could be sisters to each other in a way that Augusta had never had sisters of her own, had made her feel so happy, as if she had provided something for them beyond measure. Sighing, she sat on a stone bench. She reached down, letting her fingers trail through a clump of mint. The stalks were dark red, the leaves fuzzy green. When she smelled her hand, she went back in time to her grandmother's garden, with all the love and comfort any child could ever want. The feelings she had wanted to give her daughters and their children.

She heard a car coming up the driveway. The sound broke the spell, but Augusta stayed where she was. She knew from the sound it was Caroline's old Jeep. Augusta might have walked around the house to meet her, or gone into the kitchen to set out an extra teacup, but she didn't. She knew that Caroline finding her in the herb garden would be a good thing. It would make Caroline sympathetic to her. The herbs themselves would be an unspoken connection to the good past, to Caroline's beloved grandmother and great-grandmother.

Homer bounded off on the trace of Caroline, and Augusta knew he would lead her back.

* * *

"Hi, Mom," Caroline said.

Augusta opened her eyes. She seemed startled, as if she had been sleeping. She sat on a bench in the garden, wearing her pearls and a straw sunhat, holding a handful of herbs. It touched Caroline to see her mother sitting there in the grandmothers' herb garden, enjoying the sun and the breeze.

"Caroline!" she exclaimed, smiling.

"I thought I'd take a swim," Caroline said. "Do you feel like putting on your suit and coming down to the beach?"

"That would be great," Augusta said. "Just let me turn off the teakettle."

Caroline went upstairs to change. She used the bedroom that had been hers as a girl. It faced the beach, and from her window she could see Joe's boat. Putting on her black tank suit, she walked barefoot through the back halls of Firefly Hill. It was bare and dark in this part of the house: The floors were dark oak, the wainscoting nearly black with age. The bedrooms and living rooms were bright and overflowing with pictures and furniture. But back here, this section intended for servants, had always been spooky; walking through it had always made Caroline and her sisters feel nervous of what lurked in the shadows.

She ran down the porch stairs and met her mother outside. They walked across the lawn, through the tall grass and wildflowers. Caroline preceded Augusta down the long flight of stone steps to Firefly Beach, one hundred feet below. A quarter of the way, she heard her mother stop. "You coming, Homer?" Augusta called.

The rangy old dog stood on the top step. His head was big and proud, the sun casting golden lights on his thinning coat. From this angle he looked young and magnificent. Caroline remembered how he had loved to run on the beach his first summer there. Born a mountain dog, he soon learned to love the beach.

"Homer?" Augusta asked again. She hesitated, looking up at the golden retriever. Her pose was tense, urgent. She seemed to be willing him to move. "He's tired, Mom," Caroline said gently.

"I suppose he is," Augusta said. Without another word she followed Caroline down the stairs.

These swims were precious to both of

them. Caroline made time at least two or three times a month in the summer to spend a late afternoon on the beach with her mother. They dove in together. The water was cold and salty, and Caroline swam out to the big rock and back. She felt the sea caress her body, giving her that feeling of rebirth she got when the tide was high and she was swimming with her mother. They'd been doing this for thirty-six summers, and every time she came to Firefly Beach for one of their swims, she prayed that they would have another: another swim and another summer.

Back on the sand, they lay in the sun on separate towels. It was nearly five o'clock, but the day was still warm, the light gilded. It glistened on the sea and made the tiny pebbles, wet from the waves, look like beads of amber. Caroline watched her mother open a book and start reading. Caroline looked out to sea. There was the *Meteor*, rocking on the waves. She'd be having dinner out there in just a few hours.

Caroline took Clarissa's diary out of her bookbag. It was the actual book Maripat had given her, so she held it carefully, away from the sand.

August 1, 1769

Today counted seven schooners and one brig and one barq. Found twenty-two red starfish. Ate two joe froggers after lunch. Saw three eagles, twenty osprey, and more than a hundred herring gulls. More than a thousand herring gulls. More than seven thousand herring gulls. But no friends! No little girls to play with. Only Mama and Pa, when he's not too tired. Tomorrow morning we're going for quahogs.

August 4, 1769

Pa got four geese. The bang from his gun scared me, and I was crying, but I couldn't find Mama. She wasn't there. I found her near to dark, by the south shore where we found the whale. The last place I looked, I came upon her. Mama as sad as when Grandmother died and we had to travel to Providence to bury her, but today no one is dead. She said she wasn't crying, but I know she was, and when I kissed her she tasted like tears. I told her about the geese, thinking she would be happy because we always cook one for Christmas, but it only made her cry more.

"What's that?" Augusta asked, curious.

"An old diary," Caroline said slowly. "A little girl writing about her life. This part is about her mother."

"Does she love her?"

"Very much."

"Good," Augusta said happily.

Caroline thought of how strange it was, Augusta asking whether the girl had loved her mother. What an odd thing for a mother to ask.

What made her so insecure? Had Augusta felt that way long ago, when the girls were young? Caroline took it as an explanation for the way things happened, the fact that their childhood had been so fragmented. The hunts, the fights, the separations and reconciliations between Augusta and Hugh. Caroline's heart ached for her mother, then and now.

"The diary was written by Clarissa Randall," Caroline said. "The daughter of the woman who died on that shipwreck."

"Right out there?" Augusta asked, shading her eyes as she stared at the ships on the horizon.

"Yes."

"Dear, how fascinating!" Augusta said. "I've been keeping my eye on them. They seem to be making great progress. They work night and day. Oh, I have a great idea. . . ."

"What's that?"

"You should send the captain a copy of the diary! Wouldn't that be fun? And I'm sure he would find it extremely helpful. Maybe there's some secret code in the diary, some key to where the treasure is buried!"

"Mom," Caroline said.

"Darling, I'm serious. The captain would *love you* for it."

Caroline wanted to tell her mother the captain was Joe Connor. She felt it so strongly, the desire to explain that Joe was the ship's captain, that she had already sent the diary to him, that he was diving on the *Cambria* because of Caroline's letters from long ago. But Skye was in the hospital and her mother hated the Connors. In Augusta's mind the Connors were the enemy.

"Remember the treasure we found, honey? The gold chain?" Augusta asked, changing the subject herself.

"Yes, the one Dad gave you," Caroline said, trailing off.

"Are you going to Scotland?" Augusta asked after a long stretch of thinking about Hugh. "Didn't you say something about a quick trip?"

"Yes," Caroline said, suddenly wishing she were leaving tonight, "but I'm not going just yet."

"You pick up and go like no one I know," Augusta said, shaking her head. "Half the time I call Michele, she says you're on a plane to somewhere."

"Not half the time," Caroline said.

"I'm relieved, Caroline. That you're not going now. Skye needs you too much. I try to be there for her, but I know it's you she wants."

Caroline heard the pain in her mother's voice. She wanted to tell her it wasn't true, that she was a great mother, that Skye needed her more than anyone. But she knew Augusta wouldn't believe her, that the lie would only make her feel worse.

"She loves you, Mom," Caroline said, telling the truth.

"I know, dear. But I wish I'd done more earlier. That I hadn't missed my chance."

The words hung in the air, reminding

Caroline of the failures of love. People tried so hard, but they often missed the most important connections. Slowly she looked out to sea, toward the white boat shining in the sun. She thought of Skye drunk, wanting to see Joe. Their tragedies were linked, there was no getting away from it.

Not even by taking the night flight to Scotland.

"This is lovely. Thank you for coming over to swim with me," Augusta said.

"It was my best swim of the summer," Caroline said, wishing she could give her mother something bigger, something more.

"I'm tired," Augusta said, gathering her things. "It's been so nice, sitting on the beach with you. Being together. That's all that counts, Caroline. When all is said and done, being together is the only thing that matters."

Augusta struggled to stand. Her feet slipped a little in the sand, but she caught her balance. As Caroline reached out her hand to help her to her feet, she was filled by a surge of love for her mother, for the way her mother lived, for the fears her mother tried so hard to bury, for the things her mother would never know. Caroline felt such tenderness for her mother, growing old, she bit her lip.

Homer must have seen the women approaching. He was on his feet, and he let out a joyful bark. Standing on the top step, atop the ledge, he was the sentry of Firefly Hill. He barked again and again, full of greeting and expectation.

"He must be hungry," Caroline said.

"No, dear," Augusta said, smiling as she checked to make sure her black pearls were still around her neck. "He's just happy we're on our way home."

Caroline didn't say anything, and the expression on her face didn't change. But walking along the beach, she felt strangely joyful. Soon the fireflies would come out, begin their nightly dance. There was the *Meteor,* across the sea to her right; she had no idea what tonight's meeting would be like. But the sand felt cool under her bare feet, walking just below the tide line, and she had to hold herself back from taking Augusta's hand. She was thirty-six years old, but it still made her feel so happy when her mother sounded like a mother.

July 7, 1978

Dear Joe,

I know we keep wishing for treasure from the Cambria to surface, but yesterday something great did happen. My mother and I went swimming, and I saw some gold glinting in the sand. Just as if a firefly had dropped down! I ran to pick it up, and it was a bracelet. Not from the Cambria, but from my very own family! My father had given it to my mother a long time ago, and she had lost it last summer. So it sat under the sand all winter, safe and sound, waiting for us to find it.

Don't give up hope, Joe: next time it'll be gold coins, and I'll send you one.

With love,
Caroline

July 15, 1978

Dear Caroline,

That sand is keeping more than your mother's bracelet safe. Those old ship spars are probably still in perfect condition. It's really great about the bracelet though. I wish I could go walking on a beach and find my father's gold watch. He always wore it, and sometimes I wish I had it.

Things are weird. If you're not careful, you can start missing things you barely remember.

Take care, C.

Joe

P.S. You really *do* have magic fireflies.

Chapter Eight

That night, just before eight o'clock, Caroline sat in her car at the dock waiting for Joe to pick her up. The evening had turned cold and crystal-clear, the sea flat calm without a whisper of wind. The sun had just gone down, and the horizon was deep red and purple, the sky darkening through shades of silver to violet to jet. The ocean was a sheet of onyx.

Caroline watched the launch approach fast, its running lights glowing against the sunset. She walked down to the dock, feeling nervous. The chill stirred her blood, heightened her awareness. Her father had taught them to pay attention to fear, to rely on their instincts. The back of her neck tingled, but it could have been the night air.

Wary, she raised a hand in greeting. Joe reached up to help her down from the dock to the skiff, and she handed him the bottle of wine she had brought. She wore jeans and a soft beige cashmere sweater over a silk tee-shirt; she slipped on the thick navy wool jacket she had carried from the car.

"Good idea," he said, nodding. "It's cold out on the water."

"Thought it might be," Caroline said.

"Clear and fine," he said, looking at the sky.

"Clear nights are sometimes the coldest," Caroline replied, wondering if they'd be talking about the weather all night. She tried a smile. "Thanks for inviting me."

"Thanks for sending me the diary," Joe said, smiling back.

He gunned the engine. The eighteen-foot skiff took off so fast, it nearly knocked Caroline off her feet. She hung on to the side rail, maintaining her balance. She was not going to let Joe see her hit the deck. She had a sailor's pride, and she made note of the fact he was driving like a jerk.

Spray flew back from the bow, tickling Caroline's face. The loud engine made conversation impossible. Joe stood at the console. All his concentration was on driving the boat. She found herself staring at his wrists. He was wearing a dark green chamois shirt with most of the nap worn off, and he had pushed back his sleeves. His wrists were bare, sturdy, covered with curly blond hair. They were safer to look at than his face. Glancing across the water, she spotted Firefly Beach, its grasses glowing with green-gold irridescence.

Several larger boats appeared in the distance. Bright lights illuminated the stem of one, and the plume of sand Caroline had seen from Firefly Hill was arcing out of the sea. People milled about on deck. Joe throttled back, said something she could not hear into the microphone. Someone replied, more static than human voice. Joe slowed down even more, so their approach was a quiet slap, slap over the small waves.

Red-and-white diving flags dotted the surface in two places. Joe steered the long way around to avoid them. He made the skiff fast to a ladder in the stern of the smaller boat. They climbed aboard.

The scene was exciting, the aftermath of chaos. A compressor thumped like a steam engine; the force of sand and seawater spitting twenty feet into the air rasped like a geyser. Divers in scuba gear lined the boat rail. Others swam between the boat and the flags, their sleek black heads glossy, like seals. Two people sat on deck, using soft brushes to clean sand off what looked like barnacle-encrusted baseballs.

"Hey, skipper," one of the men called. Motioning for Caroline to follow, Joe walked over. He bent down to hear what the guy was saying. He nodded, replied. Reaching down, he handed one of the balls to Caroline. Small enough to fit in the palm of Joe's hand, it appeared to have been underwater a very long time. Barnacles and mossy green seaweed covered its entire surface.

The ball weighed more than a barbell. It tugged Caroline down, she nearly lost her grip. Joe spoke, but she couldn't hear him over the compressor. She shrugged. Joe was grinning, possibly at how she had nearly dropped the weight on her toe.

"A cannonball. We found it today," Joe said, his lips against her ear.

"Wow," Caroline said, excited in spite of herself. She bent down for a closer look at the objects. There was a pile of coins, similarly covered by sea growth. Joe picked one up. He slid the coin into her hand. The barnacles were sharp and felt rough against her palm.

"From the *Cambria*," she said. It wasn't a question.

"Yes."

She turned it over, examining it. She tried to give it back, but Joe closed his hand around hers, giving it a rough push. His grip was so hard, it made the barnacle dig into her hand.

"Keep it," he said.

"Thanks," Caroline said, peering at her scraped palm.

The lights illuminating the sea were blinding, white-blue. The two large boats were rafted together; Joe helped Caroline climb over the rails, stepping from the smaller of the two boats to the larger. It was seventy feet long, sleek and magnificent, equipped for work. Everything was gleaming white fiberglass, stainless steel, aluminum. Caroline glanced into the wheelhouse, saw instruments and gauges blinking everywhere. It reminded her of the lair of some futuristic, mad oceanographer.

Everyone was busy, but they were noticing her and Joe. He led her from group to group, shouting introductions. Caroline nodded pleasantly, shook a lot of wet and cold hands. She was aware of the fact people were sizing her up. Did that mean they were comparing her to other women Joe brought out there? Or was she unusual, did he rarely bring women out at all? What difference did it make?

She stood in the wheelhouse while Joe called everyone together on deck. He gathered them in a huddle, said a few words, and the next thing she knew, the compressor was being shut down. The lights were turned out. En masse, like revelers leaving a party, the crew climbed aboard the smaller vessel. Someone started it up, and someone else moved the skiff, tying it off to a cleat at the stern of the big boat. Then everyone waved, and the boat chuffed away.

"That's better, don't you think?" Joe asked. "Now I can hear you. It was really pretty noisy." He was about six inches from Caroline. His hair was tousled and nearly as wet as if he'd been diving himself. He had a careless, rakish smile, a sharp expression in his dark blue eyes.

"What just happened?" she asked.

"I sent them to your inn," he said. "Gave them the night off."

"Really?" she asked, suspicious. "Alone at sea with Joe Connor. Are you planning to throw me overboard?" she asked.

"No," he said. "I just thought we had a few years to catch up on, and I didn't want the whole crew listening in."

"You didn't have to do that on my account," Caroline said, although she was secretly happy. To have a man cease and desist operations just so they could have a quiet conversation together was nice.

"Would you like a glass of wine?" Joe asked, and Caroline realized that he was holding the bottle she'd brought in his left hand. "Or something else?"

"Wine, please," Caroline said. "That would be fine."

He disappeared below for a moment, returned with a wineglass, a corkscrew, and a glass of what looked like juice for himself. They went up out on deck, into the cold night air. It felt brisk and sharp. The stars were just coming out, sparks of fire in the sky.

They leaned against the rail. With everyone gone, the ship was suddenly silent and very dark. Small waves splashed the hull.

The generator hummed down below, but the sound was unobtrusive, even comforting. Green light from the loran screen glowed serenely in the wheelhouse, along with the warmth of a brass lamp. Caroline felt tension in her shoulders.

"This is beautiful," she said.

"You always loved the water," he said. "Saltwater."

"I still do."

"Me too."

"It's great that you're able to make your living out here. When did you first get the idea, hunting for treasure?"

"When I got your letter about the *Cambria,*" he said.

She laughed, sipping her wine. "No, I'm serious."

"So am I. But the thought grew stronger when I was in graduate school. I did my first cruise in the Indian Ocean, on a small oceanographic ship researching sediment and salinity. But we snagged a wreck in our dredges, a ship dating back a thousand years or so, and it piqued my interest. A lot of gold came up that day."

"A thousand years?"

"Yeah. A Turkish ship in the silk trade,

loaded with sapphires and rubies, gold medallions, statues, and ingots. Amber beads. Coins from the year 990."

"Amazing," Caroline said, imagining the thrill of Joe's first time on a ship that brought up treasure. "Did you ever actually work as an oceanographer?"

"For a few years. I worked at Scripps, in La Jolla, then at Woods Hole. But in my free time, all my reading seemed to be about wrecks. You know, local legends, failed dive attempts, anything I could find. On my vacations I'd travel to the most likely sites, size them up. I saved some money, did a real dive, and came up with enough stuff to sell and finance the next one."

"And you gave up oceanography altogether?"

Joe shook his head. "Never. I use it all the time. In some ways I practice it more now. I'm just not attached to an institution."

"And here you are, diving on the *Cambria*," Caroline said, staring at the black water.

"I never forgot it," Joe said. "All this time, no matter which ocean I was in. I'd think of the *Cambria*, lying in New England water, and I knew I had to come here."

"Is it what you hoped for?"

"Yes," Joe said, staring at the black water as if he could see through it.

"I like that you're doing it," Caroline said, surprising herself, "instead of someone else. It seems right . . . You diving on the *Cambria*. I'm surprised no one's tried it before."

"They have," Joe said. "But the ship's in a tricky spot. It takes . . . well, a certain kind of operation to do it without getting hurt."

"You're saying you're pretty good?" Caroline asked, laughing as she sipped her wine.

"It's not that," Joe said uncomfortably. "But I have a great crew and a good ship. The money to do it right."

"And now you have Clarissa's diary."

"It's complicated," Joe said, "reading the diary, then diving down, getting involved with the lives connected with the wreck."

"Does it bother you?" Caroline asked.

Joe thought for a minute, watching the stars just above the horizon. "Yes," he said. "It's disturbing. But I still want to know."

"Why is it disturbing?"

"It's hard to be dispassionate, as I have in the past. I've come across human remains before, but . . ."

"But what?"

"They were just skeletons. The people never had names," Joe said. "Now I have the diary, and that makes everything more personal. And I'm not talking about the parallels you referred to in your note."

Caroline wanted to talk about their story, hers and Joe's, but she wasn't sure how. Words stumbled through her mind, linking their letter-writing days with this moment right now. How did they get from there to here? The wind was picking up. It made Caroline's fingers cold around the stem of her glass, her cheeks and forehead sting. She shivered, and Joe saw.

"Come on inside," he said.

"I like it out here," she said, looking around. The wind was strong in her face. It whipped her long, dark hair into her eyes, and she brushed it away. She had something she wanted to say to him.

"It's how I've always thought of you," he said quietly, interrupting her thoughts. "Outside. Totally alive, with nothing touching you but the elements. Like those trips to the mountain."

"Nature girl," she said, embarrassed.

With that he laughed and opened a door. They went through the wheelhouse. Caroline felt him close behind her. He didn't quite touch her arm to guide her through the narrow passage, but he almost did. She could feel the pressure of his hand in the air between them, and it made the skin on her wrist tingle.

She followed him down the companionway; it was like entering another ship entirely. All the high-tech sparkle and gloss up above gave way to old-world warmth and elegance down below. The entire main salon was teak. The burnished wood glowed in light cast from softly shaded brass lamps. Bookcases filled with texts and navigation tables lined one wall. Framed drawings of sailing ships hung over the settees.

All the furniture was built-in and gimballed for life at sea. The settees were covered with forest-green canvas, strewn with kilim pillows. There were brass barometers, wind indicators, fittings around the portholes, everything polished to a high shine. In one corner was a small ceramic fireplace surrounded by Delft tiles, with a fire already crackling inside.

"Here's how she looked," he said. He handed her a sketch. It depicted a beautiful barquentine, a three-masted vessel with the foremast square-rigged and the main and mizzen masts rigged fore and aft.

"The *Cambria*?"

"One like her," he said, nodding. "The *Cambria* was English, carrying a load of arms, along with the gold. She went down in a gale in 1769. On Moonstone Reef."

"Right here," Caroline said, thinking of the ship lying in sand and mud however many fathoms directly under her feet. Seeing the sketch made the vessel seem more real. All shipwrecks were tragic, but as Joe had said, this one felt personal.

"It's sad," she said. "Kind of a love story."

Joe exhaled, shook his head. "What, the lady and the captain?"

"Yes."

"What about the lady's husband and kid?" Joe asked. "Or maybe I've just been reading that diary a little too closely. I got your message about the similarities, loud and clear."

"Have you ever seen Wickland Rock Light?" she asked.

Joe shrugged.

"It's desolate. You can't get on or off without a boat. She must have been horribly unhappy," Caroline said. "I'm not excusing her, but she must have been desperate, doing what she did."

Caroline gazed at the drawing, imagining a young woman who lived in a lighthouse on a rock at sea, falling in love with the master of this ship. She heard herself defending Elisabeth Randall, but was that just so she could fight with Joe? She disliked Elisabeth for what she'd done. How bad could life have been that she would run off and leave her daughter? Caroline felt contrary, fired up, and she knew it had to do with old resentment at Joe, for the unfair blame he placed on her.

"Do parents think of their children first?" Joe asked. "When they're caught up in their own plans? I think you and I know the answer better than anyone."

"Joe," she began, raising her eyes. But he had disappeared. She heard him in the galley. Caroline tried to catch her breath, to get control of her emotions. She browsed through the library, calming herself down.

She watched Joe emerge with an orange-enameled casserole dish. He placed it on the gimbaled table, which was set for two. He refilled Caroline's glass, pouring himself more juice. Sliding a hidden panel, he pushed buttons that brought Mozart into the cabin from speakers in four corners of the salon. The sound was perfect, as so-phisticated as she had ever heard. He stirred the fire.

"This is amazing," she said, pulling herself back together, trying to be nice. "I can't be-lieve I'm on a boat. A fireplace!"

"It gets cold out here," he said. "Even now, in the summer. You should come out in November. Late fall in northern waters is not our idea of fun. But I know you're the Arctic type."

"Arctic?"

"Where was that mountain he used to take you hunting? Somewhere way up in Canada, wasn't it?"

"New Hampshire," she said, picturing Redhawk. "Not quite the Arctic Circle."

The table was square, set into a corner. Caroline slid into one side of the settee and Joe into the other. Caroline felt shaky from that earlier exchange. Their knees touching slightly, Joe served them both helpings of braised lamb shanks. With it came crusty French bread, salad greens tossed in vinaigrette, and baked chèvre.

"This is delicious," Caroline said awkwardly. "Did you make it?"

"I wish I could say so, but our steward did."

"I'd like to steal him for the Renwick Inn," Caroline said, joking.

Joe laughed. "He'd never go for it. He's from St. Croix, and he lives for the day we go back down south. To him, summer in New England is cruel and unusual."

"St. Croix," Caroline said. "I went down last winter to visit a few inns. There's a beautiful place way out on a headland, in an old sugar mill. Bougainvillea everywhere, and dark sand on the beach. I loved it."

"So you go south sometimes," Joe said without expression. "Not only north."

"No, there's life beyond the Arctic," Caroline said quietly. "I'm not as cold as you think."

Joe smiled. Noticing her glass was empty, he poured her more wine.

"Don't you like it?" Caroline asked, indicating the bottle of merlot.

"I don't drink," he said.

"Never?" she asked, thinking of Skye.

"Not anymore. I used to like it too much. I didn't get in trouble every time I drank. But every time I got in trouble, I'd been drinking. The pattern was pretty clear. And I got in some trouble."

"You did?" Caroline asked, fingering the stem of her glass, picturing the bottle beside Skye in the car wreck, knowing that many of the worst nights in their family had involved drinking.

"Yeah, I did," he said. "Drinking was fun for a while, but the fun stopped. I'd drink, and it took more every time. I felt empty, and the key word was always 'more.' "

"Oh," Caroline said. The emptiness: She knew it well. Sometimes she felt such bottomless sadness and grief and need and loneliness, she'd try to fill it with wine or travel or business success or helping her sisters.

"Anyway, it got to the point where one drink was too many and a hundred wasn't enough. So I stopped," Joe said.

"I have someone I'm worried about," Caroline said. "Who drinks too much."

"I'm sorry," Joe said.

Caroline wanted to tell him about Skye, but she held herself back. She felt cautious, on guard.

They finished dinner, telling each other safe stories about college escapades and travel fiascoes and the last movies they'd seen and where they'd each been last Christmas, Caroline at the inn and Firefly Hill with her family, Joe with his crew on Silver Bank in the West Indies.

Caroline took another sip of wine, but it didn't taste as good as it had before. She glanced up and saw Joe watching her. She tried to smile. But she felt the ghosts of both their pasts swirling around the table, waiting for an invitation.

They moved closer to the fireplace to have their coffee. She took it black, strong, and hot. Topside, the wind was picking up, and she felt the boat begin to rock a little more. Joe stirred the fire and closed the glass door on it. He went up to check the anchor line. When he came back, he settled down again.

"Do you spend all your time at sea?" Caroline asked. "Or do you have a home somewhere?"

"Both," he said. "I have a place in Miami, but I'm at sea nine months a year."

"Miami is a long way from Newport, your old home, when I knew you," Caroline said, watching his dark blue eyes. Troubled, they darted to Caroline's face and away.

"Home wasn't . . ." He searched for the diplomatic explanation, but quickly gave up on it. "Well, I wanted to leave. In a way, I was surprised to find that you'd stayed so close to home. Put your father and those hunts behind you." He raised his eyebrows, acknowledging that he wouldn't drop the subject this time.

"You remember the hunts," Caroline said.

"How could I not? You wrote about them twice a year. He'd set you loose on a mountain with a canteen and a penknife and expect you to fend for yourself."

"He wanted us to be able to protect ourselves," Caroline said, surprised to find herself defending her father. She tried to remember her letters to Joe; at least one had been brutal with detail, filled with terrors of the hunt. But now, all these years later, she was revising the truth. She wished she had never told him. After all, her father had started them because of what his father had done. She drew herself up straighter.

"You were so mad," Joe said steadily. "The first time Skye went. She wasn't ready, you said. She was so scared, she didn't want to shoot a gun. Is she the one who drinks?"

"Why do you ask that?" Caroline asked, her heart racing.

"Because she crashed her car," Joe said.

Caroline sipped her coffee, but it was cold. She placed her cup on the table, looked Joe straight in the eye.

"Why am I here?" she asked coldly.

"I wanted to thank you," he said. "For the diary, for telling me in the first place. You're the reason I found the *Cambria,* after all. You told me about the wreck. . . ."

"But why did you ask me out here, to the *Meteor*?" Caroline persisted. Her heart pounded. Her mouth felt dry. She was sitting with Joe Connor after all the years of resentment, and she didn't know what to say.

"To talk to you," Joe said, his voice steady and low, "about that night."

"The night your father died," she said.

"When your sister called me—left me that message—I thought maybe she had something to tell me about what happened," he said. "Something new."

"She feels a connection," Caroline said quietly. "We all do."

"Because you were there when it happened," he said.

"I hardly remember," Caroline said. After all this time, she still didn't want to be the one to tell him.

"Tell me," Joe said again.

"I will," Caroline said, trying to keep her voice steady. "If you'll explain one thing."

"What?"

"Why did you start hating me?"

He didn't deny it. Staring at her, he spoke steadily. "Until I was seventeen, I thought my father died of a heart attack. I knew he died in your house, but I thought he was a friend of your father's from the docks, that he'd taken a break from fishing and gone off to visit him. I liked thinking he had died among friends. It made everything okay, thinking he had died with people who cared about him."

"I was a kid too, Joe. Just like you. It was too much responsibility to tell you what really happened."

"Tell me now," Joe said, looking directly into Caroline's eyes. "Please."

Caroline could summon her memory of that night in an instant. She closed her eyes, saw the kitchen at Firefly Hill. She could smell the cookies baking. She could see James Connor's eyes.

"He was sad," Caroline said. "That's what

I remember most. So sad. He was acting crazy, but it was because he loved your mother so much."

"Did he say that?"

Caroline nodded. His questions were taking her back. She could see the gun in his shaking hand, the floury fingerprints on her mother's pregnant belly. The terror in Clea's eyes.

"He cried," Caroline said. "I'd never seen a grown-up cry before. He told my mother my father didn't love her anymore. Because he loved your mother instead. He was wild."

"Then he shot himself?"

"He was going to kill *us*," Caroline said, and she could see from Joe's expression that he hadn't known that part. He looked stunned.

"You and your mother?"

"Well, and Clea and Skye too. Even though Skye wasn't born yet. She came two days later, on Christmas, so I think of her as being there."

"But why?"

Caroline stared at him. His blue eyes were clouded with apprehension, his wide mouth twisted. He's afraid to hear, she thought. Suddenly she remembered seeing that six-year-old in the picture, all smiles, in his father's shaking hand.

"Because my father had stolen what your father loved," she said steadily. "I guess he thought that killing us would be taking what *my* father loved."

"His wife and daughters. My father was going to *kill you*."

"But he didn't, Joe," Caroline said. "Your father couldn't do it."

Joe closed his eyes.

"I've always thought of him as a good man," Caroline said, her throat aching. "A good man who was desperate. Crazed by love, you know?"

"Hmmm."

"He had this with him," Caroline said, reaching into her pocket. She had thought she might have this chance, and her fingers trembled as she handed Joe the photograph of himself, stained with his father's blood.

Joe accepted the picture. He held it, staring at it for a long time. When he looked up, his eyes were angry and glittering. He wiped them.

"What the hell," Joe said.

"He loved you," Caroline said. She could

see that it cost Joe a lot to be near tears in front of her. He stared over her head, holding himself together. His eyes were closed, his dark lashes resting on weathered cheeks.

"He did," she said when he didn't speak.

In response, his mouth twitched. The seas were picking up. A line snapped free on deck, slapped against the planks like a live animal, startling his eyes open. A halyard clanked, metal against metal, in the wind. Joe's clear blue gaze went straight back to the old photo.

"I love that picture," she said. "I'll understand if you want to keep it. It belonged to your father, but I love it. It means so much to me."

"My picture?" Joe said, his voice harder than ever. "Why?"

"My old friend," Caroline said. "Joe Connor."

"I put an end to that, didn't I?" Joe asked.

"I couldn't believe it," she said, "when you told me not to write you anymore. I didn't know you thought our fathers were friends. I told myself you knew the truth. But I didn't think it was up to me to tell you the details."

"It wasn't," Joe said. "I used to think it was, but I was wrong. We were just young."

Caroline lowered her eyes, trying to stop her hands from shaking. Was he forgiving her? For harm she had never meant to cause in the first place? Why did she get the feeling that letting her off the hook, even to that extent, took a major effort? His lips were tight, his eyes hard and distant. She had the feeling he had gotten what he wanted out of her. Now he wished she would just disappear. When she looked up again, she caught him holding his picture, staring at it.

"It must have been awful," Caroline said, "for your family."

Some emotion flickered across Joe's face. He put the picture down, rested his chin in his hand. But he kept glancing at the photo. He touched the bloodstain with his finger.

"Was it?" Caroline asked. "What happened?"

"Nothing much," he said. "My mother remarried after a few years. They had a son, so she got the chance to do things right with him."

"Sam," she said.

To Caroline, sisters were a blessing. She couldn't imagine life without them. Maybe Joe felt the same way about his brother, because his eyes softened, and his mouth relaxed. He pushed the picture across the table to Caroline as if he were done with it forever. He may not have intended to send it flying, but it slid right off the gimbaled table onto the floor.

"Yeah," Joe said. "He's a pain in the ass, but he's a good kid. An oceanographer of all things, went to the same school I did. A twenty-seven-year-old know-it-all."

"Sounds like he looks up to you," Caroline said, smiling.

Joe shrugged. His smile faded as another memory took hold. He looked Caroline in the eye as if he had another bit of unfinished business. "I blamed your father for what happened," he said.

"I blamed your mother," she countered.

"He had no business putting guns in your hands. No matter what, but especially after what happened with my father. Right in front of you."

He exhaled, shook his head.

Caroline wondered how he'd feel if he knew the whole story. She wasn't about to tell him, and she doubted Skye would call him again. She closed her eyes, thinking about what had happened at Redhawk.

"I know how you feel," she began, her voice straining. She stopped when she saw Joe shaking his head.

"No, you don't," Joe said.

"What do you mean?"

"My father killed himself," Joe said. "It's pretty bad to find out your father was so miserable, he'd rather blow his head off than come home."

"I know," she said. Caroline's heart was pounding, her hands shaking. The waves had picked up, and the boat pitched beneath them.

"You don't, Caroline," Joe said, trying to keep his voice even. She could see that he thought he was alone, that his pain was exclusive, that Caroline was just a witness. "I'm sorry, but you just don't."

"I was there, Joe!" she cried, the words tearing out of her throat. If he didn't understand how that had been for her, if he wouldn't believe how much she had cared . . . "I was with him! It's one of my first memories, your father dying. I cared so much, Joe. About him *and you*." She had so much emotion inside her, she felt it bursting in her chest. "We were almost the same age, you and I—all I could think of was:

That little boy's father died." She broke off to get control of herself.

Joe watched her, not saying anything or moving closer.

"Our parents were so angry at him, and they wanted us to be too. My father went crazy knowing he'd threatened us. That's *why* he gave us guns, because of what happened."

"That's why he took you hunting?"

Caroline went on as if she hadn't heard. "My parents *hated* your father, and they wanted me and Clea and Skye to feel it too. We didn't though. You can't believe how upset they'd get that I wanted to write to you. But I had to do it."

"Why?" he asked.

"To console you."

"You were only five," Joe said. "Why should it have been your job to console me?"

"It wasn't my job. But I couldn't get you out of my mind," she said.

She felt the boat pitching. She wondered how earthquakes felt, to have the ground shift underneath your feet. She felt Joe's arms come around her. His embrace was rough at first. He pulled her to her feet. She couldn't look at him, but his hand on the back of her neck was gentle. He traced the skin beneath her hair, and she heard herself moan through her tears.

His lips brushed her cheek, and she raised her face to meet his kiss. His face was coarse with two days of not shaving, and his grasp was tight. They kissed as if they were saving their own lives. It tasted like salt: the sea, tears, and blood. The kiss was harsh and violent, and it made Caroline feel as if she were standing on deck in a storm. His touch shivered down her skin, made her tingle and shudder as he whispered her name.

Scared by the emotions she was feeling, Caroline tried to push away. Joe's eyes were dark, even more angry than they had been at the beginning of their discussion. But he wouldn't let go. He looked bewildered, as if he couldn't believe he'd just kissed her. Gripping Caroline's arms, he held her still. His mouth brushed her cheek, and he whispered something she couldn't understand. When he pulled back, his eyes were almost tender. The expression lasted only an instant. He let go of her.

"I'd better get back," she said shakily.

Caroline felt a sharp mixture of pain and longing, tension and relief. But she could breathe easier than she had since coming to the boat. Without looking at Joe, she bent down to retrieve the picture on the floor. She brushed it off, slipped it into her pocket. If he saw, he didn't say anything.

They headed up on deck to feel the wind on their faces. Cold air had swept down from Canada, and it slashed across the open ocean. Caroline pulled her jacket around her. The boat rose and fell. The wind had whipped the waves into whitecaps; Caroline could see them in the starlight, crested with foam. Standing on deck, she felt like crying and didn't know why.

The old ship lay wrecked on the reef below. The seas were high and rugged. If they waited much longer, it wouldn't be safe to take the launch. Caroline climbed over the lurching rail, her nerves tingled with danger. The black ocean foamed and chopped. Her fear had such primal power. She was an expert swimmer, but she thought if she fell in, she would disappear. Sitting close to Joe as he took the wheel, their arms touched through their heavy jackets.

He drove less aggressively than he had on

the way out, as if he had exorcised some demons. Or perhaps he was just being cautious in the building seas. Caroline's hand closed around the coin he had given her that day. Clutching it as the small boat flew across the sea, getting closer to shore, she felt it was a talisman to keep them safe. A creature slashed through the water, bright as neon, and she jumped. The fish left a trail in the water, phosphorescent fire.

When their feet were on dry land, Joe stood before her, not knowing what to say. She had the feeling he wanted to apologize for his kiss. Her voice trembled, but she spoke anyway, to take him off the hook.

"Thanks for dinner," she said.

"Thanks for coming."

"Are you sure you can make it back to the *Meteor*?" she asked, staring at the whitecaps, at the small boat tossing at the dock.

"Yes, I can make it back," he said.

Why did she feel disappointed? That kiss had started something. A feeling of heat filled her chest, and she realized that she wanted Joe to hold her again. Caroline shivered, the desire was so unexpected and strong and unfamiliar.

The waves hit the dock; she felt the spray in

her face. It cooled and soothed her, and she let it push her feelings for Joe away. A poet once wrote that cathedrals were never built beside the sea because it was so beautiful it would distract the people from praying. Caroline agreed. Most of her travels took her to other oceans, and she felt the need for another one soon. She had to get away from this.

Glancing over at Joe, he seemed about to speak. He took a step toward her, but something stopped him.

A car was coming down the road. They could hear it over the wind, and they turned in time to see a yellow cab drive into the sandy parking lot. A single passenger sat in back. He paid the driver. When he got out, he grabbed a soft black bag and an enormous backpack from the trunk.

The man stood alone, silhouetted against the dockmaster's office light. The taxi drove away.

"Hey, a welcoming committee!" the man called. His voice was exuberant, full of humor.

"Holy shit," Joe said.

Joe stuck his hands in his jeans pockets. His posture was straight, his sturdy shoulders thrown back. A small smile crossed his lips, but he did his best to keep the pleasure out of his eyes.

The man was young. He looked like a college kid; he had a baseball cap on backward. He had a lanky build, wore wire-rimmed glasses, and was coming straight toward them with a ridiculous grin on his face. Pulling off his cap, he revealed short blond hair, darker than Joe's.

"How'd you know I was coming tonight?" he asked, dropping his bags to give Joe a bear hug. "I was trying to make it a surprise. Standing out here, waiting for me. Jeez!"

"I didn't know," Joe said. He let the young man hug him for so long without getting prickly or pushing him away, Caroline started to smile. She knew a sibling reunion when she saw one.

"Hi," the newcomer said, stepping back and catching sight of Caroline. He had a wonderful, wide-open smile, and it occurred to her: Joe would look like that if he ever looked really happy.

"Caroline, this is my brother, Sam Trevor. Sam, this is Caroline Renwick."

They shook hands. Was it Caroline's imagination, or did Sam react to her last name? If nothing else, she had learned tonight that the Renwick name was evil magic to Joe, and she didn't suppose it would be any different for his younger half brother.

"Nice to meet you," Caroline said.

"Same here," Sam said, his grin back full force. "You coming out to the boat?"

"Heading home, actually," Caroline said.

"Yeah, she was just leaving," Joe said, unintentionally abrupt. Or perhaps he had meant it to sound the way it did, rude and dismissive.

"Still an old grouch," Sam said, laughing. "He tries the same thing with me, and I don't even hear him anymore."

"I didn't mean—" Joe said, looking at Caroline apologetically.

Caroline smiled. She didn't know which was the truth, Joe being mean or Joe being contrite. No matter which, Caroline took her cue. She said good night to the men, climbed into her car, and pulled out of the parking lot.

Only when she reached the main road did she see a flash of light in the eastern sky. It was bright and fast, close to the horizon. She saw another, higher in the sky. Shooting stars, she thought. It was the night of the Perseid meteor shower, and she had been too absorbed in Joe Connor, in their past and present—in their kiss—to gaze up at the sky and count the shooting stars.

Holding tight to the barnacle-encrusted coin Joe Connor had given her, Caroline Renwick drove slowly back to her inn.

August 5, 1978

Dear Joe,

I dreamed about you last night. It was the strangest thing. I was standing on a rock, in the middle of the Sound, with waves crashing all around. They were about to sweep me away, when all of a sudden I heard your boat. You were rowing out to get me. I heard your oars hitting the water, and my heart was beating so fast and hard, I thought I was going to drown. But I knew you were coming, Joe. You did too. In my dream, you looked just like you. But in real life, I don't even know if I'd recognize you. I think I would, just from your letters. Wow, I'm glad I survived that dream.

Gratefully yours,
C

August 14, 1978

Dear C,

 If I thought you were going to drown,
do you think I'd row? I'd take the fastest
motorboat I could get.

Love,

Joe

P.S. I've been thinking about that too.
What it would be like to see you in real life.

CHAPTER NINE

At the hospital, Skye wanted to hear everything. If she ignored the antiseptic smell, the nurses walking by, and Skye wearing pajamas during the day, Caroline could almost imagine they were just two sisters having coffee. Only it was tea, lukewarm, in paper cups. And her sister's face was bruised, shades of yellow and fading purple.

"What's he like?" Skye asked.

"He has an amazing boat," Caroline said. "Like a floating laboratory, so high-tech, you can't believe it. They analyze the sediment and artifacts right there—"

"Not the boat," Skye said. "Him."

"He's guarded," Caroline said, flushing as she remembered his arms around her shoulders, his deep kiss. "Very guarded . . . never mind about that. How are you?"

"Why won't you let me care about you?"

"What are you talking about?" Caroline asked, shocked by the question.

"I want to know about you, and you always turn it back to me."

"I answered you—"

"In the most *perfunctory* way, just to get me off your back. You're like this all the time. Maybe you don't even know you're doing it." Skye exhaled. "Does he realize he's in love with you?"

"Skye," Caroline said, shaking her head.

"He is. Of course he is. Why else would he come to Black Hall? Don't tell me it's for that sunken ship. There are plenty of buried treasures around the world. He's here for you. You got under his skin all those years ago, and now he's come to sail away with you."

"That's not true," Caroline said.

"Love," Skye said, staring out the window.

"Love is not the answer to everything," Caroline said, shaken by Skye's accusation. "No matter how much you want to believe it."

"Is he what you expected? After all this

time, does he match the picture you had of him in your mind?"

"I don't know," Caroline said, comparing her image of Joe as a cowlicked child with the serious blue-eyed man. Oddly enough, they weren't completely different, only the man had lost that boy's loving, open smile.

"It must be like a wish finally coming true," Skye said. "Seeing someone so important after all this time. It would be like . . ."

"Like what, Skye?" Caroline asked, alarmed by the change in her sister's tone.

Skye's head was down, but when she started to talk, Caroline could tell she was trying not to cry.

"Like Andrew Lockwood coming back to life," she said.

The sisters sat in silence. What if it were possible? Caroline could see him now, that other tragic boy from their past. His eyes were brown, not blue, and he had lived in the mountains, not by the sea. She put her arm around Skye.

"Did Homer come home? Mom was here this morning, and she said he was gone again all night."

"He's back."

"Where do you think he goes, Caroline?"

"I don't know," she said.

"Simon told me you're letting him stay at the inn. Thank you."

"Don't thank me," Caroline said, sipping her tea.

"Did Joe ask about me? The reason I called?"

"Yes, he did."

Skye shook her head. Her face was pale, and it seemed to be getting paler. Caroline knew her sister well, and she could see that she was uncomfortable, embarrassed about the drunken phone call. Caroline's first impulse was to comfort her, but she held back.

"Shitfaced to the max," Skye said. "What can I say?"

"What are you going to do about it?" Caroline asked.

Skye opened the drawer of the bedside table. She removed a gray pamphlet titled "Forty Questions." Glancing at the questions, Caroline could see that they were meant to help a person determine whether or not she was an alcoholic.

"It's rigged," Skye said.

"How?"

"It makes me seem like an alcoholic."

Caroline let Skye's statement hang in the air. In the hallway, a voice came over the public address system anouncing that Dr. Dixon was wanted in the emergency room. Someone on the floor had their television turned up high. Game-show bells and laugh tracks sounded noisy and festive.

"Dad wanted us to feel the ecstasy of life," Skye said. "Had you ever felt it, Caroline?"

"Yes," she said, thinking of the moonlit nights, the cries of nightbirds. She thought of dusty trails and thorny banks, wild animals screeching in the night, adrenaline flowing in her blood.

"It was incredible," Skye said. "I hated it, I was so scared, but I got used to it."

"To what?"

"To the surge. That feeling of really being alive. But we can't sustain it."

Caroline thought of kissing Joe last night. "Maybe we can," she said.

"I think I'm supposed to die young," Skye whispered.

"You can stop drinking instead," Caroline replied.

"It's complicated," Skye said. "You make it sound so easy."

"I don't think it's easy."

"I don't even know if I want to."

"That's for you to decide," Caroline said, sounding peaceful but feeling the opposite.

Skye didn't respond. She was staring at the pamphlet of forty questions, frowning at it as if she wished it would disappear.

* * *

Michele warned Clea: Watch out.

Caroline was in a horrible mood. She refused to accept the salmon from the fish man, she told Michele she hated daisies on the tables in the bar, and she asked a group of rowdy young artists from Montreal to keep it down even though they were making no more noise than any other rowdy young artists over the last hundred or so years.

Clea had pulled up with a trunkful of old clothes to ask what Caroline thought she and Peter should wear to the ball. She half considered leaving, to come back another day, but ignoring problems had never done anyone in the Renwick family any good. So she walked into Caroline's inner office.

"Since the theme this year is favorite

paintings," Clea said, "I thought we should go as one of Dad's. I mean, don't you think?"

"If every one of Dad's paintings burned in hell, I'd be happy," Caroline said, furiously tapping numbers into her calculator.

"Dad was many things, but he did make beautiful pictures," Clea said, stepping back and lowering her voice to speak to Caroline the way SWAT negotiators speak to hothead terrorists.

"I saw Skye this morning," Caroline said.

"How was she?"

"Weighing the options. Whether she'd rather die young or give up drinking."

"Are you serious?"

"Yes. Dying young sounds so romantic, doesn't it? Artistically drinking oneself to death. Too bad it's so messy. And it makes people so mean."

"Like Dad."

"We're not supposed to notice he drank," Caroline said. "Or else we're supposed to excuse it because he was Hugh Renwick."

"What do you mean?"

"He got away with things no one else could. He had Large Concerns. Life was dark, and brutal, and harsh, and infested with evil. You know? And he saw so *deeply* because he was this great artist. He couldn't *not* see."

"Why are you in such a bad mood?" Clea asked, struck by Caroline's intensity, by the anger in her gray eyes.

"Lies were the truth in our family, have you ever noticed?"

"Like what?"

"Like Dad drank because Skye shot a man. He was so broken up with guilt over letting her hunt, he shut himself up in his studio or my bar with a bottle of scotch. Supposedly because he loved us so much, right? Because he had wanted to protect us, and instead he'd ruined us. But what a lie!"

"How?"

"Because if he really loved us, he would have stayed in our lives. He was here, but he was gone."

"He lost hope," Clea said quietly.

"But why?" Caroline asked. "We still loved him. I don't know about you, but I still needed him. More, if that's possible."

"I know."

Caroline squeezed her eyes shut. Slashing the tears away with her index fingers, her chest shook with repressed sobs. Clea watched; Caroline would never just let it out. This was the thing they couldn't understand, the way their father had just decided to depart. He was *right there,* sitting in plain sight, but he was a million miles away, in a haze of scotch.

"He'd brought daughters into such a barbaric world," Caroline said. "So much for 'the ecstasy of life.' Too bad his philosophies were in such dire conflict. He forced us to hunt our entire childhood, and suddenly he never took us to the mountains again. It was over."

"It wasn't over," Clea said. "He was sick. That's how I see it—sick with grief."

"You're more understanding than I am," Caroline said.

"Feeling bitter doesn't work," Clea said, covering Caroline's hand. Caroline allowed it; no one could say the things to her Clea did. Maybe because she hadn't seen Andrew die, Clea was softer, more trusting and unguarded, than either of her sisters. She didn't suffer in the same way as Caroline and Skye.

"He wanted to be near you, Caroline," Clea said. "It's why he came to your inn."

"To drink!" Caroline said, holding back a sob.

"What's wrong?" Clea asked. "You sound awful."

"Am I aloof? Do I stop people from caring about me?"

"Not exactly," Clea said, alarmed by how frantic Caroline sounded.

" 'Not exactly?' What's that supposed to mean?"

"You're . . . competent. That's what it is. You handle everything so well, you give people the idea you don't need them."

"I need them plenty," Caroline said angrily, crumpling up her paper, starting over. "I need Skye to get a grip on herself."

"Uh-huh," Clea said, seeing the contradictions in her sister, the fact that even in a fury she could still not express her own needs—Caroline once again projecting her own feelings outward onto those she loved.

"I'm sorry," Caroline said. "But if you'd heard Skye, you'd understand. She is in bad shape. We have this whole family legend going about art and drinking. Skye and Dad. What a lie."

"Maybe that's why I married a minister," Clea said, smiling at Caroline. "Finally, a man I can trust." But even as she said the words, she knew they were true. She could never love an ordinary man, one who thought white lies were okay, who might believe a secret affair was acceptable if no one found out, who could lie to himself and his family about drinking himself to death.

Caroline turned her attention to her calculator and stack of receipts. Clea watched her flip through invoices, her fingers skipping over the keys. This was Caroline in action, Caroline being excellent. Clea had observed all her sister's escape attempts, and this was one of the most effective.

"Did you have fun last night?" Clea asked.

"What?" Caroline asked, her fingers stopping mid-click.

"Last night?" Clea asked, smiling. "Did you have fun?" When Caroline didn't reply, she went on. "You did go to the *Meteor*, didn't you?"

"Yes," Caroline said. She closed her eyes, gathering her thoughts. Her gray eyes flew open, and she exploded, "You should have heard him, he's just as crazy as Skye. Even more so! You'd think I'm to blame for every single person's crummy childhood from here to Boston."

"You're not to blame for mine," Clea said.

"He wanted an account of what hap-

pened the night his father died. It was horrible."

"It sounds it," Clea said soothingly.

"He basically grilled me. I told him what I
could, and he started off being very high-
and-mighty, saying I could not know how
he felt. But he must have felt sorry. I think
he did, because he pulled me over—so
hard, it hurt my shoulder—and kissed me."

"Kissed you?" Clea asked.

Caroline nodded, miserable. She stared at
her hands. Clea sat back, not wanting to
say the wrong thing. Caroline never reacted
to men this way. She was so guarded, she
set herself so apart, she never let them get
to her. Their father had schooled them in
the ways of men and women, and Caroline
had chosen her armor carefully and early.
But it was off right now, Clea could see,
plain as day.

"He shouldn't have done it," Caroline said.
"He can't stand me."

"If he can't stand you, why did he kiss
you?"

Caroline blinked. Her lashes were long
and dark. They rested for a second on her
pale cheek, then opened. Her eyes were
clear, periwinkle blue, and full of distress.

"To shut me up," Caroline said. "Animal instinct, I don't know. I think he wanted to rip my throat out, but he kissed me instead."

"You've missed him," Clea said.

Caroline nodded, miserable.

"Don't be ashamed about that," Clea said softly.

"It's still there, the connection," Caroline said. "We read each other. He knows about Skye, that she drinks. I didn't want to tell him too much, but he guessed. She's broken, Clea. I saw her in the hospital to-day, and I don't think she'll ever be okay again."

"She will be," Clea said.

"How do you know?"

"Because we love her," Clea said. "And love is all there is."

Caroline looked up. Clea smiled, filled with tenderness for Caroline. Clea watched Caroline's face change. "I told Skye the op-posite today. That love can't fix everything."

"Then you were wrong," Clea said. She believed in love. She believed in it hard and strong, with everything she had. With all the grief in their life, the methods of violence, she knew that their love for each other had saved them so far. It had made them strong. And watching Caroline right now, Clea knew that her big sister had suffered as much as Skye.

Maybe even more than Skye. And Clea believed that the love Caroline needed, the one that was going to help her, was sitting offshore right then. In a boat, on the waves, over a murderous reef within sight of the house where it had all begun, Caroline Renwick's true love was waiting. Clea knew it. Gazing at her sister, she glowed with such tender affection, she thought her face would crack.

"He has a brother," Caroline said. "I met him."

"I'm happy for him," Clea said. "Sisters are better, but brothers are good."

Caroline was silent after that. She looked everywhere except at Clea.

"So," Clea said. "Joe Connor finally kissed you."

"Hmmm," Caroline said, wiping her eyes. "What are you smiling about?"

"Nothing," Clea said, smiling even wider. But even as she said it, she knew she had just told a lie. She had used the wrong word; she should have said "everything."

* * *

On the porch that night with Peter, Clea sipped lemonade and watched her children chase fireflies. It was time for bed, but they were keyed up, and they ran though the side yard with wild abandon. They swooped and yelled, trying to stave off bedtime for a few more minutes. When they stopped, when she and Peter tucked them in, their eyelids would flutter and close within seconds.

"Why are you so quiet?" Peter asked, his rocker creaking on the wide floorboards.

"I'm worried about my sister."

"Skye? She's getting the help she needs—if she'll take it . . . you know it's up to her in the end."

"Not Skye. Caroline."

"Why?"

Clea's eyes filled with tears. "She's so armor-coated. Ever since we were little she's been that way. So busy looking out for us, making sure Skye and I were happy and taken care of."

"She's a good sister."

"The best," Clea said.

"So why are you worried about her?"

"I want her to fall in love," Clea said.

"She will when it's time."

A picture of Caroline, her eyes haunted, her arms around Skye, came back to Clea. They were at Redhawk, and Skye had just shot a person dead. "Caroline's always been there for us," Clea said. "Both times . . ."

"Both shootings?" Peter asked.

"Yes," Clea said. She had been only three when James Connor had come into their house, but she remembered Caroline holding her, standing between Clea and the gun, shielding her with her own body.

"That's because she loves you," Peter said.

"Why did God put such violence in our lives?" Clea asked, taking his hand. "Such terrible things? Why did He put those deaths in our lives?"

"Maybe to show you how much you love each other," Peter said, using his handkerchief to dry Clea's eyes.

"We do," she whispered, thinking of Caroline, wishing and praying that she would let down her guard, let someone love her the way she loved them.

"Caroline has been afraid," Peter said. "I

think we know that's what her traveling is all about."

"She acts so brave, but she's not."

"No, she's not," Peter agreed.

"How lucky we are," Clea said, sniffling. "You and I."

Peter didn't reply, but he held her a little tighter. Words weren't necessary just then. Clea looked up at the sky in time to see a shooting star. It made her suddenly feel so happy, she had to hold back tears.

August 30, 1978

Dear Caroline,

Had any good dreams lately? Maybe you don't like motorboats. I'm wondering if that's why I haven't heard from you lately.

I went spearfishing off Breton Point yesterday. The surf gets pretty crazy there, and I got really pounded. The America's Cup boats were sailing by, and I started wondering if you like sailing. Or if maybe you'd want to come to Newport to see the Cup boats. They're Twelve-Meters, really sleek and beautiful. My dad used to take me to see them. The next race is in 1980. I'm hoping I can find a way to crew on one.

Write soon. Hey, are you going out with anyone?

Still your friend,
Joe

November 24, 1978

Dear Joe,

Sorry I haven't written lately. Actually, I was embarrassed about telling you my dream. I'd never told anyone that before. No, I'm not going out with anybody.

I've never seen the Twelve-Meters in person. My father has painted them before, and he's hung out with some of the sailors. He talks about Ted Hood and Baron Bich, and this brash young guy named Ted Turner who reminds my dad of himself. He says art collectors love the Twelves.

That's a long way of saying yes. I'd really love to come to Newport. But how?

> *Love,*
> *Caroline*

CHAPTER TEN

"Man, you are equipped," Sam said, drinking his morning coffee in the chart room with Joe. His eyes were big, his tone admiring as he carefully examined the *Meteor*'s electronics. He looked over the satellite equipment, from communications to engine room monitoring. He noted the airtime access routes via nautical programs like INMARSAT and AMSC and nodded approvingly.

Leaning over the computer station, he played with the navigation software. He clicked the keyboard, displaying a chart of Long Island Sound.

"You can read the charts either north up or course up, just like on radar," Joe explained. "The program interfaces with our depth sounder and autopilot, automatically figures in tides and currents. Under way, we can upload and download to the GPS receivers and exchange waypoint data."

"That's the difference between gold hunters and federal funding," Sam said. "I'm out there tracking humpback whales on an ancient rustbucket, where the idea of modern electronics is radar and the oldest GPS in existence. Shit, Joe," Sam said, downloading bathymetric charts, watching the graphic fly by. "Blindingly fast."

Joe smiled, then took a big gulp of coffee. He had not seen his brother in a few months, and the first thing Sam wanted to do was check out the new technology. It made Joe uncomfortable the way Sam looked up to him so blatantly. The kid had a short break from his own research, but he had flown down from Nova Scotia to interview for university jobs and spend his free time aboard Joe's boat. It bugged Joe, but he couldn't pretend it didn't please him too.

"So, what's happening down below?" Sam asked. "You making progress on the wreck?"

"It's slow, but yeah," Joe said. "I'd forgotten how murky New England water is. Cold and filled with particulate, makes it hard to work."

"Pretty funny, considering you're a New Englander born and bred," Sam said.

"Been a long time since I've lived up here," Joe said stonily.

Sam laughed. "Yeah, but you still sound like one. All crusty and cantankerous. You want to be one of those Florida guys who gets fat walking the beach and fishing the Keys, but forget it. You're too much of a codger."

"A codger. Hmmph," Joe said sternly. No one saw through him like Sam, and no one else could get away with saying the things Sam did. Joe did his best to keep the older-brother barrier up, and Sam did his best to rip it down.

"That what Caroline thinks of you?" Sam asked, laughing.

"Caroline?" Joe asked, startled by her name.

"Yeah. I was kind of surprised to see you with her. I mean, she's a Renwick, and I know how you feel about the old man. . . ."

"We had some unfinished business," Joe said, his mouth tightening. "It's finished now."

"She seemed nice," Sam said. "Growing up, the way you and Mom'd talk about them, I got the idea all Renwicks were bad folks. Really wicked, you know?"

"She's not wicked," Joe said. "She's just the wrong guy's daughter."

"You gonna hold people's fathers against them, what does that say about me?" Sam asked. Joe leaned over the computer, pushing the zoom-in key for a closer look at the chart. He punched another key for the sea-surface temperature. His mouth was dry. Joe and his stepfather had never gotten along. Sam knew it, and he was driving home a point Joe didn't want to face.

"Drop it," Joe said quietly.

"It's just that I had the feeling I showed up at the wrong time last night," Sam said. "Seemed like you two were in the middle of something."

"I told you," Joe said. "We'd finished what we had to say to each other. Now, you gonna get dressed, or what?"

"I'm dressed," Sam said blankly, standing there in his shorts and WHOI tee-shirt. Behind his glasses, his eyes were wide and still sleepy.

"Get into your wetsuit. I'll take you down to the wreck, show you around," Joe said.

"Great!" Sam said, leaving his coffee mug on the chart table as he stumbled over a spare searchlight waiting to be installed. Shaking his head, Joe carried the cups down to the galley. Sam was like a big clumsy puppy waiting to grow into his paws. But he did see things. He saw through Joe like no one else.

Passing through the main salon, Joe thought of last night. He had kissed Caroline Renwick. Right here, he thought. Her perfume lingered in the air. The ship smelled like salt, diesel, coffee, and fish, but Joe was stopped dead by the scent of jasmine. He shook his head, walked on.

Caroline. He had had no business kissing her. The point was, he hadn't been thinking. He hadn't had much of a choice. His arms had slipped around her, his mouth had found her lips, his voice had whispered her name. It was as if Joe himself had had nothing to do with it.

Joe Connor would never kiss Caroline Renwick. Hate was a strong word, but it could honestly be said that Joe hated the Renwick family. He had drunk over it, guzzling scotch and feeling the ill will burn down with the liquor.

But facts were facts. Joe was a scientist, and he understood the irrefutable truth of certain data. He had stood in this room last night with his arms around a beautiful woman, their bodies pressed together and her tongue working hot magic, and he had wanted her more than he had ever wanted anyone. She had whispered shivers down his spine, mustered the hair on his arms to stand on end. He had held her with more tenderness than he knew he had; he hadn't wanted to let her off the ship.

That moment at the end, when she had told him how she had cared for his father and for Joe himself—how she hadn't been able to get Joe out of her mind—had pushed him over the edge. The compassion in her voice, all directed at him, was too much to handle. He could have walked away or kissed her; too bad anger still had him by the scruff of his neck. He wanted to be done with it; he really did. That familiar lifelong resentment.

"Ready?" Sam asked, flashed with excitement. He stood in the companionway, zipping up his wetsuit. Looking at his brother, Joe thought of the youngest Renwick sister. He had sensed Caroline's anguish, felt grateful he didn't have to worry about Sam that way.

"Wash these," Joe said, thrusting the coffee mugs at Sam. "What kind of sailor are you anyway, waiting for someone to clean up after you?"

"Sorry, captain," Sam said, grabbing the mugs so Joe could get changed. But he didn't sound sorry at all. He sounded affectionate, slightly condescending. As if he knew Joe's gruff manner was an act. As if he suspected that behind the cranky exterior was a good brother, a decent man, a lonely guy who would forgive if he could.

* * *

Skye and Simon went for a walk in the hospital garden. The paths were full of white-garbed nurses pushing people in wheelchairs. A few big maples provided shade, and the paved paths were lined with low boxwood hedges. Rows of lemon-drop marigolds and brilliant zinnias filled the geometrically positioned flower beds. Skye had rarely seen a garden she didn't want to paint, but this was one.

When they found an unoccupied stone bench, Skye sat down gingerly. She had been on her feet for less than ten minutes, but she felt exhausted. The effort made her so dizzy, she had to bend over. If there had been a patch of grass, she would have curled up on it.

Simon reached into his pocket and took out a cigarette. He lit it, blowing the smoke over Skye's head. She could hear the annoyance in his exhalation. She looked up.

"What's wrong?" she asked.

He shrugged.

She tried not to worry. She was the sick one, the person needing care. But she was so attuned to Simon's moods, to his needs and tempers. When he wanted something, she had trained herself to give it.

As a child, she had watched her father bang around his studio in a rage, or sulk in silent scorn for days on end. No matter how he acted, her mother would jump to attention. And so had Caroline, Clea, and Skye.

"How much longer are you going to let them keep you here?" Simon asked.

"I don't know. Now that my injuries are better, they're trying to talk me into signing into rehab."

Simon gave a slight laugh, an appreciative expression in his eyes. "With all the drunks and junkies?"

"Yes. The substance abuse unit."

"You're not seriously considering it, are you?"

"I haven't said yes yet."

"It'll fuck with your art, Skye. Turn you into another middle-of-the-road mediocre conformist. So you drink too much. You're not a little housewife with a carpool and a mortgage. You're a sculptor."

"Half the time I'm too hung over to sculpt," Skye said, staring at her hands, trying to remember the last time she had touched clay.

"Look at the artists who drank. The writers. You're emotional, and it shows in your work. If drinking pushes you over the top, I say let it." He moved closer to her on the bench, nudged her with his hips. "I don't want to lose my drinking buddy."

"I know," Skye said. It was one of the things she feared: If she was sober, how would she and Simon get along? So much of their relationship involved drinking. Wild nights with the ideas flowing faster than the scotch, decadent Tuscan lunches with wine and grappa when they pretended they were back in Badia on their honeymoon. Then again, there were the vicious, drink-induced fights, the nights when fine wine turned into booze. She wouldn't miss those.

"Lets you know you're alive—" Simon said, "—a great bottle of Calon-Ségur. Or a nice, fresh spring wine from Portugal. Remember that trip to the Algarve? We stayed naked for six days eating shrimp and drinking that cool white wine?"

"I remember," Skye said.

He pulled out pencil and paper and spread it out on his knee. Then he glanced at Skye and started to sketch her.

Skye leaned back on her arms and tried to relax. He was a good artist. He felt high today, because a major collector had praised his work and agreed to visit his studio. Skye felt guilty though, because the art world considered her work superior to his. She knew it bothered him, and she suffered for it.

Her eyes closed, she heard his pencil flying across the paper. It seemed like such a loving gesture—a return to their early days   him drawing her outside on a sunlit day. She had boxes full of beautiful sketches he had done of her, just as her mother had so many pictures done by Hugh. It made Skye feel proud and lovely, to be loved by an artist. Her blond hair was tangled, and she knew her face was pale, but she decided to trust Simon.

"Here," he said finally.

The sketch was beautiful. Simon's style was spare, his lines simple; the body horizontal, the hair flowing down, the eyelids closed. He had drawn Skye in death, lying on a tomb.

"You're killing yourself, staying here," he whispered. "Closed off from the world, from your inspiration."

"I need help," Skye whispered.

"You need to make art," Simon said. "That's your gift. Don't waste your passion trying to fit in with the rest of the world. Express it in clay. Otherwise you're just choking yourself. Come with me now. Walk straight out of this place."

"I can't," Skye said.

"You can," Simon said, reaching out his hand. "Do it. We need each other. Haven't we always?" He had passion in his eyes.

Skye nodded. His words were true, the path was clear. His picture was a portent of things to come, and it terrified her. Skye could not stay here alone. She would try to stop drinking on her own.

He held out his arms, and as Skye walked into them, somehow she knew she was letting her sisters down. How did Caroline do it? Never compromise for love? On the other hand, Caroline was alone. Their father had warned them to protect themselves. Their mother had taught them to sacrifice everything for men.

Skye took her husband's hand. Together they walked out of the garden.

* * *

Clea was just throwing a load of laundry into the washer when the telephone rang. She poured in the detergent and ran to answer.

"Hello," she said with a don't-hang-up breathlessness.

"Clea, it's me," Caroline said.

"What's wrong?"

"Skye left the hospital. Just walked away without telling anyone."

"Where is she?" Clea asked, feeling cold.

"I don't know. I stopped by, and she was gone. No one saw her leave—"

"Oh, Caroline." Clea heard the panic in her sister's voice. Their grip on Skye was so tenuous. Clea heard a tone on the telephone line, indicating that she had a second call waiting.

"Just a second," she said. "Maybe she's calling now." Clicking off, Clea took the other call. "Hello?"

"Darling," said Augusta.

"Mother, can I call you back?" Clea asked, her heart skittering. "Have you heard from Skye?"

"Heard from her? She's up in her room right now. She's had enough of the hospital, and she came home, where she belongs. With Simon. Now, listen. We have to talk about our costumes."

"Costumes? I've got Caroline on the other line. Let me tell her about Skye. She's frantic."

Clea returned to Caroline's line. "She's at Mom's. Safe and sound."

"What happened? Why'd she leave the hospital? If that idiot Simon's trying to svengali her into doing something crazy, I'll kill him. Is that her on the other line? Tell her I want to talk to her. Can you link us up?"

"It's Mom. I'll make it quick," Clea said.

"Sit tight, and I'll get back to you with the whole story. Okay?"

"Goddamn it," Caroline said, signing off.

"That was Caroline on the other line—" Clea repeated to Augusta, adjusting her tone accordingly.

"Marvelous," Augusta said. "I need to tell her as well. I've worked out what I'm going to be for the Firefly Ball."

"The ball?" Clea asked, wiping her brow. "Mom, what about Skye? Caroline and I are so worried about her."

"I am so thrilled you girls are close," Augusta said with profound warmth. "I am so very grateful. Do you know how lucky you are to have sisters? Did I ever tell you how much I wanted sisters when I was a little girl, how I used to play with my dolls all alone and feel so sad?"

"Yes, Mom, but—"

"Now, darling. About the ball. I thought I'd go as something from Picasso's rose period. A harlequin, in fact. Everyone will expect me to dress as a painting of your father's—they'll all just take it for granted—and I'll shock them to death! It will be the most fantastic surprise!"

"A harlequin," Clea said, giving up.

"Is it too playful?" Augusta asked. "Too whimsical for a woman my age? I mean, who would expect Hugh Renwick's widow to dress as a Picasso? A harlequin, at that!"

"It sounds perfect," Clea said.

"I'm envisioning the little black mask, the bold checks, the curly-toed slippers. Really divine . . ."

Clea listened and talked for another few minutes, until her mother was done. Augusta was at her most brittle. Focusing on the ball was easier than thinking about Skye walking out of the hospital, and Clea was glad Caroline was not there to hear it.

"You'll look great," Clea said.

"Mmmm," Augusta said.

Silence filled the line. Clea took a deep breath. Just as she was about to bring Skye up again, Augusta headed her off.

"Would you and Peter and the children like to come over for cocktails?" Augusta asked. "I could call Caroline. We really need to do something to welcome Simon back into the fold. As much as I despise what he did to Skye, he is her husband."

"Not cocktails, Mom," Clea said.

"A barbecue, then. Something festive."

"Maybe she should rest," Clea said.

"She's *fine,*" Augusta said. "You should see her. As bright as ever. God, I'm glad to have her home."

"I know, Mom," Clea said.

"Let's not mollycoddle her," Augusta said. "She needs our strength and support, not a lot of tiptoeing around. She needs to get back on her feet, back to life again."

"She's been ill," Clea began, realizing how painful it was for Augusta to accept that Skye needed to recover from something beyond her injuries.

"And she's well now. She's pulled through with flying colors. She's all better in time for the Firefly Ball. Won't Caroline be thrilled? She'd be so let down if Skye wasn't able to be there."

"I don't think Caroline would mind," Clea said, knowing how hard it might be for Skye, newly sober, to mill around a party where liquor was flowing freely, bottles of champagne chilling in tubs all over the lawn, trays of drinks being passed all night.

"Well, if you change your mind about tonight," Augusta said, "we'd love to have you all over. We could have a lovely time, planning our costumes for the ball."

"Don't drink in front of Skye, Mom," Clea said.

"Even her doctor didn't suggest anything as ridiculous as that," Augusta said shakily. "My God, Clea. Do you think the world stops just because your sister got drunk last week?"

"No, but I think it should," Clea said. She said good-bye and hung up. Then she called Caroline to tell her the details.

By the time Caroline called Augusta to throw in her warning, it was too late. Cocktail hour was under way. All was well. Augusta and Simon were having martinis, as usual, but Skye was drinking a diet Coke. Skye knew she could not drink. She didn't seem bothered at all. In fact, Augusta said, she had insisted that her mother and husband not forgo martinis on her account. That would have upset Skye more than anything.

* * *

Several nights later a bunch of guys from the *Meteor* converged on the inn for dinner. They had booked one table, but when they arrived, it was obvious they needed two pushed together. While they waited in the bar, Caroline helped Michele rearrange the dining room. They had to ask a party of four to switch tables, but they bought them a round of drinks to smooth the move.

Caroline headed into the bar, menus tucked under her arm. She tried to be cool, glancing through the group for Joe. He wasn't there. His crewmates were laughing, talking loudly about the artifacts they had found that day, excited about the progress. Spotting Sam, Caroline walked over.

"Hi, there," she said, smiling.

His grin was huge. Brushing dark blond hair out of his eyes, he knocked his glasses off his nose. Bending over to retrieve them, he spilled beer on the floor.

"Yikes," he said. "Sorry. You're Caroline, right?"

"Right. And you're Sam."

"I wasn't sure it was you," Sam said, bobbling his beer mug to shake her hand. "Last time I saw you, it was pretty dark." Still grinning, he seemed to be studying her. Caroline flinched, embarrassed.

"What?" she asked.

"You don't look evil and despicable," Sam said, peering down at the top of her head, ducking for a better look at her eyes.

"Is that what you've heard I am?"

"All my life," Sam said. "This is kind of momentous, me standing here talking to a Renwick. If I hadn't seen Joe doing it the other night, I'd feel disloyal. Fraternizing with the enemy, you know?"

"Think how it makes me feel, serving you dinner," Caroline said.

"I see your point," Sam agreed. "So, are you and Joe all made up now?"

"What does he say?" Caroline asked.

"Say? Joe doesn't say anything. Haven't you figured that out by now?" At Caroline's blank expression, Sam nodded. "Joe likes geophysics best, but he'll also talk about salinity in the water column and advancements in marine technology. He's pretty good on the subject of satellite navigation, and you can't shut him up once he gets going on new methods of carbon dating the stuff he finds in wrecks. But otherwise . . ."

"A man of few words," Caroline said.

"You got it."

Some of the scientists and pirates had

made their way down the bar. They were talking to a group of pretty women watercolorists from Atlanta, up for their annual week at the Renwick Inn. Caroline stared at Sam Trevor and felt herself starting to smile. He had that effect on her, as she suspected he had on nearly everyone he met. He had a cute gap between his front teeth. His blue eyes crinkled at the corners. His glasses were crooked, as if he frequently sat on them.

"Why do you think he came here?" Caroline asked. "With all the wrecks in all the oceans, why did he decide to dive on the *Cambria*?"

"You've got to be kidding," Sam said, jabbing her with his elbow as if she'd just made a good joke.

"I'm not," she said. "I promise."

Sam turned serious. "She's a substantial wreck," he said, "historically and from a treasure-hunting point of view. Joe goes for the gold. No matter what the other factors, if he's not going to get rich on a dive, he doesn't do it."

"Really?"

"Really. The *Cambria* went down on a shoal, so you'd think the water would be shallow. But she slid into a trench, one of the deepest in Long Island Sound."

"Trench?"

"A geological feature of the sea bottom," Sam explained apologetically. He wasn't being a showoff, Caroline could see. He was a young nerd, pure and simple. He and Joe might have shared the same field, but their styles were completely different. Looking at this bespectacled scientist, she thought of Joe, his dark tan and sun-lightened hair, his pirate eyes and sexy arms, and she smiled at how different—yet the same—two people could be. Like herself and her sisters.

"So, the hole is deep, but Joe has the equipment. The tides and currents are fluky. The water's cold, and most of Joe's crew are southerners. The wreck is unstable—the bow lies on rock, and the stern's wedged in muck—he has to constantly analyze how the structure behaves under stress. . . ."

"Sounds impossible to me," Caroline said, laughing nervously.

"Does to other salvage teams too. That's why it's good for Joe. He's got the best boat going, and a crew to match. The site happens to be excellent for his area of geological interest. First and foremost, my brother's an oceanographer. He takes risks no one else would, and it always pays off for him."

"Were those the other factors you mentioned before? The risks?"

"No," Sam said, blinking his owl eyes. "The other factor is you."

Caroline felt her face redden. She looked down at her shoes, then back at Sam. His face was kind, as if he had just broken some hard news to her and was waiting for her to absorb it.

"Me?"

"Well, yeah. You must know that. Whatever happened between you guys wigged him out big-time. Coming anywhere near you had to carry a lot of weight in his decision to salvage the *Cambria.*"

"Wigged him out," Caroline mused.

"Yeah. Frankly, I'm surprised we're having dinner here. At the Renwick Inn. No offense or anything. But the Renwick name . . ."

"Strikes fear into the hearts of pirates," Caroline said.

"Exactly," Sam said solemnly.

"Does that mean he won't be joining you

tonight?" Caroline asked, hoping she sounded casual.

"No, he'll be here," Sam said.

* * *

Caroline wasn't sure how she felt when she saw Joe Connor park his truck and climb out. She watched him stretch. She saw his tan forearms flex, his shoulder muscles strain under his blue plaid shirt. He tucked the tails into his jeans, and she noticed his flat stomach, his broad chest. He was tall and handsome, and as she remembered kissing him on board the Meteor, she felt her face flush.

But fresh in her mind were Sam's words: "evil and despicable," that Caroline had "wigged Joe out" early, that he was surprised Joe would even want to eat at her inn. She felt her back stiffen.

He stood in the lobby with his feet planted wide, his rough hands in the pockets of his jeans. She felt the tingle in her neck.

"Hi, Joe," she said.

"Hi," he said, looking surprised to see her. "You work this late?"

"I own the place," she said. "I'm around here most of the time."

"Kind of like the captain," he said, trying a smile. "You're never quite off duty."

"Your table's ready," she said, leading him into the dining room.

Everyone ordered steaks and salad, though the Renwick Inn was obviously an oyster and fois gras kind of place. Joe watched his crew swilling beer, ripping into the rare beef, telling sea stories, and he sensed the artists recoiling. Twice he told his men to lower their voices and watch their language, but the volume kept creeping up. So did the expletives.

Joe had told himself Caroline wouldn't be there tonight, but now that he had seen her, he couldn't stop watching for her. All his attention was focused on the dining room door. She drifted by twice, looking sleek in her long black dress. Both times, she glanced over at the big table. But that was probably because they were causing such a ruckus. Sam was telling a long story about raising research money from the National Science Foundation, and Dan kept interrupting with a tale about prostitutes in

Fiji. Joe hardly heard. His eyes were on the door.

After dinner they took over the bar. Several artists from New York called them to their table. They compared tattoos. The artists had flowers, butterflies, and barbed wire. The sailors had women's names, ships' insignias, and serpents. More beer flowed. A few guys supplemented theirs with shots of Southern Comfort. Joe remembered the old drinking days, could practically feel the hot burn going down. He watched Sam drink a shot and realized he had never drunk with his brother.

Without telling anyone, Joe stepped outside. The fresh air felt good. Standing around bars didn't feel right anymore. The old desires came back strong. Being at sea, he didn't get to enough AA meetings. He knew it, and he tried to keep himself out of slippery places.

Joe stood in the herb garden. The heady smell of thyme and verbena reminded him of Greece. The summer night was warm, the breeze still. The inn was brightly lit. Music and loud voices came from the bar, and he had the familiar sense of being apart from the action. Watching through the old glass windows, he saw Caroline walk into the bar. She glanced around, and Joe wondered who she was searching for. He thought maybe she was looking for him. For just that second the scent of herbs grew stronger, made him dizzy.

An old Porsche pulled up. Two people got out. They clutched each other, wobbled against their car, kissed long and hard. Pulling apart, they laughed and hurried into the inn. They stumbled into the bar, and ordered drinks. The girl was beautiful. Small and slim, she looked like Caroline, only blond. She raised her glass to clink the man's, but Caroline stepped between them. Curious, Joe went inside.

"Don't, Skye," Caroline was saying, her hand on the girl's wrist. "Do you remember Dad standing in this exact spot? Do you remember how it made us feel to watch him disappearing?"

"Caroline, she's a big girl," the man said, too cool to register any expression in his eyes. He was skinny, dressed in black, with long, dark hair falling across his sickly, pale face. Some of the artists knew him; they had walked over, then faded back at the first sign of an altercation.

"Stay out of it, Simon," Caroline snapped.

The glass was full of champagne. Joe saw it catch the candlelight. The bubbles flowed in a thick stream to the surface. The girl wavered. She looked from Caroline to the skinny artist and back again.

"It's just one glass," she said.

"Think of Dad," Caroline said, her voice catching in her throat.

"This has nothing to do with him," Skye said, fixing her sister with a wild stare. "Leave me alone."

"We can leave," Simon said. "If that's what you want. We arranged to meet *friends* here—inn guests, as a matter of fact. Trent and Anya, you must know them. They live on St. Marks Place, take their two weeks here every summer. . . ."

"Simon, shut up," Caroline said dangerously.

"I hate when you fight," Skye said. "Don't fight." She took a sip, and another. With something that sounded like a sob, Caroline walked out of the bar.

Joe started to follow her. But Sam beat him to it. Joe watched his younger brother follow Caroline Renwick out the double glass doors. She hurried through the herb garden, down the path that led to the river, and Sam was right behind her.

* * *

"Caroline!"

Moving fast, Caroline heard the man's voice. She didn't want to stop, didn't want to face anyone. Ten minutes ago she had been looking for Joe Connor, but right now he was the last person she wanted to see. She didn't want anyone trying to help her. Her eyes brimming, she started walking faster.

"Caroline," she heard again.

"I'm fine," she said, trying to compose herself. She turned to look at him, forcing herself to stay calm, and was startled to find Sam bearing down on her instead of Joe.

"Are you okay?" he asked.

"I'm fine," she repeated. Being caught off guard by Sam undid her completely, and she welled up.

"You're not fine. You're a wreck," he said.

"No, I'm—"

"You can't stop her, you know," he said.

"I could have refused to serve her,"

Caroline said. "That's what I should have done. Told my bartender to shut her off, not even give her that one glass . . ."

"She would have gotten it somewhere else. Who is she, your sister?"

Caroline nodded. She wiped her tears with the backs of her hands. With Skye in the hospital, she had begun to feel safe. Like maybe Skye would get some help, maybe there was hope. But then Simon had come back, she had walked out of the hospital, and now she was back to drinking.

"I know how it feels," Sam said. "I watched my brother nearly kill himself for years."

"Joe?"

"Yeah. I probably shouldn't tell you, he used to have a drinking problem."

"He told me himself."

"He was so miserable," Sam said. "He drank to feel better, but it only made everything worse. I didn't see him that often, but sometimes . . . He'd be home for Christmas, or one time he took me to Maine, sailing for summer vacation . . ." Sam's eyes clouded with the memory. "He was like Jekyll and Hyde. The best brother in the world one minute, a lunatic the next.

That's when he talked about you most. When he was drunk."

"Oh," Caroline said, wondering what he said.

"He was crazy, those times. Out of his mind, not knowing what he wanted, what would help."

"You must have been very young," Caroline said, feeling sorry for the little boy watching his older brother self-destruct. But was it any easier for a grown woman? She felt the tears rolling down her cheeks.

"Yeah. It sucked."

"Well . . . Joe had some bad things happen," Caroline said slowly, thinking of their conversation on board the *Meteor.* "That I suppose didn't affect you. But . . ." She spoke very carefully. "Why Skye and not me? We had such similar childhoods. The same bad things happened to both of us. Or almost."

"Maybe it's the 'almost,' " Sam said.

Caroline had never known how to cry for help. When the bad things happened, she was always the one reaching out her hand. She wouldn't change that, wouldn't have it any other way, but right now she felt very off balance.

"Who knows?" Sam went on. "I know only one thing, and that's that they have to stop on their own. We can't do it for them."

"Everything okay?"

At the sound of Joe's voice, Sam handed Caroline his handkerchief. She blew her nose. The sound was so loud, it scared the ducks in the river. They took off, their webbed feet paddling the water.

"She's okay," Sam said. He sounded oddly proud, as if he had been appointed Caroline's guardian, reporting back to Joe.

"Yeah? You sure?"

"I'm sure," Caroline said.

"Worried about your sister," Joe said. It was a statement, not a question.

"Yes."

Joe nodded. Dim light slanted through the trees. The ducks had circled around, were coming in for another landing. They were silhouetted against the moon. Across the river, a whippoorwill called.

"Would have been better if she'd decided to drink somewhere else," Sam said helpfully. "Instead of Caroline's inn."

"Wouldn't have made a difference," Joe said.

Caroline nodded, feeling miserable. She

wanted to go back to the inn, but she was afraid to see Skye. She felt scared and angry and hopeless. Sam took a step toward the inn. Joe and Caroline faced each other. Tree branches blocked the moon, but his face looked pained in the half-light.

"What are those for?" Sam asked, pointing at the Japanese lanterns.

One entire string was illuminated, stretching from the inn's back porch to the barn. The lanterns hung still, as if caught in the trees, sparking the windless night with colors of persimmon, amber, turquoise, and scarlet.

"They're for the Firefly Ball," Caroline said.

"What's that?"

"Just a party," Caroline said, swallowing hard. Joe was staring at her, and she couldn't tear her eyes away from his. Thinking of Skye, tears welled in her eyes, then spilled down her cheeks. Sam was gazing at the lanterns, and he didn't see his brother reach for Caroline's hand and hold it. Caroline's fingers brushed Joe's scraped knuckles, and she wondered what it was costing him to make the gesture.

"Do you have it every year?" Sam asked.

"Yes."

"Can we come?"

"Sam," Joe said harshly, looking away from Caroline just long enough to miss seeing the smile pass across her eyes.

"Sure," she said. "I'd like that."

"Just me? Or Joe too?"

"All of you come, okay? The whole crew. It's a costume ball."

"What should we come as?" Sam asked.

"Pirates, of course," Caroline said, staring straight into the hooded blue eyes of his older brother, the toughest pirate of all.

January 6, 1979

Dear Caroline,

How to get you to Newport . . . that is the question. I was going to surprise you, drive down to Connecticut and pick you up, but I'm sort of grounded. A bad combination of beer, my mother's car, and my little brother.

The thing is, I really want you to come. I've got plenty of charts, and I've thought about sailing down to get you. Narragansett Bay, to Block Island Sound, to Fishers Island Sound, past the Thames River, to Black Hall.

And Firefly Hill.

Shit, who am I kidding? It would take so long to get to you, and it's the middle of winter. I was an idiot, doing what I did to get grounded. The thing is, idiots usually do the same thing again. Miss you, C.

Love,
Joe

February 4, 1979

Dear Joe,

If you got hurt or if you hurt Sam in that grounding incident, I'd never forgive you. You have to come get me! It's the only way I'll get to Newport to be with you. I miss you too, so much I can hardly stand it. How can I, when we don't even know each other? Or do we? Hurry, J.

Waiting impatiently,
C.

CHAPTER ELEVEN

In the sunroom, Augusta was sewing long curls of black felt onto a pair of ballet slippers. She had an art book on the hassock in front of her, open to one of Picasso's harlequin paintings, copying it with studious diligence. She adored harlequins. So secretive, so playful: mysterious jesters! She congratulated herself again on her inspiration.

A character by Picasso would be recognizable. She didn't want to insult any of Caroline's less sophisticated guests by attending the soiree as anything too obscure. She could have chosen to be a character in a painting by Karsky or de Cubzac, artists no one had ever heard of, then spend the whole night explaining herself to people. Forget that.

And Augusta knew she had a good figure. The harlequin was long and slender, like Augusta herself, and she would look marvelous and sleek in the checked suit. It would be attractive, amusing, and witty.

The only problem was, Hugh had loathed Picasso.

As an artist, Hugh had admired his work. Who didn't? Who could look down on the man who had single-handedly revamped the twentieth century, who was the master of line, who had conjured cubism? Who could feel disdain for the artist who viewed a human face head-on and saw the profile instead?

No, Hugh had envied Picasso *for his life*. To Hugh Renwick, Pablo Picasso was "Pablo," an equal. And since the English translation of Pablo was Paul, Hugh had privately referred to Picasso as Paul. To call him Pablo, or, worse, Picasso, was to kowtow to an arrogant Spaniard.

Hugh was insanely jealous of Picasso. The women, the adoration, the adulation, the South of France, the bullfights, the legend. Hugh had had his own share of women, adoration, and adulation, but coastal New England was hardly the

Riviera, and bullfighting had all other blood
sports beat.

Fishing and hunting just weren't the same
thing, especially since Hemingway, whom
Hugh had actually known and referred to as
Papa, had already made them his province.
Hugh had taken the girls on his hunting
trips, and Papa would have laughed.
Daughters weren't sons when it came to
hunting. Especially when they were so sensitive, and life had dealt them such a
shocking blow.

Hugh was never as tough as he'd
thought. He had affairs, he killed animals,
he tried to live like Picasso. But once his
daughters were affected, he had fallen
apart. Destroying himself with drink, he had
left this world. And left Augusta.

Dr. Henderson might say that Augusta's
choice of a costume revealed a certain hos-
tility for her dead husband. Her beloved—
but resented—dead husband.

Quietly sewing her harlequin shoes,
Augusta imagined what Hugh might think if
he could see her costume. She had loved her
husband with passionate intensity. She
missed him more every day. In fact, she
sometimes admitted to herself, it was easier

to love him now than when he had been alive. Harsh realities didn't intrude quite so much. She had been a jealous woman.

Not only of the other women, but of her own daughters. God help her, she thought, remembering how she had felt watching him paint Caroline.

Hearing the kitchen door slam, she glanced up just as Skye walked in with Simon.

"Hi, dears," she said. As soon as she saw Skye, she knew: She'd been drinking. Her eyes were red, her hair disheveled. It was five o'clock, and she looked as if she had just gotten up: hung over and remorseful. Augusta's heart fell.

"Where were you last night?" Augusta asked.

"We stayed at the inn," Simon said. "Some of our old friends from the East Village are up for a few days, and we met them there."

"Skye, would you like something cold to drink?"

Skye nodded. Augusta walked to the flower room. She filled a crystal pitcher with ice water. Surprisingly, her hands were shaking. Tipping three aspirin into a tiny ceramic bowl, she placed everything on a tray and carried it back to the sunroom.

"I'm so thirsty," Skye said, drinking a tall glass. She filled another, took the three aspirin, drank the water down.

"What happened last night?" Augusta asked, shaken. "I thought you had decided to stop drinking for a while."

"I did. I stopped for a week. But it seems so pointless . . ." Skye tried to laugh.

"Pointless, ah . . . my beautiful little existentialist. Shall we discuss Camus?" Simon asked, coolly lighting a cigarette.

"Only if you make some martinis first," Skye said. "Mom, you're ready for one, right?"

"Well, yes," Augusta said cautiously. "But I'm not sure you should."

"Mom, do I really want to be one of those holier-than-thou abstainers? We hate them," Skye said, shaking her head.

"Personally, I think moderation is the best approach," Augusta said. "But your sisters have a very definite opinion on this. They think you should stop entirely."

"They're jealous," Simon said, exhaling a long stream of smoke from between his thin lips. "Of Skye's creativity."

Augusta's skin crawled at his audacity, although she considered the possibility that he was right.

"Will you quit talking about that and make the drinks instead?" Skye asked, a tremor in her voice. Alarmed, Augusta noticed that her lips were nearly white. Skye rarely snapped at Simon, just as Augusta had almost never spoken angrily to Hugh. Skye had to be under severe stress to talk to him that way, but already she was retreating.

"I'm sorry, Simon," she said, passing a hand across her face.

Simon glared at her. He looked sullen and skinny, his dark eyes sunken like some dissipated raccoon's. That he even considered himself in the same league as Hugh was pathetic, Augusta thought. She indulged him only because she understood Skye's love for him. It couldn't be explained, and it couldn't be quenched.

"I'll make the drinks," Simon said darkly.

"Simon's right," Augusta said, squeezing Skye's hand as a feeling of queasy panic rose in her chest. "You'll feel so much better when you're back in your studio."

"Oh, Mom," Skye whispered.

Nothing made Augusta feel so helpless as

trying to get through to one of her girls and being unable to.

"I don't want to be an alcoholic," Skye said, tears sliding down her face.

"You're not one," Augusta said.

"I hate the word."

"So do I."

"I want to drink less, I know I have to. I can do that, right?"

"Of course, darling. I'll help you. We'll each have one, no more. Okay?"

Skye nodded. But her tears continued to fall.

Simon returned with a silver tray full of drink things. He had even remembered to bring a tiny dish of mixed nuts. The silver shaker, the vapors redolent of gin and vermouth, the three tiny olives. Skye's eyes were dull as she watched him pour the martinis into chilled glasses. It occurred to Augusta, clear as crystal: Skye should not be drinking. At all.

Augusta felt afraid. Filled with dread, she didn't know how to stop what she had started. Caroline would be devastated when she found out.

They raised their glasses, arms extended, to clink.

"Here's to Skye!" Augusta said. "Home again, where she belongs."

* * *

Caroline sat on her back porch alone. Wrapped in a shawl, she rocked gently in the glider, thinking of last night. She had walked along the riverbank with Joe and Sam while Skye got plastered in the bar. The men had told her: You can't do anything. It's up to Skye.

A small oil lamp burned on the table beside her. The night was dark and heavy, and the artists were quiet. A dog barked in the distance; nightbirds cried across the marsh, and their sound filled Caroline with uneasy memories of long, long ago.

She thought of Joe. Last night he had been here with her. Right here, by the river. He had held her hand. They hadn't acknowledged it, hadn't said anything. Sam didn't seem to notice, and when they returned to the inn, Joe had dropped it and stepped away. But for their walk through the reeds, he had offered her comfort. And Caroline almost never took that from anyone.

Amazing, she thought. She planted her feet firmly on the floor and pushed the glider back and forth, like a boat rocking on the waves. She was sitting there, on her own porch, not dashing out of town. Amazing. Totally unlike her. She opened the folder beside her. She took out Clarissa Randall's diary.

While Joe was miles at sea, excavating the ship that held Elisabeth Randall's bones, Caroline was safe at home, reading the writings of her daughter. It made Caroline feel strangely protective of the little girl, a keeper of painful memories. Little girls needed looking after; Caroline had realized that always.

Clarissa had such small handwriting. It traced across the page, delicate as spiderwebs. She had used a quill pen. Caroline recognized this, occasionally still using one herself. As a girl, she had found a seagull feather, used her father's X-acto knife to slice a sharp point, and dipped it in India ink to write in her journal.

August 15, 1769
A very bad storm today. The biggest waves I have seen since last winter, and a wind to shake the tower and make me

feared it would blow the light out. Pa told us a ship ran aground on Wickland Shoals with no loss of life and all hands lucky to be alive. It makes me glad we live here to light the lamp.

August 17
Mama gone almost all day. I wanted to find her, so I looked all over. Imagined her blown into the sea by the gale, so I was very afraid. Pa told us about pirates working the coast, bad men who take what isn't theirs and sometimes hurt others in their selfishness. Mama has such beautiful things, I thought, what if pirates took her? She wears Grandmother's cameo at her throat always. And she has the pearl and garnet pendant Pa gave her for their wedding. Pirates would surely find such treasures irresistible. I thought what if they hurt Mama taking her things! Or what if they steal her away to sail on their ship with them and cook their meals and be a wife to their captain.

But I was wrong. Mama came home. When I asked her where she had been, she gave me a funny look. She told me women have secrets just like girls, and sometimes she needs to be alone with her secrets for a while. Her secrets keep her well, she said. What a funny thing to say! But she does seem happy. So should I be.

August 18
Again, Mama disappeared! Now it seems exciting, a game. She has a secret place! Where could it be? Wouldn't it be perfect if it was one of mine? Let's see: I have Lightning Rock, the tallest granite boulder on the north end. Also the tidal pools on the south shore, where we found the finback whale at summer's start. I have the pine barrens, the green bowl, the beacon room atop the light. Should I let Mama keep her secret, or should I find her out?

August 20
Captain Thorn of the Cambria paid a visit. He brought whale oil and lavender. Don't like him.

August 22
Windy. Went to the boathouse to play, and saw Mama talking to Captain Thorn.

*Don't like him. He is from England, and
he talks that way that makes Pa laugh.
Mama bade me not tell Pa of their meeting. Walking home, we found a lobster
shedding its shell in the rockweed.
Mama cooked it for Pa, and he let me eat
the little claws. Still haven't found
Mama's secret place.*

Reading the pages, Caroline found herself
breathing hard. Clarissa had found her
mother's secret place, and she didn't even
know it. Captain Thorn was her mother's
secret, but Clarissa's mind was too innocent to realize. Like all those times Hugh
had been away from home with Joe's
mother or some other woman, and Caroline
had thought he was somewhere painting.

August 24
*Today porpoises swam by the beach, just
ahead of a whale. I wanted to swim with
them, but Mama said no. She sat so quiet
on the sand, sad like I haven't seen her for
weeks. The tern babies begging their mamas for fish made her cry, and I said what's
wrong, Mama? Usually the baby birds
make us laugh. But she said to be a good*

girl, to take care of myself no matter what happens. That when mamas aren't there to take care of their babies, they have to know the babies will survive.

August 29
I can scarcely believe. Mama is gone! Captain Thorn took her aboard the Cambria, and she drowned on Moonstone Reef! Dear God, give me back Mama!

Caroline read the horrible words, biting her lip. The poor little girl. Abandoned by her own mother, and for what? So the woman could die with her lover at sea in a storm? Clarissa had been left to deal with everything by herself, with no help from the people who were supposed to protect her. Even worse, she had lost a parent she loved.

Across the marsh, the whippoorwill called. Seagulls cried, and other shorebirds, but the whippoorwill's song was unmistakable. It rang through the night, making Caroline think of Redhawk. That mountain trail, covered with yellow leaves, where she had begun to lose her father.

The cordless telephone beside her rang.

Caroline stared, thinking of Skye. She answered.

"Hello?"

"Hi. It's Joe."

"Hi," Caroline said. She shivered, although the night was hot. She held the phone with both hands and wondered what the sea looked like tonight.

"Are you all right?" he asked. "You were pretty upset last night."

"I'm fine," Caroline said.

"The thing is," Joe said, "you're probably not, but you can't change what she does."

"That's what you said. And Sam."

"He should know. He watched me drink for a long time."

"He's a nice kid."

Joe made a sound halfway between a snort and a laugh. "He's a character."

Caroline smiled. She had liked watching the brothers together, and she enjoyed hearing Joe soften every time Sam entered the picture. She heard Joe breathing against the receiver, and she closed her eyes. A warm breeze blew, lifting the hair on the back of her neck. All she had ever wanted was a friend, she thought. Why was that so hard?

"I called because I thought of something that

might help," he said. "Maybe it won't help Skye, but it might help you."

"What?" Caroline asked.

"Just be honest," he said. "As honest as you can, about everything."

"I am—" she said, feeling hurt.

"I know. I believe you are. But . . ."

Caroline was silent, listening to his breath. Something inside her was changing, a profound shifting of ground that had to do with her isolation, the past. She knew it had started when Joe came to town, and it had to do with Skye slowly killing herself. She had always taken care of the ones she loved, but right now she knew she needed some help of her own. She held the receiver tighter.

"Sometimes you have to go deeper," Joe said. "I can't explain it, but it worked for me. Once I figured out what I was trying to hide from, I . . . was more ready to think of stopping."

"Stopping?"

"Drinking. There's a saying," Joe said. "The truth will set you free."

Caroline nodded. She closed her eyes again, thinking of what he had said. Her mind filled with an image of Skye, ten years old, alone on the mountain. She lay in her tent. It was August, the night was cool. Beneath her sleeping bag, under the thin tent floor, writhed snakes. Outside, coyotes howled. Skye lay with her eyes wide open, clutching her knife.

Andrew Lockwood would not cross their path for several years, but death was in the air. They were so young, and they were too alone. Caroline had learned never to complain.

"The truth feels too hard," she whispered.

"No," Joe said, realizing for the first time himself that the opposite is really true. "It might feel that way, but it's not. It's freedom."

Caroline listened to the phone echo. She heard static on the line, voices in the background. Jostling, as if Joe were fighting to hang on to the phone.

"Hang on," Joe said reluctantly. "Someone wants to speak with you."

"Caroline, hey!"

"Hi, Sam," she said, pulling herself together.

"What're you doing tomorrow afternoon?"

She could hear Joe in the background. They scuffled over the phone. The headset clattered, shuffled along a desktop. She heard laughter, a muffled shout, Joe speaking in a stern and insistent tone. Sam regained control of the phone.

"Well?" he asked, as if nothing had happened. "Are you busy?"

"I have a bank board meeting in the morning," she said. "But otherwise the day is clear."

"Joe's lecturing at Yale. It's open to the public."

"What time?" Caroline asked.

"Three o'clock. At Crawford Hall."

"Does Yale offer a degree in treasure hunting?"

Sam laughed. "No, but tomorrow the treasure hunter turns back into a scientist. If you come, you'll get to hear him speaking on the joys of sediment. I'm going to teach there, you know."

"At Yale? Really?"

"Well, they haven't offered me the job, but they will once—" Again Sam chuckled, losing control of the phone. Caroline heard Joe telling him to shut up, but his tone was joking, and there was laughter in his voice.

"I'll try to be there." Caroline waited for Joe to come back on the line, but Sam disconnected first. The line hummed.

* * *

After lunch the next day, Caroline swung by Clea's to pick her up. Together they headed west, down 95 toward New Haven. Clea didn't seem to find it strange that they would be going to Yale University to hear Joe Connor lecture on sediment. She simply smiled, told Caroline she looked beautiful in her navy blue dress, pearl earrings, and bracelet.

"Thank you," Caroline said. She cast a quick look across the seat. "Am I too dressed up?"

"You're perfect."

"I'm not really sure why we're going," Caroline said. "Except Sam sounded so excited, and I don't want to let him down. He's a cute kid."

"That's a good reason to drive all the way to New Haven in ninety-five-degree heat. To hear someone lecture about mud," Clea said, smiling inscrutably.

"If you didn't want to go . . ." Caroline muttered.

"I wouldn't miss it for anything," Clea said.

Route 95 was crowded. Traffic started building in Guilford, and by the time they reached the big bridge curving past the oil tanks at the head of New Haven harbor, they had just enough time to get there.

"See that big stone tower, looks like a cathedral?" Clea said, pointing across New Haven's concentrated skyline. "That's Harkness. Right in the middle of Yale, two blocks from Crawford Hall."

"Remember coming to Yale right after Dad died?" she continued.

"Yep. He had left that painting to the museum, and we all had to put on party dresses and drink tea with the trustees. Mom told the server to fill her teacup with sherry."

"And she was outrageous so they wouldn't see how sad she was."

"How much she hated doing things without Dad."

"Let's not talk about it," Clea said, shuddering. "Let's pull a Mom and put it right out of our heads."

Caroline turned off the expressway, took a right on York Street. She drove past the colleges of Yale, the granite buildings and big iron gates, and found a parking spot on the corner of Prospect and Grove. Without another word about the past, she and Clea walked up a tree-lined path to Crawford Hall.

Granite steps led into an arched and vaulted stone entrance hall. Graduate students and members of the public milled about the cool space. Joe's lecture was one in a popular series on maritime topics; it had been publicized in local papers and *The New York Times.* People were beginning to file into an auditorium.

Sam waved them over. He was sitting in the second row and had saved a seat for Caroline.

"This is my sister, Clea," she said, and they shook hands. Sam got everyone else in the row to shift down one, and they took their seats, with Caroline between Clea and Sam. Sam wore khaki pants, a denim shirt, and a tie. His hair was neatly combed, but it kept falling in his eyes anyway. He had a notebook open, as if he intended to take notes.

Dr. Joseph Connor walked onto the stage, taking his spot at the lectern. He wore a brown tweed jacket, a white shirt, and a striped tie. His manner was comfortable, like a sexy young college professor. He cleared his throat, gripping the lectern with tanned hands. Looking into the audience, he was relaxed, as if he had stood before many students, delivered many lectures.

He talked about roaming the seas in the R/V *Meteor,* diving on shipwrecks and exploring the ocean floor. He spoke of research as a by-product of his treasure hunts. He explained how climate and sea level responded to past changes, how sediments were packed in complicated patterns of layered wedges. Cylinders of gray mud were brought up and dated by the ship's paleontologist through micro-fossils contained therein.

"Drilling holes deep in the seabed to re-trieve cores of mud and rock allows us to interpret the earth's distant past, going back thirty-five million years," he said. "Div-ing on a ship such as the *Cambria* is a way to interpret the last two hundred."

He spoke of how his work combined geol-ogy and archaeology, how he juxtaposed his interest in the sea bottom with curiosity about human behavior. At his signal, the lights were dimmed, and he began to project slides on a screen at the front of the audito-rium.

"Our current site," he said, "is a perfect example. The *Cambria* was an English bar-quentine, her holds full of the king's gold. She went down in a storm in 1769, and all hands were lost, including the captain and a woman who had fallen in love with him." Joe paused, clearing his throat.

The screen showed a three-masted ship. It was the drawing Caroline had seen hanging in the *Meteor*'s chart room. Joe clicked a button, and pictures of gold coins and barnacle-encrusted cannons appeared. Another click, and a page of Clarissa's diary filled the screen.

"The woman was a wife and mother, and she left behind a little girl," Joe said. "The child kept a diary, and recently I came into possession of a copy."

"The one Maripat gave you!" Clea whispered to Caroline. Caroline nodded, eyes on Joe.

"It gives us a context," he said. His voice was deep and sonorous; it filled the auditorium. "The record of earth's history is probably written with more fidelity in the oceans than anywhere else on earth. Except, maybe, in the diary of a little girl who lost her mother. It's historically accurate, and purely true, words of grief written by someone who never expected them to be read. Clarissa has helped us piece together the story of the artifacts we bring up from the sea bottom.

"The diary was given to me by the same person who told me about the wreck in the first place, many years ago," Joe said, and Caroline felt herself blush in the darkness. "Our own histories intersected in a way that parallels the story of the wreck. At one time you might have said we were close friends. At another, someone might have called us enemies. Everything is changeable. Even the truth, or perceptions of it as time passes. On a dig like this, that can't help but seem significant.

"We bring up a lot of artifacts aboard the *Meteor,* a lot of sediment. It's not clear until later which will be helpful and which won't. We never know until we get to the lab whether the metal we find is gold or nickel. Whether our test bores hold a decipherable record of sea-level change or just mud. But then"—he took a deep breath—"nothing is just mud."

The audience laughed, and when they realized Joe was finished, they began to clap. Caroline sank lower in her chair. She stared at Joe, and she could swear that he had found her in the dark, was staring at her. His blue eyes were bright and clear, squinting past the beam of light. The auditorium lights were switched on, and he continued to stare at her while audience members milled around him.

"That was interesting," Clea said, leaning past Caroline to speak to Sam. "Your brother is an excellent speaker."

"They've asked him to come to Yale next year," Sam said, "as visiting professor. I'm not insanely jealous or anything."

"I thought you were the one interviewing," Caroline said.

"Are you a professor?" Clea asked.

"No, but I'd like to be. I interned at Dartmouth for a semester, but now I'm on a boat in the North Atlantic, sending out résumés from every town in Newfoundland and Labrador that has a post office. I interviewed here, they haven't given me any word yet. But my brother . . ."

"Really, here? Joe at Yale?" Caroline asked, still watching Joe, wondering whether he was thinking about accepting. Would he actually settle in the area, give up constantly traveling for a while? She tried not to care what his answer would be, even though he was coming toward her with his eyes focused on her like test bores.

"You made it," he said. "Thanks for coming."

"I enjoyed your talk," Caroline said, looking straight at him. "*Dr.* Connor."

"Hope you didn't mind me using you to illustrate a point," he said.

"I guess that depends," Caroline said slowly.

"On what?" Joe cocked his head. His eyes held a glimmer of a smile. He waited.

"It ought to be obvious, Joe," Sam said.

"Really? Tell me," Joe said.

"Whether she's your friend again," Clea said. "Or still your enemy."

"God, the whole family's in the act," Caroline said, making a joke to cover her discomfort.

"My friend," Joe said quietly. "She's my friend."

* * *

Driving home, Caroline played his words over in her mind: "She's my friend."

"It was good to hear him," Clea said. "He'd make a good professor."

"Yes," Caroline said.

"Wouldn't it be nice if he and his brother could teach together?"

"It would."

"At Yale. So close by. We'd probably see him once in a while," Clea said, her voice neutral, "now that you're friends again. . . ."

"Clea," Caroline said. Her voice was stern, but her face was smiling.

Once they got off the highway, they drove through the village of Black Hall. It contained large white shipbuilders' houses with black shutters and window boxes full of red geraniums, white petunias, and blue lobelia; white picket fences; a yellow Georgian mansion with white columns, once a boardinghouse for the American Impressionists, now a museum; a gas station; stately beech and maple trees; American flags everywhere; two white churches: one, a famously painted Congregational, the other Catholic. Heading south, out of town, they passed the marshes and inlets of the Connecticut River; a third white church, this one Episcopalian; and the fish store with its blue fish weathervane.

"Want to stop by Mom's?" Caroline asked on the spur of the moment. "To see Skye?"

"Great idea," Clea said.

By keeping the steeples on the left and

the water on the right, they eventually got to the sea road. The road tunneled through a dark forest of hemlocks and old oaks, the branches meeting overhead. The ledge rose on the right, and the road burst free of any tree cover. A vista of open water spread before them, rough water dancing under sunlight, Joe's ship riding on the waves.

A long drive wound upward through the forest. Wrought-iron lightposts, each topped with an evil-looking bat, lined the way. Her father had commissioned them from an artist he knew in Vermont. They had skeletal black wings, some spread and others drawn close about their spindly bodies; when lit, their eyes glowed red. Hugh had installed them to scare intruders away from Firefly Hill, so nothing bad would happen there again.

Caroline's stomach flipped. What would they find when they got there? She told herself not to care, that Skye was a grown woman in charge of her own life. She tried to pretend they weren't stopping just to check up on her.

When they got there, Skye was drunk.

Augusta was needlepointing, looking upset. Simon and Skye were sitting together on the sofa, flipping through a design magazine. Skye could hardly hold her head up.

"Hi," Caroline said, her heart falling. Clea stood beside her, saying nothing.

"Skye spent the day in her studio," Augusta said dubiously. Her eyes were red-rimmed and haunted. She looked at Skye, then away. Skye had a bottle of beer tucked behind the sofa leg. She reached down, looked Caroline straight in the eye, and took a slug.

"All she needed all along," Simon said wearily.

"Needed you, baby," Skye whispered. "Needed your big . . ."

How drunk was she? Caroline wondered, listening to Skye whisper little pornographic promises into Simon's ear. It made her heart ache—literally—to watch her beautiful sister demean herself this way. Augusta pretended not to hear, an anguished expression in her eyes. Clea breathed heavily, as if she had just run up a hill. The whole family feels it, Caroline thought.

"Skye," Caroline said sharply.

Skye ignored her. She kept tickling Simon, murmuring her sexy words into his ear, just slightly too loud.

"Skye, stop it," Caroline said.

Skye's face reacted as if she'd been slapped. "He's my husband."

"Then respect him, and wait till you're in private to talk like that." The words were out so fast, they surprised even Caroline. Is this telling the truth? she thought. Is that what I'm doing now? Clea squeezed her hand.

Skye blushed. Simon scowled, said "Christ," and left the room. But Augusta looked relieved. Caroline watched her mother, noticed the way her mouth relaxed, her fingers stopped working her black pearls so incessantly.

"Get a man of your own," Skye said darkly.

"You turn ugly when you drink," Caroline said. "Do you know that?"

"What did you do in your studio today?" Clea asked, quickly trying to make peace.

The silence was heavy, the storm about to break. Caroline and Skye glared at each other. Homer stuck his wet nose in Skye's face. Surprised, she tossed her head. The interruption seemed to make her forget the fight. "What?" she asked.

"What'd you sculpt today?" Caroline asked. "Mom said you were in your studio."

"That," Skye said, pointing.

Caroline's gaze fell on a piece of clay. It sat on a table beside a cut glass vase overflowing with day lilies, beach roses, honeysuckle, larkspur, sweet peas, and mint. Six inches high, the clay looked like a three-peaked mountain range. Skye's work wasn't generally abstract. Her sculptures of the human figure were usually vivid and emotional; she filled her subjects with yearning. She usually sculpted women known for their fire and passion: Joan of Arc, Sappho, Lena Horne, Amelia Earhart.

"What is it?" Caroline asked, kneeling down.

Clea knelt beside her. She turned the piece around to see it better.

"Redhawk," Skye said bitterly. "Can't you see the mountaintops?"

"No," Clea said, looking into her eyes. "It's something else. Isn't it?"

Skye nodded, her eyes suddenly swimming in tears.

"Oh, the mountains," Augusta said, from across the room. "I used to feel so left out! But I wanted my girls to have their time with their father. . . ."

"It's not Redhawk?" Caroline asked, wondering if the degenerative state of Skye's art would become a permanent result of her drinking.

Skye shook her head. She was crying freely now. She reached for her beer. But she didn't drink. She gripped the bottle until her knuckles turned white.

"It's sisters," she whispered.

"Us?" Caroline whispered back, shocked, trying to shield the disappointment in her voice.

Skye nodded. "You, me, and Clea."

"I love it," Clea said fiercely.

Caroline stared at the piece. Primitive, unfinished-looking, a child might have done it. The three shapes were connected but separate. They touched at the bottom, leaned away from each other at the top. The sculpture showed none of the skill or technique that marked Skye as an artist, but staring at it, Caroline was suddenly filled with wild emotion.

"Can you see?" Skye asked through her tears. "The three sisters?"

"I see," Caroline said through tears of her own. "I love it too."

Caroline's affirmation set loose something in Skye, and her body was racked with sobs. She couldn't hold them back. She sat on the sofa, clutching the brown beer bottle, and both of her sisters climbed up beside her. The three Renwick sisters held one another as tight as they could.

We're like Skye's sculpture, Caroline thought. Three lumps of clay thrown together. Joe's sea mud. Thinking of Joe, remembering the truth, Caroline held on tighter. Sisters. Three sisters. She thought of Skye's initial explanation, that her sculpture was of mountains, and she knew that was partly true also.

With three sisters, truth doesn't come in one piece, Caroline thought. Skye's drinking might be Caroline's travel. When one sister was ready to tell the truth, the others might still want to hide. Stop hiding, she thought, holding her sisters.

* * *

After the talk at Yale, Joe couldn't wait to get back to the wreck.

"You gonna teach there?" Sam asked, his left foot stuck in the right leg of his wetsuit.

"Doubt it," Joe said, watching Sam tangle himself up even more.

"Why not?" Sam asked, yanking his foot

free and banging it on a cleat. Joe reached over, undid his brother's ankle zipper. He had a distant memory of stuffing the kid into a snowsuit.

"Why should I? I like what I do. Just because you want to teach at Yale doesn't mean everyone does."

At sea the sky was clear and the views were long. Joe took a deep breath and thought how that was exactly how he had liked his life to be: clear, with long views. Nothing crowding him. Just him, the wreck, the ocean, and the mud.

"You gotta grow up, man," Sam said. "You're out here being a pirate, and there's a university filled with students waiting to learn about muck. You know? Fossil-laden rocks and mud, telling the story of time. Just like you said in your lecture. Beautiful, man."

"Thanks," Joe said dryly. Sliding off his shirt and pants, he put on his own wetsuit. Sam handed him a single air tank, which he strapped on. They were ready to dive.

"I mean it, Joe," Sam said sternly. "Dry land's where it's at for you. Especially around here. Near Black Hall."

"Why near Black Hall?"

"Think about it, idiot. Just think about it."

Joe pushed Sam overboard. He watched him splash around, sputtering with surprise. Joe followed him into the cold water. The brothers spit in their masks, then slid them over their eyes. Sam blinked at Joe, tried to dunk him. His big brother pushed him away but he swam back good-naturedly. The water felt cold on Joe's hands and neck. He took a sharp breath, then another and another, trying to get used to the temperature. Years of warmer waters had taken the New Englander right out of him.

"Black Hall," he said to Sam, treading water. "Jesus."

"Think about it," Sam said.

They stuck the regulators in their mouths and dove.

Sunlight penetrates to a depth of two hundred feet, but to the human eye darkness takes over before that. Diving beside Sam, Joe sensed the wreck looming ahead. It hung on the reef, an outcropping of glacial moraine, a dead forest of black timbers. The three spars were broken in half, their yards and halyards trailing in the sand.

Divers, members of his crew, moved about their work like bees going in and out of a hive. There was an air of flight about them, the way they hovered and swerved, bubbles rising. They swam through a ragged hole in the ship's bow, a dark cave yawning at the sea bottom. And they swam out, holding bits and pieces of the ship and its loot.

Sam zipped ahead, eager to enter. Joe put out a warning hand to hold him back. The spotlight illuminated Sam's wide eyes behind his mask, and Joe was filled with a protective rush for his brother. The kid's enthusiasm got him into trouble every time, riding his bike into traffic, saying yes to the first job that came along.

Joe motioned for Sam to wait there. The wreck was too dangerous. Sam's eyes tried to argue, but Joe was firm. He made his face angry, his eyes threatening. Sam let out a big breath of air, backed off. Joe wished he could feel as if he had just won something, but instead he felt guilty for disappointing his younger brother.

Swimming through the silent deep, Joe felt somber—for leaving Sam behind, and because he felt as if he were about to enter a tomb. Which he was; swimming into the wreck of the *Cambria*, Joe felt a sense of duty. He wanted to honor Clarissa's mother. In his mind Clarissa was frozen as a little girl, that eleven-year-old child whose mother had sailed away and never come home. Reading her diary, he had gleaned information that made identification of her mother's skeleton possible. He tried to keep his emotions out of it.

Joe swam into the black hole. Down a long and treacherous path through the twisted and upside-down interior, he followed the dim light that marked the site. His heart skittered inside his chest, but he fought to remain steady. He was glad he hadn't let Sam come in here. It took great calm to keep breathing correctly underwater. He had watched divers suffer the bends, nearly explode from a surfeit of nitrogen built up from gulping for air, giving in to panic. So he thought of Clarissa and made himself breathe right.

Blue-bright lights glowed up ahead. They illuminated the *Cambria*'s crushed stern, the old mahogany splintered and covered with barnacles and mussels, now part of the reef itself. Fish darted in and out; the sand machine pulled debris away from the treasure site. Divers worked meticulously, uncovering coins.

He saw the two skeletons. They were clustered together, off to the side. Their mouths gaped, their bones protruded. They might have been screaming for help, for forgiveness.

Joe told himself not to feel.

He hovered about them like a fish himself, striving for dispassion. He felt his heart beating madly in his chest. Taking too much air, he looked away. Then back again. These people had died for love. They had sailed away with dreams of escape, their desire for each other pulling them away from everything else. This lady had had a daughter.

Was it worth it? Joe wanted to ask her. Dying on this reef, taken by surprise, by some sudden storm. They hadn't gotten more than twenty miles away from Elisabeth's lighthouse. Joe thought of his father, dying fifty miles from home. Of his mother and Hugh Renwick, of the mess and madness their affair had created.

Joe felt his heart hammering. All his life he had used women as a port in a storm, one after the other, avoiding anything messy or long-lasting, and this was why: Just look at the agony. He swam closer to the skeletons. Taking a light from Dan, he shined the beam down on the two gaping skulls, searching.

There it was: the object that identified Elisabeth Randall. Joe's hands were heavy, his throat ached. According to Clarissa's diary, she had worn it always. Shreds of weed clung to the vertebrae, with a solid object thickly coated with algae and old barnacles nestled in the clavical bones. Joe reached in, gently dislodged it. Over the years and through the wrecks he had trained himself to be unsentimental about death. He had done it a hundred times, reached into a pile of bones and removed a gold chain or diamond pendant or pocket watch. Clinical, scientific. He had taken the loot and never looked back.

But Elisabeth's cameo should have been Clarissa's. Time should have passed the way it was supposed to between a mother and child, with the mother growing old and leaving her most precious things to her daughter. Joe thought of his father, his gold watch, how after he died Joe had never seen it again. Parents die far from home, and they take their things with them. The things that might give their kids comfort or solace or even an answer or two.

Not that things were enough, but they were something to hold on to. Objects to hold and examine, reminders of some- one who had once loved you. And some- times they were all you had.

Joe stared at the bones. He tried to pray for the woman, but somehow the prayer in- cluded Caroline and Sam. His throat burned. His weight belt dragged him down, his breath rasped in his ears. Restless, the cameo safely retrieved, he turned to leave the wreck.

As soon as he emerged, he looked around for Sam. Not seeing him right away, his heart started pumping. *Jesus,* he thought. Diving with someone you cared about was too fucking much work. He swam around the wreck, moving faster, looking through the groups of workers.

He found Sam at the reef. Away from the wreck, unimpressed by the gold, Sam was after his own treasure. Fish. A biologist, his interest lay in pelagic species, just as Joe's lay in sea mud. A thought went through Joe's mind: What if we did both end up at Yale? What if we found a way to live near each other instead of two oceans away? What if we both did what we were trained to do and taught at a good university?

Not forever, Joe thought, because that was too much to consider all at once. But for a while?

Sam was speaking. Two hundred feet beneath the surface, his brother was swimming among the fish of Moonstone Reef, forming words with his lips. He had taken the regulator from his mouth, and he was enunciating in an exaggerated way. His mouth moved, saying the same words over and over. Watching him form the syllables, Joe read his brother's lips.

"Black Hall," Sam was saying, the bubbles exploding toward the surface. "Black Hall."

March 14, 1979

Dear Joe,

   Okay, so I got a little carried away in my last letter. I think it's bizarre, the way I can't wait to see you and I don't even know you yet. Ever since you mentioned sailing here, I keep watching the horizon for sails.

   I think something's happening to me.

Love,

Caroline

April 20, 1979

Dear Caroline,

   Something's happening to me too. Keep watching—I'll come as soon as I get my mainsail repaired. It blew out in a gale last week. I shouldn't have been on the water, but I thought I'd take advantage of the wind to sail to Connecticut (i.e., you).

Love,

Joe

CHAPTER TWELVE

Skye sat in her studio, trying to feel like sculpting. Facing north, the room was cool. Her clay was ready. She sat in her regular place, on a tall metal stool pulled close to a smooth stone table. Her roughened finger-tips trailed across the slippery surfaces. Her tongue felt thick. Her head pounded. She felt a constant, dull pain in her left temple; unconsciously, she kept touching it, prodding it, seeing if it hurt more when she pressed it with her finger.

She had fallen last night. Walking from the garden to the house, she had stumbled and gone down. She had skinned her knees and struck her head on a rock. The heels of both her hands were scraped raw. She had been covered with bits of grass; sand and tiny pebbles were pressed into her skin. When she came to, Homer was licking her face.

It scared her. She didn't feel dizzy, and a look in the mirror had revealed no new bruises. But the side of her head felt different, almost as if she had cracked her skull. It ached. Her mother and Simon had been in the house, and she had gone off . . . for what? She hardly remembered now. She had been in some sort of huff, and she had stormed out to stare at the sea. Homer had just happened along, returning from one of his journeys.

Looking at her clay, Skye felt unmoved, uninspired. The connections she needed to sculpt were missing today. They had been harder and harder to find lately. Skye needed her passions to come through, from her brain to her fingertips, to give shape and emotions to the clay she held in her hand. Drinking blocked them. Liquor dulled the pain, but it also numbed the love.

Every morning she would wake up with a hangover and promise herself she would not drink that day. Even before her fall, her head had hurt. Skye had thought of the liquor crushing her head from the inside out. But at some point every day, she would get the craving. The emptiness inside was bigger than the ache in her head, and she would know a drink would take the worst feelings away. At least for a while.

She wanted one now. She looked at the clock on her table: three P.M. She made a bargain with herself. Just two more hours. Work till five, and then reward yourself with a glass of wine. You can do that. It won't kill you.

Simon walked into the room. He smelled of cigarettes and turpentine, and his bleary eyes told their own drinking story. He stood over Skye's clay, staring at it without speaking. What was he thinking? Skye wondered. Did he know she was in trouble? The word surprised her, and she wondered where it came from. Trouble.

"How's it going?" Simon asked, pouring a tall glass of water and guzzling it down fast.

"Fine," Skye said.

"Your mother's downstairs, chirping about her costume." Skye smiled at the image, and Simon continued. "She wants to know what we're wearing to Caroline's ball. Are we even invited?"

"Of course we are," Skye said. "Why wouldn't we be?"

"Because she hates me. And she's jealous of you."

Skye shook her head. It made her unhappy when Simon criticized her sisters, and today it made her feel particularly bad. What would Caroline have to be jealous of? A hung-over, bloated sculptor who couldn't sculpt? Skye reached past her clay for one of the objects she kept on her desk. There was a flat gray stone, a pure white feather, the skeleton of a snake, a shotgun shell, and a pale and faded blue grosgrain ribbon.

"Why do you keep these things?" Simon asked, taking the stone out of her hand. "We've been married five years, and I don't know half the story. These little mysterious things—your Renwick family fetishes—you never talk about them."

"They're just objects," Skye said. "Things to look at."

Simon regarded her with bloodshot eyes. He seemed so weary. Life—drinking, art, trying to love Skye—had taken a toll on him, and it showed. His dark hair was long and stringy. He seemed to be making up his mind about something. He was letting her see his thought process: Should I stay or should I go? Simon liked to play with her mind. The worst part was, Skye felt too weak to fight him.

"This, then," Simon said, putting down the stone and picking up the shotgun shell. "Why do you keep it?"

"To remind me of the deer it killed," Skye said, picturing the moonlit night on the mountain, the doe thrashing against the tall rocks, the black blood pouring out of her throat, the sound of the dying deer's hooves spasmodically clicking against the boulder. The first creature she had ever shot. For a long time, just looking at the shell could bring tears to her eyes.

"This," he said, touching the white feather.

"It came from a swan," Skye said. "My father gave one to each of us the night he took us to *Swan Lake*."

"He gave you swan feathers," Simon said, pursing his lips, fascinated by any story about Hugh Renwick, no matter how obscure.

"To remind us of nature. That nature was the great inspiration, love and nature—even for Tchaikovsky."

"Took you to the ballet and gave you swan feathers. Awesome," Simon said, shaking his head. "The snake."

"The snake reminds me of danger," Skye said. "To be careful."

She stared at the snake's skeleton. It was long and sinuous, the largest object on her table. Its skull was flat and triangular. From a different angle, if you could look into its mouth, you would see its fangs.

"Is that the one that bit you?"

"No," Skye said. "One like it."

Simon touched Skye's head. She felt his fingers running through her hair, pushing it behind her ears. She closed her eyes and tried to prevent the shiver that shook her entire body. She remembered sleeping in her tent, feeling the snakes writhing under the polythene sheet beneath her.

"When the poison took hold," he said, "did it feel warm and sleepy, like scotch? Like smoking a joint?"

"No," Skye said. "It felt black, and it hurt. I felt the air being squeezed out of me, and I thought I was going to die. But Caroline sucked it out."

Simon made his fingers feel soft and boneless against the back of her neck, as if he wanted her to think of snakes. Skye flinched uncontrollably.

"Your father left you all alone. With no one

but Caroline to look after you. And Clea, only I'll bet she never even left her tent. He should have dropped her off in the suburbs. Talk about the blind leading the stupid."

"Stop, Simon."

She stared at the sculpture she had started days earlier. The three sisters. Caroline, Clea, and Skye. Huddled together, three lumps of clay, protecting each other on the mountain.

"Caroline was older. She should have known that you were going to pitch your tent right over a fissure like that. Didn't she see it?" he asked.

"It was covered with grass," Skye said. "Soft mountain grass. She thought it would feel good under my tent, like a mattress. There wasn't much grass on the mountain."

"A rattlesnake den," Simon said, beginning to touch her neck again. "You must have freaked when they came up through the hole. After dark, all alone in your tent, your sisters in theirs. Poor Skye. You must have gone crazy, feeling those things wriggling around under your sleeping bag. Hey, maybe Caroline got a kick out of it. She might have known, told you to put your tent there on purpose. Sick of being your mother."

"She never would."

"That's right. Saint Caroline. What's the blue ribbon?"

"Oh, the ribbon," she said, not wanting to remember. "I wore it one day."

"With another man?" Simon asked. "One you liked more than me?"

Skye shook her head.

"Where'd you wear it?"

Skye paused. "To Redhawk," she said.

"The mountain," Simon said. "The weekend you shot the guy?"

"Yes."

"I'm married to a killer," he whispered in her ear.

Skye felt the tears in her eyes. She stared at the ribbon. She had worn her hair long then, tied back in a ponytail to keep it out of her eyes. So her aim would be better.

"Do you ever feel powerful?" Simon whispered. "Knowing that you took a life?"

"No, I feel horrible," she whispered back.

"I know you do. I know how much you've suffered for it. But deep inside, under all the conscience, isn't there a little part of you that feels like God? The part that craves experience . . . wants to feel everything intensely?"

"No, Simon," Skye said. She stared at the

blue ribbon. The dark spot on one end, the patch of faded rust, was Andrew Lockwood's blood. While Caroline sat beside him, holding his hand as he died, Skye had bent down to catch Homer, and her ribbon had trailed through the blood.

"The hell you don't."

"You're my husband, you should know me by now," Skye said, her voice now shaking. She couldn't go on talking about this; she needed a drink. She wanted to feel the warm relief spreading through her head, taking the excruciating thoughts away.

"Show me you love me," he said, pressing down on her shoulders. "Come on, show me."

She climbed off her stool, falling to her knees.

Kneeling before Simon, she wrapped her arms around his waist. She placed her cheek against his thigh. She felt tired and sick. More than anything, she wanted to disappear, and she thought: How did I ever let this happen? How did I ever turn into a woman who feels this way, does these things?

"Do you want to?" he asked.

"Yes," she whispered, the lie easier than the truth.

He tangled his fingers in her hair and pulled her head back. She felt tears on her lashes. She tasted salt in her throat. He's my husband, she thought. Is this love? I'm just doing this so we won't have to talk anymore. She reached for his zipper. She tugged it down, reached inside.

Homer nuzzled her face, his big brown eyes so friendly, gazing at her with unconditional love.

"Hey, boy," she said.

"Jesus Christ," Simon snapped. "Get him out of here."

Skye tried to push Homer away, but he wouldn't go. Skye noticed that his ears were nearly bald, like a stuffed animal who had been loved so hard, his fur had worn off. Homer sidled between Skye and Simon. He pushed against Skye, edging her away from Simon.

"What the fuck," Simon said, giving Homer a swat.

The old dog just stood there, looking up at Simon with dignity in his cloudy brown eyes. Simon raised his hand again. Homer didn't flinch. He didn't bare his teeth, and he didn't wag his tail. He just stared at Simon as if he expected the worst from such a man.

"Don't hit him," Skye said.

"He ruined it," Simon snapped, zipping up his pants. "Her fucking dog ruined it. Jesus. Caroline couldn't have done better if she was here herself."

Skye felt like laughing. She kept her head down, feeling the laughter exploding in her chest, and she wondered if she was losing her mind. She was a hung-over drunk who wanted to get drunker, who'd rather do what her husband told her than face the fact she didn't like him, and she was under the protection of her sister's sweet golden retriever.

Simon stormed out of the studio. Skye heard the door slamming behind him, his footsteps on the stairs, heard him start the car and drive away. Homer lay on the floor beside her. He had long since forgiven her for the accident that had brought them together. Lying down beside him, her cheek on the cool stone floor and her hand on Homer's paw, Skye closed her eyes and wished she could forgive herself.

* * *

Caroline surveyed the inn grounds. The Firefly Ball would start at dusk, and she wanted to make sure everything was ready. A white film of heat clung to the trees, the lanterns, the inn itself. Long white linen tablecloths wafted desultorily in the slight breeze. The band had set up. The bass player stood alone onstage, shirtless in the hot sun, testing the sound system.

Bars were set up at either side of the dance floor. Champagne was chilling in the barn, waiting to be wheeled out after dark. Caroline approached Michele, who was running around with a clipboard.

"Tell the bartenders I don't want them to serve Skye," Caroline said.

"What?" Michele asked.

"She's been sick. She's not supposed to drink alcohol with her medication," Caroline said.

Michele saw through the lie. But she was loyal to Caroline, and she knew how worried she had been. "I'll tell them," she said. "Will your mother be here?"

"Of course," Caroline said, a smile breaking through the stress. "Augusta wouldn't miss it for anything."

"The guys from the boat said you invited them—" Michele said, "—the treasure hunters. They're all excited."

"Really?" Caroline asked.

"Yes, and, Caroline?"

Caroline turned to look at Michele. Michele held her clipboard to her breast. She was smiling like a proud parent.

"You look beautiful."

"Thank you," Caroline said, blushing. Knowing how much she had to do, she had dressed for the ball early. Her dark hair was swept up in a French twist. She wore a long white dress with a rustling sweep to the skirt, and no jewelry except pearl earrings.

"Are you supposed to be any painting in particular? Your father's *Girl in a White Dress?*"

"I hadn't planned it that way," Caroline said. But she knew it was true. She knew that she had dressed as herself in the famous picture painted by her father.

"That's the same dress you wore, isn't it?" Michele asked.

"No," Caroline said. The white dress she had worn while her father painted that portrait had been given away long ago, donated to the Wadsworth Atheneum for an exhibition of garments worn in famous paintings. But looking down, she realized this dress was very similar.

"So many people will recognize the picture," Michele said. "I think it's your father's best-known."

"You're probably right," Caroline agreed, adjusting a bouquet of flowers on one of the tables. But she knew she hadn't chosen her father's painting because it was well known, because a great number of guests would recognize it. She had chosen to wear the white dress because one person would recognize it.

Caroline knew Joe Connor had seen her portrait at the Met. She knew because he had told her so. It was a small thing, but it was a connection. And connections were sometimes all that counted.

September 8, 1979

Dear Joe,

I have something to tell you. It has to be in person. Why is Newport so far from Black Hall? Hurry! But make sure you're safe.

Love,

Caroline

September 30, 1979

Dear C,

Actually, Newport isn't at all far from Black Hall. The problem is, you're there and I'm here. Until we're both here or both there; well, you get the idea. A new mainsail costs more than I have at the moment.

What do you have to tell me? I think I might know, because I want to tell you the same thing. Sometimes I feel as if I don't have anyone but you, C. My mother has her new family—Sam and his father. I live here, but I don't belong the same way as Sam.

It's different with you. You make me smile like no one else. Every time I see your handwriting, I know everything's going to be okay. There's one person in the world I trust, and it's you. I know this is a long letter, but it's late and I can't sleep. I'm thinking of you, Caroline. I wish you were here. I might as well say it.

I love you.

Joe

CHAPTER THIRTEEN

All day the temperature had hovered in the nineties, and at dusk the sky was pearl white, the sun a shimmering red ball. As the sun set, the moon rose. It climbed high and white in the hazy dark sky, and beneath it the paper lanterns illuminated the Firefly Ball as music filled the night.

The raw bar glistened with fresh clams and oysters on ice. Caroline and Michele had arranged some of the shellfish like a painting by Degas. The guests had created haystacks after Monet, erected beach umbrellas and white tents after Boudin. Candles twinkled, and the band played "Every Time We Say Good-bye."

Guests milled about, dressed as their favorite paintings. Many of the costumes were old-fashioned, *The Luncheon of the*

Boating Party by Renoir and *Madame X* by Sargent, the graceful long dresses, providing the most inspiration for the women. May Taylor came as the Hugh Renwick portrait of her grandmother Emily Dunne, founder of the Bridal Barn. Her russet hair piled high, she looked sweet and elegant at once. Clea and Peter came dressed as an Irish couple from Hugh Renwick's *Galway Dance,* and Skye and Simon came in black, as themselves. Having made another of their unstable, uneasy truces, they came together, with Augusta, and they took a table between the river and the dance floor.

Caroline saw her family arrive. She hung back, watching. Caroline did not know what to say to Skye. She knew her so well and loved her so much. But somehow they had lost the ability to communicate. Their last few times together, they might as well have been speaking different languages.

"Caroline!" Augusta called, spotting her.

Smiling, Caroline went to join her family. Augusta looked mischievous, dressed in her harlequin costume and her black pearls. Everyone rose, and she kissed her mother, her sisters, and their husbands. They complimented one another on their costumes, and everyone remarked on the beautiful job Caroline had done with the ball.

"Your father would be so proud," Augusta said, squeezing her hand. Behind her harlequin mask, her eyes glistened. Augusta grew more sentimental every year. "You should give yourself a lot of credit, honey."

"Thanks, Mom," Caroline said, pleased. Her parents' approval had always mattered to her and it always would.

"That dress," Augusta said, gazing at Caroline. "It's remarkably like the one you wore . . . do you remember that sitting? On the porch at Firefly Hill?"

"Yes, I remember." How could she forget? It was late in the year, the last weekend before it snowed. Andrew Lockwood had been dead a month, and the family was in shock. It was the last real painting her father had ever done. When he completed *Girl in a White Dress,* he put away his paints for good.

"It finished him, Caroline," Augusta said.

"What did?"

"That painting. It took all he had. When he was done, he said he had nothing left inside. He was never really himself after that. But he caught something. . . ."

Caroline took a second look at her mother. She sounded bitter, as if Caroline's costume had reminded her of too much loss, misfortune, and injustice regarding her and Hugh.

"Caught what?"

"That quality you have inside. That reserve . . ."

"My coldness?" Caroline said with a touch of fear, remembering what Skye had said, wanting to be contradicted.

"No. You were young and emotional, and you were holding it all inside. The effect was very mysterious and alluring. I remember looking at the face your father painted and knowing the world would think he was in love with her. The girl in the picture."

"Mom!" Caroline said.

Augusta turned away to hide the harsh disappointment in her eyes. If Caroline hadn't known better, she would have said her mother's sour tone was jealousy. But it couldn't be.

"*Girl in a White Dress*. You look beautiful," Skye said quietly. She had a glass in her hand; it looked like mineral water.

"So do you," Caroline said.

They were shy with each other, two dogs circling. Clea leaned forward. "Listen," she said. The band was playing "Goodnight, My Someone." Skye had sung it in eighth grade, in her spring concert, and Caroline and Clea had skipped out of high school to sneak in and hear her. The song united the sisters in an old memory, and Caroline and Skye tried to smile at each other.

"Goodness," Augusta said. "Look!"

The crew from the *Meteor* had arrived. A band of pirates, dressed in torn shirts, eye patches, and salty trousers, they shouldered their way through the crowd to the bar. Polite clusters of guests parted quickly, as if the men were real pirates. The crewmates grouped at the bar, grabbing beers and surveying the party.

"Are they supposed to be here?" Augusta asked dubiously.

"They're friends of Caroline's," Clea said.

The skinniest pirate slapped his beer down on the bar and began making his way over. He moved with purpose, homing in on Caroline, as if he were swinging across the deck on a shredded topgallant. Dressed with a red kerchief tied over his short blond hair, a white shirt with comically billowing arms, Sam stood before Caroline with his hands on his hips.

"Ahoy!" he said. He had an eye patch over the left lens of his wire-rimmed glasses.

"Hi, Sam," Caroline said. "This is my family. Everyone, this is Sam Trevor." She sounded normal, and she smiled at Sam, but inside she felt something change. Sam was here, and so was Joe, and Joe's presence made everything different.

"I'm here to keep up the bad name of pirates everywhere," Sam said apologetically.

"By doing what?"

"Kidnapping you," Sam said, holding out his hand, "for a dance."

Caroline followed Sam onto the dance floor. The band was playing medium-slow, and they had plenty of room to move. Sam did his best; he really did. He knew where to put his hands and how to move his feet, but he lurched to a completely different rhythm than Caroline and the music. Caroline saw the embarrassment in his face. She adjusted her movement to his, overwhelmingly fond of him for trying.

"Sorry," he said, his face red.

"For what? I wanted to dance with you," Caroline said.

"It's dangerous, dancing with me," Sam said. "I trip."

"Do you like music?"

"I love it," he said.

"That's all that counts," Caroline said as if she were talking to a younger brother. "Just enjoy yourself."

"Thanks," Sam said. They danced silently for a minute. His muscles relaxed slightly, and he didn't seem as tense. But his rhythm was just as bad. As they moved around the dance floor, Caroline looked through the crowd. She saw the pirates drinking at the bar, but she didn't see Joe.

"How's the wreck?" Caroline asked.

"Cool. I dove on it twice this week. Joe took me down."

"Oh. Is he . . ."

There he was, the head pirate. Joe Connor stood off to the side, leaning against a tree. He wore a white shirt, ripped at the shoulders and chest. His black pants were tight, his feet were bare. He had on a black hat, low over one eye. The sight of him made Caroline shiver, as if the temperature had just dropped twenty degrees.

"We found skeletal remains," Sam was saying. "Partially buried in sediment and remarkably well preserved. We've retrieved quite a bit of the gold, in fact. . . ."

As Sam spoke, he became more excited and his dancing deteriorated. They wheeled around, and Caroline lost sight of Joe. When Sam twirled her back, she saw him again. He had started to move through the crowd. His blue eyes were dark, and they were on her. People stepped aside, watching him pass. He had an air of serious danger about him, as real as any pirate's.

The night smelled of honeysuckle and rosemary. Sam saw Joe coming, and he grinned. Caroline felt the heat spread through her chest.

"Would you like to dance?" Joe asked, looking straight at her.

"I have to let him, or he'll make me walk the plank," Sam said, stepping aside.

Caroline stood still, listening to the music play. People danced around them, jostling her. She was dimly aware of them and of Sam walking away. Joe watched her with dark eyes. He didn't appear to expect or want anything. He might have been a stranger, cutting in. Caroline nodded. Joe stepped forward, took her into his arms.

His body curved over hers, and she had to steady herself, catching her breath. They danced together, so close she could feel his breath warm against her ear. The music was slow and sweet. They did not speak, but Caroline loved the way they moved, like grass in a current, with grace and rhythm. Her throat ached, and she didn't know why.

"Thanks for dancing with Sam," he said after a minute.

"I wanted to," she said, surprised.

"The kid can't dance. He's got two left feet."

"He tries though. That's the important thing," Caroline said. Looking around Joe's shoulder, she could see her family. Simon and Skye had left the table. She hoped they would come dance, but Simon headed for the bar, and Skye stood off to the side, watching.

"Sam said you took him down to the wreck," Caroline said, wanting to put Skye out of her mind for now.

"Yeah."

"You showed him the bones?"

"Yes," Joe said, holding Caroline tighter.

She felt his arms around her bare shoulders, his mouth against her ear. He held her hand against his chest in his rough and scraped hand. Her fingers trailed through the hair on his chest and rested against his warm skin. She felt the tension in her own body and sensed it in his. They stopped talking.

The music played, and Caroline rested her cheek against Joe's chest. She closed her eyes and wondered whether he could feel her heart pounding against his.

Augusta milled around. She drank martinis. As Hugh Renwick's widow she was a big hit. She found herself telling a group of young artists that the glass in her hand had actually once belonged to Hugh.

"Hugh Renwick drank from that glass?" a young man asked reverently. Like Augusta, he was dressed as a Picasso: the bull in *Guernica*. He wore a silly, lopsided mask of papier-mâché, but he looked adorable from the neck down in toreador clothes.

"Yes, he did," Augusta lied. "Would you care to sip from Hugh's hallowed goblet?"

"If it would make me paint like Hugh Renwick," the man said, eagerly taking the glass in both hands as if it were in some way holy, trying to make it meet his lips through the absurd bull mouth-hole.

"I can't guarantee that, dear," Augusta said wryly. "Hugh would be very displeased with both of us, dressed as Picassos instead of Renwicks. He loathed Paul, you know."

"Paul?" the bull asked.

"Picasso, dear," Augusta said, glancing around for her daughters. There were Clea and Peter, so sweetly social, just as adult children should be at fancy dress balls. Skye had wandered off somewhere, making Augusta distinctly nervous. She spied Simon, flirting with a young waitress, drawing her out with that passive-aggressive depression of his. Caroline was dancing with someone, blocked from Augusta's sight by the crowd.

"I would have come as a Renwick," the bull was saying, "but he did mainly landscapes and women. I didn't feel like coming as a red barn or a nude female."

"One understands," Augusta said, spotting Caroline. She excused herself from the bull and paused to watch her oldest daughter. Caroline looked exquisite tonight. She radiated from within; her skin glowed like a peach, her wide eyes were clear and beautiful, her white dress fit her perfectly. Augusta felt stinging remorse for the old jealousy she had felt earlier. But it was true: *Girl in a White Dress,* coming so soon after the death of that young man, had finished Hugh. And Augusta had so desperately wished it had been she in the portrait, her husband's most famous picture.

When the crowd parted, Augusta got a good look at the man Caroline was dancing with.

He was the handsomest man Augusta Renwick had seen in years: over six feet tall with broad shoulders. He was one of the pirates. He looked physical enough to be a workman, but he carried it off with a sort of throwaway elegance. He had a sailor's tan and the clearest blue eyes Augusta had ever seen. But the thing that shocked her was the way he was looking at Caroline. His expression was fierce and wild, full of craving and longing.

"Mother?"

Augusta felt Clea's hand on her arm.

"Darling, who is that man with Caroline?"

"A pirate."

"I can see that. But who is he?"

"Just a friend, I think. Mom, have you seen Skye?"

"They're acting like lovers. Just look at the way he's staring at her."

"It's a slow dance. Mom . . ."

"I'm looking for Skye myself," Augusta said. She tore her gaze away from Caroline and her pirate to glance around. She sipped her martini, feeling disturbed. Was it more jealousy or just missing Hugh? She looked over again. The yearning in the man's eyes

was matched by that in Caroline's and reminded Augusta of how passionately she
had desired her husband, how intensely she
had feared losing him.

"She seemed quiet," Clea said. "Is she
upset about something?"

Augusta sighed. Why couldn't they just
have fun? Why did everything have to become so serious and moody? She hadn't
raised her girls this way. She had given
them free rein.

While other mothers watched every move,
Augusta had let her daughters explore and
grow. She had fought her protective instincts and allowed Hugh to take the girls
hunting. He had wanted to teach them to
fend for themselves, and she thought he
had done it. All those nights alone on the
mountain! Yet here they were, worried
about Skye just because she had wandered
out of sight.

"I'm sure she's fine," Augusta said.

"Look at Simon," Clea said.

He was leading the waitress onto the
dance floor. She had left her drink tray on a
table, kicked her shoes off, melted into his
arms. Simon was smoking a cigarette. He
talked with it in his mouth, the blue smoke

curling into his eyes. Augusta thought he looked evil, dirty, and stupid.

"Why did Skye marry him?" Clea asked. "It's as if she deliberately picked the one man who would treat her the worst."

Augusta groaned, watching Simon's hands on the waitress's hips. "Your father would kill him," Augusta said.

"He'd kill Skye," Clea said. "He was so adamant about men, about us being strong and not being victims of anyone. That's all he wanted to teach us."

"He taught *you*," Augusta said. Hugh had cheated on Augusta, claimed he couldn't help himself, it was what men did. But more than anything, he had wanted to save his daughters from getting hurt.

"Taught me?" Clea asked.

"You married a good man. Dear Peter," Augusta said. "You're the only one. Skye married a bastard, and Caroline's all alone."

But even as Augusta spoke, she and Clea watched Caroline on the dance floor in the arms of the pirate. He looked like everything Hugh Renwick would warn her against. He was big and cool, with a wicked sexual intensity, and he had his arms wrapped around Caroline as if he had hunted her down and intended to own her. But the strange thing, the factor Augusta couldn't quite believe and had to check with a closer look, was the expression in his eyes.

The pirate dancing with Augusta's daughter looked for all the world as if he had fallen in love.

The song ended. Caroline stepped back. Joe stood still, not saying anything. He wanted to ask her to dance again. But this was her inn and her ball, and she probably had a million things to do. Guys were milling around, probably wanting to dance with her. But she didn't move. She just stood there. She was wearing that white dress Joe remembered from her father's painting, and all he wanted was to take her down to the river alone and dance with her there.

"Thank you," he said finally.

"Oh," she said. "It was fun."

Joe stared at her. It was strange; he didn't feel angry. Not at all. For the first time in a lot of years, he could think of Caroline Renwick and not feel the resentment rising. The opposite. He felt an unfamiliar tenderness, and it made him so uncomfortable he took a step backward.

"Well," she said.

The music was starting again. The paper lanterns swung in a light gust of breeze. Joe cleared his throat. Caroline watched him, expectant. He reached into his pocket. He had brought something from the boat to show her, and his fingers closed around it now. He could ask her to dance again, hand it to her while they moved to the music. He could try to tell her what finding it had made him feel. . . .

Someone bumped him from behind.

Her brother-in-law, the creep Joe had seen drinking with Skye at the bar one week before, jostled into Joe, then Caroline. The guy had the smell of booze and drugs coming out of him. He was so busy feeling up the girl he was dancing with, he hardly noticed his own clumsiness.

"Oops," the girl said, eye to eye with Caroline.

"Where's Skye?" Caroline asked Simon, ignoring the waitress.

"She needed a walk," Simon said, the cigarette still in his mouth. Joe wanted to jam it down his throat and tell him to go find his wife.

"Dora, aren't you supposed to be working?" Caroline asked, barely controlling her fury.

"Sorry," Dora said, flying off the dance floor.

"I'm worried about Skye," Caroline said to Simon. "I want us to find her."

"I'm not her keeper," he said, watching the waitress from behind. "Neither are you."

"Doesn't mean you can't look for her," Joe said. "Especially if your sister-in-law asks you to."

"Who the fuck—" Simon asked, aggression making the cords in his neck stand out. He had the look of a beater in his eyes. He was small and mean, and Joe hardly had to use his imagination to see him hitting Skye. Quietly, Joe put himself between Simon and Caroline.

"Just look, Simon. Okay?" Caroline asked tensely.

"Fine," Simon said, throwing his cigarette on the floor. He walked away, leaving it burning. Caroline gave Joe an apologetic glance and followed him. Joe put out the cigarette in an ashtray on the bar. He stared after Caroline and then he went the other way. To look for Skye.

* * *

The log stretched across the stream. It had been there for some time. Sticks, feathers, and debris had caught on stray branches protruding from one end. The stream flowed beneath the log, lazy and blackish-green, just before it widened and joined the Connecticut River. Pine trees grew thick along one bank, while reeds whispered along the other.

Skye stood at one end of the log. The breeze ruffled her black dress. It tickled her bare legs. She watched the water move. A fish came to the surface, making rings in the dark water. Skye stared at the rings. She remembered a night on a different riverbank two hundred miles to the north. The stars had blazed low over the curving hills. Her father had dropped them off hungry, to make them hunt for their food. Sharpening a stick, she had waited in the rushes.

The frog was fat. She knew she was supposed to kill it. Stabbing down, she impaled its white moon body. Her father had shown her how to build a fire, and he had told her that cooking a frog was no different than cooking a fish. But somehow it was. The big frog had sleepy eyes and a smiling mouth. After she stabbed it, it twitched and gasped. As weak and hungry as she was, Skye had gone without eating. She had killed an animal for nothing.

"Not the last time," she said out loud now.

Haze hung over the stream, and Skye balanced on the log. She held the silver flask in her hand. Music from the ball came through the trees; she could almost imagine she was at the ballet. Skye was *in* the ballet; standing on one foot, she twirled to the music and took a sip of vodka. Russian vodka, appropriate for *Swan Lake.*

Fireflies blinked in the trees. Skye took another drink. Knowing how worried Caroline was, how much she wanted to keep Skye from drinking, Skye had brought her own. She didn't want Caroline to feel compromised, serving Skye liquor she believed would harm her.

On the other hand, Skye did not want to be observed swigging from a flask. So here she was in the woods, dancing on a fallen log, remembering the first and only time their father had taken them to the ballet. *Swan Lake.* The dying swan. Wishing he'd taken them to more ballets, fewer hunts, Skye paradoxically hated *Swan Lake.* Tragically beautiful, it rang too many bells.

"The dance is over there."

The deep voice came from the shadows. Skye was so startled, she nearly fell off the log. Backing away from the sound, she felt the panic in her chest.

"Who's that?" she asked.

A man stepped forward, watching her with racy blue eyes. Tall, with a ripped shirt that revealed tan shoulders, he appeared menacing. He was dressed like a pirate; he didn't even seem to be wearing a costume.

"Don't fall," he said.

"Stay away," Skye said.

"I will."

Skye weaved on the log. The water was only six feet down. If he came toward her, she could jump. The black water would close over her head. She could hold her breath, swim for shore. The dying, stupid swan. She could play that role. The vodka she had already drunk made her dizzy.

"Sit down," the man said.

"Don't come any closer," she warned. Was he trying to help? Or would he grab her from behind, rip off her dress, hold his hand over her mouth to stifle her screams? The thought, blasting out of nowhere, made Skye turn and run. Her foot caught on a broken branch, and she started to fall.

The man caught her. He took two steps, and he was there. His arms around her, trying to steady her. Skye fought. She screamed, scratched him, tore at his eyes. They thrashed on the log, the man somehow keeping balance for both of them.

"Get away from me," she cried, grabbing his face.

"Skye—"

"I swear, I'll kill you, don't think I won't—" Skye said. Had he just said her name?

"Skye, sit down," he said. "It's okay, you're safe. Just sit down, for God's sake."

"Who the hell are you?"

The man gripped her upper arms. Skye's feet were barely touching the log. He held her steady. She had scratched his face; he was bleeding. Shaking uncontrollably, she looked into his face. It was familiar. Skye didn't know how she knew him, but she had seen him somewhere.

"Sit down, okay?" he asked cautiously. He touched his cheek, looked at the blood.

Skye's head throbbed. Her throat ached. Her stomach lurched, and she retched into the water. She didn't trust him for a second, but she didn't have a choice. Drunk, she felt wobbly and sick. She wanted a fast slug of vodka, but she had dropped her flask. The man helped her sit on the log.

Skye sobbed.

The man reached into his pocket, then handed her a handkerchief. "Here," he said.

Skye shook her head. She opened her eyes, looked around for the flask. Maybe it hadn't fallen into the stream.

"It's gone," the man said. "I saw it go in."

Skye gave him a desperate look. How did he know what she was looking for? Leaning forward, she saw the blood running down his cheek. She covered her eyes and moaned.

"Let's get off the log," he said. Offering her his hand, he waited for her.

"Why do you look so familiar?" Skye asked, trying to decide.

"I saw you at the inn the other night. You were at the bar with your husband."

Skye stared at him. That wasn't it. She knew his face, and she had known it for a long time. He was older now, but those blue eyes . . . the strong jaw, the straight nose. She blinked at him, trying to remember. She reached through the haze of vodka, past the fear of his unexpected presence.

"No," she said. She still felt afraid, but something about his blue eyes steadied her, reassured her that he wouldn't hurt her. She gave him her hand. He helped her off the log. The ground felt steady under her feet, but the sky moved overhead. She swayed.

"Skye, I know you can't hear me right now," he said roughly.

"I hear you," she said.

"No, you're drunk," he said. "But later, when you sober up, I want you to remember something."

"I'm not drunk—" Skye said.

"Yeah, you are. But tomorrow, when your head's pounding and you're throwing up and you want to die, remember something, okay?"

"What?" she asked, her fingers trembling.

"You never have to feel this way again."

"Don't—"

"There's a way out," he said.

The man's eyes were deep and direct. He held Skye by her shoulders, and even though his voice was rough, it came out kind. He looked calm. Skye knew she knew him from somewhere, but the strangest part was, he sounded as if he knew her even better. She almost had it; she stared, trying so hard to remember.

They walked back to the party. The man held back branches so Skye could pass.

They emerged from the woods, and almost immediately Caroline came walking over. She looked at Skye, then past her at the man. His eyes changed then. They had been hard, almost angry in their intensity, but they softened when Caroline came into view.

"Skye," she said, and Skye stepped into her arms.

Holding Caroline made her feel safe. Skye trembled from the vodka she had drunk and the shock of meeting a strange man in the woods, from dancing to *Swan Lake* and from remembering another time Caroline had held her close in other woods.

"You found her," Caroline was saying.

"Yes."

"Thank you," Caroline said. Skye's head was against her sister's chest, and she could feel Caroline shaking.

"Who are you?" Skye asked. "I know you . . ."

"Skye, this is Joe Connor," Caroline said.

The name sparked something deep inside. Skye tilted her head, looked at Caroline. She may have been holding Skye's hand, but Caroline's eyes were for the man. Overhead, the Japanese lanterns bobbed on the wire, bathing them in blue and red light.

"Oh, I do know you," Skye said, her eyes filling with tears.

Joe didn't smile or move. He stood very still, bleeding from where Skye had scratched him. She thought of that smiling boy in the picture, his wide-open face, his missing-tooth smile, the freckles across his cheeks.

There was nothing wide-open about the man who stood before her now. He's tough, Skye thought. That's what's so different, why I didn't recognize him at all. Life has made him wary. Skye knew, because it had made her that way too.

"Are you okay?" he asked guardedly.

Skye nodded.

"Try to remember what I said. Tomorrow."

Skye lowered her head, ashamed that he had seen her drinking from the flask.

"You were always one of us," Skye whispered.

"What?" Joe asked.

"One of us. You know . . . like a brother. I knew Caroline wrote to you, and I always imagined you knew what it was like."

"Only some of it," he said. "I was on the other side."

Skye shook her head. "No, you weren't. Our parents were, but not us. You were one of us."

It all made such perfect sense now. The summer night was hot, and fireflies were flickering through the trees, and she was standing in a tight circle with Caroline and Joe Connor. They were united by gunshots, other people's deaths.

Her mother was coming across the lawn. Simon was with her, a sullen expression on his face. Skye could feel his anger from there, and it made her stomach tighten. She would pay for his humiliation later. Clea and Peter were right behind them. Tagging along was a young man, bedecked in his pirate kerchief and black eye patch.

"Good God, where was she?" Augusta said. "I looked up, saw her stumbling out of the woods with this pirate—"

Skye saw her mother glaring at Joe.

"First I see him dancing with Caroline, and the next thing I know, he's coming out of the woods with Skye!" Augusta said.

"Mom, he helped me," Skye said quickly to stop the innuendo. "I nearly fell in the water."

"What the fuck, Skye," Simon asked, yanking her arm. "A liaison in the woods?"

"Watch your mouth, tough guy," Joe said, calmly prying Simon's fingers off Skye's arm.

Simon was high. Skye could see it in his

eyes. They glittered with violent rage, but he was too shocked by the rebuke to reply.

"Well, thank you," Augusta said properly, restoring decorum to the situation. "For helping my daughter. Mr.—?"

"Joe Connor," he said.

The name hung in the air.

"Connor?" Augusta asked.

"Yes," he said.

"Connor." Augusta repeated the word, the cold truth dawning in her eyes.

"That's right."

"Not James Connor's son?" Augusta asked with disbelief.

"Yes. He was my father." Joe sounded tougher than ever, as if he were ready for a fight. The anger was back in his eyes. Caroline stepped forward, trying to head off the confrontation, but Joe looked past her.

"Good God," Augusta said, her eyes filling with pain.

"Mrs. Renwick," Sam Trevor said, drawing himself up to his full height. He adopted the tone of peacemaker, firm but kind. "The past is the past. You have great daughters, we're just getting to know each other. Joe and I are friends of Caroline's. She invited us here."

"I did, Mom," Caroline said kindly. "Please, they're my friends . . ."

Augusta gave her a strange look, as if she had just betrayed the family and did not even realize it. She glanced at Sam, trying to make sense of what he had just said. Then she put her hand on Caroline's wrist.

"Do you remember what happened? I know you do . . . how terrible it was. His father hurt us all so badly. Please, walk away with me. Right now."

"Mom, listen," Caroline said, throwing a look at Joe, stepping forward to stop her mother from going on.

"To what?" Augusta asked desperately. "Words don't matter. They can't take away all the damage he did. I was a mother with young children, and he came into our house to kill us."

"But he didn't, Mom," Caroline pleaded.

"Murder in his heart," Augusta said.

"That's my father you're talking about," Joe said, holding her gaze.

"Your father . . ." Augusta said.

"Joe," Sam said calmly.

"I'm sorry he threatened your daughters. But I can't have you talking about him that way. Do you understand?"

"What I understand," Augusta said

shakily, "is that I don't want you anywhere near my daughter."

"Come on, Sam," Joe said, turning.

"Joe, hang on, man," Sam said, still thinking there was a chance for peace.

Joe kept walking. He did not apologize to Augusta. He did not say good-bye to Clea and Peter, did not wait for his brother. He did not throw Simon a final look of disdain. He did not remind Skye of what he had said earlier. But mainly, even through Skye's drunken haze she could see he did not say good-bye to Caroline.

Caroline watched him go. Her hand on her breast, darkly elegant with her hair upswept and her white dress wrapping her long legs, she stood in the center of her family with an expression of total despair in her eyes, watching Joe Connor walk away.

November 1, 1979

Dear Joe,

I've never felt this way before. When I opened your last letter, I was ready to laugh because you're always so funny, or learn something new about you, or hear something about Sam.

But I didn't expect to read what I've been feeling. I love you too, Joe. I know we're young, we hardly know each other, we've never even met. Why don't any of those things matter to me?

Paintings are so strange. Sometimes I'll stand in a gallery, looking at a picture of a girl. She'll be sitting in a chair, or looking out a window, or walking on a beach, and I'll get a funny feeling in my throat. Somehow I'll know she's in love. I've always wondered how I knew that, because I'd never felt it before.

Now I do, and I know I was right all along. When I see those paintings, look at those girls, it's like looking in the mirror. It's like seeing myself, thinking of you. In love with you, Joe. I am.

C.

CHAPTER FOURTEEN

"How could you, Caroline?" Augusta asked.

They were in the herb garden at Firefly Hill, the scent of verbena strong in the salt air. Waves broke on the shoal, rolled into the beach with a gentle rush. Offshore, the *Meteor* glistened and the blue water sparkled in the bright sun. Caroline couldn't bear to see it. She turned her back, facing her mother.

"I don't even know what you mean, Mom. Joe's my friend now. I wanted him there."

Augusta shook her head. She wore a long muslin dress and a straw sun hat. She huddled on the garden bench, fidgeting with her black pearls. Bending over, she pulled weeds from the bed of thyme and burnet. Then she stopped and rearranged a small cluster of scallop shells.

"Inviting him to the ball . . ." Augusta went on as if Caroline had not spoken. "Making him welcome when his family is responsible for so much unhappiness. So much unhappiness."

"His family?"

"You know what I mean," Augusta said, pulling off her dark glasses, gazing at Caroline with injured eyes. "His mother seduced your father. It's so ugly. It hurt me so much. Your father had an affair, honey. It broke my heart, and it drove her husband crazy. Literally crazy. He came here to our house," Augusta said, pointing at the kitchen door, "and killed himself in front of my babies."

"How long ago, Mom?" Caroline asked sharply. "How many years ago did that happen?"

"It doesn't matter how many years. We're still feeling the aftershocks. I came close to ending my marriage over it, Caroline. Your father took it into his head to teach you and your sisters to shoot, and your sister killed a man. Violence begets violence, and his father started the cycle."

"Dad did," Caroline said. "If you want to go back that far. By having the affair in the first place."

"This is getting us nowhere," Augusta said.

"Are Joe and I supposed to pay for *your* past?"

"I'm worried sick about Skye," Augusta said. "And now I'm worried about your judgment."

"Don't," Caroline snapped.

"You'll get hurt," Augusta said.

"I'm strong, Mom," Caroline said.

"I know. And we all rely on you," Augusta said. "Maybe too much." She reached across the garden bench to pat Caroline's knee, and Caroline took her hand.

How could people feel such powerful and conflicting emotions for each other? How often, when she was young, had Caroline hated her parents, her sisters? While knowing, with all her heart, that she would die for them? She sat beside her mother, smelling the soothing fragrance of sage and rosemary. Her mother softly stroked the back of her hand with her thumb.

"I saw you dancing with him," Augusta said. "Before I realized who he was."

"You did?"

"Mmm. I did. And I thought—" Augusta paused, considering.

"Thought what?"

"Caroline's done it."

Caroline closed her eyes. The breeze blew off the sea, and she lifted her face to feel it. Perhaps it had swept across the decks of the *Meteor,* perhaps it had passed across Joe's boat, his skin . . .

"What did you think I'd done?" Caroline asked.

"Fallen in love with a dangerous man," Augusta said.

Caroline shook her head.

"Like your father. Just as I'd done, as your sister Skye's done. . . I saw the man, the way you were looking at each other. His tallness, his rough body. And that love in his eyes."

Caroline could not move. She let her mother hold her hand, felt the soft pressure of her mother's thumb circling her hand. Augusta's voice broke.

"Maybe that bothers me more than the rest," she said. "You've kept yourself free for so long. Free and safe. Darling, I can't bear to think of you hurt."

"I'm strong, Mom," Caroline said again, her throat aching. It was true. She had learned all the lessons, and she had kept herself free and safe and strong—and alone. Her mother had nothing to worry about. She and Joe could never be together now.

"Thank God, Caroline," Augusta said, sniffling. "Do you forgive me?"

"For what?"

"For last night. Not for my emotions, but my behavior. For being so out of control . . ."

"You were shocked," Caroline said carefully, picturing Joe's face. Sam's. Forgiveness is not the only point, she thought, remembering something Joe had said. First we have to face the truth. It is about understanding. She squeezed her mother's hand, then let it go.

"I was," Augusta said.

"Where's Skye?"

"Inside. Asleep, I think."

"I have to talk to her."

Augusta nodded. She blinked at the sun. As if surprised to find herself sitting in the herb garden, she looked around. She brushed the tops of some lavender, smelled her hand.

"Your grandmother's herbs," she said. Her eyes filled with tears. "Sometimes I miss my mother and grandmother so much. They were wise women. Not like me. They were solid and old-fashioned, real mothers."

"You're a real mother," Caroline said, laughing with surprise.

"But I haven't been a very good one."

"Oh, Mom . . ." Caroline said, her eyes filling because sometimes she had felt the same way.

"I don't know what I'd do without my girls."

"We don't know what we'd do without you," Caroline said.

"Skye . . ." Augusta said, her voice trailing off, her eyes sweeping up the white house to a window where white curtains fluttered in the breeze.

"I know," Caroline said, following her mother's gaze to Skye's bedroom window.

"I've made so many mistakes," Augusta said, her voice thick. "And so much damage has been done."

"So much good too," Caroline said quietly, thinking of last night, of Joe helping Skye, of Sam running to the rescue, of Clea and Peter helplessly looking on. "There is so much in our families that's good."

* * *

Joe stared at the sea. The waves sparkled. The day was as sunny as a summer day got, but the old anger had closed in like fog in Maine. It hung thick and heavy, and it kept him locked in place. He handled his business, but his thoughts kept returning to the Renwicks.

Coming here was a mistake. Diving on the *Cambria* was a success, but the rest left him muddled and fierce. He had wanted to put some things to rest by facing Black Hall. He had stirred them up instead. His hands in his pocket, he felt something unfamiliar. Frowning, he pulled out the cameo.

Pale and incandescent, the cameo showed the profile of a woman. Her face was noble and proud, with an unmistakable touch of sadness and strength around the mouth. Even on something so old and tiny, the emotion was apparent. Her hair was full, her forehead high. She reminded Joe of Caroline. He scowled.

"Boy, Mrs. Renwick was one mad old lady," Sam said, coming across the deck.

"Yeah," Joe said, slipping the cameo back into his pocket.

"She could go on, couldn't she?"

Joe nodded. He watched gulls gather on a school of feeding blues, the water choppy and silver with thrashing fish. He glanced at Sam. The kid seemed okay, well-adjusted, not too bothered by what had happened. In fact, he had a big grin on his face.

"Kinda spoiled a nice party," Sam said. "Chasing us away like that."

"She was right," Joe said.

"About what?"

"We had no business being there."

Sam raised one eyebrow. Behind his cockeyed glasses, it had the effect of making his frames look straight for once.

"Excuse me," Sam said, "but Caroline invited us."

Joe frowned, watching the gulls gulping down pieces of bait fish. He kept his eyes peeled for sharks. There weren't too many bad species in these waters, but every now and then a mako would come along.

"Well, she did," Sam said.

"I know that, knucklehead. But getting invited isn't the point. I should have used common sense. We had no place at a Renwick party."

"Mrs. Renwick's just pissed because her husband had a thing for Mom. So what? They had their day, Mom married my dad, Mr. Renwick became the Hemingway of painters, and life went on. What's her big problem?"

"Sam . . ." Joe said warningly. He thought

of the bloody details of his father's death, and stared angrily at the waves.

"It's not Caroline's fault, her mother being so jealous and neurotic."

"I know," Joe said. It was neither one of their faults, his nor Caroline's, that they had been born to the parents they had.

"Does this mean you won't be saying yes to Yale?"

Joe shot him a look. "I was never going to say yes to Yale."

"Shit," Sam said. "I had big hopes."

"Yeah? Of what?"

"You getting on the faculty. Putting in a good word for me."

"You don't need any good words from me, Sam," Joe said, a laugh escaping. "You've got plenty of your own."

"Still, it would have been nice. Both of us living in the area, teaching together. I wouldn't mind getting to know you a little better," Sam said, playing with a paper clip he had fished out of his shorts pocket.

"You know me fine," Joe said.

"Yeah, whatever. You left home when I was three. And then the drinking . . ."

The blues kept breaking the water's surface, flashing silver in the sun. The birds were feeding, diving. Joe touched the cameo in his pocket. It felt hot in his hand. He'd go below, look for the gold. *Yale. Jesus Christ.*

"You want to dive?" he asked Sam.

Sam shook his head. He was studying a hangnail that had apparently been bothering him. "Nah, that's okay. I have work to do. My research . . . got to get back to Nova Scotia soon."

"Yeah, I remember those days." Joe tried a smile. "Got to get the data before your grant runs out."

"No shit," Sam said, trying to smile back. For Sam, it was a weak act. His mouth barely moved. His eyes were bitter with disappointment. He went back to the hangnail. Joe blinked, tried to get interested in watching the birds again, hating himself.

Black Hall.

He remembered his last dive with Sam, when he had found the cameo. The kid had been trying to talk him into Yale that day too. He had been swimming around, making Joe laugh, bubbles floating out of his mouth, silently forming the words with his lips: *Black Hall.*

What the hell was he pushing. That he and Joe should get a place in town, recreate the family life they never had? Teach together? Discuss their classes on the long commute? Become a team of Ivy League, treasure-hunting brothers? Live in Black Hall so Joe could fall in love with Caroline?

Joe exhaled, stood up, and arched his back. It was all a bunch of crap. Sam was a dreamer, and he always had been. He thought Joe didn't know him well, and maybe that was true. But Joe Connor loved his brother Sam as much as he had ever loved anyone—if he even knew what the word meant—and that was even truer.

Glancing across the sea, Joe faced toward Black Hall. He knew she was there. He had seen Caroline's face while her mother was carrying on. Those gray-blue eyes, the color of a safe harbor, so wild with love and worry for her mother and sister, things Joe could understand but had never had time to feel. How could he? Finishing grad school, finding treasure, giving lectures at places like Yale?

Joe had seen. He had looked in Caroline's face and read it all. But he had been power-less to do anything but the thing he did best: walk away.

And he did it again now.

Leaving his brother alone on deck, he

turned his back. He touched the cameo in his pocket, and it scorched his hand. The salt wind stung his eyes. It burned the spot where Skye had scratched his face. Black Hall was far away, across the open water. Yale was for academics. Let Sam be the professor. Joe was a treasure hunter, plain and simple.

And treasure hunters worked alone.

* * *

Caroline waited for Clea to arrive.

Augusta had taken her needlepoint into the shade, as if she knew her daughters had something important to talk about that did not include her. Or perhaps she wanted it that way. Caroline and Clea climbed the back stairs. The stairway, dark and cool, smelled of ghosts and summer.

"What are we going to say to her?" Clea asked.

"I don't know."

Augusta had told Caroline that Simon had not come home last night. His car was still missing. Knowing Skye was alone, they walked into the room and stood at the end of her bed, watching her sleep. Caroline's heart was in her throat.

Skye was curled up, a white sheet pulled to her chin. She looked so young. Homer lay at the foot of her bed, curled up in a ball. At the sight of Caroline, he raised his head, eased off the bed, and stretched. His bones were stiff; he moved like a creaky old man. Trudging over to Caroline, he raised his white muzzle to be petted. They looked into each other's eyes, and Caroline saw his throat vibrating with unuttered sound. Her heart filled with love for the dog, and for the girl he had signed on to protect.

"Skye," Caroline said, her voice low.

"Wake up. It's morning," Clea said, in her best mother's voice.

Skye rolled over. She opened her eyes, saw her sisters then closed them again with a moan. Her eyes looked sunken, her mouth tight. She lay still, a rabbit trying to hide.

"Come on, Skye," Caroline said, opening the curtains. "We're going to the beach."

Skye took her time.

She showered. She fixed a cup of coffee, then felt too sick to drink it. She made some calls from the phone in the library—her sisters assumed she was looking for Simon. They did not ask. Simon was irrelevant.

Rocking on the front porch while Clea

watered the garden, Caroline remembered going to Firefly Beach as children. She and her sisters had simply pulled on their bathing suits, run outside, flown down the worn cliff stairs. Now she sat with Homer, trying to be patient. He lay on his side with his eyes open, watching her rock back and forth.

But finally Skye was ready, and down the steps they went. Homer went through the garden, smelling all the rosebushes, giving the women a head start.

"I'm sorry about what happened with Joe," Skye began. "I feel like it was my fault that Mom—"

"Stop, Skye," Caroline said. "It wasn't your fault. It doesn't matter anyway. Okay?"

Waves broke just offshore and raced in white trickles over the sand flats of low tide. The sea air felt fresh and cool on their bare arms and legs as they walked through the shallow water. The *Meteor* rocked on her mooring, way offshore, and Caroline tried not to look. She felt uneasy enough.

When they reached a silvery log high above the tide line, deep in the spartina haunted by fireflies, driftwood from many winters ago, they sat down. Sandpipers skittered across the wet sand, and it glistened like a mirror. Skye held her head in her hands. Homer had been making his way slowly down the stairs. The minute his paws hit the sand, he took off in a run, flying down the tide line like a young dog.

Caroline nudged Skye.

Skye raised her head. Her dull eyes suddenly brightened. She smiled, watching Homer chase sea gulls away from a dead horseshoe crab. His shoulders were tired, but his face was proud. Tongue lolling out, he glanced at the sisters.

"Look," Caroline said. "He wants to make sure we see him."

"Good dog!" Clea called. "Scaring all the sea gulls."

He nuzzled the crab carapace. It was a large crab, the size of a dinner plate, its stiff tail a foot long. Turning the creature over, he made sure it wouldn't bite. Then he grabbed the shell in his teeth and carried it, tail swinging like a pendulum, to lay at Caroline's feet.

"He's your dog," Skye said. Caroline knew without looking that Skye was crying.

"He loves you," Caroline said. "He doesn't want you feeling bad all the time."

Skye didn't reply. She stared at the sand between her feet. She used her index finger to wipe her tears.

"What are we going to do, Skye?" Caroline asked.

"Do?" Skye asked, looking up. Her face was flushed, tear-streaked. It bore the brownish remnants of bruises from her car accident.

"Dad died drunk," Caroline said. "We never talk about it. We say he had stomach cancer, that he died because the radiation didn't work, but that's not the whole truth."

"Stop, Caroline," Skye said.

"Let her, Skye," Clea said.

"You're in on this?" Skye asked, sounding betrayed. Clea nodded.

"Remember his last few months? How he spent all his time at my bar? How he wasn't supposed to have 'cocktails' with his medication, but he did anyway?" Caroline paused, but Skye wouldn't respond. "Drinking made him so mean, and Dad wasn't a mean man."

"He was dying, Caroline."

"But he didn't have to die drunk, Skye. He could have faced the truth, faced us. He could have let us help him. We would have told him it was okay, that we forgave him for whatever he thought we hated him for. Hated himself for."

"Don't say he hated himself," Skye said.

"He did. Last night Mom reminded me of

something. He stopped painting. Just *stopped*."

"Remember how hard it used to be to get him out of his studio, to come down for dinner?" Clea asked.

"Even for Thanksgiving or Christmas," Caroline said. "Whenever he was home, he was painting in his studio. I'd want him to play catch, or to drive me somewhere, but if he had the door closed, all bets were off. Things changed right around the time he started drinking. All of a sudden, he never worked again. He just wouldn't let himself. And Dad loved to paint."

"So much," Clea said.

"Maybe he was blocked," Skye said. "You don't know how that feels."

"It felt like he stopped loving us," Caroline said. "I don't know about you, but that's how it felt to me. Blocked from painting, blocked from loving his family. Drinking all the time. We *loved* him, Skye."

"Maybe he couldn't help himself."

"I've never understood," Caroline said. "To be such a wonderful artist, to be able to express all that—important things—and to purposely lock it inside. That's what he did. Shut us out."

"He had Mom."

"He was mean to Mom too. She loved him so much, she'll protect him forever. But he shut her out too."

"Stop it," Skye said, putting her hands over her ears. Tears were streaming from her eyes. "It's because of me, I know that. I shot that boy. Dad couldn't bear it, he felt so guilty for putting the gun in my hand. So if I kill myself, do you think I care?"

"You have to care," Caroline said, grabbing Skye's hands.

"Why?"

"Because we need you. We love you so much—"

"You don't need anyone," Skye blurted out, jumping to her feet. "You're a bitter woman, Caroline. Listen to you! Attacking Dad like this!"

"I'm not attacking him. I—"

"You should feel sorry for him, being unable to paint. That must have felt like death. Worse than death, for Dad. You're so selfish, all you care about is your own agenda. Making *me* feel bad. I tried to apologize before for what happened with Joe, and do you even give a shit?"

"Skye!" Caroline said, stunned.

"You're so high and mighty. Miss Perfect. Simon always says it about you, and he's right. I agree with him."

"Cool down," Clea suggested, touching Skye's arm.

"I'm not perfect. I never said that—" Caroline said.

"You're more like Dad than I am. So what if I drink? At least I feel! You're so closed off, so steel-plated, you won't even accept an apology."

"You don't owe me—"

"*Owing* has nothing to do with it. I feel awful about what happened at the ball. Horrible! But what's it to you? What do you care if Joe walks out of your life? So what if he takes off? He'd find out soon enough how cold you are. You don't care. You're too busy living my life."

"I don't want to live your life," Caroline said.

"You act like you do. Trying to control me all the time . . ."

"Skye—"

"Why *wouldn't* you rather have my life?" Skye asked, weeping. "I'm the one who does things. I took the chance of falling in love with someone, marrying him. You just try to get me to leave him. You're like a frustrated saint. Martyring around all over the place. *I* killed Andrew Lockwood, not you, Caroline. You held his hand, you walked me out of the woods. But I killed him."

"Skye," Caroline said, struggling to keep her voice steady. "I never said—"

"Get mad, Caroline. *React!* Jesus Christ! Don't stay so calm, don't be so fucking afraid of upsetting me."

Paralyzed with shock, Caroline could neither speak nor move.

"And stop trying to take over my life," Skye said viciously. "You don't know how I feel about anything."

She ran down the beach.

January 2, 1980

Dear Joe,

It's been so long since I've heard from you. Please write back. I miss you. I still love you.

C.

April 30, 1980

Dear Caroline,

This is my last letter to you. You knew, didn't you? All that shit about trust, about best friends, about our families, about LOVE. And you knew.

You were there. My dad died in your kitchen. I know the whole stupid story now. Your family's not the only one with a gun. Did you hear the shot, C? Did you watch him die?

It sucks, you knowing all along. Did you just think I was a jerk? Were you and your sisters laughing at me? Or did you just think I wouldn't find out?

Well, I found out.

Don't write back. I hate you, your father, that house of hell you call Firefly Hill.

Joe Connor

May 12, 1980

Dear Joe,

Please don't hate me. I kept it secret because I didn't want to hurt you. Your father came here, it's true, you knew that already. I knew, but believe me, Joe: I never, never wanted to hurt you. The opposite.

I'm so sorry. If I could take it back—all of it, any of it—I would. Please, please don't hate me. You don't know what your friendship means to me. If you can't love me anymore, I understand. But don't hate me. I'm only sixteen, and you're only seventeen. I can't stand thinking of all that life waiting for me if you hate me.

Love,

Caroline

P.S. Please write back, Joe. Anything you want to know, I'll tell you. I'm here, and I always will be.

CHAPTER FIFTEEN

Every year Skye and Clea helped Caroline clean up after the ball. It was a tradition, something neither of them ever missed. Skye was half dreading it; she didn't want to face Caroline after the scene on the beach the day before. But when Skye walked into the inn, Michele said Caroline had called in sick. She had asked not to be disturbed. Skye was on her way over, to knock on the door of her cottage, when Clea intercepted her.

"Hello, my little storm cloud," Clea said, kissing her.

"Is she really upset?" Skye asked.

"She's really tired."

"I want to talk to her—"

"She's sleeping late. Just let her rest," Clea said.

"Is it because of me—?"

"Even if it is, just leave her alone right now."

With guidance from Michele, Clea and Skye went straight to the task of cleaning up the ball. Every year it was the same thing. All the planning, the arranging, the anticipation, the decoration, had lasted for months. All year, everyone at the Renwick Inn looked forward to the Firefly Ball. And when it was over, Caroline and her sisters pulled the whole thing apart. But this year Caroline wasn't around to help.

Taking down the paper lanterns reminded Skye of taking the lights off a Christmas tree. She stood on the ladder, looping the electrical cord over her arm. Swallows swooped in and out of the barn, brushing by her hair. She felt dizzy with a hangover and shame for what she had said to Caroline. Her mad twin had been in command.

When the telephone rang in the inn, she heard it jingle through the trees and almost fell off the ladder. She had left word with her mother that she was there, and she hoped it was Simon, looking for her. He hadn't surfaced since last night. But it was just someone calling for a dinner reservation.

"Hey, Michele," Skye asked when the manager walked by, taking another loop of wire. "Are the *Meteor* guys on the books?"

"No," Michele called.

Skye watched her walk across the wide porch, through the big door with its fanlight window. She knew better than to be surprised. But she felt an ache anyway, deep inside. She had worried all along that Joe's reentry into Caroline's life had been temporary.

"Hear that?" Skye asked Clea.

"Yes," Clea said.

"Shit," Skye said sadly.

"He'll be back," Clea replied with quiet confidence.

When they finally brushed the dirt off their hands and went inside the inn, Skye's back ached and her legs felt tired. She went into the bar for a beer but took a glass of ice water instead. There, pausing for a minute, her gaze fell upon one of her father's pictures. Very tiny, just four inches square, it showed a marsh.

Skye gazed at the watercolor, its greens and golds flowing into each other, just as they did in the salt flats themselves. She recognized the scene: It was the Black Hall marshes, with the Wickland Light shimmering in the background. When Skye looked at his pictures, she knew she was seeing one very specific moment in time. The cloud would pass, or the sun would move, and everything would change.

"He was a wonderful painter," Clea said.

"Amazing," Skye agreed.

"You inherited his talent."

"Thank you," Skye said.

"You heard what we were saying yesterday, didn't you?" Clea asked, gesturing at Skye's glass of water.

"Maybe a little," Skye said, sipping the water.

"You can't make beautiful sculptures if you're . . ."

Skye smiled, grateful that Clea had spared her the end of the sentence. Caroline would have said "dead" or "drunk."

"I know," Skye said.

On the other wall were the three portraits of Skye and her sisters Hugh had done after the hunts. Skye stared at the image of Caroline holding the dead fox. The winter light was cold and blue. The snow was deep, the stream black ice. The fox hanging limp with a line of blood drizzling from its mouth.

"Clea, look."

Staring at Caroline's portrait, Skye saw something she had never noticed before: Her father had painted a tear. It might have been a shadow, but from a certain perspective it was definitely a tear.

"Was that always there?" Skye asked.

"Yes," Clea said.

"Are you sure?"

"I'm positive. I used to wonder why Caroline had one and we didn't."

Looking at the picture, Skye had always felt sad, but she had never seen the tear before. Had Caroline actually cried the day she killed the fox? Had their father guessed that the hunts were laced with tragedy, that they would doom his family, not save it? Or had Caroline?

"Dad didn't usually make statements like that in his work. He'd leave everything to the imagination of the viewer. He must have felt pretty strongly about showing Caroline crying."

"She carries the weight of the world, Skye," Clea said gently, making Skye feel twice as guilty as she did already. "Dad just painted what he saw."

* * *

Joe Connor climbed out of the sea and let the dark water stream off his body. It ran down the deck into the scupper. He felt cold and clean. Night had fallen while he was down in the wreck. The fog had closed in; it wrapped the Meteor, heavy and gray, and sonorous tones of bell buoys and the foghorn at Moonstone Point carried across the water. He looked for Sam, but he wasn't on deck.

Operations were shutting down for the night. The compressor was off. Divers were slipping out of wetsuits, heading below for dinner. Joe was glad. Let them celebrate; today they had reached the mother lode.

The chests were buried under tons of mud and wreckage. Based on measurements taken of the keel, Joe estimated the vessel to be about two hundred and twenty tons, most of it corrugated aft, when the ship rammed the reef. The site was a nightmare of broken spars, splintered planks, mountains of ballast stones. But through careful tunneling, scientific estimation, and blind luck, that morning Dan had located the first chest.

Joe was the second man on the scene. They had swum down with lights, passing the bones of Elisabeth Randall. Joe's thoughts went straight to Clarissa, to the cameo he had found, to Caroline. Reminding himself that controlled emotions were key to breathing steadily underwater, he forced the thoughts from his mind.

Dan signaled from up ahead. Joe followed. Zigzagging through an obstacle course of jagged rocks and smashed wood, they shined their lamps into what looked like a devil's cave. Pitch-black, it was guarded by notched and pointed shards of wreckage. But just inside, nestled in the sandy sea bottom, was the chest.

Black wood encircled by bronze bands, it lay on its side. Two hasps had snapped free. Some of the gold had spilled out, creating a barnacle-encrusted trail of treasure. The divers followed it to the source, then hovered outside the possibly precarious "cave," trying to determine how many other chests were inside and how safe it would be to proceed.

"What do you think, captain?" asked Dan, coming up behind him on deck.

"It was an exciting day. You did good."

"Thanks," Dan said, grinning. He took a long drink of beer from a bottle. From down

below came the sounds of the crew celebrating, retelling the triumphant moments.

"Seen Sam?" Joe asked.

"He's eating," Dan said.

Joe nodded. Sam had packed his bags.
Walking past his cabin, Joe had noticed the
knapsack and duffel bag full and stowed in
the corner, ready to go. But since the other
night, when they'd had their conversation
about Yale, Sam hadn't said anything about
leaving.

"We'll shore up those timbers tomorrow,
just to be safe," Joe said.

"I say we go in with the hoist tonight, se-
cure the chest right away. We can dive
tonight, Joe. Let's—"

"We go tomorrow, Danny," Joe said. He
spoke curtly, but with respect. He didn't like
being second-guessed by his men. He was
the captain, and he proceeded with a scientist's caution. Dan was a salvage man out
of Miami, one of the professional pirates.
He knew his stuff, but he was at odds with
the oceanographers. Pirates were greedy
by trade and by nature.

"Come on, Joe. The whole thing could
shift—" Dan exploded.

"Tomorrow," Joe said, walking away.

He stood at the rail, trying to control his anger. He'd been on plenty of treasure operations where impatience had killed the whole enterprise. Wrecks had collapsed, the gold had been lost. Crewmates had died. So you had to move with care, one step at a time. On the other hand, he knew Dan was right: Just because you had found the gold today didn't mean it would be there tomorrow. The sea never stood still.

Joe was as impatient as the next man. He wanted to get out of there, finish his mission, get away from Black Hall as fast as he could; if the wreck weren't so unstable, he'd go down right then, yank the treasure chest up with the hydraulic winch, have his money counted by sunup, and be ready to go. The temptation was strong.

"Hey, aren't you gonna eat?" Sam asked, coming up with a plate of peach pie.

"Yeah, I was checking the charts."

Sam's brow was furrowed. He tried to straighten his cockeyed glasses, and the fork balanced on his plate clattered to the deck. "Here, this is for you," he said.

"Thanks," Joe said. He took the plate, watched Sam wipe the fork on his shirttail. The brothers' eyes met, and they grinned.

On holidays, when Joe was home from school, they had always fought over washing dishes. They both hated the chore and they had both perfected ways of getting out of it.

"It's good pie," Sam said, handing him the fork.

"Hmmm," Joe said, taking a bite. "So. Were you gonna tell me you're planning to leave? Or were you just going to go?"

"I was going to tell you," Sam said, trying to use his thumbnail to tighten the tiny screw holding the earpiece on his glasses.

Joe waited. Watching the awkward kid trying to get hold of that minuscule screw was putting his stomach in a knot. He had to hold himself back to keep from grabbing the glasses out of Sam's hand.

"I was planning to leave tomorrow," Sam said, fiddling with the screw.

"Hmmm," Joe said.

"Thinking about it anyway."

"Yeah?"

Sam looked up. He was waiting for Joe to talk him into staying. Joe could feel it in the pit of his stomach. He dug into the pie again, just for a diversion. He could barely eat the stuff. His appetite was gone, and he hadn't slept right in days, since the night of the ball. He was a mess of contradictions, and he knew it.

Joe wanted Sam to stay, but he couldn't wait for him to leave either. His few moments of sleep last night, he had dreamed of Caroline, of putting his arms around her and kissing her soft mouth, but when he was awake he thought of their parents, of all the history, of the scene her mother had caused.

"So," Joe said finally, putting down the pie plate. "You can't make up your mind."

"Not really."

"Well," Joe said slowly. "Tell me your reasons for both sides."

"Okay," Sam said, perching on the rail. He was so clumsy, so accident-prone, Joe had to fight the urge to grab him by the collar and haul him off to keep him from going overboard. It was an exercise in tolerance to let him stay there. "I should get back to work. The whales aren't in the passage, but I could be taking water samples, measuring salinity . . ."

"Stuff like that," Joe said, agreeing.

"Or I could stay here . . ."

"Yeah?"

"A little longer. The gold's pretty cool, and we found the mother lode today. I'd like to be here when we bring it up."

"Hmm," Joe said, smiling inwardly at the "we."

"So . . . you can see my dilemma," Sam said. "I don't want you to think I'm after anything. I mean, any of the gold."

"I don't," Joe said quickly.

"Because, frankly, I think gold sucks compared to other things. You know? Other things matter more."

"Yeah? Like what?" Joe asked, thinking of his own list.

"Well, family," Sam said. "Nature. The ocean. Love, I guess."

Joe nodded. He looked across the water, at the lighthouses blinking on the mainland. The night air sent a chill down his back. Love. Joe whistled.

"Oh, yeah," Sam said. "One more thing for the list. Good peach pie."

"That pie was great," Joe said, nodding. "Thanks for bringing it to me."

"No sweat. Great enough to matter more than gold?"

"Tough call," Joe said.

Sam was about to give up on his glasses.

Sliding them back on, he glanced over and saw Joe holding out his hand.

"Give me your specs," Joe said, gesturing "come on," and Sam handed them over. Joe reached into his pocket, pulled out his knife. He had been away at school, absent from Sam's childhood and all the toys an older brother might have put together, bicycles he might have repaired, but standing on the deck of the *Meteor,* Joe tightened the screws on Sam's glasses.

"There," he said, handing them back.

"Hey," Sam said, putting them on. Although straighter, the frames were still crooked, and Sam was grinning.

"They look good," Joe said inanely.

"I think I need a new prescription," Sam said.

The *Meteor* rode higher on the rising waves, and the breeze was picking up. Here they were, standing on the deck of a treasure ship, talking about eyeglasses, when the feeling of good-bye was hanging in the air. *Good peach pie. Great.*

"So, how much longer you guys staying up here?" Sam asked.

The question took Joe by surprise. He hadn't thought in terms of the calendar. He had been thinking about the wreck, the gold, and some unfinished business on land. He wanted to visit Firefly Hill, see the spot where his father had died. He was his father's only son, and he wanted to pay his respects. But he knew none of it would take much more than a week.

"Ten days?" Joe asked. "At the most."

"Because," Sam said, "I was thinking I'd stick around for a few more days. Maybe help out, bringing up the gold or something. Recording sediment samples. Unless I'll be in the way."

Joe shifted his gaze from the horizon to his brother. He shook his head.

"No," he said. "You won't be in the way."

Sam nodded.

Joe wanted him there. But he wasn't good at saying what he wanted, getting the things Sam had mentioned earlier. If it was an object, if it lay on the sea bottom buried in silt, if centuries had left their mark in its metal, Joe Connor was your man. But if it lived and breathed, if it had a name and knew the meaning of love, forget it. Joe was out of his element.

And yet, here was his brother, sticking around for a little while longer. Joe hadn't even had to ask. Imagine what might happen if he tried opening his mouth. If he tried leaving his ship, heading for solid land, driving to someone's door.

Tried to say what was on his mind, in his dreams.

Just imagine.

* * *

Skye sat on the window seat in the bedroom she still shared with Simon. She loved foggy nights. They made her feel safe and protected. She believed the fog hid sins, provided a place for people to hide. Skye had felt scared and sinful for so long, and the fog had always been a refuge.

She had clay under her fingernails. Today she had sculpted for hours in her studio. Somehow the tide had turned. She didn't understand how, but speaking up to Caroline had loosened something inside. Or maybe Caroline had finally hit home. Back at work she had tried again to do *Three Sisters,* a piece that would capture the way she felt about herself, Clea, and Caroline.

It had to show their closeness, but it had to show their separateness too. Skye had tried to sculpt it all different ways: abstract, very abstract, representational, surreal. She had formed one solid mass, meant to express her feelings about sometimes not knowing where she ended and her sisters began. One angry day, she had plunked down three separate balls of clay, unformed and unconnected, to show how immature she and her sisters really were and how little they really knew one another.

But ever since the other morning, on Firefly Beach with Caroline, something new was emerging. Skye was doing a piece of three women standing in a circle. They were holding hands, with one woman looking into the center of the circle, one looking out, the other looking in.

She found the combination intriguing. Because there were three, at all times two sisters holding hands would be facing the same direction. And one would be facing a different way. No matter how you looked at it, two would always be united. And one would be separate. But which two? And which one?

Doing the work, Skye felt a little safer than she had been feeling. She knew she was struggling. She needed that intense connection with her sisters, but at the same time she shrank from it.

For such a long time she had thought her main problem was the resentment she felt about Joe's father killing himself in the kitchen downstairs, her mother offering to trade her own life—and Skye's—for Caroline's. The beauty of a wild life, she thought. With so many traumatic events to choose from, how did you isolate the one that was making you would be relieved to die?

For all these years she had thought she was the only one to suffer. The others had found a way to beat the sorrow, to escape its spell. Out of three girls, why her? They had all survived the hunts, all carried guns. Why had she been the one to make an irrevocable mistake? To kill a man.

She never talked about it, had hardly ever told a soul. Her sisters knew some, and her father, but her husband didn't and neither did her mother. The details of that day were too private and terrible. If she told anyone, if she ever started talking about it, the facts might eat her alive.

Kill, she thought now. It sounded like what it was: sharp and hard and short and ugly like a bullet. She reached behind a book on the little window seat bookcase and took out her vodka bottle. She refilled her small crystal glass and took a sip.

Drunk or just drinking, Skye had passed many hours trying not to think about the hunt, about the gun and Andrew Lockwood, about any of it. She had drunk to get loaded, to get wasted, to get happy, to get sad, because she loved the taste, because she was against killing animals, because her husband liked rough sex, because she had nightmares about snakes under her tent, because her father had stopped loving her, because she hated *Swan Lake,* because she had gone to Redhawk, because she was mad at her mother for offering to trade her life for Caroline's, because Skye herself had killed a man dead.

Working on her small sculpture that day, her impression of *Three Sisters,* Skye felt something shifting. A change in her breathing, a lessening of the pain deep inside. Prey turning on the hunter. Thinking of the worst and knowing she wasn't alone. Nothing extreme, really. Unless you considered the desire to live extreme. Skye teetered on a suicidal seesaw: some days she wanted to live, many she would be relieved to die.

Just thinking that, huddled on her window seat clutching her secret bottle of vodka, Skye thought about living. She took a sip, tears rolling down her cheeks. The vodka dulled her feelings, made her fear more manageable, but it killed so many other things too. When was the last time she had enjoyed a morning? Eaten and not felt like throwing up? Left the house and not wanted to hide from the first person she saw? Sculpted something she was halfway proud of?

"You never have to feel this way again."

She thought of the words Joe Connor had said to her, and she wondered what he had meant. She looked at her glass, took another sip. Skye no longer wanted to feel this way. She felt empty and desperate and sick and scared and ready to get better.

She wondered what she would have to do, and at the same time she wondered how a person could call a person on a ship at sea.

CHAPTER SIXTEEN

Augusta's grandchildren were spending the day with her. They were outside, running in mad circles around the yard, loving the world of Firefly Hill as their mother and aunts had as children. Augusta sat on the porch with her tray of drink things and a few old scrapbooks, wishing the kids would tire themselves out and come sit with her. If only she had felt this way thirty years ago.

Augusta had not enjoyed her own children enough when they were young. The worst part was, she had realized it even at the time. She had had no choice in the matter. Like an illness she couldn't cure, she was consumed with their father. The best she could do for her daughters, as much as she loved them, was to *manage* them. Plunk them down with paints and paper; hand them seeds and dirt and a flowerpot; tell them to write poems about their school day. Being with their father had always taken top priority.

When they were tiny she had let them bake cookies and freeze Jell-O in ice cube trays, making a complete mess of the kitchen. She had let them eat their favorite foods, never forced them to have vegetables or fish. The year Caroline was twelve, she had made herself macaroni and cheese every night.

Anything to keep them occupied, so Augusta could be with Hugh. She had been so afraid of losing him. She seduced him every chance she got. Wore negligees in broad daylight just to get his attention. Read art history, studied the collections of great museums to help him further his career. Instead of helping her daughters with their homework.

Hugh had been her obsession. When he was away, she had assumed he was with other women. It drove her crazy, dominated her thoughts. She had tried to concentrate on her daughters, but her own insecurity was much too huge. When Skye would beg for a story or Clea would need help with her music lessons, Augusta would tell them to ask Caroline. So Augusta could be with Hugh.

Augusta's eyes filled, just thinking of him. She had loved him so much, and he had been so difficult. His work came first, then his fun, and somewhere down the list, Augusta and the girls. Or the girls and Augusta. She had never been quite sure of the order, and her jealousy and guilt over this fact grew even greater after the accident at Redhawk.

Hugh's love for the girls showed in their portraits. Especially the ones of Caroline. *Girl in a White Dress,* his most famous work, had caught her beauty, fragility, and solemnity. Augusta still remembered the day he sketched her, right there at Firefly Hill. Augusta had watched, feeling like the wicked stepmother in "Snow White," seething with the wish that Hugh was painting her instead.

Caroline had worn a straight white evening gown. She had stood on the porch, leaning against one of the columns, staring out to sea. Her eyes full of troubled passion, she had the air of a girl in a Greek tragedy. Augusta remembered staring at her oldest daughter, wondering what could make her feel such deep and helpless longing. The expression on her face was authentic sorrow, and it had wrenched Augusta's heart. Hugh had captured the emotion perfectly.

Flipping through the scrapbooks, Augusta sipped her martini and called up memory after memory. She found the articles she had clipped after *Girl in a White Dress* became such a sensation at the Venice Bienniale. Glancing through the piece in *ARTnews,* she ran her fingers over the photo of the painting. The colors were true: Caroline's glossy dark hair, the near-blue tinge of her columnar white dress, the dark blues and grays of the sea and sky.

But it was the look in Caroline's eyes that still took Augusta's breath away. Stunning and haunted. Augusta, and many of the most prominent art critics of the time, had never seen a portrait like it. Staring at Caroline's face as painted by her father, Augusta still wondered: What had caused such anguish? The deaths, she was sure. James Connor and Andrew Lockwood.

Tired of thinking about it, Augusta looked up. She did penance for the past every day, watching Skye dissolve. She couldn't mend that damage, but she could try to be a good grandmother.

"Children, aren't you tired?" she called, her hands cupped to her mouth. "Mark, Maripat! Come on the porch and have a snack."

"What kind of snack?" Mark asked, out of breath.

"Lemon squares," Augusta said, holding out the blue china plate. "I made them myself."

Each child took one. So polite, they said "thank you" and chewed slowly.

"Have another," Augusta said. "Go on. It won't spoil your dinner, and your parents never need to know. Would you like to see some old pictures?"

The children nodded. Augusta made room for them on either side of her. They were towheads, with Clea's beautiful skin and Peter's serious eyes. Mark rested his head on Augusta's shoulder; it made her smile from sheer joy.

Abruptly, she put away the *Girl in a White Dress* scrapbook. And she pulled out one from truly ancient times, her days as a schoolgirl in Providence and Narragansett. She had had a simple, happy childhood. The kind she had always intended to give her girls.

"There's my mother and father, our dog, Spunky . . ." she began.

"Are those your cats?" Maripat asked, pointing at Mew-Mew and Licorice.

"Oh, yes," Augusta said. "We adored our pets. They were just like members of the family!"

"Mommy used to go hunting," Mark said proudly. "She shot a wild pig once."

Augusta blinked. "Wild animals are different," she said stoically, thinking of her daughters hunting. "They can be very, very dangerous."

Eager to get back to happier thoughts, Augusta paged through pictures of her family on the Block Island ferry, in the Arcade between Westminster and Weybosset streets, on the beach at Newport, at her ballet recital in the church hall.

"Who's that?" Mark asked, pointing at a grainy photo of a small dog.

"Oh," Augusta said. "That's Tiny."

"Tiny's cute—a Chihuahua," Maripat asked, smiling at his skinny body and oversized head, his little tongue hanging out. He sat on a satin pillow on Augusta's bed.

The children were waiting, their big eyes looking up at her.

"Tiny," Augusta said, sighing. "Would you like to hear about him?"

"Yes!" Mark and Maripat said at once.

And so, because they had asked so politely, Augusta told them.

It had all started one morning in early June, when Augusta was nine. She had gone out in her dinghy to fish for blues. The sun was high, but the day was chilly. Anchored just beyond Pequot Island, she cast her line into the water. Fish were biting. The blues were running, and they fed upon one another in a cannibalistic frenzy. Augusta caught a six-incher in the process of being eaten by a larger fish.

"The sea roiled with blood and fish guts. Seagulls screamed overhead. You can just imagine. Blues in a feeding frenzy," she said. She told them about seeing something swimming on the surface. At first she had thought it was a shark fin, heading for the blues, on the scent of chum. But it had ears.

"Granny!" Maripat exclaimed.

"Yes, darling. It was Tiny."

"A dog? In the middle of the Sound?" Mark asked.

"Swimming straight for the blues. Now, you know, bluefish have needle-sharp teeth. They travel in gigantic schools, and when feeding, they have been known to massacre anything in their way."

"Granny, we know about bluefish," Maripat said patiently.

"Fine. Anyway, I scooped Tiny from the teeth of death. He was rail-thin, shivering like mad. Half dead. The poor little Chihuahua, I thought. He must have fallen off a yacht passing by."

"You took him home," Mark said.

"Sneaked him in. We already had a dog and two cats, and my parents said *no more.* So I took him up to my room. . . ." Augusta closed her eyes, remembering the cats. She felt a catch in her throat, sipped her drink to push it down. "Tried to feed him Spunky's food, but he wouldn't eat."

"He was probably so tired from falling overboard," Maripat said, touching Tiny's picture with her small finger. "Poor little fella."

"Yes." Augusta stared at the photo. She had taken it herself, posing Tiny on her pink satin pillow. He had sat there, so compliantly. She sighed. "Wouldn't eat. Wouldn't take water. He was shivering like mad, chilled to the bone from his time in the sea. I honestly thought he was going to die."

"Did he?" Maripat asked fearfully.

Augusta paused. "No. That night I took him into my bed. I brought the kitties in with us to keep him warm. We all huddled together, like a family of foxes in a den. Nice and warm, under my lovely down comforter."

"And you warmed him up?" Mark asked hopefully. "And he lived?"

"Oh, yes. He lived," Augusta said, cocking her eyebrow. She gave the children another lemon square. Maripat hesitated, but Mark gobbled his right up.

"And he got along with Spunky and Mew-Mew and Licorice?" Maripat asked, licking the powdered sugar off her fingers.

"Well, no."

"No?" Both children asked, looking disturbed. Augusta began to wonder whether she should have started this story at all. She tried to steer it back to something sweet and cozy.

"Finally, he felt like drinking. I gave him milk from one of my doll's bottles. Then I poured some more into a bowl. I had to go to school, but before I left, I let him have the rest of my cereal."

"Oh, he must have been so happy!"

"Mmm. I went off to school with Spunky—he always followed me. I got such good marks, children," Augusta said, going off on a tangent. "My teachers said I was a star pupil!"

"What about Tiny?" Maripat asked shyly.

"Well, I left him in my room so my mother wouldn't see him."

" 'Cause you hadn't convinced her to let you keep him yet," Mark said reasonably. "Did you leave the cats to keep him company?"

"Yes," Augusta said.

"And did they become best friends?" Maripat asked, happily sensing the end of the story.

"No," Augusta said, knowing she was in too deep. "He ate them."

Maripat's mouth fell open. Mark just stared at the picture album. Trying to comfort them, Augusta scattered some loose photos. Maripat tried to hold her tears inside, but they *spilled* out. "Why?" she asked.

"He wasn't a Chihuahua!" Augusta explained, wanting their sympathy. "It was horrible for me, returning home from school and finding cat fur and blood everywhere. Cat limbs all over the floor, chewed to the bone."

"Mew-Mew, Licorice!" Maripat cried.

Tearfully, Augusta told them about Tiny grinning at the end of Augusta's bed, covered with blood. His little tongue hanging out, a demoniacal mask on his face, his fangs dripping with blood as he sprang for her throat just before she slammed the door shut.

"He was a bandicoot, darlings," Augusta said, eyes shining. "A Vietnamese water rat, one of the most bloodthirsty species of mammal on earth. The veterinarian who came to remove what was left of the cats surmised that the bandicoot had come across the sea on a freighter, whose route had originated in Asia somewhere, and had fallen into our bay."

Just then, Clea walked in to pick up the kids.

They took one look at her and started to wail. Clea dropped the bag of vegetables she was carrying. Opening her arms, she hugged them to her body. They sobbed against their mother's breast.

"Mom," Clea said, panicked. "What happened?"

"Mommy, Granny had a horrible pet that ate her cats," Mark sobbed. "An evil pet who looked like a Chihuahua but wasn't."

"You told them about *Tiny?*" Clea asked with disbelief.

"Well, yes," Augusta said defensively. "I did. They asked!"

"If they asked to play with matches, would you let them? If they wanted dessert before dinner, would you give it to them?"

Augusta tightened her lips, feeling awful. She didn't dare mention the lemon squares. All she had wanted was to spend a few hours with her grandchildren, have them love her a little more. She had thought the story of Tiny would be scary and thrilling.

"I thought children loved scary stories," she said.

Clea just shook her head. She eased Mark and Maripat off the porch, into the yard. Augusta watched her reach down, take first her daughter's hand, then her son's. She walked them toward the beach stairs, and they stood at the top, facing out toward the sea and listening to the waves. Their voices carried, and after a minute the tones of anxiety were gone and they were just a mother and two children talking.

Her chin wobbling, Augusta took another sip of her martini. It tasted warm, watered-down. She had never meant to make the children cry. Augusta had given them the lemon squares, shown them the old pictures only to make them love her. That's all Augusta had ever wanted from any of the children in her life; from any of the people, really.

She glanced around for Homer, the only creature who seemed to take her for exactly who she was, faults and all. But he had wandered off on one of his mysterious outings. Even *he* was sick of her, and Augusta didn't really blame him. She felt like quite a failure. It always seemed to work out wrong.

* * *

"I am so mad at my mother," Clea told Peter.

"What did she do?" he asked.

Clea paused. She was sitting in the curve of his arm, watching their children swim back and forth in the pool. The night was clear. The Pleiades were bright, directly over the chimney, and all the other stars spread down the sky.

"She upset the kids. She told them a really awful story about a pet she had when she was little."

"How bad could a pet story be?"

"Well," Clea said, knowing this fell in the "only in our family" category, "it eviscerated her cats and could have killed my mother in her sleep. I'd say that's good for a few nightmares, wouldn't you?"

"Wow," Peter said. "I never heard about that one."

"Poor Mom," Clea said. "She doesn't get it. She's always been the same. It's as if she wants to do the right thing but can't. She never could."

"Lost in her own world."

"She's so anxious about being loved, she ends up driving people away."

"She should have a little faith."

"In other people? I don't know . . . my father wasn't the faithful type."

"In herself," Peter said. "She's a good woman, and she should trust her instincts. I've heard her say she wished she hadn't let your father take you hunting."

"That would have been a good one to trust," Clea said wryly. Her mother had tried to please him instead of listening to her own maternal instincts. How had that even been possible?

Peter and Clea sat quietly for a while. Clea felt drowsy, lulled by Peter's hand stroking her hair and the sounds of her children playing in the pool. She could get lost in feeling sorry for her mother. How awful it must be to go through life *shielded* from the truth. To be so afraid of your own feelings, you could fail to protect your children.

"Do you want to swim?" Peter asked.

"No, thanks. I'm so relaxed, I don't feel like putting on my suit."

"Just look at that," Peter said.

"What?" Clea asked.

"How confident Maripat seems in the water this summer. Remember how scared she used to be?"

"She would never go in the deep end," Clea said. Last year, when they had installed the pool, Maripat would sit for hours on the curved steps. She would hang on to the side, pulling herself around. Or she would swim the width of the pool and only with her father right beside her—gasping for air with terror in her eyes.

But this summer everything had changed. Clea had driven her to swimming lessons every morning. While Mark played soccer or went to the beach with his friends, Maripat spent hours in swim class, making friends and swimming alongside her teacher.

Peter and Clea now watched their daughter glide back and forth, stopping to splash her brother but neither afraid nor reliant on him. She swam on her own, lost in her thoughts, her strong strokes taking her where she wanted to go.

"She loves it," Peter said.

"She does," Clea agreed proudly. She had taken steps to help her daughter conquer her fear, to help Maripat feel strong and confident in something she had decided to do. It didn't take leaving her alone on a mountain, to pitch a tent and kill her food and lie awake listening to animals moving outside. Just driving her to swimming lessons.

* * *

Caroline was out of breath. She had spent the evening climbing Mount Serendipity, taking the north trail, the one that ran almost straight up the granite ravine. The night was black. It favored the hunted. The stars had come down to strike the crest.

From the ridge she had looked southeast and seen the *Meteor*'s lights shining like stars in the Sound. Staring, she had wondered how much longer Joe would be there.

She had seen an owl flying low through the pines, starlight on its chestnut wings. Honeysuckle grew along the trail, and she now climbed down, breathing its sweet scent of summer. The trail forked halfway down. The wide path went straight to Black Hall Center. Melancholy without knowing exactly why, Caroline took the other, narrower one, that curved left toward the Ibis River.

Almost immediately Caroline saw the fox.

He was hunting along an old stone wall, skulking so close to the ground, she thought at first he was a shadow. His coat was glossy red, the tip of his tail pure white. Caroline stopped dead. She watched him stalk a chipmunk. He crept slowly, stone by stone. His ruff stood on end, his snout pointed straight at the prey. But then he heard Caroline.

They faced each other. Caroline's heart pounded. He looked so small, the size of a miniature collie. He bared his teeth. Lunging once toward Caroline, he flicked his tail and then sprang over the wall. Caroline wasn't afraid. She thought the fox was beautiful. Seeing wild animals up close was one of the best parts of hiking, and she tried to imagine how she had ever killed them. It was never a part of her personality. Yet she could recall perfectly the smell of gunsmoke, the feeling of her eyelashes against the sight.

At home, Caroline stood in her kitchen, breathing hard. She drank a glass of cool water, trying to calm down. Haunted by the memory, by the spirit of that fox, she stared out the window.

She wore khaki shorts and a long-sleeved blue shirt with the sleeves rolled up. Her hair hung loose around her shoulders. Kicking off her hiking shoes, she peeled off her clothes. She was thinking of how good the shower would feel, how she would make the water really hot, when the phone rang. Naked in her bedroom, she answered it.

"Hello?" she said.

"Caroline. It's Joe."

She hadn't expected to hear his voice. She held the phone in her hand but couldn't speak.

"Are you there?" he asked.

"Hi," she said.

"How's your sister?"

"I don't know," Caroline said. She hadn't seen Skye since the altercation on the beach.

"I hated to leave her the other night, and I'm sorry about what happened at your ball. I didn't mean to ruin it—"

"Don't be sorry," she said. "I should have told my mother you'd be there. Somehow I had thought I could keep you two apart."

The phone line crackled, and she imagined the static was normal for a call coming from out at sea.

"Our families. That's partly why I'm calling," he said. "I'd like to see Firefly Hill."

"Yes," Caroline said, understanding why that would be important to him.

"Do you think it would be possible? I know your mother doesn't want me there, and I don't blame her. But I want to visit—" he began, then stopped himself.

"I can arrange it," Caroline said. Did this mean he was getting ready to leave the area? "When would you like to go there?

"Soon," he said. "Tomorrow we're going to bring up the main chest. That should take all day. But once we get it, we'll be done. Anytime after that."

"How about Wednesday?" she asked quietly.

"Wednesday would be fine."

They arranged to meet at her place, and Caroline would drive him over to Firefly Hill. She would make sure her mother was out, so there wouldn't be any dramatic confrontations.

"Hey, Caroline—" he said all in a rush.

"Yes?"

The line was silent except for the static. It buzzed for a moment, neither one of them saying anything.

"Thanks," he said finally. Then he hung up.

* * *

Two nights later, Simon didn't even bother to sneak in. The old Porsche came up the driveway with the stereo playing so loud, it woke Skye out of a sound sleep. Entering the back way, he let the door slam behind him. He opened the refrigerator, poured himself a glass of something. When he was ready, he tromped upstairs.

When he entered their room, he had the good manners to move a little more quietly.

Not suspecting Skye was wide awake, he stood at the window for a moment, drinking wine as he surveyed the moon on the water. Probably he was thinking of the painting he would do. He would call it *Nocturne #62*—or whatever number he was up to—because he called all his paintings *Nocturne*-something. He was probably setting a price for it in his mind.

He unbuttoned his shirt, then ran his hand over his bare chest. Half turning from the window, he started unzipping his jeans. He was lost in thought. He sipped his wine. His face, illuminated by moonlight, was con-templative. Maybe he was thinking of how famous he would be. Or maybe he was thinking about the waitress he had just left.

"Did you have fun?" Skye asked from her spot in the bed, making him jump.

"Oh, you're awake?" Simon asked.

"Yes."

"Usually you're not."

That stung. Skye knew he meant that usually she was passed out from drinking too much. But she had not had anything to drink that night. She was shaking a little, her hands trembling under the covers. Her body was detoxing, and it wasn't easy. She had a dry mouth. A headache. But it was worth it. She wanted to pay attention. She wanted to see things—everything—even her husband coming home late from his tryst. Skye was tired of hiding.

"I'm awake now," she said quietly.

"Yeah. Well."

"Where were you?"

"What am I supposed to do? Give you an account of every move I make? If you wanted that sort of husband, you should have married Peter."

"I realize that now," Skye said, "but I want to know anyway. Where were you?"

"In my studio. Painting in the barn."

"Those aren't your painting clothes," Skye said.

"How would you know?" Simon asked, laughing. "They were right about the rehab, Skye. You do have a problem. You're too drunk most of the time to notice what the hell I wear to paint."

"I'm not drunk tonight," Skye said calmly.

"Whatever," Simon said.

"I want a divorce," Skye said.

That silenced him. He finished undressing. He drank a little more of his wine. She imagined that he might be wondering how he could continue to have it both ways: He wanted Skye and the comfort of her money and the prestige of her name, and he also wanted to go to bed with anyone else he desired.

Simon stood naked in the moonlight. He was tall and thin, and the blue light made his body look wet. Again he sipped his wine, stroked his chest. He started coming toward Skye. He sat on the edge of the bed, offered her a drink from his glass. She shook her head. Placing it on the table, he reached under the covers.

He slid his hands up under her nightgown. He brushed her skin, caressed her breasts. Skye hadn't been touched that way for so long. She bit her lip and arched her back. He kissed her neck, his tongue darting out to taste her skin. It felt so good, Skye thought she would moan. But she didn't.

"Um, Simon?" she said.

"Yeah?" He kept licking and sucking her neck, touching her hips and belly with his warm hands.

"Get out of my bed."

"You know you don't mean that," he growled.

"Get out of my bed," she said again. "Get

your sleazy clothes off my floor, and get out of here now. Do you really think I want you to touch me after you've been with another woman? Didn't you hear me before? I want a divorce."

"You're fucking kidding me," he said. "You can't be serious." He sat up straight, staring down at her.

"I'm serious," Skye said, her throat aching.

He yanked himself off the bed. He tore into his clothes, slamming around the room. He was swearing, hate on his tongue. He wasn't getting his own way with her. He never would again. Somehow the courage Skye had found on the beach with Caroline and Clea was following her into the rest of her life. She was putting an end to anything that hurt her.

Simon left the room. Skye heard his boots on the stairs, and then she heard the door slam behind him as he walked out of the house. Trembling, Skye reached for the telephone by her bed.

It was five in the morning on Wednesday— nearly dawn—but she dialed Caroline's number anyway. That's the way it was between them: Anywhere, anytime Skye needed her, Caroline would be there. They hadn't spoken since their fight on the beach, but Skye didn't care. She had to reconnect with her sister. Trying to hold the receiver steady she heard Caroline's sleepy voice answer.

"It's me," Skye said.

"Are you okay?" Caroline asked, worry immediately in her voice.

"I'm fine," Skye said. "Caroline, I'm so sorry to call you so early."

"I'm glad you did," Caroline said.

"I just asked Simon to leave," Skye said. "It just happened, and I wanted to tell you. Can you believe it? I told him I want a divorce. I'm just so sick of it."

"Oh, Skye," Caroline said. "I'm glad."

"I just want to get better," Skye said. As she spoke, she felt her voice getting hoarser. She knew that what she was saying was so true, but so hard. Getting better: It should be the easiest thing in the world, but at five in the morning, trembling and desiring a drink to block it all out, to obliterate the pain, she had never imagined anything harder.

"I want you to get better," Caroline whispered.

"I haven't had a drink all day," Skye said.

"I'm so proud of you," Caroline said. And Skye remembered all the other times Caroline had been proud of her: At her spring concerts, her school plays, when she was six and did the best cartwheel in first grade, when she was twelve and made her first sculpture, when she went to college, when she moved to Rome, when she had her first one-woman show in New York.

Caroline had always been there, and Caroline had always been proud. Skye gripped the receiver harder to quell the trembling in her hands.

"I'm sorry," Skye said. "About the things I said on the beach."

"Don't be sorry," Caroline said. "It kills me to admit you have a point."

"You mean . . . you're sorry?"

"Did I say that?" Caroline asked, gentle laughter in her voice.

"I'm lucky to have you," Skye said.

"Took the words out of my mouth," Caroline said. "I'm lucky to have you too."

"I'm going to try to sleep now."

"Do you want me to come over?" Caroline asked. "Do you need me to sit with you?"

"No," Skye said, hanging on. She knew this would pass. She knew it would.

"Are you sure?" Caroline asked. "I'll just be with you if you like. We can walk down to the beach and maybe go for a swim." But even as the words came out sounding sure and positive, Skye heard her stop. She was doing it again, trying to make everything better when Skye had to do it herself.

Skye laughed, and this time Caroline really laughed back.

"That's okay," Skye said. "I'm fine by myself."

"I know."

"Anyway . . ." Skye trailed off, tired now. "Everything will be okay, just as long as you . . ."

"As long as I what?" Caroline asked.

"Love me," Skye whispered.

"That's the easy part," Caroline whispered back.

CHAPTER SEVENTEEN

Caroline stood inside the screen door, where she had been watching for Joe's truck. She wore a buttermilk linen sundress and flat beige sandals, things she might wear to work. As Joe walked up the steps, she felt her pulse jump. Seeing him made her nervous, and as he approached the door, she wished she had not offered to do this.

Standing on the other side of the screen, he looked nervous himself, as if he weren't sure what he was doing there. He gave her a dazed smile. She noticed the lines around his eyes and mouth; he spent a lot of time smiling out in the sun. He wore chinos and a blue oxford shirt. Although the collar was frayed, the shirt was freshly pressed.

"Are you ready?" he asked.

Caroline had planned to ask him in, but she realized there really wasn't any reason for it. So she grabbed her bag. He held the door for her. Their hands brushed, and their eyes met. Caroline blushed, remembering their kiss. When they got to his truck, he put his hand on the passenger door handle.

"I'll take my car. You can follow me," she said, thinking it would be faster for him to return to the dock from Firefly Hill.

"That's okay," he said, pulling open the truck door. "You're doing this for me. The least I can do is drive."

He backed out of her driveway, circled past the inn, and headed east down Beach Road. They passed the Ibis marshes, where the river turned brackish and flowed toward the Sound. Stopping at Black Hall's only traffic light, they watched four teenagers fly by on their bikes. Sea gulls perched on the roof of the gas station.

Joe drove with his elbow sticking out the open window. His blond hair flew in his eyes, and he kept brushing it back. He turned on the radio, then turned it off. Caroline stared out the window, feeling so tense, she didn't know what to say.

"Did you get the chest of gold yesterday?" she asked finally.

"We didn't, actually," Joe said. "We tried, but the sea wouldn't cooperate. The wind kicked up yesterday morning, and then the currents shifted. My guys are thinking of mutiny, they're so ready to finish the job."

"What about today?" Caroline asked.

"Today I had plans," Joe said. "Besides, the currents are still fluky." He tried to smile, but his mouth was tight. His gaze slid over to Caroline. His face was drawn, and she noticed the bluish circles under his eyes.

They were on their way to Firefly Hill, the place where it had all started.

"Did you tell your mother I was coming?" he asked.

"I thought it was better not to." Caroline said. "But she won't be there. My sisters took her to Providence for tea."

"They know?"

Caroline nodded. "I told them. They're glad to help."

"No use upsetting your mother," Joe said.

"Are you okay?" she asked.

"Yeah," he nodded. He glanced over, then back at the road. They were on the stretch where it hugged the rocky shore. The driving was treacherous, but Joe didn't seem to be able to keep from glancing over at Caroline.

"This is it," she said as they rounded the bend. She directed him to turn into the driveway, up the hill into a thicket of dark trees. At the top they emerged back into bright sunlight. Caroline wanted to point out the *Meteor,* which was visible on the horizon, but Joe was staring at the big white house standing between him and the sea. He must have been thinking of his father, his last hour. James Connor had driven up that hill, parked on the rough grass, walked across this very yard.

At the sight of Caroline, Homer trotted over with his towel. He dropped it to say hello, panting up at her with love in his eyes. Joe obviously knew dogs. He offered Homer his hand. The dog sniffed it, then turned quizzically back to Caroline. She took his big head between her hands, shaking it gently. Crouching down, she touched the top of her head to his.

"It's okay, Homer," she said.

"He wants to make sure I'm not going to hurt you," Joe said.

"He knows," Caroline said.

They walked across the back porch, into

the mud room. The wainscoting needed paint. The linoleum was old and cracked. Framed fingerpaintings by all three girls hung on the walls. Caroline could have brought him in the front way, through the big hall with its sweeping stairway, but this was how the family always entered. It was the way his father had come in.

The kitchen was open and airy. Big windows gave onto the lawn, sloping to the ledge that dropped to Long Island Sound. Red clay tiles covered the floor. The big oak table had two coffee cups on it, left from Augusta's and Skye's breakfast. One wall was covered with pictures of the family in other places: Paris, Siena, St. Lucia, Colorado. Between two windows curved a silver fish, stuffed and mounted. It was a landlocked salmon, caught by Caroline at age thirteen.

Joe looked around the room. Caroline could see the pulse beating on the side of his neck. His blue eyes were steady, taking everything in. He stood in the middle of the room, a question on his face.

"Here," Caroline said, taking his hand. It felt big and rough, covered with scars and calluses. No matter what, she would have known the man it belonged to worked on the sea. Pulling gently, she led him to the spot where his father had died.

"Right here?" Joe asked. His tone was neutral. He might have been asking about some historical site that had nothing to do with him. But as Caroline nodded, his eyes began to betray him. They clouded over. His lashes lowered so she couldn't see.

"I don't remember everything," Caroline said, "but I remember thinking he loved you and your mother."

Joe made a sound deep in his throat. "At five years old?"

"Yes. Too young to understand what was happening—" Caroline paused, trying to say it right. Her throat felt dry. "But I understood the tears."

Joe wasn't looking at her. He leaned against the kitchen counter, examining some pebbles someone had left lying there.

"He was crying?"

"Yes," Caroline said, because she couldn't lie to him.

"And angry?"

"At first, yes," she said, trying to remember. She could see the man's red face, the gun wobbling in the air over her head. "But then he just seemed . . . sad. Very, very sad."

Joe moved to the kitchen window. He stood looking at the sea, dark blue against the bright sky. His hands were jammed in his pockets. Beyond the breakers, across a long stretch of water, lay the *Meteor*. He stared at it intently, as if he wanted to fly away from Firefly Hill and be safely back on it. He shot a quick glance at Caroline.

"Where were you?" he asked with his usual wariness.

"That night?" she asked, surprised. She pointed at a spot eighteen inches from where his father had stood. "I was right there."

"A lot for a little girl," he said, still cradling the pebbles.

"Nothing compared to what it was like for you."

Again, a violent breath of air. "I wasn't even here."

"Do you think you should have been?" she asked softly. "Do you think you could have stopped him?"

A shrug. He turned back to the window. The sun was going down, and the cliff's shadow fell across the wide bay. Staring at him, Caroline could read his thoughts.

"He had your picture," Caroline said gently. "He was holding it, and for a minute we held it together, he and I. I've always thought—" She stopped herself.

"Go on."

"I've always thought your father had you with him. The last face he saw was yours. And he loved you so much."

Joe turned from the window. He shook his head, and for a moment he couldn't talk.

"No," he said simply. "The last face he saw was yours. You were with him, Caroline. With him when he died."

Caroline took two steps, and she was in Joe's arms. As he reached for her, she heard the pebbles he had been holding clatter to the floor. She understood his feeling because she wished she could have been with her own father at his death, but he had shut her out long before then. She felt her tears hot against Joe's neck. His strong arms gripped her body, his hands grasping each of her shoulders. He gulped hard, swallowing his own sobs. Behind him, the sea was silver and black, a crescent moon hung over the horizon.

"We loved them," Caroline said of their fathers. "We just thought we'd have them longer."

They stood locked in an embrace. Joe's

hand stroking Caroline's hair. She had wanted to comfort him, but here he was, holding her close, whispering her name, telling her he'd never realized before, never pictured how it had been, how close she had stood to his father, how much it meant to him that she had been there.

The kitchen clock ticked loudly. Waves beat upon the beach, tumbling rocks in their wake. It was time to leave. Augusta would be home soon, and Caroline didn't want to face the explosion her arrival would bring.

Joe looked into Caroline's eyes. He wiped his own face with the back of his hand. Reaching into his pocket for a handkerchief, he offered it to her. She dried her eyes, folded it, and handed it back. She felt his reluctance at having to leave this place where his father had died, and she stood still, waiting.

Without another word, he just walked out the door.

He drove her home. As they got closer to her house, Caroline knew their time together was almost over. She glanced over at Joe. The lines in his brow and around his mouth were deep. There was something going on behind his eyes.

"Thank you for taking me there," Joe said when he caught her looking.

"Oh, Joe," she whispered, overcome.

"I'm glad I went."

Caroline nodded. Joe had recovered his tough reserve. A chilly breeze blew through the truck, blowing his hair into a windy mess.

When they reached the inn, he turned into the wide drive and continued left, down the private road that led to Caroline's house. Sharply trimmed privet hedges lined the road, and the branches of tall maples interlaced overhead. The approach felt safe and private, and at this time of day, just after sundown, it was already very dark.

Parking the car, Joe turned to her. His right arm was stretched out along the seat back. He had a strained smile on his face, as if this were good-bye. He stared at her for a long time, and she began to feel the color creeping into her face. They had come a long way, Caroline and Joe. She wished she could say what she felt, but she didn't believe he wanted to hear.

"Well . . ." she said.

"Yeah," he said, drumming his fingers on the steering wheel.

Gulls cried. Across the river, a whippoor-will began to call. Locusts hummed in the trees. The night sounds got louder.

"I have to get back to the boat, they're expecting me."

"I know," Caroline said, trying to smile.

Joe stared at her. He looked out the window. A minute passed.

"Say good-bye to Sam," she said, her hand on the door handle."

"I know I should leave," Joe said slowly. "But the thing is, I can't."

Caroline looked over, her pulse quick and light.

"We could have tea . . ." she began to say.

He opened his door even before she finished the sentence. They walked up her flag-stone walk, and Caroline used her key to open the front door. Augusta always left Firefly Hill wide open, but Caroline had locks and alarms.

Joe entered, looking around. At Firefly Hill his attention had been on one spot, but here he seemed interested in everything. The rooms were spare and cool, done in the colors of dusk. Her floors were wood, stained deep brown and highly polished.

In the living room, she had a cream-colored

sofa with a heathery dark blue throw folded across the back. A matching armchair sat by the gray stone fireplace. A single mahogany table held a blue glass vase containing wildflowers she had picked on her hike up Mount Serendipity. There were no rugs.

They walked into the kitchen, and Caroline turned on some lights. It was a cook's kitchen with a stainless steel stove and refrigerator, copper pans from Paris, plenty of counter space for chopping. The cabinets were made of warm, pale-gold natural wood. They seemed to glow from within. The kitchen table was round, lacquered black. In its center were tiny silver salt and pepper shakers, a silver sugar bowl, and a single framed picture of Caroline, Clea, and Skye.

Caroline filled a big copper kettle. She turned the heat on low, a ring of blue flame. Turning to Joe, she saw him studying the photo. It showed the three girls dressed in warm jackets, each holding a fish they had caught. Caroline was about eleven.

Replacing the frame on the kitchen table, Joe continued to look around the room.

"It's different from your mother's house," he said.

Caroline nodded, pouring milk into a silver pitcher.

"Hers is warm and cozy, all cluttered up with life," she said. "This place is . . ." She had been about to say "cool and spare, like me," but she didn't want him thinking she was feeling sorry for herself, looking for a contradiction. But the fact was, Caroline felt empty and alone, as if they had already had their tea and Joe was already gone.

"It's beautiful," he said. "I was thinking it's kind of mysterious."

"You were?"

"Yeah," he said. The woodwork in Caroline's kitchen was painted slate gray. One section of the wall was pumpkin. Joe went to the kitchen window, when he noticed six moonshells arranged there. Reaching into his pocket, he took something out. He examined it, then placed the object on the sill with the shells. He glanced over his shoulder at Caroline.

Slowly she approached. Her heart was beating fast. Caroline's desire for order was reflected in the shells, spaced at three-inch intervals in a straight line. Exactly three inches past the last shell, Joe had placed a cameo. Caroline stared at it.

"It's from the *Cambria*," Joe said in a low voice. "It belonged to Clarissa's mother."

Caroline, moving to touch the cameo, looked at Joe first. He took it off the sill and placed it in her hand. She stared at the fine rim of gold, worn to a thin line. The cameo itself was incandescent.

Held to the light, the carving was ivory, the background translucent pale green glass. The woman looked noble, with strong cheekbones and a straight nose, her hair drawn back, her chin tilted up.

"She looks like Clea," Caroline said.

"She looks like you," Joe said.

Caroline could barely see. For the second time that evening, she wiped away tears. She was incredibly moved, holding this jewel that had belonged to a family she had come to care about. She thought of Elisabeth Randall's bones lying in the eel grass, the tides sweeping in and out. The cameo felt light in her hand. It was so fragile and delicate, yet it had survived underwater for two hundred years.

"It's amazing," she said, handing it to him.

"I want you to keep it," he said, pressing it into her palm.

Caroline was stunned. She looked into

Joe's eyes, and she saw the beginning of a smile. "I can't," she said, clearing her throat.

"Why?"

"Shouldn't it go to someone else? Clarissa's descendants? Or the town?"

"There aren't any Randalls we can find. And the town . . . it doesn't work that way." He laughed. "I'm a treasure hunter, remember? I filed my claim and got my permit, and this is treasure."

"Your daughter—"

"I don't have a daughter," Joe said.

"Well, if you ever do."

Joe was staring into Caroline's eyes, his blue eyes dark and unflinching. His wide lips wanted to smile; she could see it in the corners. He was amused with the awkwardness of her gift-taking, but she was always like this. At Christmas she felt uncomfortable when it was her turn to reach under the tree.

"I don't—" she began, looking at the cameo in her hand.

"You have to," he said a little roughly.

She was thinking of all the reasons she shouldn't accept anything from Joe Connor, all the anger and hurt that had passed between them, the way they had tried a friendship this summer, until the Firefly Ball came and his true feelings had come out.

"Sometimes it's more generous to take than give," he said.

"How?" Caroline asked.

"To let the other person give you what he has to offer. If you're always the one giving, you never have to feel disappointed, because you don't expect anything in return. But it's miserly in its own way. Because you never leave yourself open or give the other person a chance."

Caroline nodded, thinking of her father. And of herself: Skye was right.

"That's what my sister says."

"About you?"

"Yes."

"It's what my brother says about me," Joe said.

"Something we have in common," Caroline said. "Smart siblings—"

She never saw the kiss coming. He wrapped his strong arms around her, drew her body against his, and kissed her as if his life depended on it. Raising herself up on tiptoe, she reached up to hold him. She ran her fingers through his messy hair, felt the insides of her forearms around his face.

The teakettle began to whistle.

Joe stepped away, turned off the flame. He faced her again, breathing as if he had just run from Mount Serendipity.

Again, he took her in his arms. His body, which had felt strong and supple when they had embraced earlier, now felt rigid with an almost inhuman tension. *It feels like hugging steel,* Caroline thought. She trailed her fingers softly down his spine. His blue cotton shirt seemed thin beneath her fingertips. She could feel his bones and muscle. The sexual passion between them was enormous, but she sensed something different as well.

This was the love that had been building up between them since they were five and six. She could feel Joe Connor absorbing her warmth and love as she herself was consuming his. He wanted something from her that had nothing to do with sex; she knew that. She touched his face, softly stroking his cheek with her left hand.

Holding his hand, she led him down the hall. The spareness apparent throughout Caroline's house did not extend to her bedroom. This was her private place, her sanctuary. She was most herself in this room, and allowing him inside made her feel vulnerable.

Everything was dark wood and white lace. The white lace curtains and eyelet coverlet had belonged to her grandmother. The dark mahogany four-poster was elaborately carved with roses and angels. The massive chifforobe and armoire came from Scotland. Bookcases were filled to overflowing, and the bedside tables were crowded with framed pictures of the people she loved.

He kissed her again. His mouth covered hers, and he wrapped her tighter in his arms. He let out a moan that sounded almost like grief as he slowly lowered her down to the bed. She could barely stand the tension that felt as if it had been building since she was sixteen years old. Caroline leaned into Joe, the full length and weight of his body pressing against hers. They kissed and kissed, undressing each other all the while.

"I'm sorry," he said when his hands touched the bare skin on her shoulders.

"Why?"

"My hands are too rough for such smooth skin."

Joe's hands were callused from hauling equipment, working underwater on the wreck, and the friction made Caroline's body tingle wherever they touched her. She felt the hair on his body, silky and fine, and she nearly lost her breath with the sexy maleness of him.

She lay back, letting him explore the soft curves and hollows of her body with his mouth and hands. He wanted her to stay still. He wanted her to lie back so he could love her, and he let her know this. "Shhh," he whispered, holding both of her hands just behind her head with one of his. "Please," she whispered, trying to get loose. "Please," he whispered back. She could neither touch him nor wrangle away. He made her lie there while he used his mouth all over her body.

He was steady and slow, and Caroline squirmed under the pressure of his tongue. Her nipples hardened. She arched her back, willing him to touch her breasts, finally reaching down to drag his hands up. His callused fingertips pinched and rubbed her nipples, sending a tense thrill straight between her legs. She clutched his head, encouraging him, bringing her hips up to meet his tongue. Everything exploded in red and blue stars behind her eyelids, and she gave out a shuddering breath.

He moved up the bed, his hands now gripping her shoulders, his flat, hard body pressing against her. She felt him enter so easily, water splashing against rock. She was so wet from her own excitement and from his mouth, and he was so hard. He moaned again. Caroline had not known a person could make such a sound of need and love and sex. She had never heard anything like it before.

They clung together, the blood pounding in Caroline's head making her feel in rhythm with Joe, their bodies hot and moist and full of fire, her legs wrapped around his waist, their love so intense, Caroline went deep inside, where she felt the connection they had always had and never really lost.

"Caroline," Joe said into her neck, his arms wrapped around her, "I love you."

"I love you," Caroline said back as Joe's eyes locked onto her gaze.

She touched his face. People weren't made to get this close to each other, she thought, scared by the depths of it. She was lying on the edge of the tallest and narrowest precipice she had ever known; if she moved left or right she would go over and never stop falling.

She had never felt this way before. She had let herself get physically close to men, but her emotions had never kept up, rarely even followed. But she and Joe had said "I love you" to each other and meant it.

"Joe," she said, again looking straight into his eyes, rocked at what was happening.

"I know," he said, smiling. His face glistened with sweat, his eyes sparkled in the cool light of night.

But what do you know? she wanted to ask. She wanted him to tell her. She wanted him to say the words, to name the moment, to tell her what *she* meant. But he couldn't do that. Only Caroline could. The feeling was there, just as it had been practically her whole life, ever since she had sent Joe that first letter. He was the boy who was everything to her, the one she had saved this feeling for her entire life.

"Look," she said, pointing.

Joe raised himself up on his elbow, looked toward the bedside table to where she was pointing. There, in the front row of framed photos, was the picture of him as a child.

"I knew I loved you all along," she said.

"I don't know why," he said, his voice rough with regret. "I made everything so hard."

"So did I," Caroline said, her throat

aching, thinking of things Skye had said. "But here we are."

Lying next to Joe, she felt the truth: She had fallen in love. For the first time in her life, Caroline had given a man the power to hurt her. Her heart skipped. Joe could kiss her good-bye. He could sail away, go to sea in search of a different treasure, and there would be nothing she could do about it.

"What?" he asked, seeing her expression change.

Caroline couldn't speak. His eyes were so clear and blue, like the open ocean in October after a storm has blown through but a solid month before the first snow would fall. She felt so scared, she was frozen in place. Was *this* what her father had in mind? Teaching his daughters how to protect themselves against life, was it this feeling of absolute love and need?

"Whatever you're thinking," Joe said, still smiling into her eyes, "it's going to be okay. It is, Caroline."

"How do you know?"

"Because it's over," he said gently. "The bad stuff is over."

CHAPTER EIGHTEEN

While the coffee brewed the next morning, Caroline walked barefoot to the inn to see what was for breakfast. A few of the guests were up early, but she breezed past them into the kitchen and filled a basket with peach muffins. Returning home, she covered the porch table with a damask cloth. The dawn light was turning from silver to rose to blue-gold, and she wanted Joe to see it. But when she went into the bedroom to get him, he grabbed her wrist and pulled her back into bed.

After a while they got dressed and walked down to the water. Fish were jumping and ospreys were hunting. A kingfisher, sturdy and blue, dive-bombed a school of minnows and came up with a beakful of silver. Joe held Caroline's hand. They stopped to kiss under the big willow tree. Walking a little farther, they stopped to kiss in a grove of pines.

"I have to get back," he said finally. "I didn't expect to be away this long."

"Will Sam be worried?" she asked.

"Sam, no. But some of the other guys will want to kill me. We're a few days behind, and they can taste the gold. I never do this."

"Do what?"

"Leave the boat overnight. Hold up the operation." He shook his head. "No one will be surprised though. They all saw it coming."

"What do you mean?"

"At the ball, the way you looked . . . I had to break a few heads—the comments they were making. They're nothing but a bunch of sea dogs, got the manners of hoodlums. Then they got on me for defending you, saying you'd hooked me good. But you did look beautiful. *Girl in a White Dress.*"

"What?"

"The portrait," he said. "It's the only painting by Hugh Renwick I can stand. I told you, I saw it once. I was walking through the gallery where it hangs, and it was there at the end of the room. I couldn't move. It was like being in the room with you. Only I wanted to know what you were thinking. There was something about your eyes. . . ."

"He painted that after we stopped writing, you and I."

"Did something happen?"

"Yes," Caroline said, thinking of Andrew Lockwood.

"Come out to the boat," he said. "Tell me there."

"I can't," she said, shaking her head. "I want to, but I have a ridiculously busy day."

"I want you there when we bring up the gold. I want you to see."

"What's it like?" Caroline asked, holding his arm, gazing at the river. "Finding the treasure?"

"I wish I could describe it," Joe said, bending down to pick up a stone. It was flat and smooth; he rubbed the surface with his thumb. "But you wouldn't believe me. You'd have to see for yourself."

"Is it more beautiful than this?" Caroline asked, taking the cameo out of her pocket, holding it to the light.

"When Marco Polo returned from China, he told about the wonders he'd seen," Joe said. "Because they were beyond the comprehension of the people of his own city, they accused him of lying. When he was dying, they asked him to confess his lies, because he was about to face God. And Marco Polo said, 'I never told the half of it.' "

Joe took Caroline's face in his hands, looked her deep in the eyes.

"That's how it is for you?" she asked, her heart pounding. He was telling her why he went to sea, the wonders he sought and found, the reasons he would always have to leave.

"Come out with me so you can see for yourself."

"I don't know," she said.

"Tonight? Tomorrow? I'll send the launch for you."

Caroline hesitated. She thought of the things Skye had said, about how she never let people close. About how she always lived her sisters' lives instead of her own. And of what Joe had told her: Generosity sometimes involved taking.

"I have things I have to do this morning," she said slowly, "but I can come out this afternoon."

"We'll pick you up at Moonstone Point," he said.

They walked back to her house. She held

the cameo in her hand the entire way. Even when she kissed him good-bye, she didn't let it go.

* * *

Someone had been in Augusta's kitchen while she was out yesterday. She found beach stones scattered on the floor. Pictures shifted on the table. Two water glasses in the sink. Augusta had a suspicion, and she didn't like it. It was late morning, and she was waiting to ask Skye.

"Sit down," Augusta instructed, offering her cheek for Skye to kiss, hustling her into a place at the table. "I have breakfast all ready for you."

"Oh, Mom, I can't eat," Skye said. "I just want coffee."

Augusta just pretended she hadn't heard. When Skye smelled the muffins, when she realized Augusta had picked tiny wild blueberries from the bushes at the top of the beach stairs, she would change her mind. The muffins were small, their tops golden brown. Augusta took four from the oven, where they had been warming, and placed them in a lovely basket lined with a checkered napkin. She set the basket in front of Skye.

"Dear, I wish I could tell you this juice was fresh-squeezed," Augusta said, filling a glass, "but that is only partially true. I realized too late that I didn't have enough juice oranges. So I mixed it with canned."

"That's okay. I don't want—"

"I'll be desolate if you don't drink your juice. It's full of vitamins, you know."

"Mom, my stomach is a little—"

"We could make screwdrivers," Augusta suggested, assuming Skye was hung over. She knew that Skye should get her drinking under control, but maybe just this once it would actually help.

Yesterday's ride with Clea and Skye had left her anxious and tired. They had invited her along, but they spent the whole day acting nervous and distracted. Augusta had ridden in the backseat, doing her needlepoint, knowing something was wrong. Arriving at home, she felt like Mama Bear: *Someone's been sitting in my kitchen.*

"Who was here?" she asked when Skye had taken some sips of coffee.

Skye didn't reply.

"Was it your sister?"

Holding her cup with two hands, Skye looked down.

"Tell me, Skye. I want to know."

"Shouldn't she feel welcome to come and go?"

"Not if she's with Joe Connor. Was he here? Answer me, Skye."

Skye couldn't speak because she didn't want to lie. Augusta felt the truth bowl her over, and she clutched her black pearls.

"I knew this would happen. Why else would he be in Black Hall, if he didn't want to come snooping around? I knew the instant I saw him at the ball."

"Maybe he wanted to visit the place where his father died," Skye said slowly. She took a bite of her muffin. Her tremor wasn't as bad as it had been the last few days. Still, Augusta couldn't bear to look.

"All this digging up the past," Augusta said. "It's horrible."

"The man was his father, Mom."

Augusta felt stung, and she wanted to strike out. She pictured Skye's studio, the new sculpture she was doing. She envisioned the talismans Skye had set out on her worktable, and she thought of the loathing she felt for them. To Augusta, they symbolized the wreckage of the painful past, every-thing wrong with Skye.

"I cleaned up your studio," Augusta said casually. "While you were sleeping."

"What do you mean?" Skye asked, look-ing up sharply.

"Those junky things. That dusty old blue ribbon, that horrible rattlesnake skeleton you had."

"Mom—"

"I threw them out."

"No."

Augusta nodded emphatically. "Surround-ing yourself with negativity, no wonder you're depressed. How can you expect to do good work, lead a meaningful life, with snake bones lying right in front of you?"

"A snake bit me once," Skye said, her eyes piercing.

Augusta breathed steadily, poured more juice. "Don't be so dramatic. Not that snake—"

"It was poisonous," Skye said, her voice a little louder. "It happened on the mountain, when you let me go hunting with Dad. Car-oline sucked the poison out."

"It wasn't poisonous. If it was poisonous, I

would have known. You would have been hospitalized, and if you think I'd let you go to the hospital without being right there at your side, you're crazy."

"Oh, God," Skye said, starting to laugh.

"What's so funny?"

"You weren't by my side, Mom," Skye said. "Caroline was."

"No, Skye. I think—"

"At the campsite, where it happened, and at the clinic later. And she was with me when I shot Andrew Lockwood, and she was with me when the police came, and she was with me when his parents walked into the inquest room and I had to look them in the eye."

"I was right here, waiting for you!" Augusta said.

"But Caroline was *with* me," Skye said quietly. "She always was. She was like a mother to me."

"*I'm* your mother," Augusta said, feeling panic rising inside her.

"But you weren't there, Mom. You never were. I was in trouble, and I needed you. Facing Andrew's parents was so hard."

"It was an accident, Skye. Even they knew that. . . ."

"You could have come. Didn't you think about how awful it was for me, seeing the people whose son I *killed?* I wanted to disappear, Mom. That's all I could think about."

"Darling, I was terrified for you. That you could be charged with murder. That was my only thought, that you couldn't go to jail."

"Mom, I killed someone! I wasn't thinking about *jail*. I was thinking they'd never see their son again. It was a beautiful sunny day, and he was *dead*."

"Beautiful sunny day? Well, I was thinking about *you*. Going to jail, with God-knows-what for a cellmate, no freedom, no liberty, no beautiful sunny days. I was paralyzed."

"I know," Skye said. "But Caroline wasn't. She was there."

It hit home, hard and suddenly. Augusta had never been present for Skye. She had wanted to, planned to, imagined that she was, but she hadn't.

Trembling, Augusta pulled out her needlework. She had been hiding this from Skye, intending to keep it a secret until Christmas.

"Look what I'm making for you, Skye," she said, solemnly, showing Skye this symbol of her love, wanting it to obliterate the horrible past. She wanted to return to the comfort of *good* talismans instead of snake bones, to the old ways that had always let her pretend she had a happy family.

Spread out on the table was Augusta's nearly finished needlepoint pillow: *Swan Lake* with its mysterious forest, blue lake, graceful swans, enchanted castle. At the bottom were two dates—Christmas of two different years, thirty years apart.

"Do you see the significance?" she asked, her voice shaking. Her arms wrapped around Skye's shoulders, she traced the dates with her index finger, as if she were talking to a small child. "The Christmas my father took me to *Swan Lake*, and the year your father took you and your sisters."

"I'm falling apart, and you want to give me a pillow," Skye said.

"Darling, you'll be fine!" Augusta said, so afraid to hear the truth. She hugged Skye, practically shaking the needlework in her face, wanting her to see it and be happy, praying it wasn't too late.

"Mom, don't!" Skye said. "*Swan Lake* reminds me of Redhawk."

"But the ballet . . . your father took you. You loved it. You'd listen to the music all night if you could, way past midnight, until I made you stop. . . ."

"You don't even know. You think what you want to think about everything," Skye said.

"Darling!"

"Mom, I hate *Swan Lake.* It reminds me of Dad. It reminds me of that fall day, of picking up the gun and shooting Andrew Lockwood. That's what I think of every time I hear that music."

Without speaking, Augusta reached for a pair of scissors. She found herself cutting the needlework in half, then in half again. She stared at the four pieces, two in each hand.

CHAPTER NINETEEN

Joe met Caroline as she stepped off the launch. He reached down to take her hand. Climbing aboard the *Meteor,* she let him pull her into his arms. He had on the bottom half of a black wetsuit. His bare chest felt warm in the sun, and salt crystals glistened in his blond hair. The crew stopped everything to watch.

"I don't bring girls out to the boat," Joe explained. "Twice."

"I don't take days off in the middle of the week," Caroline replied.

"Hey, Caroline," Sam said, bounding over in his diving suit. He shook his head, spraying water from his hair like a wet Lab. He kissed her on the cheek, apparently thrilled to see her. "You picked the best day to come out."

"I did?"

"Hell, yeah. You should see the treasure! It's like a real-life pirate's chest—ancient and covered with brass—and we've got the wires ready to hook up. Show her the winch, Joe."

Joe smiled at his brother's enthusiasm. "Right there," he said, pointing to a big stainless steel drum with quarter-inch wire spooled around. "We hit the engine and say the word, and we haul in the gold."

"We waited for you," Sam added. "We were all set to go the minute Joe got back from wherever the hell he was last night, but Joe said we had to hang tight."

"You did?" Caroline asked, blushing.

"Yeah," Joe said.

Caroline smiled.

"Got a wetsuit?" Sam asked.

"No," she said.

"Let her borrow one, Joe," he said. "You're gonna take her down, aren't you?"

Joe hesitated for a second. "Do you dive?" he asked.

"That's okay," Caroline said, laughing. She did dive; she had her scuba certification, and she had gone down on the local reefs before. But she was out of practice, and she wanted the operation to get under way. "I think I'll wait for you to bring it up."

"Okay," Joe said. "It won't be long." He zipped into the top half of his wetsuit while scanning the Sound. The blue surface was flat, painted with sunlight. It was one of those perfect summer days with no waves; the sea's only movement was its natural rhythm, low swells forming without peaks.

"Hey, skipper," one of the guys shouted. "We ready to go, or what?"

"Patience, Danny," Joe said, strapping on his tanks. "By dinner tonight you'll be packing for Athens."

"Athens?" Caroline asked.

"His next dive's in Greece," Sam said. "The brothers could've gone to Yale, but gold is gold."

"You're leaving tonight?" Caroline asked.

Joe's smile left his lips first, then his eyes. His eyes were clear, the color of deep water. "Not tonight," he said. But Caroline could see that it would be soon.

"Oh," Caroline said. Black Hall lay ten miles across the calm Sound, hills of dark pines rising sharply behind the town. Firefly Hill stood to the north. Caroline caught a glint of light and knew it was sun striking her family's picture window. She blinked, staring at it.

The pirates clustered on deck. They said a few words that Caroline couldn't hear, getting their strategy set. Then they split up and went over the side. Sam yelled goodbye, and Joe flashed her a grin. He went backward off the rail.

Caroline stared into the water. A few bubbles, a ring of ripples, were the only signs that anyone had been there. The men had disappeared completely. Last night, when Joe had seen the trouble in her eyes, he had said everything would be okay, the bad stuff was over. How could she have imagined that that meant he would stay?

Her father had armed them against danger, but he hadn't warned her about this part. Once you let yourself feel love, once you let it in, you take the risk. You lay yourself open to pure fear. The thought of Joe leaving was worse than any night alone on the mountain.

Something broke the surface. As Caroline stared, the sea began to dance with silver splashes. Two, three. A fish tail broke the surface. A sea gull circled overhead, letting out a jubilant cry. A common sight of summer: The bluefish were there. Trying to breathe, Caroline watched them feed.

Sunlight infused the top layer of water, and it twinkled above with plankton and particles of sand. The divers aimed down, flipping on lights to guide them into the murkier deep. Sam followed Joe. Diving always made him euphoric, and he'd start breathing too fast just when he was supposed to be cool and calm. *Think Tibet,* he told himself. *Meditate and focus on spiritual matters. Think anything but this.*

This. Who could believe Sam was diving with his big brother on a big-league wreck with major treasure? Sam had grown up idolizing Joe. He made no bones about it. Sam had never been good at hiding any feeling— not one—that he'd ever had. That Yale stuff, for example. Sam had been so disappointed when Joe had said he wasn't even considering the job. He had tried to act as if he didn't care, but Joe could see that he did. Sam had really blown it that time.

Just thinking about Yale made Sam's breathing go crazy. A year they could finally spend near each other, down the drain. Like all the other times Sam would show up and Joe would leave. *Don't take it personally,* he told himself. *That's just the way Joe is.* Sam's chest hurt. He pushed Yale away, straight out of his danger zone. Exhaling a long stream of bubbles, he narrowed his eyes. He peered through the dark water; ahead he could see the spars of the *Cambria.*

The wreck was a magic forest of broken timber. The divers swam in a line along the reef, circling around to swim the length of the old ship. She lay on her side, wide and austere as a great dead whale. The ribs of her black wooden belly curved out, the bow and stern tapered in. The masts had snapped off; they spiked out of the sand connected to the ship with evil loops of wire. Blackfish and cunners swam in and out.

Joe turned to face Sam. He gestured for Sam to stay put. Sam nodded assent even though he wanted to swim into the wreck behind Joe, watch the operation up close. But he wasn't in Joe's league as a diver. Sam's work off Canada's Maritimes didn't require much scuba action, and Sam knew he was present by his brother's grace alone.

In the precarious cave of the wreck, Sam would be in the way.

Joe was saying something. Sam squinted, looking through the celadon water. Air bubbles were flowing out of Joe's mouth. Mask to mask with Joe, Sam read his lips: *Black Hall.*

No way. Joe couldn't be saying what Sam thought he was. Sam himself had mouthed the same words a few dives back, teasing Joe, wanting to tempt him to stay in the area, sign on at Yale, move into the town where Caroline Renwick lived. Sam had watched the way Joe changed when he was around her.

Black Hall. Sure as hell, that's what Joe seemed to be saying. But he couldn't be. Sam grinned, letting a whole passel of air out and shrugged to indicate he wasn't getting the message. Reading the word was wishful thinking on Sam's part. Sam's brother was a loner, a pirate, a treasure hunter. He'd never let anything like a woman or a brother hold him back.

Turning, Joe grabbed the cable. It ran from the winch on board the *Meteor* straight down to the wreck. Joe and Dan would attach it to the reinforced chest, bolstered by support and wrapped in straps, and they'd pull the gold out. Joe swam into the wreck. One by one the other divers fol-

lowed. Engineers, geophysicists, archaeol-
ogists, professional salvage guys, they belonged in there, carrying out the delicate
business of easing a chest of gold from the
delicate labyrinth of old wood.

Sam had a different place in the sea. He
was a biologist. He studied sea plants,
ocean creatures. Once they got the gold,
he'd hop a plane and return to his post up
north. The cetaceans of Newfoundland
needed to be counted. Seals needed to be
observed. Herring stocks assessed. In the
murky depths of Moonstone Reef, he tried
to forget his dream of him and Joe at Yale.

Trying to remain patient, Sam Trevor saw
a school of menhaden. The tiny fish flashed
outward like an explosion of silver. Behind
them came the bluefish, pewter torpedoes,
eating machines. They pursued the bait
fish, mouths open. The biologist hung back,
observing the fish and tried to stop wondering whether his brother had actually been
saying *Black Hall.*

* * *

In her studio at Firefly Hill, Skye worked on
her sculpture of the three sisters. She wore a

black ballet top and faded overalls, and she was covered from head to toe with a thin film of clay. Beside her was a bottle of Absolut and a crystal glass. The glass was full.

She couldn't stand her feelings.

She had just destroyed her mother. She pictured her mother's face, shadowed with despair. She could sculpt it, the bust of a woman who had just seen into the depths of her youngest daughter's empty soul. Old news, but it had shocked Augusta. Skye had seen it in her eyes. Vodka was the fastest way out. She sipped her drink and felt everything grow distant.

But her new piece was filled with love. Although the sisters did not have faces, Skye knew which one was Caroline, which was Clea, and which was Skye. All three had their heads tipped back just slightly, gazing at the sky with exuberance and gratitude. That's how Skye wanted to feel someday.

Exuberant and grateful. Skye raised the glass again and drained it.

The Renwicks had made secret-keeping and lie-telling an art form. What was the alternative? It they had told the truth, they would have fallen apart. Her parents would have gotten divorced, Skye was sure. She wished she could hold on to her picture of them as a couple in love, the way the stories made it sound. They had traveled the world together, always with their children, renting houses in beautiful places for Hugh to paint. They had made a fantasy world, and now it was finally disintegrating.

Skye's name came from the place where she had been conceived, the storied Isle of Skye in the west of Scotland. When she was old enough, her parents would hold her tight and tell her about the tiny cottage, just big enough for a couple and their two little girls, with a peat fire burning all day and night. It had been a blissful time, a place where Augusta and the girls walked the sea path while Hugh fished for salmon and painted every day.

Christmas—nine months later—her father went off with another woman. That woman's husband came to Firefly Hill with the thought of killing the whole family, and that just about summed up the way of the Renwicks.

Hearing someone coming up the stairs, she turned to face the door. Simon stood just out of sight. She could see his lanky shadow thrown by the hall light, and she felt relieved it wasn't her mother. He paused out there for a long while, and she could almost feel him summoning up his courage. She heard him take a deep breath.

He entered her studio holding one red rose. Apology in his eyes. He wore black jeans, a green tee-shirt, and scuffed work boots. Very slowly, he walked across the big space, his footsteps echoing. When he got to Skye, he knelt before her and handed her the rose.

"This is for you," he said.

"Thank you," she said. She held the rose to her nose and breathed its sweet scent, trying to be unmoved.

"I picked it on my way in," he said with disarming truthfulness. "From the garden outside."

"Why?"

"I wanted to prove I belong here, that I'm part of the family. I am, you know," he said, burying his head in her lap. Her hands were covered with clay, but she laid them gently on his hair.

"Your father made mistakes, Skye, and your mother took him back."

"Maybe she shouldn't have."

"Didn't you tell me he planted those roses

outside as a symbol? He wanted to undo his mistakes, make things up to her. I'll be better to you."

Again, she smelled the rose. It was musky and sexy, like love and the end of summer. Skye thought of Caroline and Clea; for some reason, she felt tears hot behind her eyelids. She felt herself slipping away. She wanted to believe Simon. More than anything, she wanted to click into love and forget Red-hawk and the blue ribbon and *Swan Lake* and the look in her mother's eyes.

"This is wrong," she said, pushing him away. "I have to be alone right now."

"Make love to me," he said.

"Simon, no."

"What's the matter?" he asked. "You were never like this before."

"I'm tired. I want to sculpt," she said, the two lies colliding head-on. She wanted to get rid of Simon as quickly as possible so she could get plastered on vodka and sleep the rest of the afternoon away.

"Which is it?" he asked, grinning as he caught her.

"The truth is, I need to be alone," she said, thinking fast. "I had an amazing dream last night, a major inspiration for a new piece, and I really feel like working." Her desire for isolation made the lie as easy as breathing.

"Sex," Simon said, sliding his tongue down her neck, his finger down her jeans. "You need to relax."

"Stop," she said, flinching. She pushed his hand away.

"I don't feel like stopping," he said, his breath hot on her neck.

The panic came over her. Feeling Simon's hand on her breasts, his mouth on her throat made her skin crawl.

"No, Simon. I said no!"

"You bitch," he said.

Skye took a deep breath. She closed her eyes, but only for an instant. She wanted to be completely present, right there for what was happening. She didn't want to escape into her imagination, into a momentary lapse of reality. Her husband had a vicious look on his face, and he had just called her a bitch. It was almost a relief.

"If you don't leave right now," she said, standing, "I'm going to call the police."

"What do you think the police will do?" Simon asked, smacking her so hard across the face that she saw stars. "You're my wife."

"Simon!"

"You don't want to make love? Fine. Then we'll fuck."

Shocked, Skye touched her eye, her mouth. The left side of her face stung; she could almost feel it throbbing in the shape of Simon's hand. He grabbed her by the collar, tearing her shirt. She felt her brain explode, as her eyes went wide with terror.

* * *

The fish were feeding. Caroline stood on deck, her hands on the starboard rail, watching the activity. Bluefish lunged into a school of menhaden, sending the baitfish flying like pellets into the sky. It was a full-blown feeding frenzy, with teeth snapping and half-eaten fish making a slick of oils and blood trailing the currents straight out to sea.

Caroline wondered what was happening below. A few crew members had stayed on deck to work the winch and stay in radio contact with Joe and the others below. Every so often they would pay out a little more cable. Take a turn on the winch. Crank up the engine. Check the *Meteor*'s position over the wreck, and back a few meters in reverse.

She watched the fish, trying to forget the pit in her stomach. The men on deck were talking about Greece, about diving for a treasure off Mykonos, about the warmth of the water and the beauty of the women there.

"They have it!" the winch operator yelled. "They've secured the chest!"

All the guys converged on deck. The big winch held a spool of wire like a giant's fishing line. The wire ran through a long, pivoted beam that swung out over the water down to the wreck below.

"Is this very dangerous?" Caroline asked one of the men.

"Shit, yeah," he said. "Once we start pulling, you know how much tension will be on that wire?"

"Picture the wreck as a house of cards," said an older man, a cigarette dangling out of his mouth and the tattoo of a battleship on his arm. "The gold is sitting smack inside. We gotta thread the wire through the structure, keep it from touching anything, then wrap it around the chest. We touch one card, the whole house goes down."

"It won't happen," the operator said. "Joe knows his stuff. We do this all the time."

"Gonna do it in Greece next month," someone else said.

The operator spoke into the mike. He pressed a finger against the earpiece, trying to hear better. He spoke again, and Caroline heard him say "Roger. Starting the winch." He punched buttons on the control panel.

Caroline watched the wire go taut. It was pulling the chest. Thinking of the house of cards, her stomach flipped. She gazed away, out toward the thrashing bluefish. They had moved closer. Something dark was swimming toward them.

The thing was a shark.

Inside the wreck, darkness was total. No sun penetrated from the surface. Light shimmered from lanterns illuminating the chest, and Joe tried to see as he and Dan wrapped the case in cable. They had rigged up a series of metal arches, guiding the wire through the old ship. Designed to keep the cable from chafing and collapsing the wreck, the arches seemed to be holding.

Joe counted his men. He looked for Sam

and felt relieved not to see him. The kid listened, Joe gave him that. Sam had always tagged along, followed Joe like a big puppy, but when Joe told him to back off, he did. *I do that too much,* Joe thought, yanking on the cable to test it. Tell Sam to back off. Tell *everyone* to back off. He thought of Caroline waiting on deck, and he moved faster. He gave the signal to start pulling.

The cable tightened. It scraped against the metal guides and supports. Joe's heart pounded, and he felt himself wanting to breathe too fast. He was glad Sam was outside the wreck, safe and free. This was the riskiest part of treasure hunting: getting the gold out of the unstable wreck. This was the part where people could get hurt.

The chest shifted. The wire stretched. The girded chest bumped along the sea bottom. Divers surrounded it, easing the encased old box over broken spars. Dan watched the cable, gauging its tension against the metal guides. He gave Joe a thumbs-up. Joe swam behind the chest, noticing a trail of coins spilling from a crack between the protective straps.

His main concern was getting the gold to the water's surface. It was easier going now; the chest was off the sea bottom, being guided through the dark wreck. Bones lay strewn around, the remains of the *Cambria*'s crew. Clarissa's mother was among them, but Joe didn't let himself think of her. He was a pirate now, not a scientist, and he had to get the treasure.

As he swam out of the wreck, the water seemed bright. Joe felt relief. He searched for Sam, saw him waiting a safe distance away. The worst part was over. One by one his men were coming out, following the chest of gold. It hovered in the water, suspended in the hole in the *Cambria*'s hull. Half in and half out, it wasn't moving.

The cable was snagged.

Right away Joe saw the problem wasn't serious. The wire had eased between the metal arch and a ship's timber. Dan called for some slack, and the winch man let off some tension, unhooking the strap from a broken spar. The cable drooped. Joe swam over. He had just reached up to free the wire, when he saw the shark.

It was coming fast. Sleek as a jet, black on top with a white underbelly, the shark was headed straight for Sam. The creature twisted, opened its mouth to expose jagged teeth, slashed past Sam. Joe saw the startled look on Sam's face. Sam's eyes widened behind his mask. He opened his mouth, and a balloon of air bubbles escaped.

Joe grabbed a broken spar from the sea bottom. He didn't have a plan, he didn't even think. All he wanted was to protect his brother. He lunged toward the shark, trying to scare it away with his useless wooden club.

Joe's air hose caught on the metal guide. The cable had tightened up again, tugging the chest. Yanked back, Joe felt his air stop. All he had to do was slip out of his harness, leave his tank hanging where it was caught. But he was distracted by the shark and Sam. He saw Sam holding still, turning in place, watching the shark circle around. The shark flicked its tail and dodged away. Joe followed it with his eyes.

Fumbling with the harness, Joe smiled at Sam. The kid was a mess, freaked out over the shark and unaccustomed to seeing his older brother agitated. Sam swam forward, taking his regulator out of his mouth, ready to share his air with Joe.

Joe motioned him back. He had taken a big breath of air; he had plenty to take him to the water's surface. But Sam kept coming. He knew the buddy system, how you shared your air with a fellow diver in distress. Sam's eyes were focused on Joe, his mouthpiece held out like a gift.

Just then the chest swung free. It flew past Joe, on its way up. Snapping loose, the cable shook the wreck. The *Cambria* trembled, and the shock waves felt like an underwater earthquake. Joe steadied himself. He reached out, trying to push Sam away.

The wreck came down as if the ground had shifted. It tumbled in on itself, sending timbers everywhere. Divers scattered like baitfish. The school of blues exploded away, the shark had disappeared. Joe felt a timber strike his shoulder with a glancing blow. But Sam got hit hard. Joe saw the cable whip across the back of his head.

Sam's blood wafted into the murky water.

Joe darted toward his younger brother, but he couldn't swim. His arm wouldn't work.

No one had cared when Caroline pointed out the shark. They said they saw sharks all the time out here—it was no big deal, part of the job. Only gullible city people believed *Jaws*.

Caroline had laughed, knowing she should believe them. She had lived by the sea her whole life, had never heard of one shark attack in Black Hall waters. *It's like the hunts,* she told herself: *We saw bears, we saw wolves, but nothing ever ate us.*

Caroline watched the chest shimmering beneath the surface. It was the size of a dinghy, blackened with time. Coated with green seaweed and raggedy barnacles, it came out of the sea, dangling on the cable, supported on all sides by strapping. The winch man maneuvered it onto the deck, water pouring from its seams.

Four black heads bobbed into sight. The divers were coming up. She looked for Joe and Sam, thrilled that they would all be able to see the gold together.

The divers were shouting. Climbing onto the swim platform, leaping onto the deck. Someone radioed for the Coast Guard, for a helicopter. Caroline ran to the rail. She stared at the surface, praying to see Joe and Sam.

"The shark?" she asked. She was thinking of hunters and prey, her worst fears.

"The wreck collapsed," someone told her, running by.

"Where's Joe?" she asked, her heart racing. "Where are they?"

Less than a minute passed, and they came up. Everyone was clustered around Sam. His face was pure white, streaked with blood. His eyes were half closed, rolled back in his head. Blood pumped out of a four-inch wound behind his ear.

Joe gasped air. He was trying to buoy up Sam, but his left arm was hanging limp at his side. His wetsuit was torn; Caroline saw the gash in his shoulder. Dan swam to his side, held him steady. Caroline held out her arms, tried to help as first Sam and then Joe were hauled onto the deck. People flew to the wheelhouse, then came back with blankets.

"He was trying to save me," Joe said, looking from Caroline to Sam. "He was just trying to pull me out of the way."

"He's hurt bad, man," Dan said, staring at Sam. "Losing blood fast."

"Coast Guard's on the way," Jeff called. "Sending a helicopter out right now."

"Sam," Joe said, his voice cracking. The sight of his exposed wound shocked Caroline. The jagged wood had plowed through his upper arm, slicing it clear to the bone. His own face was pale, his lips blue. Joe was losing a fair amount of blood himself, but he wouldn't leave Sam's side.

Someone found a towel, dabbed it against Sam's head. Sam's blood began pooling on the deck. The crew seemed paralyzed by their captain's distress.

"We need a fucking doctor," Dan said, spitting water. "Out the fuck here at sea, sharks swimming around, and not one of us is a doctor. All these eggheads and not one of them's a goddamn M.D."

"Where's the helicopter?" a young crew-member asked, scanning the sky.

Caroline pushed her way into the tight circle of divers. She knew first aid and she crouched down, touched Sam's face. It felt ice cold. Her throat tightened. She thought of Redhawk Mountain, of Andrew Lockwood. The memories broke her heart, and she knew she couldn't afford them right now.

Caroline pulled off her white shirt. She wore a bathing suit underneath, and the breeze chilled her skin. She pressed the shirt to Sam's head. She held it against the wound as hard as she could, feeling his hot blood soak into the fabric, forcing herself to look at his face so she wouldn't see Andrew's.

"Loosen his wetsuit," she instructed Dan and Jeff. "Cover him with the blanket and bring some more." She felt the side of his neck for his pulse and couldn't find it. She knew the cut was bad, that it might have scored an artery.

"Is he going to die?" Joe asked, his eyes red and brimming with tears.

Caroline looked over at him. The effort of will with which Joe held himself up was enormous. His lips were a tight blue line. He had lost every trace of cool, of toughness. That emotional wariness she had observed ever since meeting him had vanished. It took a certain amount of courage to sit on deck surrounded by his men, tears rolling down his face, without wiping them away. He was hurt himself, close to passing out, but he hung on to Sam.

The helicopter was coming. Caroline heard the engine beating, far-off and faint like hundreds of birds.

"Is he going to die?" Joe asked again, never taking his eyes away from Caroline's face. She had to be careful with her expression. She knew how he felt about the truth. She knew that he wouldn't want her to lie, but she couldn't bring herself to say what she had seen once before, what she believed to be true. So she kept her eyes steady, her lips silent.

The tears in Caroline's periwinkle blue eyes were the only sign, the only giveaway to tell Joe that she had watched a boy losing blood before, that the answer to his question might very well be yes.

* * *

Breathing heavily, Augusta mounted the stairs to check on Skye. She would have admitted it to no one, not even to Caroline or Clea, but she felt finally and utterly defeated, a total failure as a mother.

The children had been such happy little girls. She could picture them now, running through the field at twilight, catching fireflies in their cupped hands. They were in constant motion. Augusta could see them perfectly in her mind's eye. She had sat on the porch steps, so full of love and delight, she thought she would rise like a balloon. Her daughters would dance and leap in arabesques of joy, and Augusta's eyes would fill with tears for what she had brought to life.

Whoever would have thought that twenty-five years later she would be checking her youngest, her darling Skye, to make sure she hadn't harmed herself? That she wasn't drinking straight from a bottle, that she hadn't taken an X-acto knife to the blue veins in her delicate arms? Over a death that had occurred so many years ago?

Skye, a killer.

Dear God, Augusta thought. The pain in her own family. She bowed her head, wiped her tears. How could she not have known how better to help? Her three girls, sisters looking after each other. Caroline, the surrogate mother. Thank God for her, that the others hadn't had to endure it all alone— their real mother too selfish and cowardly to protect them.

At the top of the back stairs, Augusta paused. She leaned against the banister, her arms full of white towels. She felt like a tired old washerwoman.

The door to Skye's studio was shut tight. Augusta stared at it. This was the moment she feared. When she would fling open her daughter's door, walk in, and discover Skye drunk.

Augusta straightened her spine. She took

a deep breath and put an expression of put-upon ditziness on her face. She'd walk in complaining loudly that the world would never know about the mothers of sculptors, all the extra work they did to make sure their daughters could sculpt freely with clean hands.

She pushed the door open. She stepped inside. And her heart stopped just as Skye screamed.

"My God!" she said, dropping the towels.

There was Skye, blood streaming from her nose, while Simon stood over her, breathing like a bull. He held her from behind, and Augusta could see that he had hurt her. He had his pants undone, his belt trailing to the floor.

"Leave us, Augusta," Simon said. "This is between me and my wife."

"Skye?" Augusta asked again, ignoring him. She grabbed one of the clean towels and began walking toward her daughter. Was this a bad fight or something worse? Was he about to *rape* her?

Skye's nose was crooked. A lump was starting to swell under her left eye. Augusta crouched beside her, examining her eyes, stroking her hair. "Did he hit you?" Tears were leaking from Skye's eyes. Enraged, Augusta turned to Simon. "Did you hit her? So help me, Simon, if you . . ."

She glimpsed Simon's face. How ugly it looked, all contorted and red, the veins on his neck standing out like cords. His teeth were bared like a tiger's, and Augusta felt the rush of animal instinct herself. The hair on her neck stood up straight. She remembered feeling this way just once before: when James Connor had come into her kitchen and threatened her children.

Augusta put herself between Simon and Skye. She faced him head-on, their eyes met, and she saw the blow coming. She wasn't sure whether Simon was aiming for her or for Skye, but she held up her hands to protect them both. She heard Skye cry out, and the word "Nooooo!" lingered in the air, the whistle of a locomotive rounding a long curve before entering the tunnel.

It was Augusta he was aiming for, and he connected with a thud and a snarl. Augusta heard it as much as felt it, Simon's fist connecting with the side of her head, and her other senses were alive as well, she smelled and tasted her own fear, and she saw Skye, her baby daughter, her truest artist and purest spirit, pick up a pair of scissors.

"Skye," Augusta tried to say, but her brain couldn't push the name into her mouth. "Skye." *Don't, darling,* she wanted to say. *Don't. Don't.* Augusta felt herself slipping away, the words gargling in spit or blood. She might have been blacking out or she might have been dying, but for that moment, with all her heart, she didn't care. All she wanted to do was protect Skye. Protect her now, as she had been unable to protect her fourteen years before.

Unable to speak or act, Augusta Renwick lay crumpled on the floor of Skye's studio, powerless to protect her daughter from the forces that swirled around her family, and as she drifted into a place she had never been before, she saw Skye, a howl on her bloodied face, stab Simon Whitford through the heart.

CHAPTER TWENTY

The Lifestar helicopter flew Joe Connor and Sam Trevor down the Sound to Coastline General Hospital. Dan drove Caroline by launch and truck, and she arrived at the ICU frantic and terrified. A nurse told her they were both going into surgery, that she had no details yet. Uneasily, Caroline settled down to wait.

After an hour she asked for Peter, but they told her he was busy with another family elsewhere in the hospital. She tried to call Clea, then Skye, but no one was home.

The air was too cold. The orange vinyl chair stuck to the backs of her legs. She rose every time a doctor came through the door. The doctors wore loose green cotton scrubs, their surgical masks pulled below their chins, weary looks in their eyes. They spoke to the waiting families, explaining the procedures and answering questions. Caroline watched the emotions in those families' faces, feeling her own hands ice cold with worry.

Finally a young physician came looking for her.

"Are you Caroline?" she asked.

Caroline stepped forward. "Yes," she said, reading the doctor's nametag.

"You're Joe's wife? Sister?" Dr. Nichols asked, looking at her notes.

"Neither," she said. "But I was with them when it happened. I'm his friend."

"I see," Dr. Nichols said.

"Will they be okay?"

"Yes. Joe's out of surgery now. He'll need more work to repair the muscle damage, but he can take care of most of that when he goes home. He's from"—she checked her form—"Miami?"

"Yes," Caroline said, swallowing. "How's Sam?"

"Almost out of the woods, but not quite. He lost a great deal of blood. We're pumping more in right now. He's a lucky boy. Another twenty minutes and he wouldn't be here at all. He's a regular little bulldog."

"Bulldog?"

"Yes."

"Mmm," the doctor said, checking her notes. "He woke up from the worst head injury I've seen all summer and wouldn't let us give him anything until he'd asked about Joe. Had to know how his brother was." She smiled. "Joe's the same. He's in recovery right now, wanting to know when he can see Sam."

"Brothers," Caroline smiled, thinking of her sisters.

"Joe also wants to know when he can see you."

"Am I allowed in?" she asked. "I thought only family—"

"He has you down as next of kin," Dr. Nichols said, smiling. "Go on in."

Joe was asleep. He lay on the gurney, covered with a cotton blanket. The recovery room was kept cool, and Caroline saw him shivering. She asked the nurse for another blanket. The nurse smiled, checked Joe's shoulder, then covered him. The bandage was massive, pure white, stark against his tan skin. The slight pressure of the nurse's fingers was too much, and Joe flinched from the pain.

His eyelids fluttered open. Caroline

leaned forward, touched his cheek. His eyes were bloodshot, cloudy from the anesthesia. Seeing Caroline, he smiled. A shiver shook his body, and he clenched his teeth, waiting for it to pass.

"Sam," he said hoarsely.

"He's okay," Caroline said. "The doctor said they're giving him blood, he's asking for you."

"He's okay," Joe said, closing his eyes, latching on to the important part. "Alive and okay." The nurse returned with a shot. She sent the pain medication into Joe's already-inserted IV—speeding soothing relief quickly into his veins.

"Sleep," Caroline said, touching his cheek. She kissed him, feeling the two-day growth; waking up at her house that morning, he hadn't shaved. The memory pierced her heart, and she kissed him again.

"Don't go yet," Joe said sleepily. "Okay?"

Caroline stayed. She watched him fall asleep, sitting beside him until the nurse told her she had to leave. Standing in the hallway, Caroline closed her eyes and said a prayer. She heard someone call her name. When she opened her eyes to look, she saw Peter standing there. She didn't think there

could be anything worse than seeing Joe
so hurt, but there was.

"Come with me," he said, putting his arm
around her. "Something happened; your
mother is downstairs."

Clea met her outside the emergency room
entrance. Red geraniums bloomed in tall
stone pots. Two police cars were parked at
the curb, and the officers stood beside their
cars, talking. Three nurses were taking a
break, leaning against the brick wall and
smoking.

"See the police?" Clea asked. "They're
here to talk to Skye."

"Skye?" Caroline asked, shocked. Seeing
Joe upstairs already had her completely off
balance. "Peter said Mom—"

"Simon beat her, Caroline. She told me he
tried to rape her. When you see her—"

"Where is she?"

"Inside," Clea said, pointing toward the
emergency room. "Mom got between them,
and Simon hit Mom and knocked her out.
Then Skye went after him with a pair of scissors. She hardly hurt him at all—it was self-
defense—but it's awful," Clea said, her eyes
wide. "The police—"

"They want to arrest *Skye?*" Caroline asked, her heart pounding.

Clea looked at Caroline and wiped her eyes. "They want to question everyone. To them it's just a domestic disturbance."

Suddenly the day became too much for Caroline. She had been holding up well, but now she pressed the heels of her hands against her eyes. She thought of Joe and Sam, her mother and Skye, and she leaned back against the brick wall with her eyes still covered.

"Being right there," Clea said, putting her arms around Caroline. "Seeing them right after the accident must have been terrible."

Caroline shook her head.

"I'm glad I was there," she said. "Joe asked for me, Clea. You're used to it, having Peter and the kids. Being the one someone asks for when they're hurt and scared, but, Clea . . ."

Clea gazed at Caroline, waiting for her to catch her breath.

"Joe looked for me on the boat. I saw him the minute they brought him up. He watched me while I was trying to help Sam."

"Of course he did," Clea said. "There's no one better, Caroline."

"He listed me as next of kin."

"He did?"

"Yes." Caroline looked at the sky. "Here at the hospital. They came to find me in the waiting room because Joe had put my name on the form. But he's leaving, Clea. As soon as he gets better, he's going to Greece." She tried to laugh.

"What?"

"Isn't it funny? That he's the one leaving? I finally want to stay put, and Joe's getting on a plane."

Clea knew there was nothing she could say. She just stood there, knowing that Caroline needed to feel all of the complex emotions roiling inside of her.

Caroline pushed off the wall. She linked arms with Clea. She swallowed her fear and walked with her sister straight into the emergency room. She asked the nurse on duty where to find Skye and Augusta; the nurse told her Augusta was having a CT scan and Skye was being questioned by the police. They were just about to head for the waiting room, when Caroline caught sight of Simon being led into one of the examining cubicles.

He wore a flimsy hospital gown. He stood at the far end of the emergency room, and to reach him, Caroline had to walk past many other patients, doctors, and nurses. He flinched at the sight of her. His skinny arms snaked out of the gown; his stick legs looked bony and pathetic. He had a pitiful expression in his beady eyes, and Caroline stood right in front of him, forcing him to look at her.

"Hello, Simon," she said in a normal voice.

"Hello, Caroline," he said warily.

"Why are you here?" she asked.

He pulled down the front of his hospital gown, revealing a square white bandage just below his collarbone. "Look what your sister did," he said. "She stabbed me."

"But you're walking. You're on your feet," Caroline said, trying to control the rage in her heart.

"They stitched me up," he said.

"Look at me, Simon," she said, tilting her head back to look up into his bloodshot eyes. "I'm taller than Skye."

"So? She stabbed me!"

"I'm taller than my mother."

"You're crazy, Caroline. You know that? Every frigging one of you is out of—"

"You hurt them," Caroline said, dropping her voice and reaching up to touch his chin.

She wanted to choke the pathetic sneer off his ugly face.

"You hurt my sister and mother," she said again. "They're small women, Simon. They're wonderful, and they've both shown you more love than you ever deserved, and you put them both in this hospital."

"They attacked me," he said, trying to push her hand away.

"Attacked you?" Caroline asked.

"Crazy bitches."

With that, Caroline snapped. She jumped on Simon and began pounding him with her fists. She yanked his black hair, she clawed his evil eyes. She pictured him going after Skye, hitting her mother, and she saw blood. She heard her own cries, felt her blows connecting against his chest, the chest of a monster.

"Were you trying to rape my sister?" she screamed.

"Lady," a loud voice said. She felt herself being pulled back, and she looked into the broad face of a hospital security guard.

"Fuck you, Caroline," Simon said, scrambling back.

"Hey, are you all right?" a young nurse asked, a concerned look in her face.

Caroline thought she was talking to Simon, until she saw the nurse looking at her.

"Call the fucking cops," Simon said. "I want her arrested."

"He hurt my mother and sister," Caroline said, staring at him.

"I need pain medication," Simon said. "My chest is on fire."

"Relax," the nurse said curtly. "Your doctor will see you soon."

Then, taking Caroline's arm, she led her toward the waiting area. "Leave it to the police," the nurse said. "If my mother and sister landed in here, I'd want to kill the guy too. But then you'd be in trouble, and who would that help?"

"No one," Caroline said. She was shaking. She hoped she had hurt Simon badly. She felt no remorse or regret for attacking him, only a desire to have hit him harder. Looking up, she saw Clea coming toward her.

"Can't I leave you alone for one minute?" Clea asked.

"No," Caroline said.

"You're going to get in trouble," Clea said. "I'd prefer not to visit you in jail."

"You're just mad you didn't hit him first."

"Did you connect?"

"I think so. My fist hurts."

"That's a good sign," Clea said, smiling.

Caroline shook her sister's hand, and they settled down to wait for news about all the people they loved.

* * *

Sam's head pounded. A thousand whales were slapping their flukes on the surface of his skull. Banging their tails pow. Whales' tails on the brain. He hadn't felt this bad since a sailing accident at age eight. He lay in his hospital bed, staring at a TV he couldn't see. He had his glasses, but when he put them on, his head hurt worse. When he took them off he saw three of everything, as murky as objects underwater.

Someone was coming into his room. A short, fat nun. A midget as wide as she was tall. Sam fumbled for his glasses, wanting to see her better. The nun had a very deep voice.

"What the hell are you doing, sitting up?" the voice asked. It was Joe.

"The nurse said I could."

"Bullshit. You're supposed to be flat on your back for another twenty-four hours."

"Look who's talking!" Sam said. He slid

his glasses on, wedging the eyepieces under the bandage. There was his brother, sitting in a wheelchair. "You're supposed to be in surgery again today, getting your arm sewed on right."

"I already did, smart guy. First thing this morning. It's why they're making me sit in this thing. So I don't keel over." Standing up, he gave a macho stretch and pushed the chair away. "How do you feel?"

"Great. You?"

"Great."

The brothers smiled at their lies. Bowled over by the emotion, by how close they had come to death, they stared at each other.

They shook hands, and it turned into more of a clasp—the closest they would let themselves come to a hug. They were bandaged and bruised, broken open and stitched back. They had each nearly died trying to save the other. Gazing at each other now, they seemed to be taking inventory, making sure the other was in one piece.

Sam choked down a lump in his throat. Joe had his arm all bandaged, in a sling, pressed tight against his chest. Even in his hospital gown he had that tough-guy look that Sam in his wildest dreams would never have. A pretty blond nurse came in to check Sam's blood pressure, but at the sight of Joe, she lost interest. She ended up adjusting Joe's sling. Joe just stood there, curling his lip at her, looking mean to hide the fact he had nearly cried.

"Joe, you know you ought to be sitting in that chair," the nurse said, dimpling. She pulled Joe's hand, and he pulled back. "Just because they didn't use general anesthesia this morning doesn't mean your body isn't weakened. Now, sit!"

Joe just shook his head. He did it politely, but with a definite "get out of here" subtext in his baby-blues. The nurse blushed, patted his arm, forgot all about the task she was supposed to perform on Sam.

"So," Sam said, watching her leave the room. "What was that you were trying to say to me before the wreck collapsed?"

"Say to you? I was thanking you for trying to stick your air in my mouth."

"No, before that. Before you practically strangled yourself with your air hose, trying to bludgeon the shark. It was a blacktip, by the way. Rare for northern waters, but certainly not a danger to man. Actually, I enjoyed observing it."

"Bullshit. It was a mako. Worst shark in this region."

"Blacktip."

"Going straight for your jugular."

Sam shook his head. "Harmless species. But thanks anyway."

"Damn biologist." Joe said. "You're welcome. Thanks for the air."

"Anytime. So." Sam took a deep breath. He pictured Joe before he entered the wreck. Treading water, grinning widely, mouthing the words *Black Hall.* For those first bad hours, lying unconscious or close to it, Sam had basked in the salvation of thinking that his brother had made him a promise.

Sam's body was healing, but so was his spirit. Because he had convinced himself that Joe had been trying to tell him something. By saying *Black Hall* he was really saying *Yale.* He had made a decision to give up treasure hunting, stay in New England, be near Caroline and Sam. Sam felt himself grinning, and he couldn't stop.

"When were you going to tell me?" Sam asked.

"Tell you what?"

"Caroline."

Joe turned red. He tried to suppress the

smile, but he couldn't. He nodded, a wry look on his face. "Yeah," he said.

"You're in love with her? That's what's going on?"

"It's true," Joe said, sighing as his grin got bigger.

"And you're gonna move in with her?"

"What?" Joe asked, the grin disappearing.

"*Black Hall.*" Sam said, smiling so hard it made his temples burn, his skull throb, his ears ache.

"What are you talking about?"

"I saw you, underwater," Sam said, the smile dissipating a little. He wanted Joe to get it out, tell him that he'd changed his mind, decided to stay. That their little brush with death had hastened a conversion that was already under way, that he was finally figuring out what was important in life.

"Yeah?" Joe asked, waiting for a hint.

"You said *Black Hall.* As if you were trying to tell me something."

Joe frowned. "When we first went down? Before I entered the wreck?"

"Yes, then."

"I was saying 'Go over there,' 'Wait out here,'" Joe said. "Something like that. I didn't want you inside the wreck while we were bringing out the gold. I thought it'd be too dangerous."

"You mean you're not gonna go to Yale?"

"I told you, Sam—"

"But I thought . . ." Sam trailed off. He stared at the window. Somehow he had imagined that Caroline was going to change everything. He had seen the way Joe behaved around her, turning nicer and acting as if he were finally chucking off the old armor. Finally letting his guard down enough to fall in love. Sam had thought Caroline would keep him here.

"I told you, I'm not a teacher. You're the smart one. I'm not cut out for university life, doing research and lecturing students." Joe paused. "Not even at Yale."

Sam pulled his glasses off. His head was really starting to pound; the whales were at it again. Love and a headache, the combination made him think of his sailing accident. He had been in love for the first time, and he had lost the girl. True, he had only been twelve. But now, losing Joe, he felt himself going into a tailspin.

"Sam?" Joe said, his voice too soft.

"What?"

"It has nothing to do with you. If I were going to teach, I'd want to do it with you."

"Yeah."

"I would, kid."

"Just forget it, Joe."

"We're going to see more of each other. I promise."

"You always say that," Sam said, sinking into his pillow. He was still weak and tired; he felt it now. He didn't even have the backbone to act his age, pretend he didn't care that Joe was going to leave again, go somewhere halfway around the world and see Sam only when Sam made the effort.

"I'm kinda tired," Sam tried to say. The words came out garbled.

"I mean it, Sam," Joe said. Sam's eyes were closed, but he felt his brother squeeze his hand. "This time it's going to be different."

* * *

Augusta lay in her hospital bed, drifting in and out of sleep. She had a concussion, and had suffered two seizures. An earthquake and two aftershocks, she thought of them. Her head ached terribly, but she refused to let anyone know. Caroline was sitting beside her bed, watching Augusta with that clear, steady gaze the whole family had come to rely on. The sight of her flooded Augusta with such gratitude she gave a big smile even though she had taken her bridge out.

"Caroline," she said, the word coming out as a croak.

"Are you thirsty, Mom?" Caroline asked.

"A little," Augusta said. She let Caroline push the button to raise her head, the little motor humming inside the bed. She opened her mouth as Caroline tilted the glass, poured a trickle of ice water into her parched throat. She swallowed, opened her mouth for more.

Caroline supported her head so carefully. She watched like an eagle, making sure Augusta didn't dribble on her chin. When Augusta had finished drinking, Caroline wiped her lips with a tissue. Augusta almost couldn't bear it, the love in her oldest daughter's eyes. When Augusta had given so little in return.

"Here we are," Augusta said.

"You and me," Caroline said, smiling.

"Toothless and bald," Augusta said. She was too tired to feel vain. They had shaved her head to stitch the cut, and she didn't have the energy to wear her bridge. All she wanted to do was sleep.

"You're still beautiful, Mom," Caroline said.

Augusta shook her head, but she felt better to hear it.

"How is Skye?" Augusta asked. "Have you seen her today?"

"She's fine," Caroline said.

Augusta nodded, looking away.

"What, Mom?"

"I almost feel . . . I don't have the right to ask," she said. "We turned you over to the universe a long time ago. Why should I think I can get you back now?"

" 'We'?"

"Your father and I."

"Oh, Mom," Caroline said. "You didn't pawn us."

Augusta waited for her to say more, but she didn't. Why should she? Caroline just didn't want to hurt her mother by agreeing with the truth: that Augusta had been a selfish mother, unwilling and unable to go through the hard parts of life with her three daughters. Wanting only the art and the parties, the love and the fun and their father. Augusta blinked, to focus her blurry vision.

"Mom, get well," Caroline said, such warmth in her black-pearl eyes. "Don't think about bad things right now. We need you at home."

"Have you ever needed me?" Augusta asked without rancor. "I can't see why. I was a terrible mother."

"That's not true," Caroline said, her smile growing wider. She meant it, Augusta could see. She felt tired, nearly exhausted from the effort of simply staying awake. Sleep was coming, she could feel it deep inside herself.

"Do you know, I've been lying here, thinking about it all. They're giving me medication that makes me so drowsy. But I think about you girls, and your father and me, and I keep trying to figure it all out. How it all turned out so wrong. As if there's one little piece missing, and if I can just get to it . . ."

"It didn't turn out all wrong," Caroline said.

"Our messy lives. We loved you girls so much. That much I know. He wanted so desperately to protect you. And when he couldn't, he turned away. There wasn't anything I could do to stop him."

Caroline touched her mother's forehead, soothing the worry out of it.

"What good does it do?" Caroline asked. "Thinking of that? It's over, Mom. Just get better."

"One little piece," Augusta said "I just want to put it all together."

* * *

When the time came for Joe to leave the hospital, he didn't really have anyplace to go. He had chartered the *Meteor* out to a group of physical oceanographers from Woods Hole. They intended to record wave anomalies in the Atlantic Ocean—measure the heights and periods of standard waves, hoping for the occasional rogue. They were willing to pick up the *Meteor* in Black Hall and drop it off in Piraeus, doing their research as they crossed the Atlantic.

Fine with Joe. He felt relieved to have the *Meteor* on her way over. He had to be in Greece by the first of October, Mykonos by the seventh. The weather would be favorable then, the water clear. His operation was a joint venture with an archaeologist out of Marseilles. Their permit covered thirty days, and the Greek government was not known to be flexible with extensions.

Caroline had invited him to stay with her until he left.

Joe had hesitated. Not because he didn't love her or want to spend his last days in New England with her, but because he didn't want to hurt her. He knew he would leave Black Hall as soon as Sam was better, as soon as they let him out of the hospital. He had told that to Caroline. She had listened, taking it all in, then said she knew, she didn't care, she wanted him to stay anyway. Skye was staying at her house too. Not wanting her to return alone to Firefly Hill, Caroline had convinced her to stay in the guest room.

Joe and Caroline sat on her porch glider. The night was warm, and haze hung low in the marsh. Caroline wore a white cotton dress. Joe was slouched down at one end of the glider, and Caroline leaned against his chest, away from his sore arm. Homer lay at her feet, his head resting on folded paws, utterly content to be with Caroline.

"It's so quiet," Caroline said.

"It is," Joe said, playing with her hair.

"Sam looked good today. He liked the brownies Clea made him."

"Sam's in love with Clea," Joe said. "If Peter weren't such a good guy, I believe Sam would try to steal her."

"Everyone loves Sam," Caroline said.

"Even you?" Joe asked.

"He's my buddy," Caroline said. "I like that, the way our families go—"

"Go what?"

"I was going to say together," Caroline said quietly.

Joe nodded. His chest felt tight, the way it did when he stayed underwater for too long. That afternoon Peter had asked him about Greece, and Joe had felt the tendons in his shoulder start to throb as he thought about leaving.

"I like your family too. Skye and Clea." He grinned. "Your mother . . ."

"She's very polite about you staying here," Caroline said, smiling. "But I think it's because she knows it's not going to be for very long."

"It's not?" Joe asked, surprising himself by the way his voice lifted at the end.

"Is that a question?" Caroline asked.

"I guess not," he said. "Too bad you have your business to run. Otherwise I'd tempt you into coming to Greece with me. You keep telling me you love to travel."

Caroline lifted her eyes. Her expression was direct and sharp, not soft at all. She didn't smile. "Don't tease me," she said.

Easing out of Joe's arms, she lifted their empty water glasses. She walked barefoot into the house, and he heard her moving around the kitchen. He sat very still, wondering how it would feel to live there. To not be planning the next treasure hunt. His shoulder throbbing, he shifted on the glider.

The old dog looked up at him. Reaching down, Joe petted his head. Homer leaned into his hand, making friends. They had a lot in common, loving Caroline. Joe stroked the brittle fur, gentle and rhythmic.

"Should we go find her?" Joe asked. Homer struggled to his feet, limping into the kitchen.

Joe paused behind Caroline. She stood at the sink, rinsing the glasses. He could tell by the way she stood that she was upset, that he had hurt her.

"Caroline," he said, "I'm sorry."

She didn't move. She stood there, the water running over her hands. Joe put his hands on her shoulders and turned her around. Her cheeks were wet and there

were tears in the corners of her mouth. Her
eyes were stern.

"You have nothing to be sorry for," she
said. "I'm just a little sad, okay? Aren't I allowed to feel sad?"

"You're allowed," Joe said. Because he
felt sad too.

Homer stood beside Caroline. He gazed up
at her, sensing her mood. As if he understood
her need for comfort, he nudged her thigh with
his head. She reached down to pet him, then
lowered her head to his. Joe watched for a
moment, realizing there was something eternal in the relationship between them. Homer
was very old, past the age most dogs lived,
and it hurt Joe to think he would soon die.

"Have you had him since he was a
puppy?" Joe asked.

Caroline stayed where she was. Lovingly
Homer bumped her head. When she stood,
she wiped her tears.

"Not quite," she said. "I got him when he
was about a year old."

"He must have been a beautiful young
dog," Joe said. "Why did his first owner
give him up?"

"He died," Caroline said.

"Oh, no," Joe said, petting Homer's back.

His spine was visible through the reddish coat, and he arched into Joe's hand. Caroline reached for something on the table. It was Skye's hospital bracelet. She had cut it off her wrist earlier, leaving it on the kitchen table before going to her room for a rest.

"Skye killed him," Caroline said quietly.

"God," Joe said.

"We were hunting. She was only seventeen, and she thought she was shooting a deer, but it was a man." Caroline bowed her head.

"I'm so sorry," Joe said.

"She's never gotten over it," Caroline said. "It was just an accident, but that doesn't matter."

"No," Joe agreed, stunned.

"I was with her. She was beside herself—couldn't believe what she had done. I sat with him while she stood there. Poor Skye," Caroline said.

"He died there in the woods?" Joe asked.

"Yes," Caroline continued on. "I held his hand. He had such bright eyes. He was lying there, on the trail, and I remember thinking he looked so nice and *bright*. That's the word I kept thinking. So bright."

"Caroline," Joe said, moved beyond words. She had seen both his father and that young man die. He loved a woman who

was so kind and sensitive, and all these
years he had resented her for not telling him
faster. Her father had sent them hunting because of something his father had started.
"What was his name?"

"Andrew Lockwood."

"Homer was his dog?"

"Yes. It was a beautiful day, and they were
just out for a walk. Homer was kissing him.
Licking his face all the while, trying to make
him better. When Andrew's eyes closed,
Homer just licked his eyes. He never
wanted to stop."

Joe looked at the dog's white face. He
could see him kissing his dying master, and
knew why Caroline loved him so much. And
why the dog loved Caroline.

"How's Skye?" Joe asked.

"I don't know," Caroline said. "It's with her
all the time."

"Do you think she'd go to an AA meeting?"

Caroline paused. She glanced from Joe to
Homer in that blank way of someone who
had lost hope that a tragedy could be
averted. She shrugged. "I don't know," she
said. "I doubt it."

"It helps me," Joe said.

"I wish . . ."

"What?" he asked.

"That it could help her," Caroline whispered.

"Caroline," Joe said. Something was building inside him, and he had to get it out.

"What?" she asked.

"Come with me."

"To a meeting? But—"

"No, to Greece."

She looked shocked. Did she think he was teasing her like before? He pulled her into his arms. He said it again, looking straight into her gray eyes. "Come to Greece with me."

"Don't joke," she said.

"I'm not. Tell me one reason why it wouldn't work."

"My family," she said, "I can't leave them. And I have an inn to run."

"You love to travel, everyone knows it. Michele knows how to run the inn. And your family—"

She waited. She wanted him to finish the sentence: will be fine. But they both knew such predictions were impossible, that fate played tricks on people, that keeping watch was just an illusion. You could be standing right beside your sister, and she could kill a man. You could be ten feet away, and something terrible could still happen.

"Your family knows you love them. You'll be back."

"I will?"

"Yes. I'll talk to the guys at Yale. Not this fall, but maybe next year. I'm thinking of Sam too. Watching you with your family makes me want to do better with him. I've been on the run for a long time."

Caroline stepped away from Joe. Homer had retreated to an old blue blanket in the corner of her kitchen, and she leaned against the counter, watching him. He hadn't taken his eyes off her, and her sudden attention made him raise his head, bang his tail on the floor. Caroline leaned over to pet him, and to reach into a fold of the blanket. She pulled out a small towel, battle-scarred from many play sessions. Homer bit one end while Caroline held the other.

"My father started this," she said, tugging on the towel.

"With Homer?"

"Yes. When we first brought him home, he was so upset. He cried all the time, and he wouldn't play with any of the toys we gave him. Balls, bones. Then my father gave him an old towel. It was soft, and I guess it smelled like us."

"Homer liked the game?" Joe asked, wondering what this had to do with going to Greece.

"Yes. Homer loved it. He carried the towel everywhere, and when the first one got all chewed up, we gave him another. He'd always want my father to play with him." She paused, standing to face Joe. "My father liked it too. Till he got so sick. Then he stopped everything."

"His cancer, you mean?"

"No," Caroline said. "The kind of sickness that made him drink and turn away. Like Skye now. I'm afraid to leave her."

Joe walked over to her. He felt his heart pounding. He had never wanted anything as much as this. He wanted her with him, but at the same time, he needed to help her. She was caught in a trap, trying to save someone who had to help herself. He took a deep breath, than held her face gently between his hands.

"Do you know what the opposite of love is?" he asked.

"Hate? Joe, I could never—"

"Fear."

"The opposite of love is fear," she said, frowning.

"We could be so fearful, we could let this go."

"I don't think I'm afraid—"

"You just said you're afraid to leave Skye."

Caroline nodded, seeing his point.

"And your father," Joe began. Talking about Hugh Renwick wasn't easy, especially when what he had to say was so filled with the understanding of one flawed man for another.

"What about him?" Caroline asked.

"Tell me something. How did Homer like your father?"

"He loved him," Caroline said. "It was so sad, ironic, really, that after my father died, Homer cried for him the way he'd once cried for Andrew. For days and days. He'd disappear from the house, go off on these long walks. He'd come home and howl on the porch."

"For your father."

"Yes," Caroline said, recognition dawning in her eyes.

"Even though your father had stopped playing with him. He might have turned away, but that didn't stop Homer from loving him."

Caroline nodded, her eyes briming. She bowed her head for a minute. Joe waited, wanting to touch her but knowing she needed to decide for herself.

"I'm not afraid," she said suddenly, raising her eyes. They were full of tears, the most beautiful eyes he'd ever seen.

"You're not?"

"The opposite," she said.

Joe grinned, knowing she meant love, that they were picking up where their letters had left off so long ago.

"When do we leave for Greece?" she asked.

"As soon as Sam's out of the hospital," he said, taking her in his arms.

CHAPTER TWENTY-ONE

Augusta was released from the hospital right after Labor Day. She went straight to Clea's house, because Clea was the daughter best equipped to give their mother the care she needed. The bad blow Augusta had suffered had affected her motor skills and she needed physical therapy three times a week. This meant driving her to a rehabilitation facility and encouraging her to do her exercises at home.

Caroline gave her a fabulous black hawthorn walking stick with a sterling silver handle, which Augusta thought was marvelous. Antique and Irish, like something Oscar Wilde would have used had he ever needed a cane. Since they had shaved her head at the hospital, she was growing to enjoy being bald—or at least she was making the most of it. Her hair would grow back, but for now she wore the beautiful and dramatic silk scarves her daughters kept bringing her. She twisted them into turbans and thought she looked quite regal. Divine, considering.

But Clea felt overwhelmed. Her whole family considered her the rock. She kept house and cooked gourmet meals. She ran her children from day camp to flute and trumpet lessons to the movies all day long. She was the minister's wife, she stood by Peter's side at weddings and funerals, sickbeds and prayer services.

Having her mother under her roof was making her crazy. It wasn't Augusta's fault. For once, her mother was being meek. She seemed grateful for every saltine, every glass of seltzer water. Her doctors had told her she couldn't drink alcohol while she was taking anti-seizure medication, and Augusta hardly complained. Every day at five she would say, "Time for a martini!" But Clea wouldn't bring one, and Augusta wouldn't push it.

Mainly, Augusta stayed in her room and listened to music. It confused Clea to see her mother so quiet and contemplative. One day she called Clea to her bedside. Clea had thought she was going to ask for an extra blanket, or a glass of ice water, but instead, Augusta patted the quilt and asked Clea to sit by her side. Reaching for an English bone hairbrush, Augusta began to brush Clea's hair.

"Tell me something," Augusta said, slowly stroking Clea's hair.

"Like what?" Clea said, feeling goose bumps on the back of her neck from the unfamiliar pleasure of her mother's touch.

"Anything, honey. Just tell me a story. Anything at all."

"Well, Maripat and Mark both want to sign up for a new soccer league."

"About you, Clea," Augusta said. "I love the children, but I want to hear something about you."

"Oh, Mom," Clea said, her throat constricting, hardly knowing where to start.

"Something about Clea," Augusta said. "Tell me."

"But why?"

"I'm so sorry there has to be a 'why,' " Augusta said. "That you don't think it completely natural for me to wonder about you."

"You had Dad to worry about," Clea said.

"Yes, I did worry," Augusta said, brushing Clea's hair, "that he'd find me boring, feel closed in, go off with someone else. You girls suffered for it."

"I'm fine, Mom," Clea said. "And Caroline is great." Caroline had announced her plans to go to Greece. While no one was totally surprised, the reality of her departure—for an entire year—felt daunting.

"But Skye's not."

"No," Clea said. Skye had moved out of Caroline's, back to Firefly Hill, where she could be alone. Clea had stopped by once with an extra pot of beef stew, and found her in bed at four in the afternoon, staring hopelessly out the window. Feeling her mother brush her hair, Clea closed her eyes. She tried to imagine how she would feel if she knew Maripat was suffering the way Skye was, and she knew her mother had a broken heart.

"What can I do, darling?" Augusta asked. "I know it's a case of too little too late, but I can't bear it. I can't bear to see her this way."

"I don't know, Mom," Clea said, reaching back for her mother's hand. It felt thin and frail, and when she turned around, she saw how old her mother looked. Augusta stopped brushing Clea's hair, letting her hands fall to her lap.

"With Caroline off to Greece, I don't know. . . ."

"She'll be back."

"I've let her handle so much for so long. She's taken care of Skye all her life, while I . . . wasted so much time."

They looked into each other's eyes, the two mothers of the family. They each understood how it felt to raise daughters, the special worries of letting their beloved girls out into this world full of dangers, and Clea tried to send her mother some of her own strength. Clea had gotten it from somewhere, and she liked to think some of it had come from Augusta herself.

"What happened?" Augusta said in the absent way of someone who has woken up from a bad dream. "That's what I asked Caroline. With all our gifts, all the love we have for one another, what went wrong? That's what I want to know. That one missing piece."

"Life, Mom," Clea said, holding her mother's hand. She thought "what if" all the time: What if Peter died, what if someone hurt one of the children, what if she fell through the ice in the pond? Terrible things happened when you least expected them. But so did wonderful things, so did joy. "That missing piece is life," she said.

"Life," Augusta said, tilting her head.

* * *

Skye was alone at Firefly Hill. She had agreed to have dinner with Caroline and Joe. What she wanted to do was pull the curtains, turn off the phone, and get the job done. She wanted to kill herself. She was so sick of living. Nothing touched the agony inside.

The house was a tomb. Memories everywhere. Homer's fur all over the furniture, but no Homer. He was at Caroline's, her mother was at Clea's walking with a cane and undergoing physical therapy because of the man Skye had brought into their home. Simon was in Boston. He had gone back to Biba, but he would have to face charges for assault and attempted rape in the coming months. Skye didn't care. She didn't love him anymore. She didn't need him—didn't need anyone. She loved only her father. She had recently imagined herself drinking with his ghost. Talking out loud to him, telling him how she felt, begging him to forgive her.

Someone knocked on the door. Expecting Caroline and Joe to just walk in, she felt surprised. She checked herself in the mirror: bloated face, circles under her eyes, her hair a rat's nest. She noticed a dark stain on the front of her sweater, but she didn't care. Slowly, every joint in her body aching, Skye went to the door.

It was Joe. He stood on the porch, all alone. Skye looked around.

"Hi," Joe said.

"Hi. Where's Caroline?"

"At home. Can I come in?"

Skye swung the door open. Without speaking, Joe walked past her. He waited until Skye remembered to ask if he'd like to come into the kitchen.

"What's wrong? Is she okay?" Skye asked.

"She's fine," Joe said, eyeing the bottle. Skye blushed. She hadn't drunk from it, but she had been staring at it for the last half hour.

"Would you like a drink?" Skye asked.

"Skye?"

His voice was so quiet, so calm and kind, it stopped Skye in her tracks.

"Would you like to go to an AA meeting instead?" he asked.

"AA?"

"Alcoholics Anonymous."

"You're one?"

"I'm one," he said, smiling.

"How did you know?" she asked, trembling. "What made you go?"

"It was over for me," he said. "I didn't want to do it anymore."

"I'm so tired," Skye said. She thought of the bottle, how she could drink it all night and not feel drunk, how nothing was chasing the pain away. She thought of her .22 out in a shed behind the house. She hadn't checked on it in a while, but for the last day and a half she had been imagining how it would feel to pick it up, do to herself what she had done to a man on a mountain trail.

"I was too," Joe said. "I was sick and tired of being sick and tired."

"That's it," Skye said, tears streaming down her face. "That's how I feel."

"You never have to feel this way again. Will you come with me?" Joe asked.

Skye took a look around the kitchen. There were the clay handprints she had made for her father in first grade. The bust of her mother she had done in high school. There were pictures of her and her sisters, dressed in their red-checked coats, ready to go hunting on Redhawk one Thanksgiving weekend. A picture of her father the year before she shot Andrew Lockwood; it was the last picture of him that showed him smiling. He had spent the rest of his life drunk.

"Dad," Skye said out loud.

"He'd want this for you," Joe said.

"I feel like I'm leaving him," Skye said. Then, giving Joe a defiant look, "I love him."

"Why shouldn't you? He's your father."

"Everyone blames him" she said.

"He's still your father."

Skye nodded. That's how she saw it: Before the hunts, before the shooting, there was a big man who taught her how to draw, carried her on his shoulders, took her swimming at the beach.

"You're not leaving him, Skye," Joe said, reaching out his hand.

The tears ran down Skye's face. She picked up her father's picture and held it to her breast. She felt so afraid of leaving the house. She and her father were so alike, artists who had made mistakes with the ones they loved, who drank because they couldn't bear the hurt in others' faces.

"Come, Skye," Joe said. "Please?"

She took a deep breath, put down her father's picture. If she looked too deeply into Joe's eyes, she would see more than she was prepared for right now. He was helping her out of love for Caroline, she was sure. Skye was sure Caroline knew what he was doing, that she was sitting home right now with Homer, wishing her heart out that Skye would go to the AA meeting with Joe. It would make leaving for Greece so much easier.

"You're taking her away," Skye said.

"Only to Greece," Joe said. "Not *away*. She could never go away from you."

"It's too far," Skye said.

"She hasn't left yet," he said. "She's five miles up the road right now."

Caroline leaving for Greece: another blow, another reason to take the dark path, hide out, turn away. It was so much easier to sleep than be awake, to drink than to stop.

"There's a saying in AA," Joe said. "Don't quit before the miracle."

"What's the miracle?"

"You'll know it when you see it," Joe said.

"What if I never see it?"

"If you quit, you'll never know what you might have missed."

Closing her eyes, Skye thought of the .22. She thought of her father and Joe's father; she thought of Andrew Lockwood. Their faces had been so clear, but now they were fading. She couldn't bring them into focus. Right now the face she was seeing was Caroline's.

Skye's eyes slowly opened, and she nodded.

"Okay," she heard herself saying. "I'll go with you."

* * *

Every morning Caroline found herself giving Michele a little more of the inn's business to handle. She took her to Coastal Bank & Trust, introduced her to the bankers, explained the workings of various accounts.

Michele was a quick study. She seemed eager. She learned fast, asked the right questions. Of course, she had been at the front desk for ten years, so she had a head start. Caroline noticed Tim hanging around some afternoons, taking a regular seat in the bar. Classes had started at the college, and he would sometimes drop by with colleagues or students to have a beer and talk about the artists of Black Hall. Seeing him there made Caroline happy. She knew he was at the inn to support Michele, that he would keep it up when Caroline was away.

Other days, Caroline wasn't sure she wanted to leave. How could she sail away with Joe and leave the inn behind? How could she leave her family? They needed her too much. Maybe she hadn't been the perfect sister to Clea and Skye, the perfect daughter to Augusta, but she had done her best, and so far hadn't they all survived? They wobbled along, the Renwick women, a troupe of off-balance acrobats trying to pedal bicycles across a high wire.

Sam was scheduled to be discharged from the hospital the following day, and she and Joe were supposed to leave a few days after that. Skye was now going to meetings. Caroline knew her sister's new sobriety came with no guarantees, but she had hope. She knew that she had no other option.

Caroline dropped in regularly at Clea's to visit her mother. Augusta was trying to be a good sport. She didn't like the idea of Caroline leaving, especially for Greece—especially with Joe Connor. But she held her tongue. As if she had decided enough harm had been done in their lives, she seemed unwilling to do more. She didn't dislike Joe; she resented his father for the violence he had introduced to their family.

Three days before she was going to leave, Caroline drove Augusta to the hospital for a checkup. They were in the neurologist's office, waiting to see the doctor, when Joe and Sam walked in. Augusta froze. This was her first moment face-to-face with Joe Connor since the Firefly Ball.

"Hello, Mrs. Renwick," he said, holding out his hand.

"Hello, Joe," she said cautiously. She shook his hand, then his brother's. The boys kissed Caroline, and everyone seemed very chummy.

"Looks like we have the same doctor, Mrs. Renwick," Sam said.

"Call me Augusta," she said. "You too, Joe."

"Thanks, Augusta," Joe said.

Caroline and Joe had a million things to do before they left. They stood off to the side, by the receptionist's desk, going over a checklist. Augusta and Sam sat alone, not knowing quite what to say to each other. Augusta reached up to make sure her turban was in place.

"Hey, nice hat," Sam said, grinning. His skin was pale, the circles under his eyes dark and deep. Skinnier than ever, he must have lost ten pounds. He had a big white bandage on his head, exactly like the one Augusta had worn the previous week.

"Thank you," she said demurely. "Yours is quite nice too."

"Feeling better?" he asked.

"A little shaky these days. And you?"

"Wobbly as all hell. If you'll excuse my language."

"Think nothing of it," Augusta said, peering at him. She was looking for a resemblance to his brother, but saw practically none. Joe was strapping and sexy, while Sam was thin and gawky, handsome in an English-schoolboy way. Glasses, tufty hair sticking out of the bandage, a narrow face.

"Actually, my head hurts all the time," he said, leaning closer to her. "They're giving me anti-seizure medication, and it makes me feel like sleeping."

"Me too," Augusta said. "It's awful. I feel like I'm living in fog, and I'm not allowed to drink martinis. Do you have seizures?"

"I had one," Sam said, staring at his knees.

Augusta touched the back of his hand. The poor child. He was so young. "Did you hate it?" she asked.

"Yeah," he said. "I don't want to have another. My doctor said they're not uncommon with head injuries. Have you had any?"

"Two. Nightmare roller-coaster rides. Once they started, nothing on earth could stop them."

"Wow, it rots, huh? My brother would go crazy if he knew. He thinks the accident was his fault."

"Your brother," Augusta said, folding her arms and biting her lip as she watched Joe and Caroline laughing quietly.

"You don't like him?" Sam asked.

"Nothing to do with you, dear," she said. "But certain things from the past. And now he wants to take Caroline off to Greece."

"He's a good guy," Sam said.

"If you only knew the whole story. It started with his father, you see, coming into our home one Christmas Eve and threatening to kill us all. I hope I'm not shocking you—"

"I know the story," Sam said easily. "But you're missing the best part."

"Which is?" Augusta asked. She was changing in ways she couldn't comprehend, including allowing the possibility that this skinny child, his head addled, might have something to tell her about her family's tragedy.

"Your daughter's in love with him."

Augusta turned her head to stare.

Sam shrugged. "I don't want him going to Greece either. But do you honestly think you're going to stop them? You might as well decide to play ball."

"I've never played ball," Augusta said thoughtfully.

"You'd better start now, Augusta," Sam said. " 'Cause that's what life's about."

*　*　*

"I think I got Augusta to give you her blessing, dragging Caroline off to Greece with you," Sam said. This was his first walk outside, his first day out of the hospital. Warm in the September sunshine, he and Joe were heading down a road by the sea.

"You're a powerful man," Joe said.

"She's stubborn," Sam said. "But who can blame her? Not wanting to send her daughter off with a scoundrel like you?"

"Good point," Joe said, kicking a stone down the road. "But what about you? You gonna give me your blessing?"

Walking slowly, Sam caught up with the stone. He tried to kick it, missed, scutting his sneaker on the tar. His vision was off. He closed one eye, kicked again, connected with the pebble.

"It's not forever," Joe said. "My permit's only for thirty days."

"Thirty days in the Aegean, then on to—where?"

"Lamu," Joe said. They rounded the bend and came upon a break in the trees. The Sound glittered in the sunlight, sparkling dark blue.

"Where's Lamu?" Sam asked, giving the stone an angry kick.

"The Indian Ocean. You know damn well."

"Is Caroline going with you?"

"Yes," Joe said.

Sam took a big breath of sea air, felt pain shoot down his neck. He was flying to Halifax the same day Joe and Caroline were leaving for Athens. His doctors told him his vision would improve, the pain would subside, and he'd probably never have another seizure again. But he had long ago lost the only girl who ever mattered, and he didn't look forward to missing Joe.

"You've got my blessing," he made himself say.

"Thanks," Joe said. He picked up the pebble they'd been kicking and handed it to Sam. Sam looked down at the small rock in his hand, then back up at Joe.

"What's this?" he asked.

"Objects are important," Joe said. "They remind us of things, you know? Like all that loot I brought up from the *Cambria*. Like my old man's watch—still don't know where it got to."

"What's a stupid stone supposed to remind me of?" Sam asked.

"Black Hall," Joe said.

"What about it?" Sam asked.

"A place to look forward to."

"We're here now. What's to look forward to?"

"Jobs," Joe said.

"I've got a job," Sam said. "On a research vessel out of Nova Scotia."

"I'll write to Yale from Greece, you do your part from Canada, we'll meet back here same time next year."

Sam stopped to stare at Joe. His mouth must have been hanging open, because Joe reached over to close it for him.

"Didn't you hear me?" Joe asked, chucking Sam under the chin.

"I heard. You're full of shit." Sam stood his ground. He felt like charging his brother like a bull, knocking him over, pounding his face in the dirt. Joe had teased him unmercifully as a kid, and Sam felt he was doing it once again.

"Believe what you want," Joe said, shrugging.

"You take it too lightly," Sam said roughly. "Family ties. You're what I have left, with Mom gone. So don't play around—" Sam stopped, watching Joe's smile widen. For the first time, he began to believe that maybe Joe wasn't kidding.

"I'm not playing around," Joe said.

"Swear?"

"Swear."

"Yale? You really think I should pursue the position there?"

"If you want to hang out together, yeah."

"You think I'll get a job?" Sam asked, his throat aching right into his ears.

"Probably not," Joe said.

Sam laughed, blinking at the bright sun that was making his eyes water.

"Why would they want to give the job to a biologist who doesn't even know a mako when he sees one?"

"Blacktip," Sam corrected.

"Mako," Joe said.

* * *

Caroline and Clea visited Skye, and together they walked Firefly Beach. Homer explored the high-tide line for dead crabs and old lobster buoys. The sisters knew they were saying good-bye. It wasn't time to say the words yet, but the feeling was in the air. They strolled along, feeling the hot winds of summer give way to the cool breezes of autumn, full of gratitude that Skye seemed to be getting better. Secretly they were all trying not to worry that Skye would tumble without Caroline there to catch her.

With each AA meeting Skye attended, her desire for drinking lessened. But that first meeting remained sharp, so clear in her mind.

Quivering from alcohol withdrawal for the second time that summer, Skye had gone to that first meeting with Joe. The room was small and dingy, in the basement of a white church in Eastbrook. Signs covered the walls, those little sayings she and Simon had once made fun of: One Day at a Time; First Things First. Skye had felt so scared, so nervous. But the people were friendly and kind. They made her feel welcome right away. Joe had never been to that particular group, but he spoke to one woman, telling her Skye was new, and the next thing Skye knew, she was surrounded by women, all giving her their phone numbers, all telling her things would get better, that she never had to feel this way again.

One woman had said, "I wish you a slow recovery," and that was what was happening. Baby steps. She went to a meeting every day. Sometimes she went with Joe, sometimes she called one of the women she had met that first night, but mostly she went alone. One day at a time, Skye was not drinking.

That in itself was a miracle. She cried a lot. A *lot*. Some days all she could do was eat popcorn, lie on the sofa in the fetal position, and cry. She would talk to her sponsor, an older woman who had been sober for sixteen years, whom Skye already loved more than just about anyone but her sisters and mother, and who understood everything Skye was going through because she was an alcoholic too. Skye would cry as if it were the end of the world, and her sponsor would say, "Yes, but did you drink?" "No," Skye would say. "Then you're having a good day!" her sponsor would say, sounding jubilant, and Skye would know she was right.

"Are you all packed?" Skye asked Caroline.

"Almost."

"What do you need for Greece?" Clea asked. "A bathing suit?"

"Two, I think," Caroline said.

"None," Skye said. "Just you and Joe and the sea and sun. Naked."

Caroline smiled. She picked up a flat stone and skimmed it across the shallow water: seven quick jumps. Clea tried: three blooping ones. Skye found a perfect scaler and sent it surfing the sea: eight jumps. Her hand didn't shake at all.

The sisters turned toward the steep stairway and began the trek up. Homer went first. He moved stiffly, but then he got the rhythm. He took the steps one at a time; when he came to Firefly Hill, he had taken four at once.

"You leave tomorrow," Skye said.

"I know."

"Mom's coming home, and we'll be fine. We'll be together," Skye said to set Caroline's mind at ease.

"That's great, Skye."

"Are you excited?" Clea asked.

"Yes, very," Caroline said. But she didn't sound it. Her voice was hesitant. She was trying to smile, but her forehead looked worried. Homer brushed against her as if he knew they didn't have much time left together.

"What's the matter?" Skye asked.

"I feel like I'm forgetting something," Caroline said.

"Like what?"

"I don't know." Now she really smiled, as if she had been caught in her old pose: oldest sister, perfectionist, worrywart. She was leaving for Greece with the man of her dreams. She had to just let herself go.

"Well, you have till tomorrow to figure it out," Clea said.

"That's right," Skye said. "Mom's coming home, you're leaving home. We'll have a little party."

Having reached the top of the steps, they paused to catch their breath. Skye looked out to sea, feeling free. She didn't hate herself anymore. It was so new, life without drinking. The blue water sparkled, empty without Joe's white ships. Forgiveness was possible, even for herself. Her heart felt calm, she was taking everything as it came. For now anyway. For today.

"I can't believe it," Caroline said. Suddenly she smiled, as if it were sinking in. "I'm going away with Joe."

"It's about time," Clea said.

"The longest love story I've ever heard," Skye said, "because no one will ever tell me it didn't start when you were five."

"Good-bye," Caroline said, "will be very hard to say."

Homer had been lying on the grass, taking a rest. But suddenly his head lifted, and his sleepy eyes turned eager. He sprang to his feet, his sore legs buckling only slightly. Perhaps he had heard a bird, or an animal in the brush, because his scruffy mane bristled, and he let out a sharp yelp. Then, like the young dog he used to be, he ran across the wide field toward the pine forest and disappeared into the trees.

"Where does he go?" Caroline asked.

"The secret life of Homer," Skye said.

"He probably has a girlfriend in Hawthorne," Clea said.

"A pretty girl Lab who loves to swim and doesn't mind slobbery old towels," Skye said.

"Someone for Homer to love," Caroline said, sounding so unlike the Caroline from before, Skye had to turn away, to keep her sisters from seeing the tears in her eyes and getting worried all over again.

CHAPTER TWENTY-TWO

When the time came for Caroline to leave, Homer wasn't back. Everyone else had gathered at Firefly Hill: Augusta; Clea, Peter, and the kids; Skye; Sam; Joe and Caroline. Augusta was on her best behavior, not trying to change Caroline's mind, getting along with Joe better than anyone had dared to expect. The family was together except for Homer. Mark and Maripat had been sent down to the beach to scout around for him. Perhaps it shouldn't have mattered so much that he be there—he was only a dog—but it did.

The men were loading the car. It was a bright September afternoon, cool and clear. The Renwick women had a few minutes alone in the kitchen, and they were making the most of it by sitting around the table for a cup of tea. Caroline wore her going-away clothes: a charcoal-gray suit, starched white shirt, the cameo at her throat. She had that overly composed, Carolinesque air to her. Augusta had come to recognize it as Caroline's matriarch look, and seeing it twisted her heart just slightly.

"You look great, dear," Augusta said.

"Thank you, Mom."

"As if you have absolutely everything under control, every single detail in place. I wish I could be as collected and serene as you."

"Really? I'm a mess inside," Caroline said calmly. "For some reason, I feel as if I'm about to get seasick."

"Maybe you're pregnant!" Clea said happily.

Caroline gave her a long look, blowing on her tea. "I'm not," she said. "I just feel funny, like I'm missing something."

"Don't you want to go?" Augusta asked. "You can always change your mind. It's not that I don't like Joe. You know that, don't you?"

"You've been very nice to him, Mom."

"Well, if you're not in the mood to travel, you can wait here till he gets back. Although, frankly, I wouldn't let him out of my sight. I'm being very honest with you,

Caroline. If you really love him, I wouldn't send him off to the Greek isles alone. He's a very charismatic man."

"Mom, he's not Dad," Skye said, smiling. "And Caroline's not you."

"I'm well aware of that," Augusta said. She smiled. She was being very brave about this. How could she say everything that was in her heart? Her oldest daughter was about to leave home just as Augusta felt she was on the verge of becoming a good mother.

"Mom," Caroline said, taking her hand.

"You don't have to worry about me," Augusta said, her voice strong. She knew what she had put her children through, knew how totally they had cared for themselves and each other over the years.

"We'll take care of her," Clea said.

"Or she'll take care of us," Skye said.

"Oh, Skye," Augusta said. She had been holding herself together, but hearing Skye's declaration, seeing her beautiful face nearly clear of bruises, made Augusta think she might break into pieces.

"Look what you did this summer," Skye went on. "Got right between me and Simon. You protected me, Mom."

"I did, didn't I?" Augusta said with a certain

amount of wonder. "I was never very good at it before though. Protecting you girls . . ."

"You're good at it now," Caroline said.

"I wish your father were here right now," Augusta said.

"I wish it too," Caroline said. Her throat was low, and she touched it as if it ached. "I think that's what's missing. Remember, Mom? We were talking about it a week or so ago? That one little piece?"

"Dad?" Clea asked.

"Dad," Caroline said.

"I miss him terribly," Augusta said.

"The summer's been about him, in a way," Caroline said. "With so much about James Connor and Andrew Lockwood, the hunts . . ."

"Homer getting old," Clea said.

"And me getting sober," Skye added.

"He was such an extraordinary man," Augusta said.

"And I never understood him at all," Caroline said. "So many things have become clearer this summer, but that part hasn't. If anything, he's farther away."

Her sisters looked quietly into their teacups, and Augusta sniffled loudly.

* * *

Caroline knew it was time to go.

Her mother patted her scarf, adjusting it carefully. She did look stunning, like an aging film star. Her scarf-turbans went perfectly with her black pearls, her New England–Hollywood looks. But seeing her mother, Caroline could tell that Simon's attack had taken something out of her. For the first time, Augusta looked old.

"Mom, are you okay?" Caroline asked.

"Just thinking of Hugh."

"We loved him, Mom," Clea said.

"It was never that we didn't," Skye said.

Augusta nodded. She looked tired and resigned, as if, like Caroline, she had spent too much time searching for the missing piece, the explanation that would weave it all together.

"Remember chasing fireflies?" Caroline asked. "Dad could do that with us for hours. It was always dark and hot, the middle of summer, and the stars were always out."

"Oh, sweetheart," Augusta sighed.

Caroline stared at her mother, trying to memorize her face. She would take it with her wherever she went, the image of her mother's eyes. She felt the pull of love, the eternal conflict of being a daughter.

"Remember when you were six," Clea said.

"You caught a firefly, and you were so excited, you fell and squished it?"

"I started to cry," Caroline said steadily. "My firefly was dead, and Dad came off the porch. I remember him walking through the field, through the tall grass. He looked so gigantic."

"Hugh couldn't bear to hear you cry, Caroline," Augusta said. "Ever. When you were an infant, he'd pick you up at the least whimper. The nights he was home, he would walk you for hours, up and down the hall, just to keep you happy."

Caroline nodded, touching her lips. For some reason, she could almost remember that too. It was as if the family ghosts or angels had cast a spell on the table, made it possible to remember impossible things. Closing her eyes, she could feel herself in the palm of her father's hand, smell his scent of cigarettes and oil paint, hear him singing her a lullaby. Driving her home the time she had a fever. But none of those things was the missing piece.

"Chasing fireflies," Augusta said. "It wasn't just when you were young. I vividly remember the summer Homer came to live with us, your father running through the salt hay with him, on the trail of anything that blinked."

"I loved Dad for that," Caroline said. It was true, she thought: With all the later hurt, during the years he spent drinking, she forgot the total love. "And I wish Homer would come back to say good-bye to me."

After a moment, Augusta reached for her cane. She motioned for the girls to stay where they were. She stood painfully, got used to her feet, and left the room. Caroline heard her thunking up the stairs, along the upstairs hall. She wondered how long her mother would keep the house. Firefly Hill was big and rambling, and maybe someday it would start to make sense for Augusta to live somewhere else. Somewhere smaller, more manageable.

Or maybe she would stay there until she died.

"I'm going to drive the mailman crazy," Skye said, "asking him for letters from you."

"You have to call from absolutely everywhere," Clea said.

"I've changed my mind," Caroline said. "I'm not going. Joe will have to find someone to take my place."

"Excellent thinking," Clea said. "Shall I tell him to move along?"

"Caroline?"

At the sound of her mother's voice,

Caroline turned around. Augusta leaned on her silver-topped hawthorn stick, a gentle smile on her face. Clea and Skye stood still. Their mother seemed weakened by the exertion, but happy, content in a way Caroline had never seen her before.

"Go get them," Augusta said, nodding to Skye. "Please?"

"Who?" Skye asked.

"Joe and Sam," Augusta said.

Surprised, Skye stood still. Then she ran out the door as fast as she could. They watched her run barefoot to the car, say something to Joe.

"What, Mom?" Caroline asked.

"I have something for your friend."

"Joe?"

Augusta nodded. She touched her black pearls, then she reached out her frail hand and touched Caroline's cameo. Caroline had found a length of black velvet ribbon and threaded it through the fragile gold clasps.

"Beautiful things," Augusta said, "from people we love. Objects matter."

"I know," Caroline said. She didn't know what was happening, but it began to dawn on her: Her mother was honestly making peace with Joe.

The screen door opened. The September evening was cool and a small burst of wind blew in. Skye stood there, smiling. Sam burst through the door, followed by Peter. Very cautiously, Joe followed. Caroline felt her heart quicken at the sight of him. He looked so handsome and tall, his white shirt tucked into his jeans. He smiled and said hello.

Augusta put out her hand. She stood tall and regal, her face stoic and dignified. Caroline watched Joe glancing around. His gaze lit upon the old kitchen table, the terracotta tile floor, old family photos, clay handprints of each of the girls. But Caroline knew he was thinking about his father. Caroline reached for Joe's hand, and he held tight.

"It was here, wasn't it?" Joe asked.

Augusta nodded.

"Right here," Joe said, staring at the place Caroline had shown him.

Augusta took four steps, stood in the exact spot where James Connor had fallen to the floor. "Here," she said.

Joe went to stand beside her. Caroline let go of his hand, and she leaned into her sisters, watching Joe and her mother. The moment seemed intense and private. Charged tension passed between them, the old woman and the son of the man who had died in her kitchen that Christmas so many years ago.

"He spoke of you that night," Augusta said in her low voice.

Joe nodded, frowning.

"I'm sorry, Joe," Augusta said, handing him something. "Please forgive me."

Joe examined the object in his hand. He held it up, and Caroline saw something heavy and gold.

"My father's watch," he said.

"I took it," Augusta said. "That night. If you had any idea . . ." She bowed her head, trying to control her voice. "When it was over, when your father was lying there . . ."

Caroline looked at Joe, saw him wiping away tears. She wanted to go to him, but the moment belonged to him and her mother.

"And Caroline was crying so hard, clutching your picture. Something made me take his watch. Forgive me, Joe. I don't know why I did it. I was rather crazed, you know? Your mother had my husband, so I thought I'd take something that belonged to her. I don't know."

Joe nodded. He gazed at the watch, turning it over and over in his hand. Caroline knew Augusta's explanation didn't matter. She knew what Joe's father's watch meant to him, and she had wondered: Searching his whole life for treasure, did any object compare to the sweet memory of his father's gold watch? And now Augusta had given it back to him.

* * *

"Thank you, Augusta," Joe Connor said. What he did next seemed so natural, it stole Caroline's breath away: He took her mother into his arms. Augusta dropped her cane in order to put both her arms around his neck. The stick clattered to the floor.

"You're welcome, Joe," Augusta said when she let him go.

But Joe held on. His hands still resting on Augusta's arms, he began to smile. His blue eyes widened.

"What, dear?" Augusta asked.

"Your pearls," Joe said.

"Oh," Augusta said, blushing with pride, brushing the pearls with her fingers. "Hugh gave them to me. They are rare black pearls, from one particular bay in the South Seas, near Tahiti or somewhere marvelous like that. But of course you probably know. Being a treasure hunter and all."

"Actually," Joe said, "I was thinking of how they remind me of Caroline's eyes."

Caroline caught her mother looking at her.

"Greece," Augusta said after a moment. "Hugh always said he'd take me there."

"I wish I were going," Sam said.

"They'll be back," Clea said reassuringly. "Yale, you know."

"Yale," Peter said. "Excellent school."

"Ah, Yale is just a four-letter word," Sam said. "Greece is where it's at."

"Take good care of her," Augusta said to Joe, looking him straight in the eye.

"I will," he said, gazing at her hard.

"Make sure," Clea said, standing beside Joe, her voice choked up. Skye didn't say anything, but she nodded.

"I promise," Joe said.

"He's getting better at promises," Sam said. "I swear."

"Enough out of you," Joe growled, but the look in his eyes was clear and full of love. "Why don't you get busy?"

"Get busy with what?"

"Finding that girl."

"What girl?" Sam asked, blushing.

Joe laughed. "See? You're such a damned academic, you've forgotten all about her."

"Sam's so adorable," Clea said. "There must have been hundreds of girls."

"Yeah, probably," Joe said, staying focused on his brother's eyes. "Only one who counted, though. But he's forgotten all about her."

"No, I haven't," Sam said, so quietly Caroline almost couldn't hear.

"A girlfriend for Sam?" Augusta asked. "How lovely! What's her name?"

"Hey, never mind," Sam said, now truly flustered. "We're saying good-bye to Caroline and Joe. That's all that matters right now."

Caroline smiled at him, her beloved's baby brother, and knew that some girl would be very, very lucky to have him. Then Joe took her by the arm, kissed her on the lips, and told her it was time to go. Her heart aching, she hugged them all: Clea, Skye, Sam, Peter, and the children. She told them that she loved them, she promised to write.

When she got to her mother, she stopped.

"Darling," Augusta said, "this is it."

"Thank you, Mom."

"For what?"

Caroline paused. For listening to the truth, for defending Skye, for letting Joe into their home, for having the courage to start to change, for the gift she had given her daughters that night: a way back to their father. If you start with love, can forgiveness ever be far behind? But she couldn't put those things into words.

"The missing piece?" she asked.

"Was that it?" Augusta asked, her eyes bright. "I want to feel like we found it, but I don't. Darling, I don't."

Caroline and her mother hugged, and neither wanted to let go. Clea and Skye had to step forward, to pry their mother away, whispering in her ears that it was time for Caroline to leave.

"Where's Homer?" she asked, looking around.

"We checked the beach, Aunt Caroline," Mark said. "He wasn't there."

"I want to say good-bye . . ." she said.

"He's so old, darling," Augusta said. "I don't like to say this, especially with you about to leave, but they're known to go off by themselves at the end."

"He's sixteen," Skye said.

"I want to see him," Caroline said. "We have to find him."

"There's only one thing to do," Sam said.

"There's no way we're leaving without you seeing him," Joe said.

"Let's look in the woods," Caroline said. She led the way.

* * *

They marched through the woods in swift silence. The scent of autumn was growing strong. The forest smelled of drying leaves and fallen pine needles, mushrooms clinging to the undersides of dead trees. It was the same time of year they had brought Homer here to live, and the old memories caused Caroline to feel a distant sadness, a longing for things long ago. She led her family, Joe, and Sam down the dry streambed, through the old cemetery where her father was buried, toward the curving path down the hill—the back way to Firefly Beach.

"Homer!" she called.

Her voice carried through the trees. Couldn't he hear it? Homer knew the sound of bags being thrown into cars, the excitement of travel. He had done it often with Caroline, and she believed that he realized what was happening now: that she was leaving. Old love was stirring in her, the feeling of his head under her hand, the memory of rescuing him from the concrete kennel when he was just a puppy.

A bark sounded. Was it Homer? Caroline felt the yearning. She wanted to see him for what might be the last time.

"Did you hear him?" Caroline asked, peering through the thick brambles. A bright opening led to the beach. "Homer!"

The old dog lumbered down the path from the sand, his eyes shining with love. Caroline crouched down, her arms open, watching him come. He had a big smile on his white face, his mouth drawn back and his brown eyes laughing.

"Where were you?" she asked as he crashed into her arms. He nudged his nose against her face, licked her eyes and cheeks and hands. She let him slobber all he wanted because she was so happy he was returning from his adventure to see her off. Running back the way he had come, he waited for her to chase him. He was leading her on a chase, though the thicket, over the silver green grass onto Firefly Beach.

"Where do you go, Homer?" Augusta called, following behind. "On your mysterious trips?"

"You're a traveler, aren't you?" Caroline

asked when she caught him on the beach, looking deep into his eyes. "But you always come home."

Her heart ached with love for Homer, and for her entire family. How could she leave them at all? Why would anyone choose to walk away from all this, the comfort of their old home, this magical beach, the sure love of their sisters and mother and old dog? Homer sat on his haunches by a driftwood log, looking into her face with such keen emotion, she wished she could read his mind. Gentle waves broke on the sand, whispering secrets.

"Darling, you know I'm not one to shove you along, but don't you have a plane to catch?" Augusta asked.

"We do," Joe said, sinking down in the sand to pet Homer. The old dog looked long and hard into Joe's face. He seemed to be reading it: the blue eyes, the shape of his mouth, the strength of his chin. As if making up his mind, Homer sniffed his hair. He gave Joe a slight lick, then another. The gesture wasn't love, probably not even affection. But it was open and generous, a way of telling Joe to take good care of the girl they both loved.

"I'll bring her home soon," Joe said. Caroline nodded. She gave Homer a big hug, smelling the scents of drying grasses and sea air. Then, kissing him once on the nose, she stood up.

"Let's go," she said quietly to Joe, wanting to leave before she changed her mind.

"Okay," he said.

But Homer yelped. He lay down as if he were in pain. The fallen leaves were a reminder of another trail, from long ago, and Caroline felt her pulse quicken. She crouched beside him. Her hands traced his body, wanting to soothe him, but feeling for lumps or broken bones.

Rolling on his back, he wriggled in the white sand. His face was full of play. Caroline knew he was trying to keep her near. She was about to stand, to lead him back to the house, when Joe crouched down. Something under the huge drifthood log had caught his attention, and he twisted his neck for a better look.

"Look," he said.

"Oh, great," Sam said. "Our eminent geologist has just discovered some rare beach glass that requires his immediate examination. Stand back."

"No, look," Joe said softly, taking Caroline's hand.

"Whoa," Sam said. "This could be, like, the coolest way to give someone a diamond ring—like hiding it in the parfait, only better. What'd he do, get Homer in on the caper?"

"Sam, shut up," Joe said, gently directing Caroline's attention to the underside of the old tree. Silvered by weather, surrounded by sand and seaweed, was a message, deeply scored into the wood.

The second she saw it, Caroline knew. Her eyes filled with tears. She petted Homer, and she let Joe hold her hand. She stared at the words, letting the tears spill from her eyes. Blinking, she could almost see her father's old Buck knife: its handle worn, the blade carefully sharpened before every use. It wasn't that she recognized his carving, or that he had signed it with his initials. But she knew.

"Mom?" she said.

"Yes, darling?"

Everyone gathered around. Caroline felt them crowding beside her, crouching around her. Joe's arms held her tight, and Homer licked her hand.

"Dad was here," Caroline said.

Everyone bent down to read the words,

but only Augusta read them out loud: " '*I love them all.*' "

"Dad carved that?" Clea asked.

"Certainly," Augusta said, eyes shining.

Skye put out her hand, touched each letter. Her shoulders shook with sobs, but she looked straight at Caroline, smiling.

Behind them, wind moved the reeds. A seagull began to cry, wheeling overhead. Slowly the beach became more alive. The birds were getting used to the humans' presence; very cautiously they began to come closer. Dusk settled on the sand, the last light evaporating into the violet sky. Caroline heard a twig crack and looked up in time to see a deer, approaching the creek. She thought of her father, of his love for nature. He had brought them somewhere beautiful after all.

"Why didn't he tell us?" Skye asked quietly, staring at the words. "Instead of just carving it?"

"It was right here, the whole time," Caroline said. How had Homer known? Had he followed her father? Had he heard him cry, watched him drink his whiskey, tried to console him as he walked down Firefly Beach and knelt down to carve his message?

Augusta nodded. "This is just an outward
sign, but—"

"Outward signs are good." Clea grinned.

"Especially when they're the missing
piece," Caroline said.

* * *

It was time to go, that eternal moment between saying good-bye and actually leaving. Everyone had promised to write and
call, everyone had kissed and hugged.

They were a close family. Was it possible
to hold on too tight? All these years, living
near Firefly Hill, Caroline had never wanted
to go too far away for too long. As if in her
absence shots would be fired. Someone
would get hurt, the old dog would die. All
her beloveds would disappear without her.

Now she knew that wasn't going to happen. Missing pieces do more than complete
the puzzle, they fill an empty space.
Caroline's heart was full of the knowledge
that her family's love wasn't going anywhere.

Stepping away from the house, Caroline
held Joe's hand. They stood still for a moment, breathing the salt air and the last
herbs of summer. The waves rumbled over

the tide flats. Gulls cried out at sea, and one lonely whippoorwill called from a distant marsh. Sam walked ahead.

Caroline looked toward the shoals, where the wreck of the *Cambria* still lay. She closed her eyes and thought of her father, whose ghost had been such an important part of this magical night. She wore Clarissa's cameo around her neck; Joe had his father's watch in his pocket. The stars were out, and she found one for Andrew Lockwood. Their dead were with them always, showing them the way.

"Caroline!" Clea called from inside the kitchen. "Look!"

"Look!" Skye said.

When she turned back to the house to see what her sisters were talking about, Caroline saw a firefly. It was September. The night was cool; fireflies should have been long gone for the summer. But there it was, undeniable, darting through the grass above the beach. Green-gold, it glowed like magic, like a whisper from the past. The firefly zigzagged through the night. Homer chased it just like when he was young, playing on the sand with Hugh.

"Good dog," Augusta called. "Good, wonderful dog."

Caroline gazed at her sisters and mother. They stood inside the kitchen, shadowed by the screen door. Homer walked slowly to the porch. He sat down, facing her. They watched each other for a long time. The sea broke on the shoal, and the waves rushed in. Joe squeezed her hand. Caroline squeezed back.

"We'll take care of him, darling," Augusta called.

"I know," Caroline called back.

Turning away, she walked with Joe Connor through the tall grass of Firefly Hill. He held the door of the car while she climbed in. Once inside, Sam gave Caroline several reassuring pats on the shoulder.

"Ready?" Joe asked, his clear blue eyes smiling.

"Ready," she said, waving to her mother and sisters.

"As ready as we'll ever be," Sam said. "We'll be back in a year."

"A year," Joe said. "Only a year."

"A year's not so long," Sam said.

"No, it's not," Joe said.

Joe started the engine. He pulled away slowly, so he, Caroline, and Sam could wave.

Beach stones crunched under the tires. She had the missing piece in her heart; it would be there always. Homer followed the car down through the dark and graceful tree canopy to the ocean and roads that led away from, and back to, Firefly Hill.

"I love them all!" Caroline cried out the open window.

The night was silent as the car sped away, but she could swear she heard her mother's voice calling the same thing back.

November 6, 2000

Dear Everyone,
We made it!
   Greece is beautiful, just like the postcard:
white churches, rocky cliffs, the bluest
water in the world. But it's not home, and
none of you are here. Homer would
understand. We have the missing piece in
our hearts, and it will bring us safely home
to Firefly Beach.

                    WE LOVE YOU ALL,
                    C+J

ABOUT THE AUTHOR

LUANNE RICE is the author of *Dream Country, Follow the Stars Home*—now a Hallmark Hall of Fame feature presentation—*Cloud Nine, Home Fires, Secrets of Paris, Stone Heart, Angels All Over Town, Crazy in Love,* which has been made into a TNT Network feature movie, and *Blue Moon,* which has been made into a CBS television movie. She lives in New York City and Old Lyme, Connecticut, with her husband.